The Wind from Nowhere

On his ranch in the vast wilderness of the great northwest, where he alone was black, dwelt Martin Eden, man of conquest. The strangest love story ever told.

By

OSCAR MICHEAUX

The Black Heritage Library Collection

BOOKS FOR LIBRARIES PRESS
FREEPORT, NEW YORK
1972

First Published 1941

Reprinted 1972

Reprinted from a copy in the
Fisk University Library Negro Collection

Library of Congress Cataloging in Publication Data

Micheaux, Oscar, 1884-
   The wind from nowhere.

   (The Black heritage library collection)
   I. Title. II. Series.
PZ3.M5809Wi [PS3525.I1875]   813'.5'2   72-4810
ISBN 0-8369-9109-5

PRINTED IN THE UNITED STATES OF AMERICA

To

My Sisters

IDA, MAUDE, OLIVIA, ETHEL, and GERTRUE;

and to the memory of

VEATRICE, who is dead.

LEADING CHARACTERS
IN THE ORDER OF APPEARANCE

NELSON BOUDREAUX
Deborah Stewart's grandpa.

MARTIN EDEN
Around whom the story is built.

JACK STEWART
An old Scotchman.

DEBORAH, HIS DAUGHTER
Born with the gift of second sight, who foresaw the tragic events that were to befall Martin Eden.

JESSIE BINGA
With whom Martin was once in love.

LINDA LEE
Who loved him dearly, but lacked the courage and strength of her convictions.

HER MOTHER
Who was likewise.

TERRY, LINDA'S SISTER
A "hell-cat," who hated Martin Eden.

THE RT. REVEREND DR. N. J. LEE
Linda and Terry's father, an hypocritical rascal, who was the cause of all the trouble, and shared Terry's hatred of Martin Eden.

EUGENE CROOK (White)
A banker, whose bank has since gone broke.

PLACE: *The former Rosebud Indian Reservation, an immense plateau laying between the Missouri River on the east and the Black Hills on the west, in Southern South Dakota and Chicago.*

TIME: *The present.*

*"To him that hath shall be given, and to him
that hath not shall be taken away — even that
which he haveth."*

—St. Paul

The Wind from Nowhere

CHAPTER I

NELSON BOUDREAUX, an elderly man, sat on the porch of a house on Vernon Avenue, a street in the Negro section on the South Side of Chicago. He was deeply engrossed in a letter. After perusing several lines, he smiled and raised his eyes thoughtfully, somewhat musingly, while his mind recalled a woman he knew, it seemed now, ages and ages ago. While thus reminiscing he heard a pair of footsteps coming slowly, a bit unsteadily, along the sidewalk in front of the house.

Upon reaching the walkway that led up to the porch upon which the old man was sitting, the person paused. This brought the old man reading the letter, back to himself and coming quickly out of his reverie, he adjusted his glasses and looked to see who it was. But the glasses, he forgot, were for reading only, so all he saw was a dark shadow across his vision.

Meanwhile, however, the owner of the footsteps was moving towards him up the walkway to the porch and by the time the old man removed his glasses and tried to focus his eyes on the other, he heard a deep booming voice:

"Well if it ain't Nelson Boudreaux, you old son-of-a-gun!" The old man recognized the other's voice and exhorted:

"Ned Washington, if I'm alive!" and beckoning with a swing of the hand, he directed: "Come on up here, have a seat and rest those creaky old bones, you stinkin' old relic!"

They were close enough now to reach and grasp hands. Laughing jovially, Boudreaux swung the other around onto a seat.

"I'm sure glad to see yuh," he cried, placing an arm around the visitor.

9

"Sorta hard on yuh to even walk up a dozen steps, eh? You look like an ole' weasel. It's been years and years since I saw yuh and I thought you were dead." Washington had caught his breath and wasn't puffing and breathing so deeply, as when he came up, so turned now to the other, his old eyes a bit watery as he squinted at Boudreaux closely, a bit searchingly.

"You're on borrowed time yourself, you old vampire," said he; then pausing as his eyes happened to fall on the letter, he pointed at it with a shaky old finger:

"You were reading a letter as I came up and I saw you pause to smile like it made you happy. Musta been something interesting. Wha—whats it all about, anyhow?" Looking down at it, Boudreaux started a bit, then relaxed; he perked up again with:

"Oh, yes, yes, the letter. I'd sorta forgot. Mind ain't so good as it usta be—I forget rather easily, and quickly, but gettin' back to the letter." He picked it up and looking at it a moment, turned to the other with an idea for some fun.

"I'll bet that you couldn't guess who its from in a hundred years!" and then in an undertone: "You must be a hundred already." Laughing, he shook the letter in front of Ned's face. The latter leaned away like a person who didn't like to play.

"And I ain't gonna try, neither," retorted Ned. "I'm through with hard thinkin'. It hurts my head, so quit kiddin' and tell me who its from."

"Got a mind not to, you old fossil. You admit you don't like to think—just like the most of us Negroes; but if you tell us so, we wanta get mad and he't up about it." Boudreaux relaxed, turned to the letter, and shuffled back to the first page as he said:

"Well, I'll tell you about it, but it all seems so long ago that I fear you may have forgotten."

"Gwan and read the letter, man. You've said so much about it you done got me all worked up and anxious. Gwan and read the letter." Boudreaux laughed at this and turned to him with a tolerant smile.

"All right, old kid. Here we go," then he paused again. "Do you recollect my first wife? The pretty little Creole girl I brought with me to Chicago when I came here? She was just a kid, then, if you remember?" Turning on him as if in surprise, Ned queried:

"Agnes, you mean?"

"Sure, sure—of course! I didn't think you could remember that far back." Washington picked up the cane he had hobbled up on and drew it back, while glaring at Boudreaux:

"I bet I'm gonna kill you!" Then relaxing and in a changed voice: "Forget that gal—the prettiest little thing that ever came outa New O'leans! Well, what about her? That musta been fifty years ago. You told me, if I remember correctly, that she was dead, and that's been a long time ago."

"Yes, it has; but this letter's from her grand daughter, our grand child."

"What're you talkin' about, anyhow?"

"I mean (see you *have* forgotten something) that its from, not our daughter, for she's dead, too; but from our daughter's daughter." Washington leaned back and sighed, then shaking his head:

"This is gettin' too deep for me. Whatever is it, man, that you're tryin' to tell me, anyhow?" He struck his knee with his fist, impatiently. The other patted him on the shoulder.

"Calm yourself, old one, please and listen. I'll explain."

"Then please do before I fall clean out with ye, and get up and leave."

"Just this, Ned. When my first wife, Agnes, and I parted, we had two daughters." Washington nodded his head now as if recalling.

"Yes, I remember now that you did have some kids. Weren't big enough then for me to remember if they were boys or girls."

"They were girls, both girls."

"All right, now go on. Then what?"

"If you can be quiet long enough, I'll explain all about it." He turned and glanced at the letter, before going on.

"We agreed between ourselves that she should take one of the children, I the other." Looking down and trying to follow him, with it becoming more clear, Ned nodded his head up and down, very much interested.

"So she took hers with her to Iowa. She went to Waterloo and got a job waitin' table in a restaurant. I suppose it was a white restaurant—she was very light, you know."

"Looked jes' lak a white girl—could even pass for one without any trouble."

"She could that; but I don't think she did, or even tried to pass. She just asked for a job and got it. Any way, she was workin' in this restaurant when she met the man she later married. This much I *do* know. She didn't try to fool him. She showed him the little girl and told him that its father was a colored man. The child she had was a bit darker than her."

"Yes, but she was light, too," interposed Washington. "As I remember her, white people would never notice the difference."

"But not light enough to fool a Negro," said Boudreaux.

"Oh, I guess not," commented Washington. "You've just got to be white to fool a niggah." Boudreaux laughed.

"Even *you* could have, in those days, gone down town and been mistaken for a Spaniard or a Cuban. And you were *one* handsome darky, too, I'm tellin' yuh—niggah women were fightin' all over the South Side about yuh."

"Oh, well, that got me nothing. I'm old now and I gotta 'bring it with me' like any other spook. Getting back to the story—she wrote me that the man told her when she explained about herself and the kid that it didn't make any difference; that he loved her because she was good and kind and would make him a good wife. As for the child, he proposed that he adopt it and raise it as his own, so that was that.

"Well, he married her and they went to live on a farm in the country. Out there, Laura, our daughter grew up, married a white man and they had one daughter and two sons, then she died. Her husband took the children and moved to Indiana and

rented on a farm there, where they have been until just re-
cently, which brings me up and back to the letter." Stamping
his foot, and raising a protesting hand with impatience, Ned
argues:

"Just a minute, Nelson. In all this marrying and dying and
movin' back to Indiany, was the children, as far as you know,
ever told that they had a 'streak'; that there was Negro blood
in their veins?" Boudreaux looked around at him, thought a
moment and raised his head which he shook in the negative.

"I doubt it. After all, they were just poor people and discussing their lineage was perhaps about the last thing they
would have been talking or thinking about. Where they lived
in both Iowa and Indiana, there was no 'race' problem, at least
locally, so they just thought they were white people, lived as
such and the fact that they have Negro blood, has perhaps
never been brought up." Agreeing with the other by some nods
of the head, Washington motioned him to go on.

"The letter is from the girl. She writes me once in a great
while. I haven't seen her, and if I never do, she'll never know
the truth, for I'll not tell her. Meanwhile, her name is Deborah
and being the oldest of the three children—just old enough
when her mother died to keep house and take care of her brothers, she did manage to get through and graduate from high
school which accounts, perhaps, for her writing now and then.
She probably hasn't much occasion to use her education otherwise. Now I'll read the letter to you." With this, he adjusted
his glasses, raised the pages and began:

"Dear Grandpa:
    You may be surprised to hear from us, but we've left
Indiana and moved to South Dakota, so I thought it best
to write and let you know where we were and what we are
doing.
    This part of South Dakota is known as the Rosebud In-
dian Reservation, which was thrown open to settlement a

few years ago, and papa came out and registered for a claim but failed to draw one.   Poor papa, he never seems to have any luck, but a Mr. Watson, who came with him, drew one. He came out, filed and proved up on it and returning to Indiana, persuaded papa to come out here and rent the place. So here we have settled and hope to do better."

As Boudreaux read the last words, our story flits 800 miles westward to a scene on the former Rosebud Indian Reservation, and to the ranch home of the only Negro to have settled there and acquired any large amount of land. He was young, was this Colored man, virile and a hard worker with a definite objective in life. His name was Eden, Martin Eden, and his life had been lived very simply.

Once a Pullman porter, he had saved his money, something like $4,000, which he brought there to start with. He had worked hard from the day he settled there; had saved the money made, bought more land, fed cattle and hogs and now was about ready to make a shipment of two car loads of corn fed steers and one of bulging fat hogs to the market.

A neighbor, by the cognomen of Preble, passing by in his old Ford car at this moment, came to a stop beside the feed lot and greeted Eden, as farmers are given to greeting each other, in a loud voice. Martin had just finished dumping a load of corn into the troughs for the steers, so crossed to the fence and greeted Preble with:

"Hello, Ben. How's your hammer hangin'?"

"Kinda low, Eden." Both laughed. Then, as if recalling what he had stopped for, Ben perked up:

"By the way, Eden. Have you decided on who's to look after your stock while you're away?"

"In a way I had, but yesterday, I decided otherwise."

"Exactly what do you mean?" inquired Preble, a bit puzzled.

"I mean that I don't altogether trust the parties who have offered to do so and whom I was considering. Was told that they sell your feed, run your stock on the range, and the last people who had them looking after their stock, found it half starved and half frozen when they returned. So I'm not after any of that kind of service for my stock."

"I don't blame you; which brings me up to what I've stopped to tell you."

"Oh, something to tell me, eh? Shoot."

"Yeh. A family has just moved onto the Watson place, from back in Indiana. And old Scotchman with two sons and a daughter—and speaking of daughters," he pauses to wink, "looks like a mighty good catch for a prosperous young bachelor by the name of Martin Eden." Preble paused to wink again and laughed, before becoming serious and continued:

"They impress me as being honest and reliable and just who you need to look after your stock for you while you're away."

"Humph. Sounds interesting," commented Eden.

"I was talking with the old man yesterday and he told me that he would like to hire one of the boys out. I don't think they're holding much, so perhaps need the money. Why not drop by, see him and talk it over?" Eden thought for a moment then raising his head, asked:

"You say they're on the Watson place?"

"Yep. Handy for you, too—just this side of your Swanson place, southeast."

"More interesting still," observed Eden, straightening up to go back to his work; he turned and said:

"Well thanks, Preble, I'll go down and see him." Preble started his motor. Before stepping on the gas, however, he turned to call loudly:

"And don't forget what I said about the girl. She's a humdinger—and easy on the eyes, oh boy! Here's your chance. You may not have to go east to look for a wife any more! Just wait until you see her—yeah, man!" He started to move now, slowly, and strained his ears a bit to hear Eden above the roar of the old motor.

"Who said I was looking for a wife!" cried Eden, loud enough to be heard. For answer, Preble just laughed long and loudly and waved a hand as the old car picked up speed and sailed away down the road.

Eden smiled patronizingly and waved back as Preble looked over his shoulder and continued on his way.

In spite of the fact that Eden was a colored man, his white neighbors insisted on kidding him about the girls, all of whom were white, in town and in the neighborhood around him. Yet, they were all nice to him, just as nice as they could be. He almost never heard the ugly word of "nigger," so currently used by white people in referring to one of his race. They seemed to understand that to use it was an insult, and he was surprised to see how much they abstained from using the term.

Every white girl in the country knew him very well and most called him by his first name. They always smiled in passing him; engaged him in conversation whenever the opportunity afforded, and were ever solicitous regarding his health. He knew of no place where he could have had better neighbors and lived so happily. Indeed, he was far more popular, on the whole, than any individual white man. That he was a hard, forward vigorous worker and was succeeding, added to his popularity, and the fact that he was colored, seemed to single him out for attention.

Martin Eden loved his wilderness; he had dedicated his life to helping to build it to the great and successful farming section that it was destined to become—and expected to make it his home forevermore!

Yet with all this, he kept the fact that he was colored well in mind socially and had no thought or intention of misunderstanding the way the white girls treated him. Regardless how courteous and kind and considerate each was, his interest was limited.

No thought like that of "going with one" entered his mind. He knew that just as soon as he showed signs of transgressing this unspoken rule, he would begin to be confronted with embarrassment. The customs of society had long since decreed that he go his way and they go theirs. Eden thought of this as he went about his work and soon forgot what Preble had suggested.

At the end of each year since he came to the Rosebud Country and had made it his home, however, it was his custom to go back East, when he could manage it, just before Thanksgiving and stay until after the New Year. During this time he socialized with those of his group to his heart's desire.

He had been in love once, very much in love, with a young girl. He had fallen in love with her long before he had thought or was prepared to come West. This love for her had continued through the first years of his life in the Rosebud Country. His ambition from the beginning had been to acquire and own a section of land. During the year about to end, he had purchased the final 160 acres that completed the section, and was now the happy owner of 640 acres, or one entire square mile.

He now planned to build a nice house for his bride. A house where they could live in comfort and continue his work with her helping him. He pictured a large, warm barn for his stock with adequate sheds for the cattle which he would feed in the future. It would take fully a dozen or more outer buildings to complete the estate of the large and successful farmer which he aspired to become.

It would take several years, perhaps, before he could hope to make such a dream come true. He would have to, by dint of sacrifice, hard work, and the exercise of a keen and alert mind, take advantage of it when the opportunity was at hand, to ultimately possess all that. So he tried to make himself fit to do these things of which he dreamed.

His trips and association with his people in Chicago didn't help at all in completing this plan. As a group, his race had little—almost no conception of what it took to succeed; to acquire, to have, nor to hold. Free and easy going, they did not impress him as ever thinking anything out deeply enough nor far enough to get anywhere. A few were buying homes in Chicago; some had more than one house, and, here and there others had even more, and were considered well-to-do—but that was far as it went. Few were in trade, commerce, or industry.

All around him in the Rosebud Country were Germans, Russians, Poles, Bohemians, Moravians, Slovaks—Scandinavians —in short, almost all kinds of Northern Europeans, all struggling to a common end—success! Practical success and security —but Negroes, they didn't even seem to think of it—much less starting to try to make it work.

At the end of every visit he returned to his wilderness where there still was real opportunity, cold and discouraged. He couldn't restrain the inclination to criticize their failure to the members of his race; at times he became severe and some said that he was "hard on his people." To which he would answer, hotly, "you're hard on yourselves! What'll become of us should there be a great economic change?"

The economic depression had come and left the Negro race, above all other groups who also suffered their share, prostrate.

Suffice to say that Martin Eden had been in love; and that he had realized his ambition to own a section of land. He hadn't gotten around to building the house, the barn and necessary sheds. Those were the "things to come." He had been planning, soon as these buildings were up, to marry Jessie, bring her hither, and *"live happily ever afterward."*

In the midst of this, Tripp County, adjoining the one where he lived, on the west, was thrown open to settlement; throngs came—more than 100,000, and took a try at securing a 160 acre tract. Even a few colored people came up and tried. This had just taken place that year. Ten months hence, the land would be open to general settlement. Then, those who wanted the land to live on, build up and develop as a home or investment, could do so. Those who sought it only as a means to make some quick money, were expected to sell their relinquishments

to those who wanted it, for a considera ion. This changed Martin Eden's plans. He had one unmarried sister, and a grandmother, both with homestead rights to exhaust. He would buy
relinquishments, and put them on it. "Now why can't I put
the girl I will some day marry on one and get another 160
acres" thought he. Which brought up Jessie again.

Had their relations, at this time, been as they once were, it
could have all been settled expeditiously. But it couldn't be
at this stage because the last time he had been to see her back
there in southern Illinois, he found her ill—sick in bed. She was
suffering from "inflammation of the womb." People asked,
"how could a young girl, just graduated from high school have
such an inflammation, unles —" And they left it to the imagination to explain the rest.

Martin Eden had returned to Dakota, having agreed, at her
request, not to believe the things he had heard; but he was a
considerably changed man thereafter. He hadn't tried to quit
loving Jessie, for she was young and she was beautiful and she
was sweet and he wanted her. He had been saving to give her
the great love that was in his heart—then suddenly this had
to happen! Ugly thoughts then became mixed with his beautiful thoughts and all became jumbled and confused. They upset
him—detracted his trend of thought and mind and left him
unhappy.

That had happened more than a year before. He had almost
become reconciled to a bachelor's fate. As he prepared to call
on the old Scotchman, and knowing that he would soon be on
his way to Chicago, Eden just considered that he had no girl,
had no love—but was quietly looking for both.

As he got into his car, preparing to call on the people to whom
he had been referred, Eden thought of what Preble had told
him about the girl and he smiled a bit ironically. "Wouldn't it
be fine," he thought to himself almost aloud, "if she were a nice
colored girl?" A beautiful colored girl out here in this wilderness and a young ambitious colored boy, with a definite objec-

tive in life, would most surely soon find an interest in common.
They would most surely soon fall in love and they would most
surely, understanding each other, soon marry and they could
hardly miss being happy.

"But," he sighed as he started the motor, "she is white, while
I am black—so forget it." He did—before he even got there.
But he thought of some other people; a colored man, married
to a white woman in a county lying to the north of him. He
had met this man in a saloon in Gregory, his post office, that
same fall and had had a long talk with him. The Negro had
told him that he was married to a German woman, had two
daughters of marrying age; but he hadn't invited Eden to come
up and see them. Oh, no; because his two daughters were *going
with white men*, poor white men, so he was told, but white men
nevertheless—and he knew the story. They *wanted to be white*.
No man stood higher in the estimation of the white people in
the country than did Martin Eden; and especially did the best
white people respect him. But he *was colored* and he knew that
this was the reason this Negro had not invited him up to meet
his marriageable daughters. It was because *all wanted to be
white*. Being so, they had no respect or admiration for anything but a white face—*even if the dark face had wealth, intelligence and was of the highest standing*. He hated them for it! As
he recalled all this, his face darkened and he muttered aloud:

"Dirty old sonofabitch." Driving along the dirt road, he
thought of the old Negro again. His face grew darker with
anger, and again he muttered an oath: "*Dirty old sonofabitch!*
That's why I don't want anything to do with a white woman.
It's niggahs like him that makes me that way. But they'll never
have a chance to make a fool of me—never! For I'm not gettin'
soft or fallin' for any, regardless how nice they treat me. I hate
them—hate them!" And then he relaxed.

This wasn't true. He thought of Olga Kloke, and Marion
Martin; of several white girls that he knew and recalled that
they were more than nice to him. They were almost sweet to

him; but they gave him no cause to try and transcend the established social custom. Everything was working out all right, just as it was, so why couldn't it continue that way? He had never thought of it, perhaps never would have, but for his meeting this old Negro; this old Negro that he hated! Then after a time, he said to himself, this time aloud:

"Skip it." So by force of will he put it quickly out of his mind. By this time he drew up in front of the Watson house and looked across the yard, with its prairie grass lawn. Then, getting out of the car, he went through the gate, crossed the yard and knocked on the door.

A moment later the door was opened. Before the old man who stood there could speak, the caller said:

"Pardon me, but my name is Eden, Martin Eden, and I've been asked to see you."

"Mr. Eden, indeed I'm glad to meet you," cried the other, while swinging wide the door: As Eden stepped inside the Scotchman grasped and shook his hand, before continuing:

"Stewart is my name, sir. Richard Stewart is what I was christened in Scotland. They've been calling me Jack, old Jack Stewart, so long, however, until I've almost forgotten what my real name is; but come up to the fire, Mr. Eden, and sit down. I'm glad to meet you and I welcome you into our little home." His tone was entirely sociable and Eden liked him at once.

To provide a home for a renter, old Watson had built an addition to his claim house—a nice three room frame structure, painted white, which stood just in front of the old claim shack so that they could use the old house as a kitchen. One had, however, to step down two steps to get into the kitchen from the new part of the house.

Deborah was Jack Stewart's oldest child, and only daughter. She was also the grandchild of old man Boudreaux, who, as already known, was a Negro. When Martin Eden's car stopped outside, Deborah had just begun preparation of the evening meal. Naturally the arrival of the stranger aroused her curiosity. As her father admitted Eden she hurriedly gained a vantage point in the shadow of the kitchen, where she could hear everything that was being said. Moreover, she had a full view of the visitor, who was unable to see her.

To Martin Eden the Stewarts were simply a white family with a boy for hire. He was there to determine if the latter was satisfactory for his purposes, and if so, make him an offer. Little did any of these principals dream that Deborah and her brothers were third generation descendants of Negro Nelson Boudreaux. Naturally Eden did not know it. If so he would undoubtedly have associated them with the views and practices of the Negro whose daughters were engaged to white men. Furthermore, he would never have called on the Stewarts at all. "The streak," nevertheless, was in Jack Stewart's children, who were entirely ignorant of it.

As she peeped out at her father and Eden, Deborah was filled with mixed emotions. She had heard of him. He was one of the first persons mentioned by anyone in discussing the Rosebud country, a sort of novelty, as it were, which most of the residents took pride in telling their friends and visitors about. Because the Negro is so rarely taken seriously, Eden and his accomplishments in the West were always considered interesting subjects.

So she watched him from her vantage point and listened to him curiously. She observed that he was tall and straight, had a good forehead, a strong determined chin, and thought to herself that he must be interesting.

"We've only been here a little while," her father was saying.

"So I hear," replied Eden. "Well, I hope you like our wilderness—that's what I call it," and he laughed.

"We do. You have such fine, rich black soil out here; as rich as any of that in Indiana, where the land is so awfully high— I mean the price of the land. Too high for any poor people to ever hope to own."

"Very true," agreed Eden. That is why this is considered a haven for us poor people."

"*Us* poor people?" echoed Stewart, looking across at him, not understandingly. Eden looked back at him quickly, and in some surprise.

"Yes, of course. That's what I meant, *us poor people*. Why?"

"But from what I hear, you are not poor at all, Mr. Eden. They tell me that you own four quarters of land. Thats a whole section! A mighty lot of ground for one man to own anywhere." Looking at him curiously, Eden relaxed, broke into laughter and cried:

"Oh, me. Well, I didn't mean it that way. That is, I wasn't exactly talking about myself—and yet I was. I haven't had the land long—nobody here has had anything long. The country is only five years old. We all considered ourselves poor when we came here. Some of us have gotten hold of a little something since, but we don't consider five years quite long enough to develop a feeling of being anything else but poor, see?"

"Yes," said Jack, nodding his head weakly; "but still you do *own* the land and anybody that owns 640 acres of land as fine as yours—well, I just can't think of them as being poor. I—"

"I'll tell you what let's do, Mr. Stewart," said Eden, reaching over and touching him. "Suppose that we say nothing more about it, yes?"

"Well, I—"

"I *know* that I am poor, even if I am holding 640 acres of land. What I came to see you about, however, is to explain that I'm going back East for a spell, and I need somebody to look after my place and my stock while I'm away, and your neighbor across the road told me about you—you understand who I mean, do you not? I'm referring to Mr. Preble, Ben Preble," jerking a thumb over his shoulder in the direction of the house across the road where Preble lived.

"Why, of course I understand, Mr. Eden. He's a fine neighbor, too,—a fine man, this Mr. Preble."

"He is that—big hearted and honest and most obliging."

"Very true."

"Well, he says that you have a boy, your son I suppose, that you are interested in hiring out; I'm in the market for some one. I've said what I want done—so that's the story."

"Yes," said Stewart, "I do want to hire one of my boys out. Mr. Preble said that he thought you might be able to use him, so I'm open for a deal. As I understand it, you have some stock over on the Swanson Place and some cattle and hogs, too, up where you live."

"Some chickens, a dog and a cat," Eden assisted. They both laughed loudly at this.

"It'll be mighty convenient for you, and most helpful to us, if you hire my son. You see, we're just poor people out here from Indiana, trying to get along. It took everything we had to move out here, the expense and all that, so you can understand? That's why we can use a job for one of us."

"Perfectly, Mr. Stewart. If your boy is any good and will look after my stock properly during my absence, that is all I expect." And then in a changed tone, Eden explained, "I'm about to make a shipment of stock to Chicago. I usually stay there until after the holidays. So taking it for granted that you'll see that everything is looked after properly, I'll consider it's a deal. It's a winter's job though not much to do; the pay is only $40 a month and he must board at home. Is it acceptable?"

"I accept," said Jack; "now I'll go and fetch Bill, that's the boy's name, and you can look him over yourself and explain what you want done."

Stewart rose. He hadn't been sure that Bill would get the job. The truth was that the Stewarts were hard pressed. Moving from Indiana had depleted the little money they had saved, so it was most important that some source of revenue be found to keep the wolf from their door. It would be many months before their first crop. Meanwhile, there were four of them and they had to live.

As Jack Stewart started toward the door to call Bill, the voice of Deborah stopped him.

"Father," she called. He looked around quickly and saw her beckoning to him from the kitchen. Her face was serious. He crossed the room and stepped down into the kitchen toward her. As he came down, she moved away towards a corner and he followed.

"You're so forgetful!" she whispered in a severe tone; as he came up. "You know how much getting this job for Bill will mean to us. Why don't you play up to Mr. Eden? They told you that he batches, so go back there and invite him to stay for dinner. Try to flatter and please him by being so nice he'll be persuaded to hire Bill, anyhow."

"Why of course, dear, of course!" he exclaimed, overly nervous with anxiety now. "I was so excited until I clean forgot." He started away, then turned and took her by the arm exclaiming: "Now you must come in and meet the young man, also, my daughter. You—"

"No, no," she protested, emphatically. "Not now! I'm looking too—oh, too unkempt!" She was the one that was nervous now, and a bit distracted. She finally got her bearings and, taking hold of him, cried: "Now here's what you do, however. Take him with you and find Bill and by the time you get back, I'll be tidied up a bit and hope to look presentable. Besides, I'll also make the house look more habitable."

"Yes, yes, that's the thing to do, Deborah," said Jack. "I'll do what you say and"—He broke off suddenly, leaned over and kissed her on the cheek impulsively. She returned the caress by pulling her father to her and embracing him. Both were more happy than they had been for a long time. She almost pushed him toward the entrance now in order to initiate the business at hand, meanwhile, keeping studiously out of Eden's sight, the while.

On returning to the big room, Jack found Eden standing patiently, his back towards the fire.

"Now Bill and George, my other son, are doing a little work across the creek. Supposing we go over there and let you size Bill up while he's working?"

"Okeh, Mr. Stewart," replied Eden and they stepped toward the door. A few minutes later they came upon George and Bill, typical farm boys with their coarse clothing and weather beaten skin. Eden could see before he even got to them that Bill was what he needed and made up his mind then to hire him.

"Bill," called his father, as they came up. "Shake hands with Mr. Martin Eden, the man we've been hearing so much about." Smiling, tolerantly, Martin stepped forward.

"Glad to know you, Bill," said he, extending his hand. Bill stammered some words and took the proferred hand.

"Your father and I have just entered into a deal for you to work for me—but excuse me," Eden interrupted himself while turning first to George—who was waiting to be recognized and introduced—and then back to Bill, "is this your brother?"

Jack stepped into the breach by introducing his older son. "George, this is Mr. Martin Eden."

"How do, Mr. Eden," said George, who, in addition to being a trifle silly, was fond of talking and craved attention. These traits caused his father and Deborah to be ever shunting him into the background. Whenever George had as much as half a chance, however, his mouth was a hard one to keep shut.

"Aw, I've heard so much about you, Mr. Eden," he cried, happily, "until I feel like I know you already. Everybody's been telling us about the 'rich' colored man they have out here and everybody likes you, too."

"George!" cried—and all but begged—Jack, trying to get the boy's eye. Eden rather sensed what he was like so stood smiling patiently, while George, ignoring his father, continued:

"We're going to like you, too, Mr. Eden—that is, if you'll let us."

"I hope you will like me, George. I try to treat everybody right. I shall try to be fair to you, your brother and your father."

"And to Deborah? That's my sister. She's smart, too, Mr. Eden. She graduated from High School back in Indiana, she reads a lot and knows a lot. I bet you'll like her, too."

"Thank you, George," said Eden, still smiling, appreciatively.

"You will—everybody likes Deborah. She's a good girl and takes good care of all of us."

"George, will you please hush?" cried Stewart, taking hold of him and all but putting his hand over his mouth. Then turning to Eden with an apology:

"You must excuse George. He's affected with the running off at the mouth. He'll talk you to death if you'll let him, so ignore him, please."

"He's interesting," commented Eden, still smiling patiently. Jack turned to Bill with an expression of pride:

"Now Bill here, he's quiet. He almost never says anything, speaks only when spoken to, and is very dependable. I hope you'll like Bill."

"I like both the boys—and George is all right," said he, looking across at him, "eh, George?"

"I sure am, Mr. Eden. Of course I'm all right," then turning to Bill and his father, triumphantly, "what'd I tell you? You see what a smart man, who's just met me, says. See?"

"Yes, we see, George, but if you'll only give Mr. Eden a chance to check on and talk to Bill, whom he is here to see, maybe we'll get around to you later."

"Oh, I'm sorry," said George, apologetically. "I—I didn't understand."

"Now Bill," said Jack, turning to the quiet one of the pair. "Mr. Eden is considering hiring you. He's going away—" he broke off now to turn back to Eden. "As I understand it, you're shipping out a couple of car loads of cattle and one of hogs, very shortly. Is that true?"

"Right."

"And you'll need Bill, maybe, right away?"

"From tomorrow morning on," replied Eden. To all this Bill was silent, listening, however, and nodding when they turned to him, that he understood. Jack Stewart further explained:

"Mr. Eden is agreeable to hiring you, but is here to satisfy himself as to whether you're any good." Eden laughed at this, and even silent Bill smiled. George, it could be seen, would like to say a whole lot; he could have prolonged it for an hour, but knowing that anything he might offer at this time would be considered out of place, he swallowed what he wanted to say with an effort, and kept quiet. Meanwhile, Stewart turned to Eden:

"How does he stack up, Mr. Eden? Do you think you can use him?" Eden looked at Bill a moment, and the hearts of all the others seemed to stand almost still with anxiety while they awaited his decision. They relaxed after a moment, when a broad smile overspread Eden's face.

"I think Bill'll do." All three Stewarts heaved a sigh of relief and Jack turned to Bill:

"Well, Bill, he has decided to try you. You will start work tomorrow morning. Your salary will be $40 per month, which I accept, so if you're satisfied, then thank Mr. Eden and we'll go back to the house."

"Thank you, Mr. Eden. I'm glad you're giving me a job. I'll do my best trying to please you."

"You'll please me, Bill. I can see that you're a good boy and won't quit work until what you know ought to be done, has been completed."

"Well, if that's all settled, we'll go back to the house and have dinner," said Jack, turning to Eden.

"You must stay and have dinner with us, Mr. Eden, then we'll all go up to your farm and check up on the work."

"Well, I thank you very much, but—"

"No buts, Mr. Eden," broke forth George again at last "You must by all means stay and have dinner with us. My sister's a good cook. She took a course in domestic science and home economics while she was going to high school, so she's—"

"George, if you don't hush your big mouth, I'll have to gag you," cried Jack. Eden was forced to laugh, as Stewart, losing patience, drew back as if he'd like to strike George. Eden patted George on the back.

"No, he won't, George, and you're all right. But suppose we chase up to my place first. Your sister hasn't had time to fix dinner yet, so we'll go up there in the meantime. What do you say to that?"

"Oh, I'll sure be glad to go, Mr. Eden. I'll be glad to," he cried, smiling all over, as they started toward the house.

When her father and Eden left to seek George and Bill, Deborah not only tidied herself up, but the house as well, and had just finished this task when she heard their footsteps returning. She rushed into the kitchen, but not quickly enough to escape her father, who observed that she had on another dress; her hair was done up and he knew that he could invite her to meet Eden now without embarrassing her too much. So before she could get out of sight, he called:

"Deborah!" whereupon she stopped and turned. "Come forward and meet our neighbor." Plainly excited and blushing all over, in spite of a great effort to appear nonchalant, Deborah came out of the kitchen, stepped up into the main room and advanced a few steps. Her father stepped back a foot or two and she found herself standing face to face with Martin Eden.

That was, for reasons that will explain themselves later, perhaps the most exciting moment of her uneventful life. Within hand-shaking distance of him, she paused and looked up at her father, as if afraid to meet Eden's eyes, which were upon her. She'd been thinking about him every minute while he stood across the creek, talking with her father and brothers. Face to face at last, she was almost afraid to meet him. Her knees actually trembled and her heart was all aflutter.

"Mr. Eden," her father was saying, and his voice, seemed to come from far away. "Please meet my daughter, Deborah. Deborah, Mr. Eden."

As she turned and raised her eyes to meet his, she realized how tall he was, how strong he seemed; and still frightened, she was conscious of extending her little hand and trying to say something proper, and of his reaching quickly, as though this courtesy were unexpected on her part. She felt a thrill run the entire length of her body and wondered if he could feel her trembling.

But Eden, too, in spite of his declaration of an hour before, to let no white girl excite or make a fool of him, was conscious of a strange excitement within his breast. And while he knew most of the white girls who lived in the Rosebud Country, had often met and had been offered their hands like this, he had never before felt as he now did. Here was one who was too nice and too sweet even to try to dislike, much less plan to hate. He heard her saying in a low voice:

"I'm pleased to meet you, Mr. Eden," and holding her hand, heard himself reply:

"And I'm pleased to meet you, also, Miss Stewart."

It was over. Yet still he seemed to keep holding her hand. He didn't—it merely seemed that way. This, he *did* know, and he remembered, for it passed through his mind many times afterward, and he perhaps never forgot.

He looked into her eyes and thought they were blue, but something in them seemed to strike him, infinitely. He was then uncertain as to their exact color. There appeared to be something about them that bewildered him; yes, overpowered his resistance, and he was conscious of being drawn toward her in some strange manner. When he had loosed her hand, both stood still for a moment, emotionally upset.

These two kindred spirits—unable to fathom their disturbed reactions—had but to understand Deborah's Negro lineage. She was descended from Nelson Boudreaux and his Creole vife, and something in this man—a Negro also—seemed to arouse in her a feeling never before experienced, in the limited contacts she had made with men.

As he viewed her closely, Eden saw that she was not tall and still not short, nor was she stout or slender, but of that indefinite type called medium. What impressed him most of all, however, was that the girl was pretty—simply ravishing in her sex appeal and personality. In short, Deborah Stewart, was infinitely and definitely beautiful.

In the fleeting seconds they stood there, which Jack Stewart made possible by a line of talk of which neither was even semi-conscious, Eden seemed to see something in this girl that he had never been conscious of in a white girl before. Whatever that subtle something, there was, also, something strange and mysterious about her.

"My daughter," went on Stewart, "is possessed with a rare sort of gift; the gift of second sight. Things that are going to happen to us, she seems to foresee. She didn't develop it. Just born that way, I believe." At this remark Deborah only lowered her eyes and smiled modestly.

"Most remarkable," commented Eden, looking at her anew and curiously. "I hope she never tells what is going to happen to me. For if it is bad, I wouldn't want to hear it, and if it is good, I wouldn't want to believe it."

"If she ever tells you that something is going to happen to you, I'm telling you now to believe it, and if it is possible for you to keep it from happening, then try to stop it, otherwise it will surely occur."

Deborah, back to normal again, turned to her father:

"Now, father, Mr. Eden, I am sure, is not interested in listening to any psychical resume. I'll bet he could become more interested in some good food," whereupon all broke into laughter, which immediately eased the tension.

"Your daughter," ventured Eden, turning to Stewart, "is not only interesting and charming, but she is also beautiful."

It was so sudden, yet said with such sincerity that it was convincing. Nevertheless, Deborah turned on him boldly, and queried:

"Who, me?" pointing to herself. "Why Mr. Eden! Of all that we've heard about you, we hadn't been told that you were—a flatterer!"

"Oh, really, Miss Stewart, but I am not," said he protestingly.

"I appreciate your modesty, nevertheless it pleases me to say that I think you *are* very beautiful."

"I won't listen to you any longer," said Deborah, affecting to pout, and hurried away toward the kitchen. At the door, however, she paused, turned back, and looked at him. He was standing where she left him, gazing after her. In that moment he forgot that she was white and he was black; he had forgotten everything except that she was a woman, a beautiful, charming woman with a magnetism he was finding it hard to resist.

After two seconds, with her eyes on him and wearing that heavenly smile, she managed to become calm enough to turn to her father and say:

"Did you ask Mr. Eden to stay for dinner, father?"

"I did, Deborah." She turned again to Eden, who thought she looked so sweet, as she asked:

"And—are you going to, Mr. Eden?"

"Of course he's going to, Deborah, dear," insisted her father.

"Well, father, I just wanted to be sure," said she.

"Can you imagine any man who has to keep batch, turning down anybody's invitation to cook a meal for him?" asked Jack.

"Especially when a charming young woman like you is going to do the cooking," said Eden smilingly.

"Oh, Mr. Eden!" she cried, stepping down into the kitchen, but not before she had given him one wonderful parting smile, free of everything but a great delight in her heart, for the chance to serve him—and then she was gone.

"Well," said Eden, placing hat on head and turning to Stewart who came toward him, "I guess you, myself and the boys can chase up to my place and check on things, eh?"

"Already to go, Mr. Eden," and they started away, but a movement and voice from the kitchen, arrested them:

"Oh, father!" Deborah called before her eyes fell on Eden, to whom she turned now and addressed:

"Are you fond of, and would you care for—biscuit, Mr. Eden?"

"Not unless you are going to make a plenty of them and have enough butter to spread over all that I can eat." She laughed cheerfully at this.

"I'll remember. That's one thing they say that I *can* do well, so I'll try mighty hard to please you."

"You and the girl seem to get along so well, until I guess I'd better get you away from here while I can," grinned Stewart, taking him by the arm. They walked toward the door.

In the kitchen, Deborah went about her work now with a light heart. While she pretended not to be flattered by what Eden persisted in saying, she had been nevertheless. It pleases any woman to be called beautiful and in Deborah's small life she had had little opportunity to hear such wonderful words about herself. He seemed to have cast a spell over her and she couldn't quit thinking about him, regardless how hard she tried.

Bill came into the house for something after Eden and her father had left. She looked out of the kitchen, and seeing who it was, called:

"Bill! Send George in here to help me while you and papa go with Mr. Eden."

"But George's expecting to go, too. He's out there in the back seat of Mr. Eden's car now, waiting."

"Of course he would be," complained Deborah, fretfully; "but it doesn't matter if he is. Tell him to get right out—no," she broke off, thinking up a better way. She came out of the kitchen and close to Bill, glancing out at the car, to see George relaxing in the back seat.

"Yes, he's out there and as usual, running off at the mouth." Then turning to Bill: "Here's what you do. Simply tell him that I want to see him. Don't get into any argument about it, but if you can get him out of the car, the minute he is inside the house, have Mr. Eden drive away, see?"

Bill understood, and getting what he came in for, returned to the car, opened the door and said:

"George, Deborah says come to the house a minute. She wants to see you."

"Me?" asked George, desisting in his gab, and pointing to himself. "What does she want to see me for?" He was plainly annoyed, not to say a trifle suspicious.

"How would I know?" lied Bill. "Get out and go see."

"I—I," began George, sputtering and more suspicious now than ever.

"Shut up George and hurry," cried his father. By this time he was out of the car and Bill crawled in. He closed the door behind him and this made George even more suspicious.

"Now don't you all go way and leave me," he admonished, pointing a finger towards his father; his eyes turned on Bill, who looked away. "Remember, I wanta go up to Mr. Eden's place, too." With this he turned and ran toward the house. Just before entering, he glanced around quickly to see if they were about to pull away. They were looking at him and Bill was waiting. As soon as he entered the house Bill turned to his father:

"Deborah says to go on without him. She needs him to help her."

"Then step on the gas and hurry, Mr. Eden, please," said Stewart. Eden complied and the car shot away, before Deborah could detain George from leaving the house with a loud:

"Eh, you all! What—" but the car was too fast and before George could get half way to the gate, they were over the hill

and out of sight. Meanwhile, Deborah had come to the front
door and when George, with an oath, and a swing of his arm
to emphasize his feelings, turned, she was standing in the door
looking at him disdainfully.

"All right, young man," she said commandingly. "Don't
blame them. I planned this strategy. You're staying right here
and helping me."

"I ain't, I ain't," cried George, swinging his arms about,
all out of sorts. "I wanta go up to Mr. Eden's place and since
you got them to go without me, I'll walk. I'll get there before
they start back. I'll—"

"And if you do, you'll eat no dinner tonight."

"Now Deborah. I—"

"Get right out to the barn yard and catch a chicken. Get
that one like you, which is always crowing. He's crowed his
last time. So get right out there, catch him, ring his neck and
while he's hopping around without his head, go down into the
cellar and get a pan of turnips and potatoes and hurry."

With that she turned and slammed the door, leaving George
only himself to argue with.

When Jack, Bill and Martin arrived at his place, the steers
and hogs, bulging with fat, had about eaten their fill, so were
beginning to lie down for the night. Eden led them around the
place, through the feed lot, pointing out and explaining
matters as they went.

"I'm shipping everything in this yard out to Chicago tomorrow, Bill. The cattle you're to feed are out there in the
pasture. Some are on the way in now," he said, pointing to the
fields, where, forming as they had been trained, the cattle
and the horses were gathering into one long line that lead up
to the barn, and were soon on their way in. "You put them
up at night, and then gather up the eggs around the barn and
straw pile. You're to come up and let the cattle out in the
morning. Close the doors, but don't lock them in at night nor
tie any of them up. I've trained them to know where they
belong, and in case of fire, they've all been taught to come out."

"Splendid, Mr. Eden, splendid," complimented Stewart. "A most practical idea, I do say."

"I did it because I get lonesome out here alone and often stay in town late at night, at a picture show or hanging around a saloon, listening to others tell lies and helping them by telling a few myself." Everyone laughed. Eden turned to Bill:

"After I've gone, you're to drive the cattle from the Swanson place up here and run them in on feed where these are feeding now," said Eden, with a swing of the hand toward the steers and hogs, beginning to fall asleep from carrying their own fat. "Do you understand, Bill?"

"Yes, sir, Mr. Eden. I understand everything."

"And I do, too," said Jack. "We'll be careful to carry things along just as you have them planned."

"Fine," said Eden, pleased to hear that they did.

"Now supposing," suggested Stewart, "that we go around and gather the eggs while you're here, so that Bill will know where all the nests are."

"No sooner said than we start doing it," replied Eden.

"Then what are we waiting for," said Jack, leading the way, tho' he didn't know where.

A few minutes after gathering the eggs, they were on their way to the Swanson place, where they checked on the cattle for the night and returned to the Stewarts' house for dinner.

When the trio entered the house, they found Deborah setting the table feverishly. She had brought out the family's best table cloth, silver, and napkins, which had not been used since they came to Dakota. She had, in the meanwhile, worked George so hard that he had no ambition to talk—not even to complain about their having gone and left him.

A few minutes later everyone was gathered about the table. Eden was seated directly across from Deborah, where he could look into her face at will. Hungry farmers have little time, until they have become filled, for ceremony and ostentation. Deborah had prepared a sumptuous meal and Martin Eden ate his fill. The closest way to a man's heart, so 'tis said, is through his stomach. If so, Deborah had the right of way to Eden's from the outset. At times during the meal Eden happened to meet Deborah's eyes as if by prearrangement.

She was so much unlike the average country girl, especially the poorer ones, that any one had to notice her. She seemed to him to be very intelligent and refined and that was what he liked in women.

When the meal was over Bill and George helped her clean the dishes while he and old Jack talked of land, crops, cattle and hogs. Jack took him to the highlands of Scotland, as it were, from where the elder had come to America many years before. Eden then related some of his experiences all over America from the days he had acted as a Pullman car porter.

"How," said Jack, curiously, while Deborah looked on and listened with the keenest interest, "did you ever happen to settle here, Mr. Eden? That's something everybody asks everybody else when your name is brought up."

"Oh, I don't exactly know. I guess it just happened. I was about to buy a farm and settle out in Washington or Oregon. I wasn't used to the kind of farming they do out there, else I guess I would have gone there. I was born and raised on a farm in southern Illinois. When I came to Chicago, many of my associates were going back to school, preparing to become doctors and lawyers. They tried to get me to do the same thing, but a profession had never quite appealed to me. So at a loss to know just what I ought to do, I decided that it would be to my best interests to go where the country was new and unsettled. Get there, begin with the beginning, and grow up with the country. That was my idea, so here I am."

"How interesting," commented Deborah, looking straight at him with admiration.

"Not only interesting but practical. Good common sense, that was all," said Jack approvingly.

"I should say it was," said Deborah, warming up to him as they talked.

"So one night, out of Omaha on my way to Chicago from Portland, Oregon, I happened to see in a paper an advertisement reading 'Rosebud, Government Lands,' and it interested me. Immediately I checked on what it was all about—and decided to come here; and that's my little story."

"Your *little* story?" exclaimed Deborah.

"Your *big* story, you should say," said Stewart.

"A great big story and interesting, very interesting, I'd say," said Deborah, looking straight at him out of honest, admiring eyes. "You should write a book some day about yourself."

"A book?" he mused. "Maybe I will some day, but nothing that I have experienced so far would be enough to make as interesting a book as I would wish to write. It's when you've had trouble, plenty of troubles, great troubles, and can put yourself into the third person, or even maybe into the first person and tell what has happened to you, those subtler things, I mean, that one can write an interesting book."

"Are you fond of books?" she asked.

"Very fond of them. I read all the time. At times that is the only way I can endure this lonesome life I've been forced to live up there in my little old sod house."

"And do you—get very lonesome?" said she, curiously. He looked at her and in such a way that she was forced to lower her eyes. He wanted to say that if he were near her he would never get lonesome! Instead, he shifted the conversation:

"I've been doing all the talking, Miss, so suppose you do some, too. Tell me about yourself, some of your experiences."

"Me?" she echoed. "My experiences? Why, Mr. Eden, you make me laugh. What ever kind of experiences could I have had?"

"Why, I don't know. Every girl must have had some kind of an experience. There is always, more or less, for instance, the boy friend," said he suggestingly. She looked across at her father and burst into laughter.

"She hasn't had any experience that would be worth relating, Mr. Eden," said Jack Stewart, glancing at her fondly.
"She has been nowhere, seen nothing. Why, where we came
from was only eighty miles southeast of Chicago, and she
had never even been there until we came through the city
on the way out here." Eden looked at her and felt rather sad.
He could understand now what it meant to be so poor. Seeming
to sense what he was thinking, Stewart went on:

"But she's a good girl, Mr. Eden. No finer girl ever lived.
Without her I don't know what I'd have done. Her mother
passed away when she was just a little tot; George and Bill
were not much more than babies. Well, to make a long story
short, she raised herself and both of them. She put herself
through high school back there in Indiana. So while she has been
nowhere except from Indiana here, she's a good little girl and
her father's darling." He got up, crossed over to Deborah and
patted her cheek fondly, while she looked up at him with love
in her eyes and, placing her hands on one of his, caressed it.

Eden was greatly moved by the display of love between
father and daughter and considered it appropriate to make his
departure. He rose to indicate his intentions and said:

"Well, folks, it's time for farmers to be in bed, especially
since this one must be up early in order to run that stock into
town." Everyone walked toward the door. Deborah's waist
was encircled by her father's arm. "Meanwhile," continued he,
"let me thank you all for a mighty happy evening."

Deborah had a sudden thought and asked:

"By the way, Mr. Eden, you spoke of reading so much.
Do you happen to have any—literature up at your house
that we could 'borrow' while you're away? It doesn't matter
if it is old."

"Lots of everything, Miss Stewart, old and new, soiled,
too." They all laughed. "And you can have it all."

"Oh, thank you, Mr. Eden," said she, gratefully. They
crossed to the door and she decided to tease as he turned
back a moment.

"Can Bill get it or will you give it to him?" she asked.

"I'll give him all he can bring home, if I think about it. If I forget it, he can bring it."

"I hope you'll think to give it to him, for if you forget and he has to bring it, we might accidentally find and read some of your 'love letters.' Lost between the pages, you understand." She was chiding Eden and it brought a big laugh from him.

"Love letters," he sighed, and shook his head. "Think of the 'forgotten man' getting love letters."

"Forgotten man!" She exclaimed teasingly. "You're not going all the way to Chicago to keep company with cattle."

"There is nobody waiting for me back there," said he sadly. "I did have a girl who I thought liked me once, but this wilderness and life out here was too much for her, so she quit me."

"I don't believe it," she protested, promptly. "No girl would ever quit you, oh, no."

"Really? I'm flattered, but I'm sorry that you won't believe me."

"We've wondered at your living out here all alone, Mr. Eden," said Jack. "It would seem that you'd get married."

"He will soon enough," chided Deborah. "Don't let him fool you." She was anxious to find out if he did or did not have a girl. She didn't understand just why.

"I'm all alone, honestly, I am. All the girls I meet and know live in Chicago. They don't understand my life out here in this wilderness; they wouldn't appreciate it."

"There may be some truth in that," said Stewart, turning to Deborah.

"That's possible," she observed; "but I can't seem to believe him. I'd be willing to bet that when he comes back here, he'll have a wife on his arm." Knowing that she was mistaken this time, he turned and cried:

"That's a bet! What's the stake?" She blushed now and conceded. She believed that he was speaking the truth, so she decided to say no more. For reasons she could not even explain to herself, she felt relieved. She was glad to feel that she could look forward to seeing him returning as he was going away—single.

Before he left arrangements were made for them to help him drive the cattle, load and haul the hogs to Gregory on the morrow to be entrained for Chicago, and the market. This completed, he stepped out into the night but turned to call:

"Well, good night, folks—see you tomorrow." While all bid him good night, Eden was conscious mostly of her voice, coming to his ears, softly:

"Good night," then he caught one fleeting smile from her before the door closed, and he was gone.

It was still dark when Jack Stewart and his two boys drove up to Eden's little sod house on the claim the next morning to help him get his stock to town and aboard the eastbound freight for Omaha, where the cars would be shifted to a fast, through freight for the windy city.

The hogs were hauled to town and crowded into a car first, after which the cattle were driven in and placed aboard two cars.

"Well," said Stewart, "it's nearly three hours before the train pulls out. I told Deborah to prepare dinner, so if its all right with you, we'll spin out to the farm and have a good dinner before you leave."

"I'm always ready to eat," said Eden, "so let's get going." After the meal, it was necessary for Bill to drive Eden to town and bring the car back.

"Suppose you all ride in, see a movie and shop around a bit, eh what?" said Eden, pleasantly.

Deborah looked at her father; it was obvious that she wanted to go, and in a few minutes they were at the freight yards, waiting for the train to get under way. It was not long before they saw the conductor wave his lantern as a signal to go. They were near the caboose. Deborah sat in the car. As the train began to move, he looked out and his eyes met hers. She raised a little gloved hand. He waved back and, as the cars pulled away, continued to watch her while Bill got into the car. They were soon lost in the semidarkness.

As the freight sped eastward Martin Eden dared not feel that he had at last met the One Woman, but he knew that whatever came, he would never be able to dislike Deborah Stewart.

CHAPTER II

It took the freight train all that night and the next day and night to reach Chicago. Eden's sleep in the caboose was too often disturbed; it was fitful, broken a dozen times each night by stops, switchings and shrill whistles. He was good and tired, therefore, when he met the agents of his commission merchant at the Union Stock Yards on Halsted Street, shortly after his arrival.

By ten A.M. his cattle and hogs had been sold, bringing close to top prices. He completed his committments back to the Dakota bank, which had advanced the money for his purchases and feedings. He had over $2,000 clear for his labor and investment and hurried, a few block east on the South Side to where the Negroes live. He bathed, shaved, and went down to the great Marshall Field Stores where he was fitted with two new suits, a natty overcoat, and a semi-western hat; then returning to his hotel he went to bed and enjoyed a long, restful sleep.

Eden arose at seven thirty P.M., had dinner and decided to call on an old friend by the name of Bowels—Joe Bowels, with whom he used to run on the road.

"Martin Eden! Of all people," exclaimed Bowels, upon opening the door in answer to Eden's ring and finding him standing there. Grasping his hand warmly, he pulled him into the house in a rough, joking way, and closing the door, called out loudly:

"Hattie!"

"What do you want, Joe, and who is it?" yelled his wife, equally as loud, from the rear. By this time, Bowels had hung

up Eden's coat and hat and was on his way to the sitting
room when he met his wife, who stopped dead still upon seeing
who it was. She held out her arms and cried:

"Why Martin Eden of all men! Come and let me hug you,
you handsome sinner!" The next moment she was in his arms
and he took the liberty of kissing her on the lips, with a full,
resounding smack.

"My, my, what sweet lips—um, um," she cried.

"The first woman I've kissed since the last time I kissed
you," he answered bashfully.

"Liar," she said, softly, looking up at him.

"Honestly."

"Really?"

"M-m."

"Then try another. I kinda like them myself." They kissed
again. A girl sitting at the table, looking on, cried:

"My, oh, my!" Then turning to Bowels, warned: "Joe,
who's this tall and handsome? You better look out. Remember,
that woman is still your wife."

"Not only have I not kissed a woman since I left here last
January, but I haven't even seen a colored person, not counting
an occasional porter on a train," continued Eden.

"Well, people!," chirped the girl sitting by the table.
"Where've you been, Mr. Man? In jail?" At this all broke into
laughter, and Bowels said:

"No, honey. This man has perhaps never been in jail.
He's a rancher, lives out west in South Dakota. I want you to
meet him. Mr. Eden, please meet Miss Eunice Janis; Miss
Janis, Mr. Eden."

"A pleasure, Mr. Eden."

"Same here, Miss Janis." And he looked at her with a joke
in his eyes. "In jail," he laughed again, and was joined by
Bowels and his wife. They had just finished dinner but had not
cleared the table.

"Sit down, Martin, and have something to eat," invited
Hattie. "Draw him up a chair, Joe."

"Sure, sure," cried Joe, finding one and pulling it up between his wife and Miss Janis.

"Just got up from the table, folks; but I'll sit here between your charming wife and the young lady and listen while you tell me all the news which I'm longing to hear."

"Well, Eden, things aren't nearly as good on the road as in the old days."

"No?"

"Naw—absolutely, not."

"And it's me and the children that know it," cut in his wife.

"Oh, the children. I knew there was something missing. Where are the little ones, anyhow?"

"At a party over at the Leachs'."

"And the Leachs, how are they?"

"The old man died since you were here."

"Oh, that's sad."

"Yeh; but he had seen his day. He was 78."

"Seventy-eight! Well, we can't complain if we happen to live that long. And Mildred?"

"She married a porter—you remember him. Minis is his name."

"Sure, Minis, I remember him. Lawrence Minis."

"That's him."

"That fellow had lots of education."

"Sure," said Mrs. Bowels, "like my husband; and all he could do with it was to run on the road—is still running on the road."

"Well, running on the road isn't so bad."

"No, but what does it get you?"

"Joe seems to have done well," commented Eden. Hattie looked across at Joe.

"Pardon me, Mr. Eden," asked Miss Janis, "but—have you a cigarette, and may I have one?"

"He doesn't smoke," interposed Hattie. Eunice's eyes opened in mild surprise.

"And he ain't no sissy, neither," said Mrs. Bowels. The girl relaxed, and Eden turned to her:

"I'm afraid you'd like to have me wrong. I'm *all* man, understand, little sister?" She smiled back at him, temptingly.

"Maybe you'll get to take her out while you're here and prove what you're saying," suggested Mrs. Bowels with a twinkle of the eye. This suited Eunice, who looked at him with an expression that was inviting.

"Here's one," said Bowels, attracting Eunice's attention.

"Thanks," she replied while looking inquisitively at Eden again:

"A light?"

"Give her a light, Joe," said Mrs. Bowels. Joe struck a match and held it across to Eunice.

"Never ask a man who doesn't smoke for a light," complained Mrs. Bowels.

"No harm done," said Eunice and smiled across at Eden.

"I'm thinking you want to *make* my boy," said Mrs. Bowels, eyeing the girl. Eunice refused to comment. "Well, give him a little time. We're old friends, he's got lots he wants to talk with Joe about."

"Just as you say, Hattie," and Eunice took a deep whiff from her cigarette.

"As I was saying, things aren't good on the road any more at all. Too many automobiles; those people with the big money are going by plane, so we get only the middle class who can't afford to spend much."

"Bad for tips, I imagine."

"Worse," replied Mrs. Bowels.

"Your salary, however, is much better than when I used to run with you," said Eden.

"Well, that helps, some," remarked Joe.

"But tell us about yourself? Forget about the road—it's the same old seven and six. Your case is far more interesting because something is happening with you. What has happened since the last time you were here?"

"Yes, tell us all about it," encouraged his wife.

"All about what?" asked Eden, looking around. "Nothing has happened to me that would be of interest to you."

"Well, I don't know," said Hattie, then looking straight at him. "Martin Eden, why don't you get married?"

"I don't see how you can stand it out there alone," added Bowels. "You're in the prime of life. You need a wife."

"I'd either find a wife or leave that place," said Mrs. Bowels emphatically.

"And why should he," argued Bowels, a bit seriously, looking hard at his wife. "It's the man's living, his future—his whole life."

"But however can he stand it out there alone? No one to cook for him, sew for him, comfort him and love him," argued Mrs. Bowels.

"Is he the only man who has ever had to live alone—for a few years?" countered Bowels, who then turned to Eden:

"And listen, Martin," emphasizing his speech by pointing a finger, "When you do marry let it be some Swede, Norwegian, or German woman or some of their kind out there. Don't *ever* marry a colored woman, *never!*"

"Well, people!" exclaimed his wife, completely on the war path now.

"Well, *what*, Hattie? It's good advice I'm giving him. *Never* marry a *colored* woman, Martin, and I mean that."

For answer his wife just glared at him, too enraged to say anything. Joe continued:

"This boy has a future, a definite purpose in life to fulfill, he's headed somewhere and in the right direction. I want to see him continue to go in that direction. But the day he gets mixed up with a Negro woman, that's the day he curves, starts back—and in the wrong direction!"

"If I had a brick, Joe Bowels, I'd throw it straight at you;

at your fat head." She paused as if to gather more force, more invective. She turned to Eunice, and though addressing her, meant the words for her husband:

"Can you *imagine* such a thing? Have you *ever* heard such words from one of our own men and that man *my own husband?*" She faced Joe now, and raved on:

"Listen, Joe Bowels. If I hadn't been married to you for twenty years and dependent on you to feed and clothe our children I'm sure I'd be justified in killing you for such an expression—yes, killing you; shooting you right through that big, meaty head of yours!" Bowels laughed at this, and was joined by Eden, but Mrs. Bowels didn't laugh. The way she felt then, she meant it. Her husband had tramped on her toes; put his heel right on a corn.

"But you know it's good advice, Hattie," he argued, jokingly, a smile on his lips. "Now take our case—yours and mine—and just look what happened to me, for instance." Mrs. Bowels spoke up immediately:

"You went to school, graduated from college, thought you knew everything and when you found out you didn't you figured out what the matter was. You decided that you needed some more education. So you went back to school, starved yourself for three years more while you studied law and graduated in that."

"Then what did I do?" he asked, pointedly.

"Well," she answered a bit hesitantly. "You said you were in love; in love with me. All you needed to become a Max Stuer, a John W. Davis or a Martin W. Littleton, as you saw it, was to get married. 'Marriage keeps a man steady,' you said; 'makes him conscious of grave responsibilities to his clients.' So you asked me to marry you—and like a fool, I did."

"Like a fool, eh?"

"Yes, like a fool."

"Then what did you do?"

"Not what did *I do;* but what *you tried* to do."

"And what was that?"

"What was that? Joe Bowels will you *ever* forget what *that* was; will you ever, until the longest day you live, *forget?*" Bowels remembered and hesitated now, so Hattie, thoroughly angry, decided to *tell it all.* She turned to the others.

"It's not a long story," she began, "it's short, very short. Joe went to Des Moines, Iowa, and took me and two of the children. There is one thing he *did* do after he got married." Eden smiled. He found it amusing and interesting, so he asked: "What was that?"

"He loaded me down with children—three in four years!" Everybody laughed.

"That was the finest thing he could have done," said Eden.

"It was the finest—also the *only* thing he did with all of his education; his practice amounted to nothing. Plainly, and simply, nothing."

"Was that my fault," protested Joe. "Could I help it if the Negroes had no money with which to pay a lawyer?"

"No," turning to him. "It wasn't your fault that they had nothing; but it was your fault for not finding it out before you went there; before you spent all those years, the best ones of your young life to become a lawyer. Had you been smart, you'd have seen that Negroes had no money to pay lawyers, in Des Moines, or anywhere else!"

"But Hattie," he tried to protest.

"But Hattie, the devil! It wasn't *their* fault, no, and it wasn't *their* fault that you were a dreamer—a man who used up the best years of his life, dreaming. Instead of a lawyer, you should have tried to be a writer; a novelist who gets paid for dreaming!"

"Listen, Joe and Hattie," interposed Eden at this point, "take it easy and don't get so excited."

"I'm not through, Martin. Joe started this, I intend to finish it. I must tell you what happened to us in Des Moines."

"Well, dear, what *did* happen?"

"We liked to have starved to death! *That's what happened!*
Some day I want to write a book. It would be entitled, 'MY
HUSBAND *WAS* A LAWYER!'"

"But he *is* a lawyer, isn't he? He is still a lawyer."

"Yes, but a *better* porter. He gave up that 'law' business,
came here and got a job running on the road—and has been
at it ever since. So now he wants to give *you* some of *his* good
advice."

"Well, I think Joe's advice about getting married is all
right," said Eden.

"To a *white* woman?"

"Oh," said Eden, laughing. "He didn't mean that and I
don't mean to marry a white woman."

"Be sure that you don't. It seems to me that when a Negro
man gets a little money, the first thing he thinks about is to
tie up with some old white woman—but to think that my own
husband would so advise you is too much!"

"I didn't tell him to do anything of the kind," cried Bowels.
Again she glared at him.

"Then since when did *we* become Swedes, Norwegians and
German women, eh?"

"Oh, Hattie, you like to go off half cocked. You said some
'old' white woman. You don't seem to appreciate Eden's
position. He isn't living here in Chicago. He's living in what
was, a few years ago, a new country, a wild and undeveloped
country. You just heard him say that he'd hardly seen a
colored face since he left here last winter. Isn't it obvious to
you that the average colored girl might not appreciate his life
out there? Think of the sacrifices in comfort and conveniences
that Chicago affords as against life out there; sacrifices that
they might be called on to make—and you know how far
Chicago's colored women are willing to go when it comes to
making sacrifices. If there's no colored people up there, then

there must be a reason; and the reason is clear. It's 'all Greek' to them and to avoid making a bad marriage and maybe spoiling his whole life and what he is working for, Eden should marry some one who lives out there, some one who under- stands the life and his needs and who could and would be willing to help him."

"Well, aren't there plenty of colored girls—"

"Naw, naw—and you know it! Martin's working out his destiny; he's making some money, but he needs all that he is making, I venture—and a whole lot more." Hattie looked at Martin and he nodded his head in agreement with what Joe was saying. The latter continued:

"He isn't going to stand still. He's either going forward or backward. I know that he wants to go forward. He's not interested in marrying any woman, colored or white, who would be interested only in spending his money. But that's what he'll get if he isn't mighty careful. If he were in Chicago, running on the road like me, it would be another story. We can only make so much money and you women understand that. You manage the little money we make so as to have the rent, or you know that you will be put out. You know that you must have food or starve. If you don't provide for warm, com- fortable clothing, you know that you'll suffer—you might even freeze. In short, our women understand life here in Chicago and how to get along, but not many of us have more than a home. But you neither understand or appreciate Martin Eden's needs; Martin Eden, a man of conquest, trying to get somewhere—go places.

"Those are some of the things, I mean, Hattie. Since there are no colored girls where he lives, it'd be better, under the circumstances for him to marry a Swede, a Danish or German woman than to risk his future happiness and prosperity by getting crazy and coming back here and marrying somebody— like Eunice, there, for instance." The others turned to Eunice, who had been listening, but not very keenly. She was a girl incapable of absorbing anything very serious, but on hearing her name called, looked up.

"And why must Eunice's name be brought into it, and how do you know whether she might not like it up there?" asked Mrs. Bowels.

"Now folks," interposed Eden, "don't you think we are carrying it a bit too far?" Perking up with an idea at this point, however, Mrs. Bowels turned to Eunice:

"Listen, Eunice," hoping to have somebody agree with her to counteract her husband, who seemed to be getting the better of the argument. "If you loved a man truly, wouldn't you be willing to go with him anywhere?" Eunice tried to think, drew away at her cigarette which was only a butt by this time, and drawled lazily:

"I don't know. Maybe." Mrs. Bowels bit her lip in vexation as her husband smiled.

"If you loved him *dearly*, I mean—*loved him better than your own soul*."

"But that couldn't be," she said, looking across at Mrs. Bowels.

"Exactly what do you mean, Eunice?"

"Love a man better than myself. That *couldn't* happen in my case. I might love him some, a lots, maybe; but not better than myself. I could never love any man that much. Oh, no, not better than myself, nevuh!" She finished, leaving Mrs. Bowels flustered, while her husband was about to burst from laughter. Eunice looked around apparently oblivious as to how she had disappointed Mrs. Bowels. She raised the cigarette to her lips, but found it too short for one last puff; she looked at the others and inquired:

"Got one, anybody?"

Bowels passed her one; Martin rose to go and Mrs. Bowels followed, glaring at Eunice when the latter's eyes were turned.

In the hall with Eden about to leave, Mrs. Bowels sighed unhappily. She had lost the argument, so Eden placed his arm about her and said:

"Now don't be discouraged, dear. I'm going to marry soon—within two years, perhaps." She looked up at him tearfully.

"And it isn't going to be to any German or Scandinavian woman, either. It's going to be one of our own. I'm checking up on one or two on this trip and may make some progress before I return home."

"I'm so glad to hear you say that, Martin. How long do you plan to be here?"

"Until after Xmas day, anyhow."

"Then we'll be seeing you again. I know some *good* gir's, some sensible girls; and before you leave I'm going to have you to dinner and you can meet them."

"Oh, that'll be fine," he cried, enthusiastically. He kissed her for it and she helped him into his coat; Eunice came into the hall from the rear as Eden bid them all good night and stepped out into a chilly Chicago night.

CHAPTER III

IT WAS ABOUT a week after Eden left when Deborah, at work in the kitchen, heard a shrill whistle. Stopping and listening a moment, she hurried to open the front door, and looked out into the road.

The rural mail carrier had stopped and was standing beside his car with a package. Upon seeing her at the door he waved his free hand and pointed.

"Got a package for your father," said he, as he came up, lifting a slip with his pencil. Will you sign for it, please?"

"Of course, thank you." She scribbled her name upon the slip and took the package. With it were a newspaper and a post card, which she read in a flash. It was from Martin Eden, postmarked "Chicago," and carried a picture of one of the tall buildings there. On the address side, opposite her father's name, was scribbled:

"Hello, Mr. Stewart:

Having a wonderful time and am sending you and the family something nice to read. Hope you will like it. Will help you out by perhaps reading some of it myself when I get back. Wishing all a merry Xmas and a happy New Year, I remain,

Cordially,
MARTIN EDEN"

The card and the package were both for her father. She felt a bit peeved to think that he had not written and addressed the package to her. But since it was to her father, he knew that she would read the books, which were perhaps in the package.

Her father was not at home, and she was too curious and anxious to see the gift to wait until he returned, so boldly she cut the string, broke the carton and withdrew the contents.

It was filled with books, and a roll of magazines had been thrown in for good measure. She had been thinking about him every day since he left. She wondered and asked herself if he, maybe, had thought of her. Then she decided that he must have, when he bought the books, for it was she who had talked to him about books. He would hardly have been interested in sending them to her father, although the package *was* addressed to him.

She examined the magazines first. There was a variety of them. She surmised that he must have bought them to read himself and then, rather than throw them away, thought of them.

She inspected the books. There were exactly one dozen. Mostly popular copyrighted novels, the best of the best, published two or three years before. Then there was one that was not of popular copyright. She singled it out, looking at it curiously and read the title aloud:

"THE AUTOBIOGRAPHY OF AN EX-COLORED MAN"
She sketched the introduction:

"The Autobiography of an Ex-Colored Man," she murmured to herself, half aloud. "A strange title, must be a strange book. I'll bet it's interesting." After deciding to read it first Deborah continued through the others, filled with delight. She knew that she would broaden her knowledge—with almost an endless number of books to read. With what they had brought from his house there were enough to keep her reading until he came back.

In her happiness, she skipped around the room. Then pausing, with her eyes upraised and holding a book to her breast, with both hands, she allowed herself to think of him aloud, and without restraint.

"Oh, Martin, you're the finest man I ever met—the very

finest man in all the world." She kissed him, then, imaginarily. She pictured him there in the big city where so many people lived, and all the noise and music and theatres and the excitement that went with it. And with all this around him he took time out to think of her and to go downtown, select, and send such a choice lot of gifts. She felt that if she hadn't fallen in love with him already, she most surely would very soon.

She was still in this state of ecstasy when her father burst into the room and surprised her. He, himself was startled when he saw her standing, holding a book, her eyes uplifted as if in prayer.

"Deborah!" he cried, and looked at her curiously. She relaxed quickly, a bit embarrassed. "What were you doing?"

"Oh—just posing."

"Posing?" She thought quickly and had to make up a little lie so crossed to the table where the books lay.

"See, father? Just look what Mr. Eden sent us." He turned and for the first time saw the gift.

"Oh," he cried. "Books. My, that's nice of him."

"I think so, too." Then he looked up at her with a question in his eyes. She sensed what he was thinking so countered quickly:

"He sent them to you," pointing to his name on the label. He turned the box so he could see his name, then said:

"Very thoughtful. We can all read them. I thought he sent them to you."

"To me? Oh, no . . . Why?"

"Oh, nothing. Just heard you and he talking so much about books before he left, that when I saw so many pretty ones, I wondered." She became silent and wondered if her father was seeing through her or understood how she felt toward Eden and, if so, what was his reaction. She decided to find out:

"Father?"

"Yes, dear?"

"What do you really think of Mr. Eden?"

"What do I *really* think of him?" he repeated, looking at her in surprise. "Why, Deborah, are you so curious? You *know* what I think about Mr. Eden. The finest man I ever met—100% through and through. That's what I *really* think of him. But why?"

"Well," as if feeling for words.

"You mean be—because he's a colored man?" this was a question.

"Yes."

"Why, Deborah," he exclaimed in surprise. "You're not—."

"I'm *not*, father. You must understand that I—"

"No. I *can* understand everything; but you were asking me such funny questions. I began to wonder if you was thinking that because he *is* a colored man that should make any difference. It surely doesn't with me and I'd be most unhappy if I thought it did with you." She placed her arms about him, her face lit up with delight.

"I'm *so* glad to hear you say that, father. I was afraid that you—but now that we understand each other, we can talk about him as much as we want to, can't we?" said she. "I think he's a wonderful man, too, father. That's how I feel about him. He seems to have such a big heart and a fine, patient disposition."

"He can even put up with George," said Stewart, "so speaking of patience, that proves that he has aplenty."

"Yes, *even* George," she sighed. "Just think of all the fine books he sent us, father." Her father was running through them, and, picking up the one which had attracted her attention, he paused, reading the title half aloud:

"The Autobiography of an Ex-Colored Man." He opened it and scanning the pages, said: "That's a strange sounding title."

"That's what I thought. It sounds so intriguing."

"Like it should be very interesting."

"That's what I think, too. I decided to read it first."

"Please do—and to me, aloud."

"I will, father."

"In the meantime, we must write and thank him," said Stewart.

"We must," agreed Deborah. "When, now?"

"Well—"

"It's easier if we do so right now. If we wait we'll most likely neglect to."

"Then let's do it now." So saying she hurried into her room and returned with pen and paper, and sitting down.

"All right, father. What'll I say?"

"Well, head it first."

"Oh yes," laughing at her forgetfulness, which she knew was due to excitement. The scratch of the pen was audible as she bent to write the heading.

"How'll I begin? 'Dear Mr. Eden'?" Jack concentrated his thoughts to dictate a letter.

"Receipt of your postal card from Chicago, advising that you were having a wonderful time and sending us your kindest personal regards, we acknowledge, and for which we thank you." He paused a moment.

"How's that?"

"Fine, father. Direct and to the point, yet courteous."

"Thanks, dear. I used to write a very intelligent letter, but old age and trouble have took something out of me."

"You're doing all right. Now what else are we going to say? We haven't thanked him for the books."

"Oh, yes, the books. That's why we are writing him. The books. Very well." He walked a few steps, then stopped near her.

"Permit us to thank you for all the nice books and magazines that you sent us, also, and which were received in the same mail. Words are insufficient—"

"No, father, 'inadequate' is the word, there."

"That's right, my daughter. Inadequate *is* the proper word.

Thank you for correcting me. Don't hesitate to do so when I use the wrong one. Now let's start over again."

"I've got it all up to there," suggested Deborah. "You said: 'Permit us to thank you for all the nice'"—she broke off with a new thought. "Instead of 'nice,' 'delightful' would sound so much better, don't you think so, father?"

"I do. Bully for you. Between the two of us we'll send him a letter that'll make him think we are smart people, we—"

"Oh, no, not 'smart,' father. Maybe intelligent. He would like that better. Intelligent is the word."

"Now you'll have to start all over again."

"No father, I have a better idea. We'll correct this as we go along and then when we have finally finished it, I'll copy it all over. How's that?"

"Great, dearest—great!"

"All right, now let's get going for good," said she, a bit judiciously.

"We ought to say that this leaves us all well."

"That's old, father. If we were not well he'd expect us to say that one of us was not, and state which one."

"That's right, of course he would. Well, since we *are* all well, we'll—"

"Just leave that out."

"Sure, just leave it out."

"There is something we must say in the letter, however. We must ask him about the eggs."

"We sure must. In the rush of his leaving, we all forgot to ask him what we should do with them. His hens seem to have a laying spell and we have several dozens already."

"Why not sell them," said she. "That's what he'd do if he were here, wouldn't he?"

"I guess so," answered Stewart, thoughtfully. "Those that he didn't, he'd eat."

"Meaning that *we* should—"

"No, Deborah. That's taking too much for granted."

"It is, father. We must account for every one of them. I'd say sell them and keep or send him the money but first tell him what we have done with them and ask him if we shall send the money to him or keep it."

"Eggs are high. On account of Xmas being so near, I guess."

"Well, father, now that we have practically decided what we want to say, suppose I go ahead and write the letter."

While Jack cleared his throat, bent on further dictation, she finished the message, which was mailed and duly received.

In Martin's reply he requested them to apply the egg money on account for Bill's pay, and to inform him before the end of the first month the amount so applied, to allow keeping the account balanced. Permission to use this was decidedly a boon to this needy family.

CHAPTER IV

IMMEDIATELY AFTER Christmas day Martin left Chicago. He had not been in Harlem since settling in the West but within twenty four hours he was in New York City.

Once in Harlem, that Negro city within a city, with its population of almost 350,000 black people crowded within less than two square miles, he saw enough Negroes to arouse a vivid memory for years to come, even should he see no more blacks after returning West.

Accustomed as a farmer to early rising, he stood one morning at 135th Street and Lenox Avenue, watching the dense crowds pour into all four entrances of the IRT Subway. Contrariwise, hundreds seemed to be on their way to their living quarters, apparently just returning sleepy and exhausted after turning night into day. Countless others were still carousing in the taverns. Evidently there were thousands who could not sleep at all during the night, becoming drowsy only with the coming of daylight.

On the other hand, far more *had* to sleep at night, to conform to the morning rush schedule of the crowds pouring into all four entrances of the subway station where he was watching.

"What do all these people do?" he thought. Dismissing consideration of the rank and file, his mind turned to the occupations followed by the aristocracy of the Negro population—a few hundred school teachers, a handful of city job holders, and the approximate 6000 employed in the greater New York Post Office. There were also the doctors, the preachers, some lawyers. Only one with sufficient influence could meet this privileged class, who—especially the wives—are accused of being "hincty" and "dicty."

61

He recalled also the richest class of Harlem—the "numbers" bankers—known before Dutch Schultz's seizure of the nefarious practice as the "big shots." He sketched to himself the course of this "numbers" racket up to the time Dutch Schultz "took over."

"Banking the numbers" is the simplest racket, perhaps, in the realm of racketeering, to figure out. It includes three numerals, running from and including, ooo to and including, 999—exactly 1000 numerals in all. If the "suckers" who insist on playing it could or would do any figuring at all, they could easily understand that when he pays 500 to one, the "banker" is giving the players, as a group, 50¢ of each dollar he plays, back. But the "sucker" rarely ever thinks of this. The catch is in the fact that you can take a chance with as little as a penny. That's the lure—$5.00 for a little "bitty" ole' penny.

Some day a man banking the game, or for several days, may be "lucky." He may not get "hit" for much over two or three cents a day for days. If he allowed that he would be hit as he should, and provided for such an emergency as a legitimate banker would, he couldn't help making lots of money. But most bankers are merely graduated "hustlers," with ambitions to "show off" by keeping and maintaining many women—expensive women, notoriety women. He is fond of trips to Atlantic City, riding there in specially built bodied cars, fur coats and diamonds for their beautiful women—mostly yellow ones—and they, like the players, are always "taking a chance." In the case of the "Banker" it's often on *not* getting "hit" too heavy.

The day of reckoning, however, had to come when several bankers were hard hit with "paying off" obligations they could not meet promptly. They sought a loan from the "honorable" Mr. Flegenhiemer, relating the facts about the "numbers" business. Dutch's bootlegging business had been cut short by the repeal of prohibition, and he was looking for a new shady practice. These men provided it. "Great goodness!" Dutch has been quoted as saying: "Funny I've never been told the inside of this racket before." He lent them the money they asked for and they hailed him as "sure one nice white man."

A few days later he ordered most of them, including many who had not even come to see him at all, taken for "rides."

None were killed. Most anybody who knows Negroes know that you do not have to "kill" him to convince him. Just give him a good scare, which is what Schultz did—but meant it and they *knew* he meant it.

In time, he took a few back as "Lieutenants" and "muscle" men; but his entry into the policy racket marked the end of the Negroes reign there as a major racketeer.

Martin's heart ached over the limited advantages of his race, and their gullibility in dealing with the unscrupulous.

After watching the scramble into the subway which took some to the Bronx; some to downtown Manhattan, Brooklyn, Queens, and transferred many to the Jersey Cities across the river. He strolled out to the intersection and ventured conversation with the Negro cop. A tall, powerfully built man and as black as he was tall and powerful, he was equally as short in his answer to Eden's queries—at first. He was also, "mean" looking. Perhaps it was because of the traffic which he had to watch, carefully. The street soon became filled also with school children.

Later, Eden was told that he just "looked" that way to discourage other Negroes who would like to *be mean*. It kept this officer from having to exercise his "mean" looking disposition. Fearing him, they respected him and he rarely—even in Harlem, had to "get tuff."

"Hello, officer."

" 'Low."

"Nice day," said Martin.

"Is it?"

"I think so," countered Eden, looking up. It was cloudy and wasn't a nice day at all. He felt that he *had* to say something, however, now or keep moving. He looked at the crowds pouring into the subway.

"Everybody seems to be in a hurry," he tried, pointing to the rushing hundreds.

"They'd better be," said the officer shortly, keeping his eyes on his work.

"Yes?"

"Yeah."

"It's rather interesting to watch them."

"Negroes goin' tu work—niggah work."

"Negro work?"

"Yeah—niggah work, cheap jobs—portering downtown; cooking in Brooklyn; runnin' elevatahs in the Bronx. That's what the mosta these niggahs youah lookin' at do."

"More interesting."

"What's interesting, Mistah?" commented the officer, glancing at him briefly, perhaps for the first time.

"Why, all these people rushing to work, to earn the right to live."

"Or face the right to die—drop dead from starvation on the sidewalks of Harlem. Nothing interesting about niggahs when you have to look at'm every day as I do."

"It is to me," said Eden. The officer glanced at him again.

"They ain't rushin' because they want to, or like to."

"No?"

"Naw. It's because they *have to*."

"Oh, because they have to, eh?"

"Where you live? You ain't from aroun' heah?"

"No," replied Eden. "Out West, on a ranch in South Dakota."

"*Great goodness!*"

Eden looked at him quickly. "What do you mean 'great goodness'?"

"Oh, nothing," said the officer. "Just s'prized to meet some Negro from so far away—except Jamaica."

"Jamaica?"

"Jamaica, West Indies."

"You have lots of West Indians here, I notice."

"Gangs ov'um."

"I hear they're more ambitious than we—American Negroes. Is that so?"

"Yeah."

"Some people don't like them?"

"They don't."

"Why?"

"Nobody told you?"

"No."

"Well ask. You'll find out."

Feeling that he had intruded long enough, Martin turned to the officer "Well, I'm very grateful for the information?"

"Glad to give it to yuh. Goin' to be heah long?"

"A few days."

"Drop back here between six and seven tonight."

"What'll be going on?"

"Nothing."

"Nothing?"

"Except these same niggahs'll be comin' from work then."

"Oh."

"They come out fastern' they go in." Eden laughed.

"Nuther thing."

"Yes, officer?"

"Drop down on 126th Street and Seventh Avenue. You'll see another sight that'll interest you, too."

"Well, thanks chief—and so long."

"So long, brother."

Eden strolled away through 135th Street, west to Seventh Avenue, which rises and is 20 feet or more higher than Lenox. On a corner where Rockefeller had just closed a bank where he hired all Negro help, he paused. People were turning the corner and hurrying westward, where, two blocks away, in an angling direction, ran St. Nicholas Avenue, under which streaked the Independent, City owned Subway. From where he stood, even at so great a distance, he could see more Negroes pouring into a "hole" in the great rock thru which ran this section of the 8th Avenue subway. Its lines spread all over the great city like veins, through Washington Heights into the Bronx, downtown through 8th Avenue, crossed under the East river through two great tubes, spreading all over western Long Island.

So his people went north, hurried southward, riding the fastest subway trains in America, to earn their livelihood, in the kind of work that the "wages and hours law" did not apply.

"My people, my people," he sighed to himself. After his long years, a lone wolf out there in South Dakota, it was truly an interesting sight to him to see how so many of his folk made their living. Out there, he was a novelty and a diversion, because he was colored. Being so was no novelty nor diversion in Harlem, for they were *all* colored—an endless stream of "color."

He now strolled southward toward 126th Street, wondering what it was that the officer had directed him to see, and said he would find interesting. As he crossed 127th Street, the tail end of a double line of Negroes greeted his eye, headed west. He paused to look at them and wondered what it was all about. They would move up a few steps at intervals, then stop again and stand awhile before moving on. Meanwhile, others would fall into line, which came nearer and nearer to Seventh Avenue, despite the fact that the line kept moving forward.

In a sort of quandary, he moved on down Seventh Avenue to 126th Street, and looked to his right. There, less than fifty feet away, he saw what the line was all about. They were headed into the relief station.

He stood and looked at the sight for a minute before moving up 126th Street on the left, to gaze across the street at the unhappy sight before him, on the right side of the street, heading east. Here he paused to watch them go in, get their little dole in groceries and meats and coming out, hurry away, glad to get out of that long, double line which, from where he stood, didn't seem to have any end.

His curiosity aroused, he decided to see how long the line really was; and to study the character, nature and expression of those in the line. So on the opposite side of the street, he walked westward through 126th, to 8th Avenue, perhaps 800 feet.

While the masses were Negroes, for it was in a Negro neighborhood, there was a liberal sprinkling of white people, which gave him food for thought. They seemed, in this line, odd to him. Before relief became a great "American misfortune" as it were, the Negro was considered as given the least of all groups to begging. Now that it has become an "American Institution," he leads, because of being the first to be fired, the last to be hired, when hard times come. He heads all groups now in the burden of relief.

This makes the sight of white people, in a relief line preponderantly Negroid, seem odd—or at least it did to Martin Eden—and out of place, and more noticeable. So as he moved along the street, he studied them closely and was surprised to see that they were, more or less, as well dressed and looked not unlike those he had just seen rushing into the subway to work, who had jobs. He was told later that those in the relief line had just as good clothes, too—but at home. They were too sensible to get into that line in their "Sunday's best."

He was also told, that to get into that line was not easy—in fact, it was hard. It often took weeks to get through all the red tape and there were many, entitled to relief, who couldn't qualify, and could not, therefore, join this seemingly, endless procession.

To his surprise, the line did not end at 8th Avenue and then he realized that the one he had seen on passing 127th Street, was the tail end of this, ending in the relief station on 126th.

He turned, and as the sidewalk is very wide under the Elevated, on 8th Avenue, he walked to 127th Street, directly beside the line on 8th Avenue. He then turned into 127th Street to follow the line, which came out of that street, turning the corner into 8th Avenue.

In the few minutes since passing 127th, headed South, the line had increased and now reached to 7th Avenue, and was in the act of making a curve back into 7th, there. He stood and, watching it continue to increase and stretch down 7th Avenue, shook his head.

At the distance he lived, back there in South Dakota, people pictured Harlem as anything but what he had seen that morning and what he saw that night. As he watched them come up out of the subway, on their ways back home, many of them virtually ran on reaching the sidewalk; they were in such a hurry, after coming "out of the hole."

He knew there was another side to Harlem; but much of that had "gone with the wind," too. Harlem seemed gorgeous and bizarre when throngs of whites with money came there to seek novelty, diversion; to slum and to see Negroes in the origin. But Negro hoodlums, with which the place is filled to overflowing, wrought such damage to their fine cars, trying to steal something, that it had become unsafe to park in many spots. So out of fear on the one hand, a loss of interest, perhaps, on the other, Harlem is not what it once was, although growing larger all the while by an increase in the Negro population.

A few days later, having seen enough for this trip, Eden left and went on his way.

CHAPTER V

DELIA FORBES, small, slender, weighing less than 100 pounds and possessing among other things, a pair of peculiar grey eyes, was born in Carbondale, a bit over 23 years before, and had lived there all her life. Her father died when she was very young and her mother had married a man named Gay, while Delia was still quite small. He was a coal digger and worked in mines near Carbondale. He was a sensible miner, a conservative man, and he had prospered; he had saved, and he was, as Negroes go, "well-to-do."

So Delia had been thoroughly educated, lived in a nice, comfortable home, and had much of what she may have wanted. She was of marriageable age now, and along with her mother's interest in her, she "wanted to get married."

There wasn't an oversupply of marriageable Negro men— even in Chicago, and still less in Carbondale. So that ideal man whom Delia was looking and waiting and praying for, was rather delayed. But on this particular morning, on hearing the mail man's whistle and going to the door, Delia received, among various letters and papers, mostly advertising something to sell, a letter that was postmarked New York. There was something familiar about the hand writing on the letter, which was addressed to her.

Returning to the living room, and examining it curiously, she broke the seal, withdrew the contents and looked at the salutation, which was rather bold, as it began "Dear Delia." This meant that the person who had written it must have known her. She turned to the end of the letter—and then almost screamed aloud with delight and excitement. She restrained herself long enough to read it through, then in a flurry of joy, she called loudly:

"Mama, oh, mama!" and danced gleefully around the room. Of all the persons she knew, the letter was from the man she was most delighted to have write her. Meanwhile, her mother, a matronly woman, who had once been beautiful and could be called handsome still, came forth from the kitchen to "see what it was all about."

"Delia," she cried, coming up with curiosity and watching Delia going through her antics, "Why all the excitement? "What's happened?"

"This letter, mother, this letter!" swinging it under her eyes. "It's from Martin Eden, it's from him!"

"Hump. Martin Eden?" Her mother took the letter, looked at the heading and read the salutation.

"It's from him, all right; from him in New York," chimed Delia.

"In New York?" repeated the mother in surprise. "I thought he was in South Dakota. I—"

"Oh, he lives in South Dakota, yes, mother; but he's in the East, visiting—and just look—read what he writes." and then in a changed tone, reaching and taking the letter back, "I'll read it to you.

'Dear Delia:

'Just a few lines to say hello. Hope you are well and enjoying life as I have been. Am here in big New York City. I left home in Dakota a few weeks ago, had a grand time in Chicago, then came on here, where I have been for the last few days. Will leave here soon, however, and plan to stop off for a spell in Carbondale to see you and others there whom I knew before leaving Southern Illinois.

'This is to ask you, therefore, to please find a place for me to stay, if your mother shouldn't happen to have a spare room which I could occupy while there.' "

She paused here and smiled up at her mother out of her large and peculiar looking grey eyes. The mother nodded and commented:

"Very nice letter." She paused to look at the daughter, who for the moment, was lost in thought.

"Wonder why he's stopping off here instead of going on to Murphysboro. That's—"

"All over," cried Delia, sharply.

"What's all over, Delia?"

"His affair up there."

"What affair up where?" affecting innocence. She knew what was referred to but she was feeling her daughter out.

"Oh, you know what affair I mean, mother! His affair with Jessie Binga. He's not going with her any more. He's stopping off here to—to see—me."

"Oh, you, eh? To see you."

"Yes."

"Did he say so in the letter?"

"Didn't I just read it to you, mother?" She shook the letter impatiently.

"He said you and others that he knew, or used to know." Delia bit her lip in vexation. She had always liked Martin Eden but he had been so completely, so desperately in love with Jessie Binga that he had never paid her any attention; just as if she didn't live in the world. She hadn't dared try make a play for him. In fact, he had never given her a chance—but now.

"Those 'others' could mean anybody," her mother went on. "It could include Jessie Binga. . . ." Her mother, she thought, was surely harassing.

"I tell you, mother," cried Delia, stamping her little foot, "his affair with Jessie is over—all washed up! They've never been—that is, he hasn't been very sweet on her since her mysterious illness of last fall, a year ago. Being the kind of man he is—broad-minded, you understand, and, very busy, he never went to the bottom of why she was ill like that—but everybody else knows all about it. How could a young girl like her, for instance, have inflammation of the ovaries if she hadn't been playing around—and not with Martin Eden, for he wasn't anywhere around to play with."

"Anybody else, except a man like Martin, with an overwhelming ambition to do things—get some where financially, would have asked some questions; he would have found out, but I doubt if he did. Still, his love for her seemed to cool a great deal after that. I don't think he's even writing to her any more. If he knew all the truth about what was the matter with her, he most assuredly wouldn't write her any more at all. And now, with him coming to see me, I shall make it my business to see that he knows the whole truth about it before he leaves."

"And drive him right smack-dab into her arms."

"The idea, mother! How can you think such a thing?"

"Woman's intuition; an old woman's."

"Nevertheless, I shall make it my business to see that he finds out."

"That's different; but be sure that it's not *you* who tells him. No man likes a gossip, much less a tattle tale, when what is tattled is about a woman that he once loved. People who once loved each other dearly can fall out—do fall out—and they can also make up—do make up."

"I've thought that all out during the minutes we've been standing here, arguing. Mine are well laid plans and they will work."

"Don't be too sure."

"I won't be."

"Counting the chickens before they have hatched has always been a bad thing."

"I haven't counted mine."

"Then don't think too much about what he's going to say to you before he gets here. Wait until he has *said* it."

"Trust me, mother; but in the meantime, regarding a room for him. I've decided to give him—mine."

"Oh," echoed Mrs. Gay.

"Why not, mother?"

"No reason for you not to at all."

"Then why do you cry 'oh' like that?"

"Just happened to, that's all."

"I want him to be comfortable while here. I shall see that he enjoys himself."

"Naturally." Delia looked up at her, but her mother, apparently oblivious, continued:

"Now with him here, staying there in *your* room, it won't be so hard to check on his movements. You will be able to see and *know* what he does and when and if he goes up to Murphysboro while here. . . ." This was too much. Delia swung her little arm in a demonstration of extreme impatience. The truth was striking too close to home to leave her comfortable.

"Oh, mother," "*Why must you!*" and stamping her foot, this time in a rage, she left. Going to her room, she slammed the door loudly. Mrs. Gay knew her daughter; knew that she was selfish and cynical—and cold. For that reason she had resigned herself to the girl's fate with regard to getting married—especially to the right kind of man. She smiled as she turned back to her work, comparing Delia, as she did so, with Jessie Binga.

Jessie Binga was warm and soft with a flood of sex appeal; she was a girl that it would not be hard for any man to fall in love with. She was 25 pounds heavier than her daughter, with a well-rounded body, soft dark eyes—in short, she had *everything* men liked in women, while Delia, she sighed, had little! Yet, she was glad Martin Eden was coming to see her. Men were often peculiar regarding choices. One could never tell too much about them, so she decided to be patient and wait and see—but not to suffer disappointment if "nothing" happened.

A few days later Eden arrived in Carbondale, carrying his bag, and was met at the door of her home by Delia.

He looked into her odd grey eyes, as he had years before, and smiled. She always wondered if he was laughing with her, or at her. Anyway, this time, he leaned and kissed her. Off to a good start, so far, so good, she thought.

After bringing her mother and going through the usual formalities, she led him to her room, which she had redecorated for his convenience, and making him comfortable, said:

"It's about dinner time and I'll bet you're hungry."

"I lose that bet before the race starts. You win. I am."

"I guessed aright, and in a few minutes, dinner will be served."

"Oh, my!" and leaning forward, he kissed her again.

"Why, Martin Eden!" she exclaimed, affecting embarrassment with a flash of those odd, grey eyes. Turning to hurry away, she waved back at him fondly before disappearing from sight.

Eden knew that he was expected to be nice to her, and for three days he paid her as passionate court as he could bring himself to play. He knew long before the end of the three days, however, that he didn't like Delia the way he wanted to like a girl that he would one day marry. As has been explained, Martin Eden *had* to make a marriage deal with some girl, or lose an opportunity that he had planned for almost two years.

He was of the opinion that any girl would as willingly accept as reject the financial opportunity to file a claim in South Dakota, the relinquishment of which he would buy, then marry her. However, he wanted to love the girl involved in the deal and realized that, though time was short, he was making slow progress toward finding and falling in love with her. He knew that love was spontaneous, could not be staged and acted like a drama, but must be experienced inwardly.

He *tried* his best to fall in love with Delia. Of all the girls that he might meet, she was one of the few whose people had enough material wealth to appreciate what his responsibility was. Others didn't. Jessie didn't, despite the fact that her father had been a mail carrier. On her mother's side there were some aunts whose reputations were most unsavory. He couldn't trace her father's side very far, but her father was charged with gambling; he was a poor business man. Martin had often wondered, when he was truly in love with Jessie, if she had any background that would make her dependable as the wife of a man with a purpose in life. Perhaps this was why he tried hard to fall in love with Delia.

After three days of it, however, he was still unconvinced. He was eager in some way to "pep" his search up—to get a "feel" that he hadn't found. Then all of a sudden he decided to drop the bars and go to Murphysboro and see Jessie.

He told Delia of his plans. It was only eight miles away. She looked at him oddly, and would have liked to argue the matter, but he disconcerted any plan, by smiling, breaking into a laugh, and catching her to him, embracing and kissing her. She was too intelligent and restrained to say that she wished he wouldn't. He knew what she wished; but she couldn't confirm it by doing what she knew he expected her to do.

He didn't say why he was going to Murphysboro, nor whom he was going there to see. There could be but one person, however, and one reason—and Delia knew the answer to both.

CHAPTER VI

It was a saturday afternoon when Martin went to Murphysboro. The Bingas, as has been shown, were not very steady people; they were forever moving. People said it was because Alfred Binga, the father, gambled his money away and wouldn't pay rent. So on arrival there, Eden had to inquire the way to their house. With the direction finally clear, he started out. On the way, coming towards him, he met a rather attractive girl, dressed neatly, a bit expensively. He had never seen her before and it struck him that she wasn't a resident of the town, else he must have heard of her before. He wondered who she could be.

As they passed each other, both raised their eyes, which met squarely. He nodded slightly, and she nodded back at him. In a second it was over. He went several steps before he dared to look after her over his shoulder, only to catch her doing likewise. Both turned their heads quickly and guiltily and hurried on. She, however, was near a corner and on reaching it, turned, slowed up and looked sideways, to see where he was headed. She went a few steps till the corner of a house hid her and watched him until he mounted the porch of the house where Jessie lived, and knocked.

Relaxing, she continued on her way, deciding as she did so to call on Jessie shortly. She knew she could do so with equanimity.

The door was opened in answer to Eden's knock, and of all the people who might have answered it, there stood Jessie herself:

"Martin! Why, *Martin Eden*, of all people!" she cried.

"Jessie!" he exclaimed, and stood for a second, his mouth open, frozen, as it were, to the spot. When she swung the door wide enough for him to enter, he stepped through, she closed the door behind him, and the next moment she was in his arms, with both murmuring soft words, kind words, tender words.

In that brief moment, all they had lived through in the years gone by came back to both with a rush. Both their hearts were hungry and had longed for this moment. They moved into the parlor in a sort of daze, intoxicated by their own emotions. They sat down, close together, and he placed his arm about her waist. They began to talk, all the while looking deep into each other's eyes.

Jessie Binga was a beautiful girl, of that dark, olive complexioned type; her eyes were like bottomless wells to Eden. Her expression had a touch of sadness. Her body was soft and shapely, seeming to have no bones to obstruct the soft, downy feel as his arm drew her close, while her lips were the softest and the kisses they exchanged seemed heavenly.

He wondered how he could have waited, yet now he *had* to wait. She was all a woman could offer a man—in the flesh. He couldn't even think then what stood between them. Afterward he knew some fundamental lack in her character was responsible for his subconscious drawing back. At the moment *the flames of fleshly passion* dominated both, but his strong will power and practice of self control still restrained his emotion. Otherwise he would have taken Jessie directly to a minister and married her.

He acknowledged to himself as he held her close, that he had made a mistake and it was *his* mistake. He should have married Jessie immediately after he settled in the West, married her while he was really madly in love with her, and before any ugly rumor had raised its evil head. Then he could have been enjoying all that love makes possible between a man and a woman. He said to himself now, and more often subsequently, that the time to marry is when a boy and a girl love with equal fervor.

Out there in his wilderness, alone together, adjustment would have been mutual. He was realizing now that in waiting as he had, he had developed ideals—and he had no patience with idealists.

In the few minutes they sat there holding hands, he was more than ever conscious of his mistake in not marrying her when he really cared, and he was deeply repentant. Even now he was tempted to forget everything and tell Jessie how much he loved her. Then his conservative self said: "Having waited this long, you can wait a little longer; control your emotions, Martin Eden, control yourself. You are young."

Notwithstanding, it was a great thrill to feel these emotions once more. Again and again he squeezed her hands and drew her as close as he could, feeling the beating of her heart as he did so. He was more aroused than he could ever before remember. At last he managed to whisper hoarsely:

"Jessie?"

"Yes, Martin."

"I—I never realized you were so lovely, so beautiful and so— sweet before."

"Oh, Martin," she sobbed—and again he embraced her, held her close and smothered her face with hot kisses.

"I—I've—got lots to talk to you about, Jessie—lots to talk about."

"Have you, Martin?" she said softly.

"Yes, Jessie, yes."

"But why haven't you written to me, Martin? Why—why didn't you write me that you were coming here? It seems that you could at least have sent me a card," she sighed complainingly.

"Yes, I know now that I should have, Jessie. But I didn't know that I—that I still cared so much for you until I—I saw your face at the door just now. Then it all came back and more."

"More, Martin?"

"More, Jessie. You must try to forgive me, dear; forgive me everything as I want to forgive you."

"You—you forgive me—at last, Martin?" This was said in such a low voice that he could hardly hear her. But both knew what it meant. She understood that while Martin had agreed to forget the ugly rumors of more than a year before, he had *not* forgotten. He was a man, their love had been unsullied—and then that *something happened*. She was sorry. She would have undone it all—if she could.

"As to what you said you had lots to talk about. Are you—you quite sure that you want to, Martin? I've been awfully unhappy since—since you quit writing to me. I've been very unhappy and—at times, almost—desperate."

He looked down at her when she said this, but she had lowered her eyes and was close to tears. He clasped her close and could feel her breast, with the pent up emotion, heaving against his. He was in a crack now; he *had* to say *something*, do something, or leave and forever hold his peace. He was too much of a man to be unfair to Jessie. After all, her environment had not been the best. He didn't expect the whole Negro race to change its condition because he had made an effort, and was still making one, to change his.

While he had succeeded in lifting himself by his boot straps, he hadn't expected Jessie, or any other girl, to do likewise. She had been born in Murphysboro, lived there always, knew no other life nor environment. While he had gone West and achieved a measure of success, she had to stay here and make the best of her limited opportunities.

Murphysboro had been founded over a coal mine, was drab and inert. What *could* this poor girl do to better herself? If in her madness, she had erred a bit, therefore, he felt that he should forgive her. This was what he had decided to do, but after he forgave her, there was no alternative but to love her again as he once had. Could it be the same? He decided to try it. Turning to her, his face afire with emotion, he opened his mouth—when both heard footsteps on the porch and a knock. They sat up quickly, listening. Then with an "Excuse me," she rose, crossed the room, into the hall and opened the door. The next moment Eden heard a surprised exclamation.

"Why, Miss Linda Lee, you?"

"Yes, me, Jessie."

"Then come right in," said Jessie, cordially. As she closed the door they exchanged a deceitful kiss.

"And how are you, anyhow?"

"Oh, fine, kiddo, fine. How are you?"

"Fit as a fiddle, as the old folks say." They both laughed "Rest your things and come in the parlor. I want you to meet somebody."

"Oh, do you have company?" Linda simulated surprise. "I'm not going to stay long enough to rest anything. I just ran by to say hello and see how you were doing."

"I'm certainly glad you came. Well, come on in and meet my friend." Taking her by the arm she brought her in and a moment later, rising, Eden was face to face with the girl he had passed on the street. They stared at each other as Jessie continued:

"Miss Lee, please meet Mr. Martin Eden, of South Dakota. Miss Lee, Mr. Eden."

"Mr. Martin Eden!" echoed Linda, in surprise, stepping closer and holding out her hand. Taking it, he echoed:

"Miss Linda Lee!"

"I'm surely glad to meet you—at last," she cried.

"And I'm more than glad to meet you,—in person and also at last."

"I've been hearing of you so long I feel that I know you," said she.

"Which is mutual. I'll tell you by and by how long ago it was when I first heard of you."

"Incidentally," said she, turning to Jessie, who had stood by courteous and smiling, "I passed him on the street a while ago. I suspect now that he was on his way here then."

"Just where I was headed," he added.

"Didn't I tell you," she said, with a nod of her head at Jessie. Jessie stepped forward.

"Incidentally, I want to remind you both that I have chairs, and since you seem to be so pleased at meeting each other after 'so many years', I command that you both be seated and finish 'getting acquainted' while I go and fix you a bit of ice cream and cake. Now do sit down, please!"

They found seats and moved closer after her exit.

"Could you, perhaps, guess where and when it was that I first heard of you?"

"I don't want to delay being told that long, so I won't guess," said she, happily. "Just tell me—please!"

"Well, it was many years ago—shortly after I left these parts and went to Chicago."

"Really?"

"Yes, Miss Lee, really."

"This is *so* interesting. Please go on."

"Do you remember a boy named Dewey?"

"Lawrence Dewey?"

"The same."

"Oh, sure. I've known him all my life. His mother is a very good friend of my fa—I mean, of my parents," said she, enthusiastically.

Martin Eden was to learn that she meant what she had started to say; that Dewey's mother *was a very* good friend of her *father*, not particularly, the family.

"Well, it was he who first told me about you."

"Indeed."

"He also spoke of your sister. There are two of you, are there not?"

"Of course. The other is Terry. She's my sister. There are only two children."

"So he told me."

"So very interesting. Why didn't you make him bring you then and make us acquainted?"

"Do you know, that is what I wanted him to do. Started to ask him several times; but then I was only a kid; I was filled with plans to get started. I didn't lose much time with any girls those days—much less going out of my way to meet one."

"That's awfully mean of you," she pouted. He smiled and looked quickly at her. She met his smile with a more tempting one, so he smiled again. He felt he had to say something; to say more.

"Your father is a preacher?"

"M-m," she mumbled and nodded, sweetly.

"Was once the pastor of our church."

"Oh, yes? Where?"

"At Metropolis."

"Metropolis! Now come to think of it, I heard that was where you came from, Metropolis. Is that where you've been?

"No. New York."

"O-oh! New York. My, but you've been places."

"Oh, no. Just on a little trip."

"And where are you going from here?"

"To Kansas."

"Kansas!"

"My parents and sisters live there."

"Really!"

"I'm paying them a visit, and from there I return to my home in South Dakota."

"South Dakota," she mused. "That seems so far away."

"It isn't," said he.

"No? I heard it was."

"Would you call a thousand miles a long way?"

"That would depend." He laughed at the trend the conversation had taken, which was exactly nowhere.

"Getting back to your father, and the time he was the pastor of our church. That was about the time I was born."

"Also me."

He looked at her again, closely. "Then we are about the same age."

"About," and she laughed.

"I remember seeing your father once, in fact, several times." She looked at him in surprise. He understood, and laughed.

"Oh, no, not then, of course." She relaxed with a sigh.

"I wondered."

"It was a few years later. I think I must have been about five then."

"And you can remember back that far?"

"Faintly. Some things, not everything. They held the conference in Metropolis that year and that was where I saw him."

"You're joking."

"Think so?"

"Yes."

"Then see if I am describing him correctly."

"All right. Remember, if you fail to, I'll say you're not as smart as you seem to be."

"Very well, here goes."

"Shoot."

"I remember seeing my mother talk and joke with him. I remember asking her who that preacher was—there were so many preachers at that conference and my mother knew lots and talked with them; but I remember this one in particular."

"I'm listening."

"He was a very tall man. Over six feet."

"Right. He still is."

"He wore his hair in a massive pompadour."

"Getting hot."

"He had a white spot on top of his hair."

"Shake my hand, Mr. Eden. I'll never call you a liar if I get to know you for a long time. That was my father all right. His head is almost entirely white now."

"I'll bet it makes him more handsome still. He was a most impressive looking figure, that I remember."

"Well," and she lowered her eyes modestly. "He's my father. I'd rather let somebody else describe him."

"There's another thing." She looked up at him questioningly.

"You look just like him, mouth, nose, eyes." He pointed at her and she laughed.

"You win on all points. It's true. I do look like him, just as you described. My, but you have a wonderful memory. Not only a great memory, but I'll bet you're smart." He laughed, then changed the conversation to a more personal trend.

"What are you doing here?"

"Teaching."

"Oh, teaching. Then you're a school teacher. My sister used to teach here.

"So I've been told."

"Do you—like teaching?"

"Well, yes," not altogether convincingly.

"It's funny, but I always imagined that I would like to marry a teacher."

"Why, Mr. Eden!"

"My sister, I thought, was so smart. I have imagined all teachers were like her—smart. That's why I suppose that I imagined I would like to marry one."

"But that isn't true—no, not by a long shot."

"You mean that all teachers are not—smart?"

"By no means,—including this one," pointing to herself. She looked straight at him this time; her expression, however, was modest. He liked that.

"Maybe some day I may find that out—meanwhile, where do you make your home—I mean, when you are not teaching?"

"In Chicago."

"Oh, in Chicago. I spent Thanksgiving and Xmas there."

"You did!"

"Yes."

"I spent Xmas there myself."

"I went to New York right after Xmas day. I spent New Year's in New York."

"I envy you. I want so much to visit New York. I've never been there."

"Just another great big old city. Since you live in the next largest one, you're not missing much."

"Did you—go up to Harlem while there?"

"Stayed up there—in the middle of it."

"How is it, anyhow—what does it look like?"

"Oh, somewhat like Chicago, except the houses are closer together, but fewer houses and more flats and apartments. There are 350,000 of us up there, crowded into less than two square miles of space. Otherwise, just a lot of Negroes, scuffling to make a living."

"I guess."

She looked at her wrist watch and he did likewise. Rising, she called Jessie.

"Yes, Miss Lee. Coming."

She turned to Martin who had risen and stood waiting, as Jessie entered.

"Oh, you're not going?"

"Got to, girlie," said Linda, stroking her dress with her hand.

"But I have the cream almost ready. I'm depending on you helping eat it. Please sit down again. I won't be long." Linda looked across at Eden. He nodded assent. She was glad, for she was finding Martin Eden most interesting. They both sat down.

"So you will soon be back at your 'home on the range'," she said, singing the last phrase.

"Back to 'my home on the range'," sang he.

"Away out West on a ranch—life on the range! That sounds so romantic. I'd like to go out there," dreamily.

"You think so?"

"Yes, I've so often pictured life on a ranch. Are there lots of Colored people up there?"

"No, none at all. In fact, I'm about the only one up where I live."

"The only one! Great goodness! No Colored people up there? But—but—how can you stand it? Who do you associate with?"

"Oh, the white people."

"White people!"

"Sure. There are some Indians, too."

"Indians!" She exclaimed, horrified, her eyes open wide in fright. "Wild Indians?" He laughed at this.

"No, no, my dear. They're not wild."

"Not wild? I thought all Indians were wild!" horror still written across her features. Eden laughed uproariously.

"Why, they have schools for them and have had for a long time—even before they provided schools for us. So you see you're away behind the times."

"Well, I don't know," she said, like a person not entirely convinced. "But I think I'd be afraid to live up there—at least by myself as you say you do, no colored people either. Some of those Indians may be tame, but—"

"Tame? Why Miss Lee! You shouldn't use that word about any human beings in America. Suppose somewhere out West where they never see one of us, and would refer to us as 'tame'. That wouldn't sound very nice, would it?"

"No, it wouldn't; but we're not Indians."

"No, but we were once savage, weren't we?"

"Well, that's what they say." Before they could continue the subject, Jessie returned with three dishes loaded with ice cream, glasses filled with wine, and a plate of cake.

"At last," said she as she set it on the piano stool, moved a table to the center of the room, spread napkins and bade them partake.

Ten minutes later the trio stood by the door, with Linda about to leave.

"It has been a delightful visit, honey. I can't remember when

I have enjoyed myself so much." She turned to Eden, who took her outstretched hand.

"I'm awfully glad to have met you," said he warmly, continuing to hold her hand. As she turned toward Jessie, he released it, while she went on:

"Everything was going along fine until he brought up the Indians."

"Indians?" repeated Jessie, with a question in her eyes.

"Yes, Jessie, Indians. He says there are lots of Indians up where he lives, and that they are tame, not wild." All laughed again, and Jessie interposed:

"Are you tame, Miss Lee?"

"No," cried Linda, "I'm wild—a wild Indian with feathers in my hair, and I have horns on my temples! Look out, here I come!" She gave an imitation of an Indian, as she saw them, charging into action, which brought forth the biggest laugh of the afternoon.

Eden lingered a few minutes after Linda had left. Jessie gave him a photo of herself, and he left one of himself that he had taken in New York. The emotional spell was broken and he returned to Carbondale that same night without having declared himself, and was strangely glad that he had not.

He found Delia waiting for him when he got back to Carbondale.

"I was wondering if you'd return tonight," said she, feeling him out.

"How could I stay away from you, darling?" and kissed her.

She looked at him out of those odd grey eyes, as if clear through him, but he seemed to have become womanproof, and only laughed as she gazed at him.

"You've been kissing somebody else since you left here," she said, still trying to look through him, but he only laughed and prepared for bed, forcing her to leave before she was through. She had definitely decided on a long talk, during which she hoped to wrest a proposal from him, so she left greatly disappointed.

Two days later, on a Monday, Eden left without proposing, but promised to write. He spent a month visiting his parents and friends in Kansas, then returned to his home in South Dakota—and to hard work.

CHAPTER VII

On his return to South Dakota, Martin was relieved to find that Stewart's had taken good care of his stock while he was away. The cattle from the Swanson place had thrived so well and were far enough along in feeding so that Eden would be able to ship another car load of steers to the market by middle of the spring. These would only be shipped to Omaha, which was the most popular local market. Eden had merely shipped through to Chicago before because he was going there for a visit, and would get enough more for the shipment to pay the expenses of his trip.

He was in no mood to go back to batching after his return. Deborah he thought, was more beautiful than ever. Stewart was so happy to see Eden pleased, that he insisted on his coming to board with them for at least a week, until he "got used" to South Dakota again. It ended by Eden being asked to board with them for good.

"Your land is not together, Eden," argued Stewart. "You have some southeast of us, northwest of us, and you live in the middle of it all. It takes but a few minutes to get here from your little shack, so why not just drive on down here and get your meals? What do you say to it, my boy?" Martin looked at Deborah, who was standing near, smiling. He wanted to be sure that it would be all right with her, since she had to do the cooking.

"You're the cook, Miss Stewart. I want to hear from you first. Will it be all right if I come here to eat?"

"Oh, I'll be glad to have you, Mr. Eden."

"Then that settles it. I don't need a second invitation."

He turned to Deborah again, "Remember in commiting your-self, that I'm a hearty eater, so better think again before you decide."

"We decided about that, Mr. Eden, while you were away," said she, coyily, blushing as she replied.

"Now what's this? A plot to spoil me?" he chided. "You know if you go to making it easy, that might spoil me. I might become hard to get along with."

"Oh, no you won't. You aren't built that way," said De-borah, smiling up at him warmly. She was glad that he was back; she had missed him all the while that he'd been away. She thought about him every day, every hour in the day. Now that he was back with his fine personality, superior will power, his courageous disposition, his considerate treatment of everybody, she was supremely happy. She was glad of a chance to serve him. It was a way in which she could, she hoped, show her gratitude for all he seemed so willing and anxious to do for them—and they needed it so badly. It would still be months before they would harvest a crop. The little money that they brought from Indiana was long since spent; they were, in truth, subsisting entirely on the money Bill was receiving from Eden.

His coming to board with them would add to the help he was already giving, so why shouldn't she be happy? Yet this was not the only reason. His presence seemed to create in her a peculiarly pleasant sensation, a strange indescribable emo-tion. The thought of seeing him three times a day, sometimes even playing checkers with him as he lingered long after the evening meal, seemed to make life more interesting and worth living.

This particular spring turned out to be very wet. Back east in Illinois, Indiana and Iowa, crops were badly retarded by the cold, wet weather. The papers were filled with stories of the fear of poor crops, so prices shot up. The wetter it was in the East, the better it was for farmers in the beautiful rolling lands of the Rosebud country. While day after day went by, and they were unable to work because of the rains, Eden was happy. He had managed to get his fields all seeded before the rains started, so he was able to relax happily as he saw the crops growing. He was perfectly content to lounge around Stewart's living room, talking with Stewart about divers things, including lands, cattle, railroads—and even listening to his tales of dear old Scotland.

In the afternoon he would play checkers. Stewart was older at the game and as they played Deborah would sit close by, watching their moves with amusement when one outsmarted the other. It brought her closer to Martin, and before either realized it (though after discovering it they were unable to acknowledge it) both were subconsciously becoming more than just friends.

Then one day Eden received a letter. It was from Jessie. She wrote him briefly that a gulf had been growing between them that would be hard to bridge. It was so hard, in fact, that she had despaired of ever bridging it, and so had, therefore, married one she felt would more fully understand her.

He was not altogether surprised. In a way he had expected something to happen, and he merely sighed to himself and said "Oh well."

"Looks like you've had bad news," ventured Deborah when she had an opportunity to speak to him alone. He handed her the letter. She read it through and cried:

"Great goodness!" She was sorry for him then, but didn't know just how to express herself.

"Remember what I said just before going away last fall?"

"Yes," she answered, hoping this would give her a chance to express her sympathy, "I remember."

"You can believe and understand it now."

"Yes." She wanted to say more. He made it possible.

"I'm all alone out here now. As time goes on they continue to fail me. This life, as they try to think it out at their distance, is all vague and indefinite. They don't understand it; they don't understand me—result, as the years go by, I become more lonely. I don't know where it will all end."

She dared take a step nearer him to lay a consoling hand on his arm.

"I'm *so* sorry for you Mar—Mr. Eden."

"You can call me by my first name," said he.

"Thank you. I'm sorry for you, Martin." She had to pause then. Calling him by his first name gave her a queer feeling, but she managed to go on.

"I'm so sorry be—because it's all such a dreadful mistake. I mean—about the others, those who don't understand you. I'm sorry and I wish I could—help you, somehow." As she finished, he was on the verge of tears. He felt as if he didn't have a friend in the world, and shed a tear in self pity. Thereupon he strolled over by the window, his back to her.

She stood for awhile, looking at him from that distance, then crossed to his side.

"Please—don't take it so hard, Martin."

"I feel like—like I haven't a friend in the world." He turned away, for his eyes were moist now and he had a hard time keeping his face straight. This was more than she could stand. She knew he was a strong man; that he was not emotional, yet he was a man with a heart and a soul, and now she was more sorry for him than ever. She had to say something and she had to do something, so she placed one hand on his shoulder, the other on his arm, and looking up into his face said, softly:

"Don't take it so hard, Martin. I can't stand to see you this way—so sad. You don't deserve it, and don't say that you haven't a friend in the world; don't feel that you haven't, for you have." There was a strange silence before she could go on.

"You *do* have friends, Martin, two dear friends. Father and I, Martin, we are your friends, your real friends. We would do anything to help you—anything!"

Tears were so near again and he didn't want her to see him becoming weak, so he turned and went out without saying another word.

He didn't come back that evening for his dinner. Deborah insisted that they wait. Her father called to her:

"Deborah, give Bill and George their dinner and you and I will wait. I'm worried about Martin. He's always here waiting. I'm worried about him and miss him."

While George and Bill fell to eating, she beckoned to her father from the kitchen.

"What is it, dear?" he asked in a low voice, coming up to her. When Eden left so abruptly, he forgot to pick up the letter. She showed it to her father.

"It's this, father. He got it today." She stood silent while he read it. When through, he cried.

"Oh, and so that's it? No wonder. I can see why, now."

"Isn't it too bad? I'm so sorry for him."

"And so am I."

"Remember what he said before he went away last fall; that they didn't understand his life out here?"

"Yes, I remember. I didn't think much about it at the time."

"I took it as only a joke," said she.

"And now it's come true. Poor fellow."

"You know, father, he *is* lonely. I wish we could do something to make him happier. He needs it."

"Wonder what kind of a girl was she?" said Stewart.

"I don't know; but I don't think he was depending on her too much. It seems that about two years ago they were very much in love with each other—and then something happened and his love sort of cooled.

"Then it seems he saw her last winter while he was away, and they sort of patched it up. But you see, it was of no avail."

"She got married on him," said Stewart, thoughtfully.

"I don't think that surprised him, or even hurt him so much," ventured Deborah, "for in a way he was expecting something to happen."

"Then what upset him so?"

"The feeling that none of his people will ever understand him or his life out here."

"And he loves it so much," sighed Stewart.

"It's his whole life—his everything. I'm so sorry for him."

"After Bill eats, we'll drive up to his house and see what's happened," suggested her father.

"Please do," cried Deborah, anxiously. "Meanwhile, I'll fix his dinner and send it to him."

"Bully, dear—that's the thing to do."

"When he comes out of it, he'll want something to eat. Then he would never think of coming back and asking me to fix it. So hurry up there, father." She went to prepare Eden's meal.

They found him in his little shack, in bed. Appreciating what had sent him there, Stewart was careful not to say so, and pretended to think that he was ill.

As it happened, Eden *had* overcome his attack of emotion and his vitals were gnawing with hunger when they arrived.

"I was feeling so bad," he lied, "that I didn't care to eat dinner."

"That's too bad, my boy," sympathized the old Scotchman.

"But I feel better now and think I'll drive into town and get a bite to eat," said he, starting to rise.

"You don't have to do that, my boy." Stewart set down the basket Deborah had packed for him, whereupon Eden's eyes opened wide with delight. Stewart spread the food on the table before him and sat there while he devoured it, almost ravenously.

Next day Martin was his old self again. It rained that afternoon and they couldn't work. Bill and his father decided to go to town, taking George with them, which left him alone with Deborah again.

"Well," said she, "I'm glad to see that you came out of it and are your old self again. How do you feel by this time?"

"Fit as a fiddle, Deborah. I must apologize for that burst of emotion yesterday. I don't know what you must think of me, going off like that."

"We all have a bad day now and then."

"Yes, but that shouldn't be as regarding me. I'm ashamed of myself."

"Oh, why should you be? It was rather interesting to me to see you that way. I didn't think you could be," said she, smiling. He looked at her quickly. She met his eyes and after a moment he turned away.

"Well, anyway, that's all over and done with."

"What'll you do now?"

"What'll I do now?" He shrugged his shoulders. "I don't know. What can I do?"

"And she—was she—your only girl?"

He looked at her as if to ask whether she thought he had a harem. Then, on second thought, he understood her.

"She really wasn't my girl any more at all—hadn't been for almost two years. I did see her while I was back East, and for a time I thought we might make it up; but my life out here is rather foreign to her; to most of them, I'm afraid. So that's the end of that chapter in this old life of mine."

"You've grown away from her. Recalling what I've heard you say, she was rather out of your realm, she no longer fit into your scheme of things."

"I guess that was it more than anything else. In the end it amounts to the same thing, however. I guess it means maybe that I'll continue as a bachelor, get cranky as I grow older so that no woman could ever put up with me and in the end, die and soon be forgotten."

"You like to joke, don't you, Martin?"

"I haven't a very good sense of humor."

"Not when you are like you were yesterday, but when you are yourself, you have a splendid sense. You not only make one laugh, you keep us laughing even long after you have said something funny."

They talked on books then and current events, after which he took his leave, fearing to be too long alone with her.

That night in his little sod house that stood on the hill, Martin Eden thought about Deborah. "The one girl in all the world for me—and she had to be a white girl!"

He sat alone and looked at nothing, then all of a sudden, he thought about something else. It was now May and in October he was due to bring his sister and Grandma to the Rosebud to file on the new lands in Tripp County. Then what about the other claim; the claim the girl he was to marry was to file on?

So there he sat, wondering what was to become of him, with October less than six months away—and he didn't even have a girl!

He rose and walked the dirt floor, trying to figure out what had happened to him. Twenty-five, brown, free, single, disengaged—and not a soul in the world to call his own! He sat down, and in doing so, kicked over a letter received shortly after he returned from his trip. It was from Jessie. He picked it up, opened it, and reread it, idly. One sentence attracted attention. "Miss Linda Lee was by today and asked about you. She often asks about you; asks about you until I'm getting jealous." He started and murmured:

"Linda Lee". . . then of a sudden, "Why not?" His head in a whirl, he repeated: "Linda Lee, Linda Lee!" Yes, why not —WHY NOT!"

Why not write to Linda Lee?

"Damned if I don't," he cried, and sitting down, wrote her a nice, formal letter, which he mailed the next day.

CHAPTER VIII

WHEN LINDA'S SCHOOL closed in Murphysboro and she returned to Chicago for the summer, she told her mother about meeting Martin Eden during the winter.

"For years," said she, "he's been madly in love with Jessie Binga. They've expected them to get married for the longest. Then, last winter he came to Carbondale to see Delia Forbes. Delia made it her business to spread it all around that he *might* marry her. Jessie heard about it before he arrived in Carbondale, but didn't let on to him, so I don't think he knew when he called on her, that she heard he had come to Carbondale, supposedly to see Delia.

"Anyway, Jessie was furiously jealous, but cooled off considerably when he showed up in Murphysboro to see her. Now here's a coincidence. On his way to Jessie's house, in Murphysboro, I passed him on the street but didn't know it was he because I'd never seen him before.

"When I happened to *drop by* Jessie's house to see her a half hour later I ran right into him, which is when and how I met him."

Her mother nodded indulgently, with a smile that spoke more than words!

"You were careful to *drop* by—that is, 'to just happen to' drop by when you *knew* that he would be there." She patted her daughter's cheek and Linda, who was a poor liar, lowered her eyes guiltily. "Please go on, my dear," said her mother. "I'm listening and am interested."

"Well, as I started to say, that was how and when I met him, and oh, mother, he was *so* interesting. I'd never met a man whom I thought more interesting. He was so broad, so well informed and knew so much to talk about instead of the usual common 'jive' our men are so given to handing us.

"When I dropped in, I think it rather upset their little applecart. I think that he and she were about to get things patched up. Jessie has plenty of sex appeal and that gets most men—especially at the outset; but if a man like Mr. Eden after being around a while and began to hear about her aunts and that her father loses most of his salary trying to gamble, he would likely begin to wonder if she had the necessary strength of character.

"From what I could gather from his talk, he seems to be planning some sort of land deal out there during the fall. He intimated that he would like to have some nice girl visit up there this fall when his sister and grandmother plan to be there.

"Anyway, for a month or twò after he went on his way, Jessie was full of going to South Dakota, and talked about it all the time. Meanwhile, she'd been keeping company with a young, no-account nobody ever since she's been big enough to know anything. Like her aunts and in a degree, her father, she's inclined to be of low estate, anyhow. Then one day some man came to town and met her—and in a few days she was crazy about him.

"He was twice her age—more than old enough to be her father. One of these old fakirs who tend to mystify you until you 'know' them awhile, but until you have found them out, they sort of sweep you off your feet. Well, this is what happened to Jessie—he swept her off her feet and before anybody knew what was going on—she had married him!"

"Hush your mouth!" exclaimed her mother.

"I'm telling the truth. She married him and followed him off to some little town and started to live with him."

"Well I declare. Meantime, what about this—Martin Eden she was supposed to be so much in love with?"

"Yes, what about him? That's what I'd like to know. After what she ups and did, I—I've tho't about him. As I see it, he was too far out of her class. Without saying it, he was demanding too much of Jessie; he was too far to the right, with her on the extreme left, so she despaired of bridging the great gulf that lay between them. His ideals regarding womanhood and high character were just too much for Jessie."

"So you're interested in him now?"

"Me? Oh not directly, mother. I only met him that once. When I was in Carbondale, I called on Delia and after a talk with her, it was my opinion that his affair with her was cold, too. So, as I said, I've been thinking about him. You would too, under the circumstances, had you met and talked with him as I did. He is so entirely different from the current run of our men. Reminds you of a high class white business man—and I know that he *is* a high class man and a business man. Everybody says that about him—no time for foolishness or playing around.

"Well, from what you say, I'm a bit interested and rather curious about him now myself."

"I'm sure you'd be greatly impressed. I've only dreamed about the kind of a man he impressed me as being—I'd never even hoped to meet one."

"Do you have his address in Dakota?" Shaking her head in the negative, Linda sighed and continued:

"If I did, I'd try to think up some excuse to write to him about. He must be lonely out there, as much as he seemed to like it."

"Maybe he's got a girl up there."

"No, he hasn't, for there's no Colored people up there."

"No Colored people up there?"

"That's what he told me. He had no occasion, I'm sure, to misrepresent the truth. If I had his address, I'd sure find an excuse to write him."

"But you must not do that, my dear. That would never do."

"I know it wouldn't mother. It's too much to hope, but I'd shout for joy if he remembered and happened to write to me."

"That would be the proper way to resume your acquaintance with him; for him to write to you."

"Of course, mother, dear. Nevertheless I just keep on thinking about him; I've lived through his few minutes with me last winter until I seem to know everything he said by heart."

"I can't understand how he can manage to make himself content, living so far away from his race—his people," ventured Mrs. Lee.

"He says in the five or more years he's made his home up there, that there never has been a colored person on his land; that other than a baseball team or a traveling show, he never sees one; but that there are lots of Indians."

"Indians!"

"Yes, mother, Indians."

"Great goodness alive! Why—how can he stay there? Those Indians, supposing that they should break lose and go on the warpath? They—why they might—scalp him!" Linda laughed.

"No, mother. They're civilized like everybody else, now."

"How do you know?"

"He told me."

"He seems to have told you lots. I thought you said you only met him that once."

"That was all; but he said there are plenty of white people and that they are very nice to him; that they are good neighbors."

"But who does he go around with—a young man like him?" She changed now, alert with a sudden idea.

"You don't imagine," she said in an undertone, "you don't suppose that he's—he's going with a—a white girl, do you?"

"Oh, mother, no. How can you even imagine such a thing? No."

"How do you know—how *would* you know?"

"I just know, mother. He isn't that sort of a man. After all, he doesn't *have* to go with somebody. Men, many men have to live alone—for awhile at least. It is not always convenient for them to have a woman around. Think of the men who went to Alaska and other far away places. They had to go first and provide a place for their women and then either come back after, or send for them."

"Maybe he's living out there alone because he doesn't like Negroes; maybe—"

"My poor little mother. You can think up the most peculiar things. But come to recall some things he said, he *did* criticize Negroes in a general way. Said they could do so much better than they are doing, if they'd try hard enough."

"We've made lots of progress since we've been free, the greatest progress of any race in the world in the same length of time. We have that," defended Mrs. Lee.

"That's what I told him, but he said that we've lived in a progressive age; that the whole world has made greater progress in the last seventy-five years since we've been free, than in five hundred years previous to that."

"Well," sighed her mother, "guess I'd better get back—" The door bell rang at this moment.

"It's only the postman, dear. That's his ring. So go get the mail. It'll only be some advertising. I'm going back to the kitchen and start dinner."

Linda walked towards the front door. All of a sudden, she thought of something she'd forgotten to do upstairs. Catching her mother by the arm, she cried:

"Listen, mami. You go get the mail. I've just tho't of something that I forgot to do—it ought to have been attended to. I'll go take care of it now while it's on my mind."

A moment later as she came back downstairs, she paused at foot of same to meet her mother, with the mail, looking curiously at one letter.

"What is it, mother?"

"A letter for you, dear. I was trying to make out where it was from, but I can't. Anyway, it's for you, so here it is. Now I guess I can go and start the dinner."

"Yes, you may, dear Mami," said Linda as she took the letter and examined the envelope. The fact is, the letter had been dropped into a mail car, which explained the obscure, indefinite post mark.

Giving up hope of deciphering the smudgy stamp, Linda went into the sitting room where there was a secretary, and a letter opener. Not realizing that within that envelope was what she had been waiting, longing and praying for, she was in no hurry, having concluded that it was from one of her pupils of the winter before, she sauntered over to the desk. Just then, she happened to think of something else she forgot to do up-stairs, so laid the letter down and went up to attend to it, while "it was on her mind."

Linda stayed upstairs, doing other things and forgot all about the letter. Thirty minutes later her mother called her downstairs to dinner. Just as she sat down, her sister, Terry, entered and called as she turned into the sitting room, after depositing her coat and hat on the hall tree:

"Hello everybody."

"Where've you been," called Linda, over her shoulder.

"Dinner is waiting, Terry. Will you please hurry before it gets cold," said Mrs. Lee.

"Yes, do," added Linda. "Lucky you came in when you did."

"I'll say so." Terry started toward the dining room, but decided to go by the secretary first and see if she had any mail. They kept it there. There was none for her, but she saw the one for Linda and called:

"Linda?"

"What do you want?" from Linda, starting to eat.

"Did you know you had a letter?"

"That's right. I did receive a letter. Well, it's from some of my students in Murphysboro about nothing. You know how students are. Always a lot of no-account ideas."

Meanwhile, Terry had been studying the post mark on the letter.

"Will you forget that old letter and come on to your dinner?" cried Linda, impatiently. By this time, Terry had sat down, still trying to decipher the post mark.

"Humph. That's funny."

"What's funny, Terry?"

"The post mark on this letter."

"Confound the letter. It doesn't mean a thing—skip it and get to eating. Your soup is getting cold."

"I can make out the word Omaha on it. I—"

Linda started, straightened so quickly that she swallowed a mouthful of food unchewed.

"Omaha—did you say, Omaha?"

"Sure," replied Terry. She held the letter under Linda's wide, excited eyes. "See. You can make it out, Omaha. It must have been mailed on the train." That's as far as she got. The next moment Linda had snatched the letter from her hand, so excited she couldn't take time to ask for it. She tore the end with fingers so nervous they trembled, and withdrew the contents while the others looked on, curiously.

Unfolding the sheets inside, she read:

"Gregory, South Dakota," and jumped to her feet for joy, with:

"South Dakota—oh, great goodness. I'll bet it's from him, from Martin Eden. Oh, me, oh, me!" She was too nervous to read it.

"Linda!" cried her mother, frowning, getting up and going around to her side.

"Well I never!" exclaimed Terry, sitting across the table, watching her sister perform.

"Great goodness, great goodness," sobbed Linda. Then to Terry:

"Here, Terry, you read it to me—it's from him, from him, I know it is—it couldn't be from anybody else.—Oh, great goodness, great goodness, great goodness!"

"Please calm yourself long enough at least to give it to me," said Terry, taking it from her trembling hands and reading:

" 'Dear Miss Lee:

" 'You may be surprised when you read this—even wonder who it is from and have to turn to the end to see.' "

"Turn to the end," cried Linda. "Oh, isn't he stupid! Turn to the end to see who it's from." She buried her face on her mother's shoulder. "Oh, mother, I'm so excited and nervous I can't—"

"Calm yourself, darling, and let Terry read it. Please listen." Nevertheless, Linda continued to utter incoherent words, while Terry read on:

" 'I'll save you this by saying in the first paragraph that I'm the man you met in Murphysboro last winter. My name is Martin Eden. Maybe you'll remember me now.' "

"Remember him now—how could he think that I would ever forget him!"

"Please hush, dear," begged her mother, "and let Terry read it."

" 'Whether you remember me or not, I am writing to say that I have thought of you very often since and decided at last to become bold and dare write you.' "

"The darling," sobbed Linda.

"Linda!" exclaimed Mrs. Lee, and frowned deeply.

"Oh, how sweet of him. Why didn't he start writing to me as quickly as he got back there. Imagine how much we've both have missed."

"How can your sister ever finish the letter if you continue interrupting her?"

"Oh, I'm so happy, mother, so happy and I'm *so* glad he has written. Read on, Terry, I promise to be calm now and listen." Terry tried again.

" I hardly know what to say that might interest you,' " the letter ran: " 'I'm afraid that what I have to say and am most deeply interested in, you may not understand, and if you do not, it will, of course, bore you.' "

"You could never bore me, Martin Eden," cried Linda, still sobbing. Terry laid the letter down.

"Be patient, Terry. You understand," said the mother. Terry understood all right and picked up the letter, trying to find where she left off.

What both understood was that although Linda was now twenty-six, hungering for love, she had never had a real beau. Her father, the Rt. Reverend D. Lee, had an emotional love for Linda which few young men could tolerate. After calling a few times and having to witness the demonstration of this peculiar paternal affection they became discouraged and their attentions ceased. In view of these existing conditions, Linda's excitement on receipt of a letter so ardently desired was easily accounted for.

Terry tried it again.

" 'I must say this, however, so that you may not misunderstand me. My whole life is bound up with the development of this wilderness.' "

"So romantic. Every word he writes," cooed Linda.

"Please, oh, please hush, darling," begged her mother.

"From the way she's carrying on, one would think she's in love with the man already—in love with a stranger; a man she's met only once."

"Only once, Terry—but *what a once!*" from Linda.

"She's crazy, mother—gone completely insane," sighed Terry.

"Yes, I am, Terry," said Linda, her eyes raised heavenward. "Crazy with happiness."

"But you've met the man only once. What do you know about him?"

"Enough to be almost mad about him! People have been known to fall in love at first sight."

"Well, I never," said Terry, and sitting down, gave it up. Mrs. Lee set Linda on a chair, picked up the letter, adjusted her glasses and tried to find where Terry left off. Linda reached for it.

"Give it to me, mother. I'll read it all over again from the beginning." Mrs. Lee interposed, directing her remarks to Terry.

"He seems to be rather a thoughtful and respectful sort of person, but I want Linda to take it sensibly and not make herself ridiculous."

"I promise not to, mother, I've never defied nor embarrassed you, have I?"

"I can't say that you have and you've always been obedient —sometimes too obedient, I think, with regard to your father." At this Terry looked up.

"This matter concerns only Linda and me, Terry. If you're through now, we'll excuse you. I would like to talk to her alone." It was an invitation for Terry to go.

"Well," snapped Terry, "you needn't act so funny about it; but if you don't want me around, I'll go. Good day!" She strode away leaving her mother and Linda alone, both of whom sighed with relief. Neither got along well with Terry, who had ways like her father, but looked like neither parent.

"They say I'm just like you—that is, my ways, mother."

"Yes, I admit you have the same ways and that is what worries me—constantly. I'm sorry you have," sighed Mrs. Lee.

"But you have sweet ways, mother. Everybody likes you."

"Except your father."

"Mother!"

"I know, dear, it's a hard thing to say, but it's the truth and you know it, and everybody else who knows us that well knows it." Linda remained silent.

"Being like me might, before the end, not be the best thing for you. There may come a time when you need to have more fire and be able to fight for what you know is right. I didn't have the fire to do that and you know, better than anybody, what has happened to me. You know that I have not been happy, that my husband does not respect me and has no patience with me."

"I wish you wouldn't talk about it, mother."

"I oughtn't to at this late date."

"I'm sorry for you, dear mother."

"When a woman fails a man, he seeks what she does not have in some other woman. That's what your father has done. He has always sought it and is still seeking. All my life I've had this flaunted in my face—and I've had to put up with it and say nothing because he's a minister of the gospel—and I'm his wife and have had to suffer humiliation from the beginning. I dare not flare up or show resentment, for fear people will talk about him." She began to cry and Linda, at her side, tried to comfort her.

"There, there, mumsy, dear. Don't do that. I'm sorry now that I didn't restrain my excitement. Had I done so, you wouldn't have come to this. You're the sweetest little mother in the world and I love you so much. Men are different, dear. The chances are that the one I marry won't be like father at all and may like me just as I am."

"I hope so, dear. I would be most unhappy if he turned out to be like your father. It would be better, in such a case, if you never married, never!"

"Mother!"

"I hate to say it, Linda, I hate to admit it—but it's the truth, so help me God!" And again she fell to weeping. Linda put an arm about her, then moved over by the window.

"Please mother, let's say no more about it at all now."

"I agree with you, dear, let's not. It's been a long time since I went off like this. I'm forever praying after each spell, that I never will again. Forgive your poor old mother, Linda."

"That's a good little mother," cried Linda, patting her shoulder. "Now let's go back to the letter and I'll read it all from the beginning to you. Meanwhile, I'll read the last paragraph first. I didn't entirely get that."

"Yes, let's do," said Mrs. Lee, trying to be cheerful.

"There isn't much more. I think I was on the last page."

" 'I shall be pleased to receive an acknowledgment of this letter, if you care to acknowledge it. Until then, I feel that I have said enough and shall await your pleasure.

'Cordially and sincerely

'MARTIN EDEN'

"Oh, fudge. Why did he have to be so formal? I can't picture him being that way. I wanted a long letter.

"At least you've heard from him and that is what you wanted most. Perhaps the next one, after he has heard from you, will be longer."

"My reply will be longer. I wouldn't want him to be as disappointed when he hears from me."

"But you must, above all things, darling, observe the formalities. I wouldn't for anything, want him to feel that my daughter was anything short of a lady, a dignified lady. If he's the kind of man you say, and his letter seems to confirm that, then I am sure he would appreciate that much more."

"I can appreciate that. I'm sure that's the way he would like to feel about me or any other girl he became interested in. He'll be skeptical enough after what Jessie pulled. Still I'd bet that he'd say it was for the best, after all. Jessie had all a man might crave, sexually, but not otherwise."

"Yes. After sex comes the other side and that is more important in the long run," said Mrs. Lee.

"As I see him, he's a man with a definite objective in life; with courage and will power enough to execute it. The girl he marries, if he can find her, will have to come up to this high ideal—and that girl wasn't Jessie Binga."

"Then answer him, dear. Write him a nice, interesting letter and I'm sure it will please him."

"I will, dear mother; but you won't mind if I put a little feeling into it, will you? I—"

"You must let him feel that you were glad to hear from him; glad enough to encourage him to answer. After that, we'll see."

"Thank you, mami, dear." She embraced her fondly and kissed her cheek.

That night, after having read his few lines over and over again, Linda wrote to Martin Eden as follows:

"Dear Mr. Eden:

"I received your kind letter and was *so* glad to hear from you. Of course I remember you—how could you think I would forget? I knew it was from you the moment I opened it and the first thing I tho't about was Indians, 'Wild Indians' (smile) and how you made me laugh, telling me not to refer to them as being 'tame.'

"Your letter found me at home and well. I can't say happy, for the old city seems rather dull to me. I returned here after my school closed more than a month ago, but regret to advise that I will not return, for I have decided not to teach the coming session at all.

"Again permit me to say how glad I was to hear from you, and that I will be at home in Chicago indefinitely and will look forward to hearing from you again. My mother, who says she knew you when you were a baby (I can't imagine you as ever having been a baby at all) joins me in love to you.

"Hoping that I may hear from you again and that you are, and will continue in good health, I beg to remain
"Very truly yours,
"(Miss) LINDA LEE."

CHAPTER IX

IT WAS HARVEST TIME in the Rosebud Country and to reap his biggest crop since coming there, Martin Eden hired several men, all white, boarded them at Stewarts', and became quite friendly with one, who seemed more intelligent than the others. No doubt this man observed the interest Deborah showed in Martin.

During noon hour one day, while they rested and talked, he referred to a conversation he had had with Deborah, when Eden was late for dinner the day before, and she had asked him where the "nigger" was. The incident was related with such nonchalance, that he didn't seem to be meaning an insult to Eden at all.

Happily, Eden was as adroit, and ignored it—in spite of the fact that it stabbed him to the quick and kept him disturbed almost constantly thereafter. He couldn't say anything. The man was only a hired hand and Eden realized that he couldn't condescend to upbraid him for it; only ignore the whole remark as he did. Furthermore, it was not what the man had said; he was supposed to have quoted Deborah.

Eden couldn't believe that Deborah would use such a word to inquire about him. Yet how was he to know that she had not unless he asked her? It was hard to find a way to do this and for the time being he kept silent and avoided saying much to her. But late that afternoon, when he was forced to come to the house for something, she took time out and spoke to him. Walking up to him:

"Martin. You seem worried or annoyed. Has something happened to upset you?" She was looking straight up at him when

she spoke; she continued to look straight at him, her eyes asking the same question. He was forced to say something. This
was as good a time as any to bring it up. Without looking at her
directly, he replied:

"Well, yes and no."

"That's very indefinite. Exactly what do you mean?"

He paused and looked straight into her eyes, bravely now.
She met his gaze unflinchingly.

"It's the word you used when you inquired regarding me of
that fellow, Richards, when I was late for dinner yesterday."
Her brows contracted. She lowered her eyes as if trying to recall, then raising them, looked straight at him, her face still
registering surprise.

"I asked where you were, that was all." Her eyes were questioning. "Why?"

"How did you refer to me when you inquired?"

She started, her lips apart. She suspected something, which
he misunderstood. His face became cold and hard, but still
not understanding what he was trying to get at, she continued:

"I said 'where is Mr. Eden'?"

"You used those words?"

"Those were exactly the words I used." He looked at her,
then turned his eyes away, a bit puzzled, still wearing an expression of doubt.

"Did somebody misquote me, Martin? Did *he* do that?
Please tell me the truth, Martin. Did he say that I said something else; called you something else?"

He turned and faced her squarely. She was looking straight
up into his eyes now with anxiety.

"Yes," replied Martin. "He said that in referring to me, you
asked 'where's the nigger'?"

Her jaw dropped.

"Great goodness alive!" she exclaimed and flew into a rage.
"Do you mean to tell *me* that he said *I* asked for you like that?"
Eden nodded in the affirmative.

"Oh, Martin Eden. *Can you imagine such a thing?* Such a terrible story, no—a malicious lie! I've never used that word in all my life, Martin, not since I was born in the world. So you —you know I couldn't have used it in referring to you."

She began to walk the floor, like an enraged tigress.

"And I even liked him a little; I thought he was rather nice and all the while he was nothing but a deceitful liar, a cad. I—" she stopped short and walked up close to Martin.

"I'm sorry Deborah; but it annoyed me so. Not that I cared so much about what somebody called me. I've been called that name before—all we colored people have and we can take it. But to be told that *you* called me such a name. I know you didn't now; but I could not be satisfied until I heard *you* say that you didn't."

"And to think that he would make up something like that, then say that *I* said it." She faced him squarely. "You should discharge him—fire him *now!*"

Shaking head in the negative, "No. I couldn't let him feel that I have thought about it at all. If he repeats it, I'll punch him on the nose, but I won't let it go to debate. I only hope he doesn't make up another such story, for then I'll have to let him feel that I know it."

"I have it! To convince you beyond any form of doubt, when he comes to dinner tonight, I'm going to call him and ask him to repeat that I said it—right before you."

"No, don't do that, Deborah. Consider it a closed incident and we must both forget it."

"But I can't forget anybody telling a lie like that—then putting it on me." She turned to him seriously. "Since *you* couldn't be satisfied until you asked *me* if I did, why can't I confront him and make him admit that *he* lied?"

"Because you're a woman and a lady and I don't want you mixed into it any further, so skip it. Just so long as I can feel that you didn't say it, I can forget it easily; but remember, if he tries to pull another fast one, he'll hear from me and when I hit, I believe in hitting hard." He patted her shoulder and departed before she could argue further about it. As he passed out the door, he turned and looked back at her. She was standing still, hurt to the core. Two big tears were on her eyelids, about to overflow.

When the door closed, she hurried into her bedroom, closed the door and fell across the bed, weeping without restraint. During this outburst, her father happened to come in, and hearing her sobbing, went to her to see what the matter was.

"My lassie," he cried, "What has happened? What *is* the matter? Why are you crying like this?" He forced her to a sitting posture and tried to dry her tears, but they flowed too fast, as she wailed:

"Oh, father, father, it's terrible—terrible!"

"Terrible? What's terrible, my lass? Explain!"

"That man Richards."

"Richards? What has he done—did he—insult you?" half rising as if to start something. Shaking her head in the negative, she said:

"No, but he told Mr. Eden a terrible story—a lie!"

"A lie, Deborah? I don't understand what you mean. What kind of a story has he told?"

"He—he—told Mr. Eden that I called him a dirty name— Oh, I'm so hurt—" and she burst into tears again.

"A dirty name—you, called Martin a dirty name? That couldn't have been, you, call Martin—what, Deborah?"

"He told Mr. Eden that I—that I called him a—a nigger!"

"Heaven help us!" exclaimed the elder.

"Can you imagine such a thing, father?"

"Who *can?* But did you, by any chance, do so?"

She sat up straight, and looked at her father in amazement. "Why, father, you—even you think I—Oh, father!" falling upon his breast and weeping more than ever.

"Of course you didn't, Lassie, of course you didn't," he cried, patting her shoulder and trying to stop her tears. "But what ever possessed the man to say you did?"

"I don't know, father, I don't know—I can't even imagine why." Jack was thoughtful a moment. Studying her, he rose and took a pace or two, then turning back, went on:

"Maybe he's a Southerner. You know down there they don't eat and drink with Colored people like they do up here. Everything is separate—even on the trains. The whites ride in one coach, the Colored in another. Now seeing you treating Mr. Eden with so much respect and courtesy, annoyed him; it would be against the customs down where he comes from. So when I come to think of it, I've never quite liked his eye. It's deceitful. So he thought that up to make Mr. Eden feel bad. I can see through it all, now."

"Yes, but why would he try to put me in the middle? If he was out to make Mr. Eden feel bad, his effort is a boomerang. I'm the one who's hurt; I'm the one who's feeling bad."

"How'd you come to find out?"

"Martin has been acting rather cold since it happened, so I asked him what was the matter. He didn't want to talk about it at first, but I forced it out of him."

"That's too bad. What's he going to do about it? Is he going to let Richards go?" She shook her head in the negative.

"What? You mean to say—"

"Said he didn't particularly care what Richards called him. It was Richards saying that I referred to him as one, that made him angry."

"I can appreciate his becoming so. Meantime, I came here to get something and I've forgotten what it was now."

"Was it—twine?"

"Twine is right, dear. Four balls—and I must have them quick."

"I know where they are. I'll get them for you," and she proceeded to go for them.

A Bohemian family by the cognomen of Vosika, announced a harvest dance and invited the neighborhood from all around to attend. They had just finished a large, fine new barn where it was to be held. Eden was invited and when he hesitated about accepting, they would have none of it.

"We'll have a dozen kegs of beer, a few bottles of schnapps, lots to eat, so you be there or else we won't think you're a good neighbor. So if you don't want us to feel slighted, be there and come early, stay late. It's on a Saturday night, you won't have to get up early Sunday morning, so that is that."

Vosikas didn't know the Stewarts, but told him to ask them, which he did. They expected him to go with them, but for reasons of his own, he preferred to go alone.

He found the place packed when he got there, with everybody dancing and having a good time.

"Why aren't you dancing, fellow?" everybody seemed to ask him. He made no attempt to do so and made first one excuse and then another, but he mingled with the men and drank beer freely with them. He ate freely, drank more beer and was really enjoying himself. During the early part of the evening, he glanced across the large floor, and his eyes fell on Deborah, sitting with the wife of one of his neighbors. She was looking at him and bowed; he returned the bow. He would have liked to dance, he was fond of it. Deborah wished he'd ask her. By and by he encountered Ed Vosika, who caught hold of him.

"Why aren't you dancing, Eden? There's lots of girls here to dance with, young ones, pretty ones. Get busy."

"After a while, maybe," said Martin. He'd run out of excuses by this time. Just then Ed's sister, about 18, came strolling by with two other Bohemian girls, all pretty, young, vivacious. Ed was starting away when he ran into them. Thereupon he grabbed his sister, bringing her up to Eden:

"Here, Sister, give Martin a dance," and shoved her all but into his arms.

"Okeh!" She waited, looking up at him smiling. He was in a crack.

"Really, I—I don't care to I—don't know how to dance the way they're dancing out there. I—"

"Then teach him, Elsie—show him how," cried Ed.

"All right, Mr. Eden," raising her arms. He was in a still deeper crack.

"Please don't, Miss Vosika. Dance with one of the other boys. I'm afraid I'd step on your toes."

"They've been stepped on a plenty tonight already," she laughed. "A few more times won't hurt."

At this point, a neighbor happened along, about half intoxicated, and striking him on the shoulder, cried:

"Hello, Eden. Having a good time?"

"Sure, John. Meanwhile, you're a good dancer. Give Miss Vosika a turn."

"Sure thing." He pushed them together and went outside. He wasn't dancing with any white girl, for everybody to be looking at them. He ran into Bill and George and their father shortly, and they teamed up and had some more beer and some more food.

Across the floor, Deborah had seen Eden's action, and thought about him. She began to understand his strange position. She could see now why he had broken down and said that he felt he hadn't a friend in the world. Everybody knew him, everybody liked him. She saw that he was welcome to dance with any of the girls there, including herself, yet he had adroitly avoided doing so. She wished she could find a way to tell him, to show him that he should not take it that way.

But she never knew. In her little life she had never encountered that most ugly of all things, race prejudice. To her, one person was the same as another—all alike. She was so effected by these thoughts that she had no spirit to dance and during the whole affair, she accepted not a single invitation.

Just before they were ready to leave for home, she encountered him. She could see that he was slightly intoxicated and she could appreciate why. Maybe he wished to forget some things.

"Well, Miss Stewart," said he, a bit unsteadily. "Are you enjoying yourself? Having a good time? Everybody's having a grand time, so are you?"

"Yes, Mr. Eden, I am," patting his arm, reassuringly. She smiled sweetly up into his face. She would do all she could to make him forget what she feared he was thinking.

"Then that's fine," and started away. "Just wanted to know that you were, that's all." And he staggered away, with her eyes following him, fondly.

CHAPTER X

EDEN WAS CHEERED the following Monday when the mail carrier brought him, among others, a letter from Linda Lee. His heart leaped for joy. He was finding it hard to have no one to think about, no one to turn to for a word of kindness, a word of love. The greatest love for him of all was right in the house where he boarded, but there was that line of demarcation, the line no one dared to cross.

Linda's letter was most encouraging. She was a nice girl, a fact he had found out; and he had also found out that her father, a Presiding Elder, was considered, in spite of his office, very much of a rascal. His name was linked with women, many women—and one woman in particular—Lawrence Dewey's mother. This was an affair of long standing. Twenty-five years before, she was one of the most beautiful women, black or white, in Chicago.

Martin Eden had been told most of this when he mentioned having met Linda before leaving Carbondale. He then remembered Mrs. Dewey from some years back, when her son and he had been friendly, while boys together in Chicago. He remembered that even then, he thought she was a most attractive woman. And they told him that she was the concubine of the Rt. Reverend Dr. N. J. Lee.

He did not in any way let this gossip compromise the good name of Reverend's daughter, Linda. Before he went West, while he was still a boy, he learned that it was nothing uncommon for a preacher—many of the biggest preachers, to be looked up on and called a rascal. Nobody thought of including their wives and daughters with them; but it was said that if you wanted to find a young man that was good and bad, just look for the son of a preacher. This didn't, of course, include all the sons of preachers.

Linda was perhaps six months older than Eden. She was dark, like her father, not tall, nor short, with a wealth of coarse, brindle-like hair. Yet for some reason, which he couldn't understand, it was hard to picture himself marrying her. Perhaps it was because her father was a preacher. Martin Eden had never spent much time with Negro preachers. They didn't altogether fit into his idea of dependable and unselfish Negro leaders. He had fully decided, however, that if he was to find some girl to file on the land, who liked him, and whom he could like well enough to marry, then he had better start finding her and that very soon. There wasn't time enough left for even hoping to fall in love with one now. He would simply have to select a nice girl who was intelligent, nice looking, and as agreeable as possible with his point of view, file her on the land, then marry her and take a chance.

The great passion that he once felt for Jessie Binga was to be no more. Every man and woman wishes to love the marriage partner, but with him, it seemed that marriage had now become strictly a business proposition. If he should happen to fall in love, so much the better, but if he didn't, he'd have to marry and make the best of it.

One thing he had decided about a long time ago, and he had stuck to his convictions regarding it ever since. This was, that he would never allow himself to fall in love with any girl, regardless how beautiful or how sweet she might seem, until he had checked on her character. For one of either sex to become infatuated without first finding out if the loved one were worthy, was something he could never condone.

He had checked carefully regarding Linda, and her character had stood the acid test—in this, she was perfect. She was educated. She was all that he could ask for in a girl that he could wish to marry, so what? During the weeks that followed, he found himself weighing her in the balance, and continued to weigh her by day and far into the night. They were exchanging letters almost weekly now and she gave him every encouragement. Then, when she read that he was planning a trip to Chicago, especially to see her, on a matter of considerable importance, her happiness knew no bounds. She showed the letter to her mother.

"Do you think he plans to—to propose to me, mother; ask me to marry him?"

"Well," said her mother a bit judiciously. "It sounds like it, but it seems to involve much more than just a proposal."

"Yes, it does; but remember when I first told you about him I said that he had some plan to tie his marriage up with some land proceedings out there."

"Yes, I remember."

"I remember his saying that he was going to place his sister and his grandmother on some. Now maybe he means to put the girl he plans marrying on a place too—I guess that is what it means."

"Perhaps that is what he is coming to Chicago to explain."

"Perhaps."

"In such a case, maybe, it's only a business deal?" ventured her mother.

"Let's not jump to conclusions. I'm sure, however, that an ultimate marriage in the same connection is a part of his plans. Anyway, he hasn't proposed yet and since his letter states that he's coming to see me he will, while here, no doubt, explain what it is all about. So the only thing that I can do, as I see it, is to wait until he comes and hear what this matter of 'great importance' is."

"Yes, that is all you can do."

"Then I will write him that I am happy and glad that he is coming to Chicago, and that I will be glad to listen to anything he might have to say regarding the matter," said Linda, as they arose. Her mother paused.

"By the way, dear. Have you written him anything about your father?"

"No, I haven't, mother. But father has been told so much about him down there in Southern Illinois that he must almost know him by now."

"I hope he hasn't heard as much about your father; but what I was thinking of was, your father's towering vanity, his monumental ego. If Martin in some way could be brought to flatter him, when and if they ever meet, it would make it easier for all of us."

"When father comes home, I'll undertake to acquaint him with Martin's position; but until he does, (you know how hard father is to explain anything to; to make understand anything intricate) I'll just say nothing about it. You know what I mean?"

"How *well* do I know. I've been trying to make him understand lots of things ever since we've been married—and haven't succeeded yet." And then, with a change of tone, "Did he say in the letter when he plans to come to Chicago?"

"Early in October, mother."

"That'll be a fine time. Your father will be at conferences all that month, so whatever it is that the boy friend has to talk about and explain, we will be free to listen to it, and if it should call for a trip up there and is fair and reasonable and will not jeopardize your character or good name, we might be able to put something over before your father comes home."

"You're so sweet and understanding about everything, mother. I don't know what I would do without you."

"I want to see my girl happy. It's time you were married if you are ever going to. I'm sorry to say your father is such a stumbling block in this respect with his 'love' that it's got me worried. I hope if anything is to come of Mr. Eden's friendship, that we can manage to keep your father out of it—at least as long as it is possible. He's run every boy that ever tried to go with you off, for ten years—oh, that husband of mine; that father of yours!"

"Since Mr. Eden is so much broader and so much more sensible than any of the boys who have tried to go with me, maybe he will appeal to father and then it will be different, mother."

"It'll be worse if anything. I've a feeling that in the end, he and Mr. Eden are not going to hitch so well. But I don't think that Martin can be run off as easily as the other boys."

They talked far into the night about Martin, and when Linda retired, she hoped that she might dream of him—and she did.

CHAPTER XI

At last eden's plans were complete. He sent his sister a draft to pay their grandmother's and her own fares and provide expenses to Dakota. Then he made ready to go and see Linda as planned.

On the afternoon of the day before he was to leave, he found himself alone with Deborah. She had been strangely silent after he told her he was going away. She guessed what he was going for. Nevertheless, she prepared him a nice lunch. She put it in a shoe box and tied a string neatly around it.

All day she had been silent and a bit nervous and distracted. Eden noticed it and expressed concern.

"You don't seem yourself today, Deborah. Don't you feel well?"

"Yes, I feel well," and went about her duties mechanically, offering to say no more. His eyes followed her. This was not the Deborah he had known for most of a year. He was not satisfied. Something had changed.

"But you—you don't act like you do."

"Don't I?"

"No, Deborah, you do not."

"I'm sorry."

He was at a loss what to do or say for a moment, but becoming more concerned the while.

"I've never seen you like this before."

"Maybe you don't know me."

"Don't know you, Deborah? I thought I had learned much about you this summer. I say, you've never been like this before. Won't you tell me?"

"There's nothing to tell." She continued moving about mechanically. Something had come over her and he knew it. Regardless what she was saying, Martin Eden had learned enough about this girl to know that she was not telling all. He was going away, perhaps out of her life forever, and he didn't want to go and leave her like this.

"I'm worried about you, Deborah."

"Why worry about me?"

"Deborah, please!"

"Please what?"

"Deborah, I can't stand it."

"Can't stand what?"

"You must know how I feel. . . ."

"How do you feel?"

"Miserable."

"Miserable? Miserable about what? Why should *you* feel miserable?"

"But I do feel miserable. I don't like to see you acting this way—I don't want to leave as long as you keep acting like this."

"You're going away to be married—at least to get engaged. You have nothing to worry about. You must be in love."

"I'm not in love."

"Not in love?"

"How could I be. I haven't known her that long."

"You'll learn to love her."

"Maybe."

"Oh, you will."

"I'm not thinking about myself. I'm thinking about you now. I can't bear leaving and remembering you as you are now acting."

"I can't see that it is any concern of yours how I act any more."

"Do you want me to remember you as you have been? Or do you want me to remember you as you are now?"

She kept silent, trying hard to appear busy.

"You know why I'm going away," he ventured. He thought he saw her flinch. "Whether you do or not, I know that I wouldn't be going if fate hadn't been so cruel to me. I wish I didn't have to go. But I can't go on forever like this. I've got a heart like everybody else. I'm still a young man."

"Martin!" she cried, standing straight, with something flashing in her eyes that he had not seen before.

"Yes, Deborah?"

She drew close, her breast heaving. He could see that she was laboring under great stress.

"You speak about yourself."

"Well, Deborah. Wha—"

"What about me?"

"About you, Deborah?"

"You don't understand?"

"I—I don't think I do."

"Aren't you looking at me?"

"I am looking at you, Deborah."

"And what do you see?"

"What do I see? I see—a beautiful girl." He suggested, still at a loss to know what she was driving at. She stamped her foot impatiently.

"I don't want flattery, Martin Eden—I want truth. You know that I am not vain. What you see standing before you is a woman, a young woman. Hasn't it occurred to you that I, too, have a heart; that I, too, am lonesome; that I, too, crave that which you are going away to find? Hasn't it occurred to you, that—that *I love you*, Martin Eden? I, oh—" She could say no more. Bursting into tears, she turned her back and wept.

"Why, Deborah!" He exclaimed, taken aback. "I—" She turned again, her face stained with tears.

"I understand and in spite of how I feel, I know why you are going away. But Martin, I'm a girl, a sad, lonely forgotten girl and I—I hoped that you'd feel sorry for me, as I have for you."

"I do feel sorry for you, Deborah; but Deborah, you—you're *a white girl*, while I—I am black. That is why—why I can't speak; why I've never been able to speak; but you must have felt—you must have even known how I could feel about you if it were not as it is. I—"

"Oh, isn't it cruel, Martin, I love you so and you love me, I know you love me, Martin, but you won't say so. You're afraid to—be weak—even in love, because of that—that ugly thing; that thing you called 'demarcation.' The line of 'demarcation' standing between two people who love each other;—two people who understand each other; two people who need each other—two people who could love and succeed together—all because of 'the line of demarcation'! Oh, I hate society and its customs, I hate it, I hate it!" She threw her arms into the air and paced the floor like a great actress. He looked after her sadly.

"But do we *have* to stand it? Is there anything on earth as important to two people as their love?"

"Nothing, Deborah," said he, sadly.

"Then why do you have to conform to such a custom?" He straightened, he placed a hand on her. He looked into her weeping eyes.

"If life ended with just you and me, Deborah, that would be one thing, but you, we, are only the medium, progenitors of lives that are to come. I will tell you a story, Deborah, so let's sit here at the table, across from each other.

"Down the railroad that leads to Omaha there lives a family who are part Negro, part white. They are more white than colored, so according to majority rule, they should be accepted as white and nothing said about it. But they are not. All the way from where they are known North and West and East and South, people talk about them to their backs. One is a banker, controls the credit of many people who wish to please him, so they dare not express their opinion to his face, unless ready to go into financial oblivion. Yet because they don't want to be known as black, they claim they are white, but everybody talks about them—to their backs. For years this has been going on and in all the years to come, they will be whispered about; and they know it and it makes them mean, and evil and spiteful, and I imagine, unhappy.

"This, as I've explained, won't stop with them, but it will be handed down to their children, their children's children.

"Only this summer during that carnival in August, I almost got into trouble on their account. I was in a saloon with some friends when I happened to look through the window, and I saw a handsome young Colored man perhaps two years younger than I. He was about my color, if I was not so tanned. I started to him joyfully, because I felt that he was somebody that I could welcome and perhaps have a long talk with and enjoy some racial contact. Pointing to the young fellow through the window, I started toward him and had got almost to the door, when my friend came running, grasping me by the arm and laid a finger across his lips. He led me back and across the room to one side and whispered:

"You can't do that."

"I can't do what?" I asked in surprise.

"Speak to that fellow."

"That fellow?" said I, jerking my thumb over my shoulder in his direction. "What's the matter? Why can't I?"

"Because he is one of the Woodsons, don't you understand; the Woodsons from down at Manila."

"Oh," I echoed. "One of the Woodsons!"

"Yes, the younger one. He's colored all right, but they don't own to being colored. They don't want to be. They associate with white people. He'd snub you if you offered to speak to him. They don't own to being colored—and they *hate* colored people."

She sat silently listening to this; and she listened to his story about the other Negro, who was married to a white woman with daughters his age, going with white men, and of how much the families wanted to be white.

"So you see, Deborah, what I mean. In spite of how we both may feel, we'd have to consider the children and these children's children, and if they, too, wouldn't be like the Woodson's. It is too great a price to pay. Besides, I have never desired to 'cross the line,' that is why you've seen me exercise so much discretion, so much restraint." She recalled then what she had seen at the Vosika barn dance. At last she nodded her head sadly.

"We can't blame the people we know for this. It was here when they came; it will be here after you go, I go, they go. A custom founded when the country was born, it is a part of our system, and woe be unto those who try to transcend it; to them can only come misery and woe. Think of children, perhaps into the third or fourth generation to be whispered about—and they will be, no fooling ourselves about that. It's cruel, I know. But—"

"I would be good to you, Martin."

"Please, Deborah."

"I understand your problems, your life, your needs. I would make you happy."

"*Please*, Deborah."

"You don't love this girl you are going to see."

"I hope to learn to. I once loved Jessie."

"And you see what she did to you. She didn't do it because she no longer loved you. She simply didn't understand your life out here, your needs—your everything."

"I know all that, Deborah."

"And neither does Linda. She is sweet, she is kind, she is pretty; but—"

"Deborah, you are hurting me."

"You are going to suffer greater injuries, Martin. I see it. I see something terrible catching up and overtaking you. I saw this some days ago. It came to me from nowhere. I see that if you go to Chicago, a change after a time will come over your life; I see great suffering, sadness, humiliation, chaos!

And before it is all over—destruction, Martin, destruction! I can't stand it—I can't stand to see all this happen to you, a good man, a kind man; a man who has never done a wrong thing to any other person. I can't stand to see this happen to—the man I love."

"I am suffering the agonies of death, Deborah," cried Eden.

"But you will suffer far greater agonies when what is going to happen to you, overtakes you. That will be more cruel than death itself. You will suffer almost unto death."

"God help me."

"He cannot. It is written in the infinite," she went on, now looking into space like a great mystic, "that you will suffer and that you will all but die, still you will try to go on. And it will all be, not for what you have done, but for what you tried to do;—tried to do only what was right and fair and honest; it will be done unto you because a vain person will choose to misunderstand you. I'm sorry for you, Martin Eden."

"But Deborah, can't I do something to escape all this? What can I do, *what must I do?*"

She turned slowly, looking straight at him but hers wear a far away expression, "You will not obey me. I don't expect you to. I wanted not to say these things to you, Martin, that is why I tried to act as I did at the start when it was all but breaking my heart.

"The only way you could avoid this catastrophe, Martin, would be not to go to Chicago. If you go to Chicago, it must happen, it *will* happen; and still—"

"Still, Deborah? Still what?"

"You will go. It is predicted that you will and I know you must. You are committed to a procedure; you have laid out a schedule, and you must follow that schedule, for you were a long time formulating it; to try digress from it now would upset and annoy you.

"More than two years ago you conceived the plan to settle the girl you would marry on a claim that you would provide.

You neglected to marry the girl that you were then in love with—you pushed the marriage date forward, until after the land you desired had been acquired. But before that could come to pass, something happened. What that something was, you experienced and know.

"But your plans have been carefully laid—you *have* to see them through. This is why I say that you will go to Chicago, you must; because all this is a part of a well thought out plan, a sensible plan; a commendable plan. Yet, having to go to Chicago and propose to Linda, bring her back here, file on this land, and marry her, will in the end, be the plan that will lead you into chaos. I can't see yet how it will come out. When this *something* of which I am unhappily possessed gets there, it becomes confused. But I do clearly see suffering for you, Martin, untold suffering, and misunderstanding, deliberate and cold plotting against you. All this I *can* see and see it *now*."

"And is there no way I can avoid all this?"

"A strange way, a peculiar way."

"But what way?"

She looked straight at him and he understood.

"I see you understand what way. The way that you cannot take, because in the end, the custom of the country and its social laws might bring about all you have related. I understand, dear Martin, and bow to it. Fate has willed one way, fate will·have to save you in the end. The irony of it all is, that it could be so easily avoided.

"I could file on the land, I could prove it up for you and I would. I could give it to you then, and you could do with me the same as you will with your grandmother and your sister. They understand you and you trust them. No papers have to be signed, a whole lot of trips do not have to be made. That is because there is a simple, unspoken understanding between your grandmother, your sister, and you, and it is all being carried out so easily and simply.

"This could still be done as regards the other claim if you hadn't bound this up with marriage plans—even when you do not love the girl. But I understand and appreciate all this and it is just as well. You do not love her but you will honestly try to and you will make her a good husband. She will want to be a good wife to you; but you do not love her and it will always be hard to succeed, because you love me, Martin. You can't say it and I won't ask you to, but you *do* love me as much as I love you, so I can only let you go on your way, feeling sorry for both of us because fate to us is cruel."

"Oh, you are so kind to me, Deborah."

"You have been kind to me, Martin."

"I am unhappy," he sighed.

"I am also unhappy, Martin."

"Maybe, Deborah, when it is all—this that you say you see—is over, there may be a new life."

"There may be a new life, Martin. I feel strangely about something; but it is in the future, so far away it is not clear. I cannot discern what it is now—it's obscure and indefinite. I just feel there is something; but you will have to go through all that I see will soon envelope you. What ever this something is, it will come after that.

"Our being close to each other is about to end, Martin. It is time that you were going. Don't despair. You are strong and brave, and in the end, I feel that you will endure somehow. I don't know. That is one of the visions that is not clear to me yet—still vague, still far away." He stepped to the door and laid his hand on the knob. She called his name, softly.

"Martin?"

"Yes, Deborah?" turning to face her.

"Soon, dear, you are going to meet and be strangely enveloped by something! This *something* will foreshadow your life soon to come—maybe your destruction—your doom. I beg you, Martin, to be strong and brave and try to endure and overcome this strange something you will soon meet.

If you succeed, if you withstand this thing that will envelope you, you may endure and in the end, triumph over all.

"And now, as a farewell to our happy but brief days together out here in your wilderness, as you call it, will—will you—do something for me before you—you leave me?"

"Anything you ask, Deborah."

"You have—have—never—kissed me; you have never even tried to." He was silent, not knowing what to do or say.

"Then, be—before you go, will you—you please—kiss me, Martin?"

He looked down at her, into those deep sad eyes that seemed to have no bottom. Her lips quivered, and he could see two tears welling up. He drew her closely, so close until her breast heaved with emotion against his and then he found her soft, sweet lips; the kiss from which he was not to soon forget. After a time which may have been an age, it was over, and he was gone.

Between his little sod house and the house where Stewarts lived, rose a high hill which Eden always had to cross to get to his house. When he left Deborah, he walked to the top, then paused to look back for the first time. He didn't see her for she had closed the door and stood by a window, but she saw him. He looked back sadly at the house which had given him more happiness in less than a year than he had ever before known. He sighed and turned, suddenly feeling a wind. It was a hard wind, a driving, cold wind which almost upset him, and blew with the velocity of a hurricane.

He struggled to stand for it drove him back several feet and he maintained his equilibrium with the greatest difficulty.

Deborah, watching him from her window, started; her mouth opened, and then she remembered. She had seen this wind and recalled that when he reached the hill it would meet him. She watched to see if it would throw him, for if it did, the storm Martin Eden was destined to meet, would destroy him. She watched his struggle with anxiety. He *had* to stand on his feet else he was done for.

"Oh, God," she pleaded now. "Save him, protect him, don't let that wind fell him—please don't, oh Lord."

The wind, a strange wind which had enveloped Martin Eden, and which came as if from nowhere, was about to level him to the ground. Then, as she watched, so eagerly, so anxiously, from her window, she could feel at her distance his power of will. It seemed to combine with his great strength, and with almost a superhuman effort, he forced himself to stand erect. He could not go forward. All the while, her heart in her mouth, she was praying for him to succeed. If he fell now, she knew it would be the end of Martin Eden. He would never rise again.

At last, he balanced himself carefully, lest the wind, when one foot was raised, should upset him and he should lose the battle against this strange thing, this wind from nowhere. At last he was about to make it, and she breathed a great sigh of relief and pressed her hand against her bosom to still the terrible beating of her heart.

He was getting started at last. *He was moving!* One step, two steps, three steps, four steps and then she knew that he had mastered it. She saw him vanish slowly until he was lost to her sight on the other side of the hill.

Then, as she lingered to watch, the wind which had come as if from nowhere, and almost blew Martin Eden to the ground, broke up, scattered, and ceased blowing. The sun, which it had obscured, reappeared. It was calm and beautiful outside again and Deborah turned away with a sigh and began a long effort to forget Martin Eden, who, like the wind from nowhere, seemed to have passed on and out of her life.

CHAPTER XII

It was saturday when Martin Eden arrived in Chicago. After finding a room, he proceeded at once to Linda's home on Vernon Avenue. She met him at the door.

"Oh, Mr. Eden," she cried in glad surprise, as she swung wide open the door. He stepped inside and turned to face her with a smile.

"It's a pleasure, Miss Lee," extending his hand.

"I'm *so* glad to see you again," said she, joyously, taking his hand and squeezing it in both of hers. Hat and top coat hung in the hall, he followed her into the parlor.

"I wasn't sure what time I would reach here, so I didn't wire."

"I'm glad you didn't, for telegrams frighten me. I always associate them with death," at which he laughed.

"Now just make yourself comfortable while I go bring my mother. She's anxious to see you since you've 'growed up'."

"And I to see her."

A few minutes later she returned, leading her mother, a matronly old lady who it was to be seen at a glance had when young, been a pretty woman.

"And this is little Martin Eden, grown into a fine, big man. My, how things can change. I knew you when you were a baby and my husband was the pastor of the church in which you were christened. In fact, he baptized you."

"Baptized me?" echoed Martin, a bit incredulously. "Now this *is* news. I didn't know that I had ever been baptized." They all laughed.

"That's been a long time ago," remarked Linda.

"Only twenty-six years," said Mrs. Lee. "Isn't that just about your age?" looking at Eden.

"Right."

"Linda here," turning to her daughter, "was born six months before you."

"Mother!" from Linda, flashing her eyes, shocked.

"M-m," cried Eden, making eyes at her, "so I know how old you are."

"I'm surprised at my mother—talking too much."

"It was merely a coincidence, my daughter. Forgive me."

"Never!" Her mother patted her cheek.

"Pity your poor old Mother." Mrs. Lee affected hurt, whereupon Linda kissed her quickly, then glanced up at Eden and blushed.

"Now since we have chairs and a sofa, why can't we be seated?"

"Excuse me, mother. I forgot. Won't you please be seated, Mr. Eden?"

"Thanks." He assisted Mrs. Lee to a seat on the sofa beside her daughter. He then pulled an occasional chair forward and sat down facing them.

"I'm glad you sat there," said Mrs. Lee, pointing at him, "so I can look at you. Linda here, has been talking so much about meeting you in Murphysboro last winter that I'm anxious to look at you; see what kind of man you are and hear you talk." He laughed.

"He can ply more questions—ask people all about their business. Why, you'd think he was a prosecuting attorney, examining a prisoner at the bar," giggled Linda.

"I like to ask questions," answered Eden. "It helps you find people out—go to the bottom of them and learn their ways, their weaknesses—their strength."

"But supposing they asked you a lot of questions, the same way? Wouldn't you think it, at times, a bit personal?" countered Linda.

"Not in the least—especially if they were intelligent questions, questions with a real interest, material questions. I
like to be asked those kind of questions. I'm always glad to
answer them. Would you, or your mother like to ask me some?
Maybe there is something you'd like to find out about me;
things you, perhaps, have the right to know.

"Go ahead, ask me anything you wish; anything that may
be on your minds. I say, if there is anything more interesting
to me than asking questions, it's answering questions. So go
ahead, ask anything about me that you want to know. I'll
try to answer."

They looked at each other, then back at him. Catching
Linda's eyes, his twinkled, then he smiled, which brought a
smile from her and another blush unseen.

"My daughter is no good at asking questions and I am not,
either. I'm thankful to you, however, for offering yourself for
examination; it is surely frank and honest. I'm still thinking
about you as a boy. I've got to have a little while to become
accustomed to you grown up. How is your mother, anyhow?
I knew her and your father, very well."

"They're well. They moved to Kansas several years ago."

"So I heard. You had three uncles who went out there
away back in the eighties, I recall."

"All pioneers, yes. So you see that I come of pioneer stock.
It seems to run in our family and blood to make conquest."

"This is indeed very interesting. Like father, like son. And
so you're a pioneer now, too."

"I love my wilderness off there in Dakota, the 'hollow of
God's hand', I sometimes call it."

"I'm curious about it. I've been trying to picture a young
man like you, going away off there, settling all by himself
and living alone. Now just how do you manage it? Who cooks
for you?"

"Until last spring when I returned home from my trip,
I cooked for myself. Kept batch."

"Kept batch? That is *real* pioneering. But you—you must get lonesome, do you not?"

"Well, sometimes, when I'm idle; but that's not often, for I'm always very busy."

"Very busy? You look like a very busy sort of person. I expect you've been so busy you—you haven't taken time to get—married. Is that so?"

"Well," said he slowly. "Yes and again, no."

"It isn't quite clear." Mrs. Lee's face wore a puzzled look.

"I mean," he explained, "that I've wished to tie my marriage up with something; something that would make both worth while, and the time has not been convenient until now—but maybe real soon now."

It was still not clear, except to confirm what he had hinted at when he met Linda, and what he had written her in his last letter. Again they looked at him, a question in their eyes.

"I'm in Chicago in regard to that matter and will perhaps get at it while here. If the bridge to be crossed is sufficient, I may start across it while here. He looked at Linda when he finished and said no more, but Mrs. Lee caught the hint. She excused hereself and left them.

After Mother Mary, as he later began calling her, had left them, he moved over beside Linda. She looked at him, turned away and again blushed unseen. Presently she inquired:

"How did you happen to go away off there to settle anyhow? We've talked about it and I said that as quickly as I had a chance, I'd ask you."

"As I said, my uncles went West as boys and grew up with Kansas, maybe 'twas in my blood to repeat what they had done."

"Yes, but from what I have learned, none of your brothers, and you have three, so I hear, has gone to the wilderness and made conquest of anything. That's what makes your case much different. That's why I'm curious to know how you happened to be like you are when they, born of the same mother, reared in the same environment, still are not at all like you."

"My brothers," said Martin, "chose like so many of our group, the line of least resistance, and as a result, have 'gone with the wind', as it were."

"Now you're coming to the point. Tell me all about yourself, please," getting a bit closer. I'm *very* much interested."

"Really?"

"Really."

"I would like to have you tell me something about yourself."

"Myself? Oh, really, Mr. Eden, there is hardly anything to tell. I've done nothing except going to school, graduating from Wendell Phillips High here in Chicago and then spending two years attending the Normal so that I could teach. I've taught three years, so that's my little story. Summed up, all in one paragraph—a short one at that. So you see I'm just a girl and that's all."

He laughed a little, and she joined him.

"Are you a nice girl?"

"Well," slowly, "I try to be. Why?"

"Oh, nothing. Just wanted to hear it from your lips, that's all."

"Have you—asked anybody else if I was?" she queried, looking up at him sideways so that it made her seem coquettish. He smiled, and placed his hand on hers and she did not draw it away.

"I'm waiting for you to tell me your story. You're young and you've been places, done things. That must be interesting. I want to know about it; hear some of it at least from your own lips."

"I don't like to talk about myself."

"And why not?"

"Oh, it sometimes leads to people talking about you; calling you boastful and egotistic."

"Oh, no. Not when you have actually succeeded in doing

something—like you, for instance." She curled up and glanced at him again with that coquettish slant. Again he smiled. He was beginning to like her. He squeezed her hand; she squeezed his, and they exchanged another glance. He decided to talk, to tell her what she had asked.

"Are you sure you want to know why I went up there to my wilderness? I'd hate to bore you."

"Oh Mr. Eden, why say that? You could never bore me if you talked—all night; you could not bore me if you talked forever. I think you're just that interesting."

"Well, after such a send off, I guess I'll have to say something, but I'm not going to take long. It never takes me long to tell anything, do anything. I even imagine that when I fall in love it will be right quick."

"Think so?" she drawled, a twinkle in her eye. Maybe after all she was what he wanted. At least she was not hard to sit near, listen to, talk to, look at.

"Well, here's my little story."

"Do tell it, please." She took a new grip on his hand, even got a little closer.

"A few years ago every colored boy with any purpose at all seemed fired with the ambition to return to school, study and learn to become a doctor or a lawyer."

"That's very true. And Chicago is full of both, loaded down with education and degrees and starving to death—not one in half a dozen is making a decent living."

"Is that so?"

"So? Too much so, but go on. Pardon me for interrupting you."

"I never somehow took to such an ambition. It was singular that so many wanted to become the same thing."

"It wasn't ambition, it was an illusion which ended in grand delusions—please go on."

"The point, as I saw it then, still see it, was to succeed, and a man didn't have to be a lawyer or a doctor to do so."

"The way it's turned out in Chicago, that seems a good way *not* to succeed."

"With the race so poor, it seems difficult to get very rich— to even have a profitable practice with the kind of clients, like most of us, few having any money.

"You said it. Negroes have no money—they don't make much, so how can they have much? It takes more than most of them make to live half way comfortably. But I can't seem to quit interrupting you. I *do* want to hear your story, all of it."

"As I saw it, then, a man could be as successful in some other line, maybe more successful if he worked hard enough and used his efforts wisely. There is just as good, if not a better chance to get along in trade, commerce, agriculture or industry."

"Sure, why not?"

"I was running on the road; I was a Pullman Porter. So I saved my little tips and salary, put them in the bank. The Rosebud Country where I now live, was about to be thrown open to settlement; it looked like a chance for a young man to get in on the ground floor, and to make good with the growth of the country. So I went up there to grow up with it—and I'm still growing—and so is the country!"

"Very direct and to the point, I'd say. And you like it up there?"

"I love it."

"How does it happen that there are no colored people up there?"

"Ask them. The Negro, from my observation and experience hasn't much spirit, or ambition these days for trying to do things. Since relief has become available, he seems content to just 'get along'—he doesn't even like to think very deeply, very seriously."

"He does not! In fact, he isn't going to do either if he can keep from it," she agreed.

"You know, after I met you in Murphysboro, I thought you were very hard on your race. You seemed to be real severe and very impatient with them. But now as I talk to you, and get your point of view, I can see that you are not. You just seem to like to face the issue squarely and take what's coming to you and we all know that, as a group, we try to shirk all responsibilities that we can. So I can see that it is not you who is hard on us. It is we who are hard on ourselves."

"It's up to every man to stand on his own responsibility. Running from it isn't getting him any nearer. Ultimately he must face the music, so why not at once and have it over with for good, is how I see it."

"You see it correctly and are facing it the same way. That is most admirable of you."

"Thank you."

"You gave me more to think about in our conversation last winter and today than I can express. Being a minister's daughter, you can't imagine what one has to put up with. The lives of those you meet and have to tolerate are so limited, so petty, so—oh, so everything to put you in the doldrums. Then there is so much deceit and pretense and hypocrisy and so little sincerity and courage. You're just bound to feel that you're going back half the time, yet you go on because people must live. They can't die until the time comes, so why spend your whole life waiting and preparing for that day when you will finally die?"

"And go up to heaven."

"Yes, heaven, that infinite somewhere from which nobody has ever returned to tell the story—but I'm drifting away from my teaching. I said that I was a minister's daughter, so you can understand what I am supposed to conform to."

"I will relieve you on that subject by talking about something else; about ourselves, for instance."

"Yes, about ourselves. Well, I'm listening. Where do we go from here?"

He continued: "How little did I think, and I bet you've thought about it since, that, when we passed each other on the street last winter it would be you that I'd be coming to see within the year!"

"And not Jessie Binga," she chided, whereat he looked embarrassed. Immediately she was apologetic.

"Oh, pardon me. I didn't mean to embarrass you."

"Oh, that's all right."

"But I'm sure glad it has happened this way. Did it—pain you very much when she—did what she did? It happened so suddenly; nobody even suspected it—when it—then it just happened."

"I never was deeply impressed with the dependable side of Jessie. Personally, I take heredity and environment rather seriously. Jessie's heredity wasn't very good; her environment was worse. I felt sorry for her. I think she was a victim of both."

"I believe so, too, now that you analyze it as you do. You know, of course, that it's all over; that they have parted." He turned toward her in surprise.

"I didn't know. Is that so?"

"Oh, yes. Quite some time ago."

"Oh, that's too bad. I'm sorry."

"It was a miss match. It couldn't endure."

"No, I had a feeling that it wouldn't turn out well when it took place. Oh, well, Jessie was a sweet girl. There was so much good in her."

"There was, but as you say, heredity and environment must have their day in court, and Jessie's have had their first session. We continue to go off on tangents; we can't seem to talk about ourselves. Now we're talking about your old love."

"And she is no longer in the picture. This has to do with you and me," he complained.

"Yes, you and me. Well, I'm ready to talk about anything you wish to." She wondered if he was ready to talk of that matter of "great importance." If so, she was in the mood to listen. Instead, he remarked:

"Personally, I'm feeling the pangs of hunger and could do some eating. How do you feel?" She smiled at him agreeably, and replied:

"Well, I'm not to say exactly hungry, but I will be bye and bye and am willing to go with you, and maybe when I smell the food and look at you eat, I may be able to do so, too."

"Thanks. When do we start?"

"Now if you like. You are my guest. I want to please you."

"Thanks, again, it is mighty sweet of you to be so considerate of me. I like you for that."

"And I like you for asking me to—and for a lot of other things." Their hands touched and he held hers for a moment. She squeezed his again and then dashed away upstairs, to change her dress etc., excusing herself and leaving him to walk around the room and look at pictures on the wall, on the piano, and other what nots.

CHAPTER XIII

LINDA TOOK EDEN to a cozy little restaurant, a sort of tea room on South Parkway. The place had booths. They became seated in one, and found themselves alone, which pleased them.

"I've heard of people eating with a coming appetite, which is what I seem to have developed," said she as she partook of a small steak and all the trimmings. While she sipped at her coffee, they continued the conversation, started at her home.

After an hour they returned. Darkness was approaching when they entered. Linda found Terry, her sister, who had a reputation for ostentation, and introduced her to Eden, who let her do most of the talking. It was clear as he listened to her, that not much love was going to be lost between them, and he was relieved when she excused herself and left them alone.

He lingered by the piano and Linda sang for him, what he thought a charming, tho' old song. *"Dearest Memories."* It seemed to soften their mood and when they seated themselves on the sofa he felt the urge. More serious than he had been since arriving, he began:

"Now, Linda, if I may call you by your first name."

"I want you to," hardly above a whisper.

"I promise to on condition that you call me by mine."

"Do you want me to?"

"I do, Linda, most earnestly. It will make me seem as if I know you; make you seem closer to me. I would like to feel closer to you; I don't like to be so formal—in short, I've journeyed here to get better acquainted with you, dear." Then he stopped.

"Oh do go on—you may even call me 'dear'— that is, if you think you'd like to—and mean it," she said, invitingly.

"Thank you, Linda, dear. There, I've called you both," and he laughed awkwardly, nervously.

"And—did you—mean them, Martin?

"Both, Linda."

"I'm so glad," and she nestled closely.

He had done a lot of planning over a period of years, and now the time had arrived for him to do some executing. He had to be back in Gregory before the end of that week coming and have his people with him to take over the claims, relinquishments on which he had purchased—and paid for. So it was up to him now to deliver.

His sister and grandmother were on their way from Kansas to Dakota, and would be waiting there when he got back. He intended to take Linda back with him, so to the task. He turned to her, his face more businesslike now than emotional.

"What I'm going to say will take some effort, my dear. It is going to be a strange proposal of marriage."

She started. This *was* a strange *something*. But it certainly didn't sound like a proposal. She had pictured the way the man she would some day marry might propose to her—she had pictured many ways—but none, most assuredly, had been pictured like this. Well, he had begun, and while she stared with her lips parted, she hardly knew how to react. She did the best she could.

"Of marriage, Mr.—I mean, Martin."

"That's better, thank you," with an attempt at a joke, and he smiled at her awkwardly. She tried to smile back, but with an effort. All she could do was to listen, so she listened.

"Now, you haven't known me long enough, nor I you, for me to propose in the usual way, the way you have, perhaps pictured some man would. It is not the way I have thought that I would propose, myself. Yet, I ask you to believe me when I say that, as odd as it may seem, this will be the first time that I have actually ever asked any girl to marry me, to be my wife." She was surprised. She was sure that in all the while he and Jessie had been sweethearts, he must have talked of marriage.

They had—but he was telling the truth. He had never asked any girl to actually marry him. She believed him and softened toward him.

"That's why it is going to be hard. I am not going to ask you if you love me, nor am I going to say that I love you— yet. Love to me, seems like a most sacred thing."

"It *is* a sacred thing, Martin.

"I've been waiting a long time. to be really in love with a girl. But my peculiar position, living off there by myself, alone, has forced me to the conclusion that if I am ever to marry (and I want a wife; I do want to marry) I'll just have to tie it up with business and take a chance if I can find a girl willing to meet me half way."

She was listening intently.

"I've decided I must do that if I am ever to marry, because I haven't been where I could court a girl like the boys here in Chicago, and finally after a period of the usual courtship, decide that I love her and propose the way she pictures that I should.

"If I fell on my knees and said 'I love you, Linda, love you more than my own soul. Will you marry me, dear?' that would seem to be acting, and I am sincere in what I'm going to say. At least it is my hope that you will appreciate my trying to be frank about it all."

"I do, Martin."

"I thank you, dear. Now may I go on?"

"Please do."

"Well, I like you very much. I like you better than any girl I know. I like you so well that, with your consent, I'm sure I will come to love you dearly soon. I am hopeful that you will find it possible to love me, too, and real soon, in return."

"I will try to, Martin."

"I thank you for that, too. As I started to say, I have always felt that it would be very fitting and proper for a man and a woman to check on each other; to find if the other is fitted as to character and viewpoint to what you feel is your particular need. I think this would be a good thing to do before they fell in love. Then, with all this settled, it would be much easier than to become infatuated and find out later that the one was just impossible according to the other's point of view."

"I think that is sensible, and I subscribe to the same principles."

Both smiled. He found her hand and she let him hold it. He continued:

"I hate poverty. From as far back as I can remember, I disliked squalor and poverty and the misery of being poor. I am more willing to labor until I fall in my tracks than to submit to the poverty in which I see most of us colored people hopelessly sunk. It takes so much out of one—penury and woe are terrible things to face—and a limited income is not pleasant to anticipate, either.

"But the only way to change all this is for a man to be willing to develop some sense of judgment, labor and continue to labor, and to learn to wait, carrying on ceaselessly while doing so!" She squeezed his hand to indicate agreement.

"You say such logical things. You will make any sensible girl learn to love you—and it won't take long."

"As I see it, it's bad enough to be a Negro with all we have to put up with; but to be a trifling, good for nothing poor one, is too much.

"I like to work; night comes too early, morning not soon enough. It gives me the biggest thrill of all to feel that I am getting somewhere, changing my condition for the better. I want cash in my pocket, money in the bank. I want to be something, have always wanted to stand for something, be appreciated and respected by my friends and my neighbors. To have this, you must possess something. A successful man is always more popular and interesting than an unsuccessful one."

"Are you telling me!"

"Then here is what it is all about, Linda," folding his arm about hers, and holding both her hands.

"I have, by the hardest kind of work and what some people call sacrifice (I don't consider I've made any. I only feel that I'm trying to do what I ought to be doing) made some progress. I have four farms. I owe some money on them, but they are in my name, I'm paying the taxes. I have improved them, and though I have no house that a wife could live in on either, I can and will, when the time comes, build a house.

"Meanwhile, an opportunity developed to acquire three more farms. I can only acquire them by acting now. The same opportunity will not be possible six months from now — not even two months from now. It is government land, taken over by the government from the Indians, and under a certain set up, I have secured an option to three of these so-called quarters, or 160 acre tracts."

"I am following you; I understand what you mean. Please go on. I'm deeply interested."

"I'm glad Thank you. It makes it easier.

"Under a decree these lands have to be homesteaded and improved upon. Every American citizen over 21 years old, a woman, if single, may enter on and claim a 160 acre tract. I have exhausted my right. I am having my sister and grandma use their rights, each on a 160 acre tract. For the third, I have planned that the girl I will marry may use her right. To do this, she has to go there and make the entry while still single, after which she could marry the next day. Now do you understand what I am trying to tell you?"

"I think I do. Now see if I have it right," loosening her hands and using them to illustrate.

"You want me to go with you to South Dakota and file on a claim, then—marry you afterward? Is that what you mean?"

"Yes, Linda."

"I see," said she, thoughtfully. Meanwhile, he tried to make it more clear.

"You see, had I known you longer, we would have had time to talk it all over and work it out together. It's hard on me, for I'm so afraid that it seems, not like a proposal of marriage, but a cold business arrangement. I—"

"No, I think it sounds all right; I think it *is* all right. You said something about it last winter and I remembered that you had some plans like this. I didn't, at the time, of course, think that I would be the fortunate girl to be chosen out of all the other girls that you could offer it to."

"I want you to know, Linda, that I made up my mind to ask you to marry me several weeks ago," said he.

She moved close to him, squeezed his arm and in a low voice, said very softly:

"Oh, did you—Martin?"

"I did, Linda."

"Oh, that sounds so beautiful. And you are not—not asking me to—to marry you just to—have somebody file on the land?" she asked, and laid her head against his.

"That's what has made it so hard to explain, dear. I've been so afraid you might misunderstand my motive and that could make it—so unpleasant. Life can't always be just like we might plan it. A man has to provide, and to do so more adequately, he must plan, but because he plans and tries to execute doesn't mean that he—that he has no heart. I have a heart, a heart that has been craving for love and comfort and understanding ever since I've been struggling to get hold of something and hold it."

"And your heart is hungry and you want love, a woman's care, but you know at the same time that she must have food and clothing and shelter. So while you've been thinking about love, you've thought about these other things, too. Is that what you mean, Martin?"

"That is exactly what I mean, Linda. I'm so glad that you can· see this thing in a broad light. What I am asking you to do—before we marry—is only what hundreds of white men and their girls are doing. They planned it just as I have, only they had a girl to plan it with. I've had to plan alone."

"Because you didn't know me well enough and long enough to ask me to help you plan, is that what you mean, also, Martin?"

"Yes, dear, and now I'm so afraid that somebody may misunderstand it all, and—" She looked up at him and was so sweet he lowered his head and their lips met with a kiss, a sweet tender kiss.

"You know, dear Linda, if we could just be left alone together to work out our own affair in our own way, we could start from here, do the things I have planned and then marry. We would find great happiness and soon learn to love each other dearly."

"I know we would, Martin. I agree with you that right from here we could go along together and never have a quarrel or a misunderstanding of any kind. Because I trust you, you are willing to trust me and I'm too fond of you already to do or say anything that would annoy or hinder you."

"But, unfortunately, you are, as you've said, a preacher's daughter and we are not going to be able to just work this thing out in our own way."

"If I was not we could leave here tomorrow—and we would —for your wilderness and I would just wait and do what you asked me, for you know best. Not much more than a boy, you are an old man, I can see, in the way of management. If I was unfettered I would be ready to go with you, do what you want and when you said the word, marry you and go live with you in your little sod house that stands on your claim. What would anything matter if I loved you and you loved me? We could be happy anywhere."

"Well," he sighed. "I knew before I came today that it couldn't be that way. I can see now, that that was the thing that made me hesitate. I must have been thinking unconsciously, of what we will both have to go through and put up with before we can do what we want to in a plain, simple way. Then before we can marry, which I won't ask you to do until next spring, we will have to go through with a lot more ceremony.

"I am not holding that against you. While I'm a poor man for ceremony and ostentation, I'm willing to put up with it if you are with me. Fighting is my forte. All my life I've had to fight, until I stay in a fighting mood, so to speak, to keep from having to go into one." Whereupon she laughed.

"In your case, I've got to be patient and do a lot of waiting and meet a lot of people in whom I am in no way, and never will be, interested. They won't understand my little life and effort and are not going to try to do so. They are going to conclude that I am rich, which I hate for any body to think. Colored people have an odd way of checking up on ownership. If somebody would say he's worth $100,000, they'd consider it was all in cash, in your pocket, or at least cash in the bank, and that the first thing to do would be to spend some of it. You would be expected to draw $10,000 of it and take some of them out—maybe a lot of them, and blow it in having what they call a good time. They have nothing, never had and never will, but they feel they are smarter than you because they think they know better how to spend it. They can, faster, but the irony of it is that a man may be worth $100,000—and not have a hundred dollars he could afford to spend in cash for foolishness. He most likely might need another $100,000 to help hold, and promote, that which he is already holding, or lose it. All this, you see, is too deep for them; they could never figure it out rationally, so won't get any headaches by trying. When you try to show them what it is all about and why you cannot throw anything away they bark loudly: 'Jive! I thought that ole' niggah had somethin'! He ain't nothin' but 'jive!' " It was comical and they both laughed.

"You see, in time it puts us who are trying to actually do something, in a bad crack—embarrassing crack, and makes us, also in time, try avoid saying too much to them. And this, mind you, can come from the so-called 'best people' except they would not say it in broken English. So I don't like to say much to them about what I'm trying to do. It's a cinch they would never understand it well enough to try helping you; they are almost sure to misunderstand it. If you try to tell them that I have four large farms and am expecting to acquire three more, they're most likely going to declare that I'm rich, and will expect me to start blowing it. 'Money is made to spend' is their philosophy. That is how they view it and as I said, worth, quoted to them, is always viewed as in that much cash. So I would like to ask you now to please not tell them that I have any lands, if you can keep from it. I don't want to be misunderstood, which means that you will, too, if I don't give you a five-carat solitaire for an engagement ring, when and if we become engaged, which I can in no way afford. It will strain my cash-on-hand reserve to give you a single carat stone that is costing $250. I really have no cash of my own at all, but I have borrowed quite a large sum to put this deal through. I will need every dime of it for that purpose and will be borrowing much more before it will be complete. This will be sooner than I want to, and who knows that by that time I may be in a position where I will be unable to borrow more. So in such a case, I'll just have to get along the best way I can when that time comes."

"My; but your life is filled with so much to do, Martin. It is, such a big life—"

"—burdened with cares and responsibilities which take away so much of the would-be joys that, if you marry me, dear, you may have to put up with me for days, unhappy and distracted, because, and, on account of, all this."

"It is then that I will try to do so much to make you happy, dear."

"That is when I will need your care, your patience and your everything, Linda. If you marry a man who is trying to get ahead in life, it won't be nearly as easy at once as it would be if you married one with just a job."

"But he would stay that way; there would be nothing to look forward to; nothing to thrill and cheer me in life."

"Not as much. I have no qualms about foregoing necessities, personally, and am sure you won't, but these friends of yours are going to have a lot to say about it when the time comes, mark those words. And some of these people may be right in your own family."

As he talked, she was thinking; thinking about her father, who had no business experience at all. But he was tall and commanding and handsome and considered himself one of the "race's leaders." He was fond of giving advice to people who had nothing to be advised about. He would expect to give it to Martin and if Martin didn't want to be bothered with it, he would quickly say that he was ungrateful. He even might, when the time came, say a lot of things that this man sitting there beside her, wouldn't care to be bothered with at all.

The thought of this was already beginning to annoy her. She hated to have to think about it. Her heart had gone out to the man beside her. Whatever her raising, she was a *woman* and it was the *woman* in her that was dominating her feelings for this man; this man who needed a woman's care so much, so she felt the urge to help him, here and now.

"Martin," said she, caressing him. "You have impressed me deeply with your frankness and sincerity and I want to say something to you that I never thought I would say to a man unless he spoke first." His face was a puzzle as he looked at her.

"You said that you liked me very much and I'm satisfied to wait until you say, of your own volition, that you love me. But Martin, dear, I—I feel that I am in love with you already.

I think I fell in love with you when I met you last winter. Please don't think I am—immodest because I am telling you this. I guess I wanted to because after all you've said, I know you need it; you deserve it, so now that I have told you, I'm strangely satisfied. Please go on."

"And you love me, Linda? Oh, that is so sweet and makes me so very happy. I don't think it is immodest of you. I need your love, I need your kindness. I have a heavy task before me and it will require great strength and power of will. This, *I* will provide, and if you give me love, that will be food for the strength I will have to have to carry on, dear. I'm mighty fond of you, precious," and they exchanged another kiss and then another.

"Now I know you want to talk this over with your mother. That will be all right with me—in fact, I allowed that you would. What I want to ask before you do so, however, dear, is, do you consent? Are *you* willing to trust me enough to go with me to Dakota and do first what I have asked you; then do you consent, under this condition to—marry me, Linda?"

"Bless you, Martin, of course I do. When I became so bold as to tell you that I love you, that meant that I am yours, heart, body and soul—yours forever if you want me. So I consent to everything. I will tell my mother and give her the satisfaction of saying that I may go and that I can marry you."

"Thank you, darling. Am sure that your mother will consent; I have a feeling that she and I are going to get alone fine together."

"And she likes you, too, dear Martin. I will try to explain everything to her so that she will understand."

"After you have done so, then I will do so again." They stood up then, faced each other and for the first time, oberved their comparative heights.

"Oh you're so tall—away up there," she cried, raising her hand and standing on her toes to indicate how tall. He placed an arm about the shapely curve of her waist.

"My, it seems that this waist was made for me to put my arm around and—" They embraced affectionately and their lips met in a prolonged kiss. It was many minutes before he finally took his leave, leaving her free to tell her mother at last.

CHAPTER XIV

GETTING INTO BED beside her mother, Linda crawled up into her arms.

"Well, mother. He has proposed. He has asked me to marry him; to be his wife."

"My darling!" Her mother was too happy to say more, so drawing Linda to her, kissed her fondly.

"What else did he say; what did he—attach to the—proposal?"

"Well, he explained about the land—oh, he didn't ask me to marry him just to have me help him get more land. All that I have to do is to go up to Dakota and file on the land. I must do this before we marry; but we can be married the next day, then, if we want to."

"Oh, the next day."

"Yes, mami—in the next hour, but he said that he would not ask me to marry him until next spring."

"Until next spring?"

"Until next spring, mother dear. And he's going to give me a ring; a half carat solitaire for my engagement. He says it is costing $250.00."

"My!"

"But he is waiting for your consent, of course, first, mami."

"Did he say that?"

"Why, of course, dear mami. He likes you. He says that he thinks you and he are going to get along fine."

"That's nice. I rather like him, too."

"I know you do, mother, and you know how much I want you to. Don't you think he's really a wonderful man, dear?

So courageous, tenacious—so determined. I do want you to like him lots, mother, for I—I'm so fond of him. I really love him, mother."

"Did you tell him that you did?"

"Yes, mother. I did tell him. Was that nice?"

"If you felt that way, yes. Did he say that he loved you?" Again Linda hesitated.

"Please let me explain—for him, dear."

"For him?"

"It is like this, mother. He said that he was very fond of me and that he knew he would love me dearly real soon, for he knew that as nice as I was to him, he couldn't help it."

"But you told him that you loved him without waiting until he said he loved you. Why, my—"

"Please mami, let me explain."

"How can you explain such a thing? I—" Aroused, she sat up in the bed. Linda got out and ran around to the other side, sitting beside her with an arm about her, almost pleading.

"You must not blame him, mother. He is all man through and through and I didn't want him to say that he loved me until he was ready to do so on his own volition, then I would believe him and know that it would go on forever."

"But—"

"Oh, mother, I don't want you to misunderstand him. That's what we've been talking about so long downstairs. He's so afraid he will be misunderstood because of this land. He is just frank and honest and truthful and I want to take him at his word and encourage him to always be that way. Why should I make him lie to me just to please my vanity if I knew that he did not mean it? But if he is honest enough to simply tell me that he likes me very much; better than any other girl, then I know he means that. But if he fell on his knees and said a lot of words about love when we have not known each other long enough, nor closely enough to do that, then I would know he was playing a game."

"But why did you have to tell him that you loved him. Did he ask you if you did?'

"No, mother, he did not. I—"

"Then—"

"—why did I have to tell him that I did? That is what you were going to ask me. Well."

"Well, Linda, what?" Her mother was very severe and Linda was close to tears. Still she made another brave effort.

"You see, if you had heard all that he said, it would be different; you would understand better why I told him."

"Humph!"

"Oh, mami, you're breaking my heart. Why won't you trust me and believe me? After all, he and I talked for so long and about so many things I could never relate it all. But after he said a whole lot about what he had been through and what he had suffered, I was so sorry for him; my heart went out until I just had to tell him how I felt—loving him as I know I do, I had to tell him mother."

"So you told him."

"Yes, and I'm happier ever since."

"After all these years I thought I knew you better than you know yourself, you fool me."

"I love Martin Eden so that I fool myself. But it makes me so happy, mother. I have never been so happy in all my life! Mami, why don't you encourage me when you know I feel so happy? I've waited such a long time to feel like this. I never knew how much a man could be in my life before and such a wonderful man as Martin. I'm so happy I feel oh, I feel that if I died now I would not have lived in vain."

"Well, I guess there's nothing I can do or say that will change you."

"Nothing, mother, nothing; no living person could. I just love Martin Eden until if he told me to go out there and kill myself, I would be willing to do so I love him that much." Deploring such madness, as she viewed it, Mrs. Lee adjusted the covers and looked down upon Linda.

"When does he want you to go to Dakota?"

"Next week."

"Next week!"

"Please, mama. We went over all that, too."

"What is it that you didn't go over, my child?"

"Nothing. We went over everything. We even talked about all the time we would have to lose and things we would have to endure because of others. Not ourselves. We agreed that if it wasn't for others, we could go on to Dakota tomorrow and after I filed on the land, we would marry right away and I could stay out there and we'd live in his little sod house until we could build a better one."

"And you'd be willing to do that?"

"All that and more, yes mother."

"Then you must surely love the man."

"I love him mother; better than my own soul."

"God help us!"

"I'm sorry mother, but that's exactly the way I feel."

"But what about your father?" At this Linda sighed deeply.

"He would never understand it—even if he was right here and Martin tried to explain it, as he did explain it all to me. And as for me going with him to Dakota, the best that could be hoped for would be to take him with us."

"Well, that wouldn't be fair to Martin. After all he is not marrying your father."

"That is what is worrying me—my father—and it is worrying Martin, too. I think somebody must have told him about father.

"He hinted that somebody, maybe in my own family would slow us up. It is so unnecessary, when he and I have arrived at a complete understanding about everything. I think, with your consent, we just ought not to say anything about it to father until it is all over with—that is, until I have gone to South Dakota and returned."

"I agree with you there; but we've got to bring somebody

in on it. He'd have something to lay me out about until he died if I let you go without getting his consent, and if anything at all should happen."

"It's me that knows that, and *how well do I know it!*" There was a silence, as both thought of the woman who could act as an intermediary. Presently Linda spoke

"I was thinking of Mrs. Dewey." She knew this was treading on dangerous ground and that her mother would never bring Mrs. Dewey into anything she had to do; but she was in a crack now and had to shift the responsibility to somebody else's shoulders. She knew that Mrs. Dewey could take the responsibility and account to the Elder better than her mother.

"That *is* a way out," said Mrs. Lee, thoughtfully. "Meanwhile, it is getting late and we both need the sleep. Supposing we let it go over until—say, Monday, then get in touch with Mrs. Dewey?"

"Thank you mother."

"This will leave you and Martin free all day tomorrow to enjoy yourselves, and not burden you with even thinking about it on Sunday. Take him to church with you."

"Thank you, mami." The next moment she had turned on her side and was soon asleep.

Sunday was a beautiful day and Martin Eden, for the first time in years, was marched into church. He was made to listen to an intelligent sermon, which he enjoyed so much that he insisted on complimenting the minister who preached it.

"Did you say from South Dakota?" inquired the minister after Martin had been introduced to him.

"Yes, Dr. Greer," explained Linda. "From South Dakota."

"My, my, but that seems far away." He looked Eden up and down: "And what do you do, may I ask, away off there, young man?"

"I'm engaged in farming and ranching."

"Farming and Ranching—that sounds more than interesting, it's illuminating. You seem to have taken up Dr. Washington's teachings."

"I'm a disciple of it. I always liked his philosophy of common sense. I'm trying to apply it."

"How interesting, how *very* interesting indeed," said the minister, admiringly. Linda smiled happily. It would mean very much to her if Dr. Greer talked with her father about it when he came to town. Her father was a close friend of the Rev. Dr. Greer, who would, she knew, most assuredly talk to him about meeting Martin when her father returned to the city after the conferences.

Linda took Eden on a tour of the South Side all that afternoon; they had dinner together again at the little tea room, then went to a theatre and enjoyed a good show together.

Early the next morning Mrs. Dewey, whose husband was superintendent of an apartment building on the West Side and had their quarters there, got an urgent call from Mrs. Lee, to come to Vernon Avenue at once.

"I'll come over right after dinner," said Mrs. Dewey in reply to the call. She was pleased to be called by the man's wife, the man with whom she had been friendly for years. Whenever this happened she knew Mrs. Lee was in a hole or in distress, and being unable to work herself out of it, called on her for help. On such occasions she always felt it confirmed her feeling that she was smarter than Mrs. Lee.

Mrs. Dewey was at the Lee's when Eden arrived that Monday afternoon. She remembered Martin well enough to kiss him in a motherly way.

"You kept shooting away until you struck something, eh, Martin?" Martin was modest about it.

"How's Lawrence?" he inquired of her.

"Oh, just so so. I'm disappointed in him. I don't see why he couldn't have gone ahead like you. You were such friends, he forever talks of you, how smart you are and all that—still he hasn't gotten any where—just a porter in a barber shop on the West Side."

"Lawrence is intelligent and interesting."

"But it's got him nothing."

"Maybe it will in time."

"Never. Especially now."

"So? Why?"

"He's gotten married!" Eden was surprised.

"Well, that's fine. Give him my congratulations. I'm trying to do that myself." Mrs. Dewey looked around at Linda, who lowered her eyes, bashfully.

"Yes, but you're marrying right—one of *our* girls."

"One of *our* girls? Well, what about Lawrence?"

"Married a white woman."

"Oh, a white woman?"

"Yes, a white woman, can you imagine such a thing?"

"Perhaps he loved her."

"He had no right to."

"I wouldn't say that."

"I am, nevertheless. Not only a white woman, but she's got three children."

"A widow, eh?"

"Yes. I feel like killing him."

"You shouldn't feel that way."

"Well, I do and I'm not going to have anything to do with either of them." Eden was thinking about Deborah now.

"I think that is very unfair."

"I don't. That is something which is strictly forbidden—and to think my son, my only one, should go pulling something like that—but enough about Lawrence. I hated to tell you about him. I'd never spoken had you not asked me. I'm here to see what this is that you and Linda want to do, is all about. So sit down and tell me, please."

Mrs. Dewey was not as smart as she was reputed to be, but seemed to understand Eden's story more readily than the others. When he was through she winked, pointed her finger at Eden and said:

"This boy was born trying to get somewhere. And to think,

why, he and Lawrence were as close as two peas in a pod. Now here he is at 25 holding whole tracts of land, machinery, cattle, hogs and horses—and my son's holding a white woman!" she shrugged her shoulders, disgustingly.

"Shows you what some men can do. At least I give my son this much credit. He isn't envious; he admires Martin; says he's one Negro in a million and said he'd get somewhere some day—perhaps end up a millionaire."

"Yes, a million of rags, flying in the air," echoed Eden, deprecatingly.

"But Martin," cried Mrs. Dewey. "Just look where you are already—in five years. Give you ten years more and—"

"Please don't go to estimating. I may be broke and begging—who knows. Things have turned out that way before."

"But not with men like you. Where there's a will, you'll find the way. But getting back to Linda's case, if she goes to South Dakota and files on this land, then what?"

"I want to marry her."

"Oh, you want to marry her." Linda blushed furiously and turned her eyes away. "Why, Linda, you. My, my!"

"Please Mrs. Dewey, don't," she whimpered, close to tears.

"You see, Mrs. Dewey, we think it best if it is agreeable with you, that she should go and not say anything to Dr. Lee about it until he returns to the city the last of the month."

"That is right. We'd have a time explaining this to him right here, much less from this distance." After a moment of thought she rose and beckoned Mrs. Lee to follow her upstairs.

"Excuse us, please. I want to talk this over with Mrs. Lee, privately. We'll be back." Upstairs a few seconds later:

"I want to keep them in suspense for a while; but it's a wonderful break for Linda. That boy is 100 percent. I know it from all Lawrence has said about him. Good habits, neither smokes, drinks, gambles nor runs around. One man in a million and Linda should grab him and run."

"I rather like him myself. Seems so serious, clean and manly."

"He's a business man; a money maker. I wish I'd had such a chance when I was her age."

"Then you think that I should let her go with him?"

"With me. If I go, the Dr. can find nothing to criticize. If he will pay my way and provide expenses up there and back, along with Linda's, I'll go along with them and act as chaperon."

"Oh, that'll be fine. Then it's settled—if he's agreeable to handling it that way."

"By all means."

"All right then. We'll go back downstairs and tell them."

"Better let me handle it."

"Just as you say. I'm leaving it all to you and the Dr. will have to hold you responsible."

"That's understood."

They returned to the parlor.

"Now, Martin," said Mrs. Dewey, when they were again seated.

"We, Linda's mother and I, think it will be all right, but I want to explain about her father."

"I've explained all about him, if that is what you are referring to, Mrs. Dewey," interposed Linda.

"Oh, you have; and about how hard it is to make him understand anything intricate and all that?"

"All that and more."

"Then I can come directly to the point. If Linda went up there alone, people—"

"—would talk about it. Yes, I know they would and I have not expected her to."

"Oh, and you have thought of that, too."

"Oh, yes."

"Then I can explain what we decided still easier. If you are willing to take—"

"—fine. I'll take you both and pay all the expenses if that's what you and Mrs. Lee agreed on."

Mrs. Dewey beamed with admiration.

"The man thinks not right along with you, but away out ahead of you. All right, dear, it's a deal. When do we start?"

"Tomorrow at six thirty."

"Tomorrow at six thirty?"

"Had that all thought out, too, Martin." This made him laugh. "Or did Linda help you to do so?"

Martin invited them all to dinner. Mrs. Dewey suggested that he give her some money to go out and buy something to cook and have dinner there, which is in keeping with the way people do things in Chicago. The suggestion was agreed upon and after the meal the session ended.

CHAPTER XV

EVERYTHING WAS UNDERSTOOD and their tickets waited for them at the Northwestern Station. Eden was compelled to return to South Dakota a day ahead in order to get matters arranged before all would arrive. So Linda, accompanied by Mrs. Dewey, followed him West to his wilderness, as he called it, but which they chose to call, his "home on the range" in South Dakota.

His sister and grandmother had arrived while he was away and when he returned he found them waiting for him in his "little sod house that stood on the claim," which was his original claimstead.

All had to stand in line before the land office all night to be on hand to make their entries as quickly as the time limit had expired. Eden relieved them at intervals of four hours, permitting each one (his sister Olive, his grandma and Linda) to go to a room and get some sleep between times. They were therefore among the first 100 entrants to file on their claims, and took no chance of having the relinquishments that he had bought for them, become involved in a contest case by people who sought lands but had no money to pay for relinquishments, nor did they have the $6.00 per acre fee that was demanded of each entrant by the government. They all made their entries and soon left the land office, with the proper papers to their claims, which totaled 480 acres and were the finest lands that ever "laid out of doors," free and clear.

It would take a minimum of fourteen months' residence by each one to "prove up" on their claims. His grandma and sister had no interest in staying there any longer than required to prove up. They remained in Dakota. Eden erected shacks, as claim houses are called, on their claims, gave them a team and moved both on to their land, and they began their residence at once.

As to Linda's, she had six months before she would have to begin actual residence, and since she was to become his wife, he arranged to return her to Chicago forthwith.

"It is all so simple and practical now that I am here and see what it's all about," said Linda. "It is just as you said and I'm so glad now that I believed you and made it as easy as I could for you to acquire that much more land."

"Thank you, dear," said Martin. "Now that you have been on the ground and can understand it from first hand, you can see that what I asked you to do was nothing unusual at all."

"It was not—just a sound, sensible move, and you would have been very foolish not to take advantage of so wonderful an opportunity. After what I now know, I feel that I could criticize you severely had you not done this." They were alone in the parlor of some white friend's home in which he had found for them to stay while there.

"Does it make you happier now that you have been able to help me?"

"It surely does, sweetheart," kissing him fondly.

"By helping me you are also helping yourself. As you now see, it was the simplest kind of procedure. Many people in Chicago, however, even at this distance, could and would make a lot of capital out of it. In fact, if you are not very careful, they will make capital out of it yet."

"Oh, not so, dear. How can they when it has all been so simple, direct and sensible on your part to have taken advantage of? How could anybody possibly misunderstand it now?"

"I wouldn't know, but they can, and they will. Watch and see if they don't even yet; but I won't worry about that bridge until it is before me to be crossed."

"But Martin, dear?"

"Yes, Linda?"

"I want to know—"

"Skip it, baby. I may be wrong. Let's hope I am, at least; but 'just in case,' I want you to please remember my admonition."

"Oh, fudge," she pouted. "If they do I'll—"

"Maybe punch them in the nose. I hope when the time comes you'll be brave enough to do that—if it ever comes."

"And if it does—" she doubled her fist and struck at a shadow.

"Now, sweetheart, I've got something for you."

"For me?" anxiously. He nodded, withdrew a small velvet box from his pocket, and springing it open, displayed a blue white, sparkling solitaire. The light caught it at the proper angle and it shone brilliantly.

"Oh, my!" Her mouth remained open while she took the ring and holding it at a distance, gazed in speechless admiration.

"And from you to me?"

"From me to you."

"Oh, that is beautiful—*beautiful!*" She was as delighted as any engaged girl could be. He took it from her hand and as she held out the proper finger he slipped it on.

"Oh—oh—oh!" she threw her arms about him and almost smothered him with her kisses. "I love you, I love you, oh, I love you, Martin, my Martin!" Then she repeated the performance. She was too happy to remember that he had not yet said he loved her—though he was becoming more fond of her each day.

She extracted his promise to write as often as convenient. She had asked that he write every day, but being a practical man, he showed her how that would be impossible.

"This is still a wilderness, and days may pass before I could get to letter writing, my sweet."

So Linda, with Mrs. Dewey, returned to Chicago, the

happiest girl alive, with Mrs. Dewey filled with pride in having helped put something over.

Out West, Eden had a busy session, getting his sister's and Grandma's houses built and moving them in and fixed up for the winter, which is often severe in South Dakota, especially if it should start snowing early.

In spite of Linda's promise, given with the best of faith, to say nothing about him or the lands out West, back in Chicago Mrs. Dewey had said plenty and before they had been home a week, Martin Eden was reported all around the town as being "rich." About this time, The Reverend Lee returned from his conferences and heard all about it. Vain to the core and full of ostentation, this pleased him to the nth degree and he capitulated, after he had pretended to upbraid them all for letting her go without consulting him.

"Looka heah, Dr. Lee," said an old sister, stopping him on the street, "what's this I heah about your darter, Linda, going off out West and getting engaged to some rancher?" To this the Dr. said, "tut, tut," nonchalantly, yet bristling all over with ego as he did so. This put him in a class ahead of everybody else.

"Honey, they tell me he's rich!" went the word around. As positive confirmation of the report was the sparkling solitaire that Linda was wearing.

"And it ain't no Loftis Bros' 'on time' ring, neither! M-m."

The Bowels heard about it and helped to confirm it. Said Mrs. Bowels at a tea party one afternoon, during this seige of reports regarding her friend:

"Why he was here last winter with a 'whole train load' of cattle—and I saw his check. It was for—oh, so much that I couldn't count it."

"M-m, m-m!" everybody was singing. "The 'Rich' Martin Eden—The big rancher from away out West—M-m, m-m!"

So everywhere Linda went, she was the object of curious eyes, sometimes admiring eyes, mostly envious eyes—but always and every where, the center of attention.

"Why don't you introduce me to one of his friends, Linda," said one. "I'm free, single, unengaged, and I can give him plenty of lovin', honey. Come on. Don't be so stingy."

"But there's no colored people up there except him," she protested.

"No, what?" Then, from the more sensible:

"Well, what'd you care? If he's got the dough, you can come down to Chicago and have *your fun*. There's plenty of pretty boys to be had in Chicago by doing a little paying. Their business is making love. They're experts at playing 'hearts'." Then laughter.

During all this, with a full month's vacation on his hands, Dr. Lee called on his friend, the high and mighty Bishop Brooks.

"Well, well, Newt. I'm hearing great news about your daughter, Linda."

"Gossip," said the Dr., deprecatingly.

"Oh, no, not gossip."

"I'll say not gossip, this time, Dr. Lee," exclaimed Mrs. Brooks, entering the room. She had two marriageable daughters.

"Why, Mrs. Brooks, You don't mean to say that you've been listening to all these silly tales about my daughter, too!"

"Listen, Bishop," turning to her husband. "Mrs. Dewey was here no longer than yesterday from the West Side and told me out of her own mouth all about it."

"You see, Dr. Lee," chuckled the Bishop, turning back to Reverend Lee and nodding his head, and keeping one ear open for his wife's report.

"Mrs. Dewey was up there and saw and heard all about it and she told me herself that the white people said he was well to do—almost rich, and that he commanded the respect of all the best people up there. This was what she said that *white people* told her about him, and you know what that means."

"Why it means that it's the truth, of course," commented Bishop Brooks.

"White people told her that," Mrs. Brooks went on. "Not boggies. If you had a $20 bill wrapped around twenty-five or thirty ones, a Negro would call you a millionaire; but when *white* people say that a Negro's rich, then he's got to be rich."

Mrs. Brooks was so emphatic, that the Reverend had to give in. Especially did that tickle his vanity more than words can express. The Bishop and his talented wife had two daughters who had given them plenty of trouble. Both had been expelled from a half dozen schools for girls, including Vassar, where they had been sent to complete their education. The public had about concluded that kindly and brilliant Bishop Brooks two daughters were just "bad" like so many ministers' children. Anyway, neither he nor his wife could do anything with them, as much as they had tried.

Then, the girls tried marrying for a change. One fell desperately in love with a pimp, and ran away and married him before anything could be done about it. They brought her home and put through a hurried annulment before he could put her "on the block."

If the "pimp" could have kept the Bishop's daughter long enough to connect with some of his white customers, who were always in the market for "fresh" ones, with a Bishop's daughter "available," business would surely have been very good with him—for a while at least.

In view of what had happened to the Bishop's daughters, the Reverend Lee swelled up with pride, when the people compared Linda's engagement with the unhappy plight of Bishop Brooks' daughters.

There was one who kept studiously quiet while all this was going on. That person was Terry. As ostentatious as her father, she was not basking in any of Linda's glory. 'Twas said, Terry was so "ornery" that no sane man would put up with her foolishness, so she had been married more than a year before to about the only one who would have her and put up with her. Her husband, whose cognomen was Glavis, was the son of a jack-legged preacher from the backwoods of Tennessee. He was an honest, hard working fellow and likeable; but it had taken all the effort she could muster to "graduate" him from a porter at a downtown novelty house, to "shipping clerk" which she told the people that he was. In truth, Glavis was still doing the porter work, while his wife was referring to him as the "head shipping clerk." But even this in no way compared him with the "rich" rancher from out West that poor, simple Linda, as Terry would refer to her, when angry, had become engaged to. So Terry had a 'bone to pick' and was simply biding her time as to when to strike. It would come as everything comes if we can wait.

Mrs. Dewey had "tipped" Martin off as to the kind of letter to write his father-in-law-to-be after he heard from him. Remembering this, after he got a letter from the Elder, asking to be told more about coming to Chicago and taking such liberties with his daughter during his absence. Eden answered, being careful to "flatter" the Dr. at the opening of his letter, apologizing for taking such "liberties" in the middle, and flattering the Elder again in closing. This "jumped" him into high favor with her father right from the start.

Out West, in the meantime, Deborah, still living down on the Watson place while Bill looked after Eden's properties, assisted in that county by her father, had watched the proceedings. She had seen Linda when Eden brought her to Gregory to register, but she had not met her. These were long sad days for her. Life had been as empty as a dried gourd during these weeks.

She couldn't seem to get interested in any white man after Martin Eden went out of her life. It was empty and she was very despondent. There seemed so little to live for and she knew then how much he had meant to her.

The lands in Tripp county had put double responsibility on Martin and he was a virtual slave. He had to get matters into shape so that he could leave for Chicago to see Linda during the holidays, so he decided to give his sister and grandma more Xmas than they could have on their claims, by inviting them down to stay at his place while he was away. They met Deborah and became so friendly that she shook off her despondency and found a new life while they were there.

Eden was very much embarrassed when he arrived in Chicago, to learn that he had been elevated to the position of a "rich rancher" without his knowledge or consent. It was doubly annoying when he knew that soon he would be hard pressed to meet his interest charges and commitments. Modest by disposition and possessing no thread of vanity or egotism, he said to Linda:

"I'm so sorry such a rumor has become widespread."

"Honestly, I didn't put it out, Martin. Please believe me when I say that I did not."

"It'll prove a boomerang before it's all over. I dislike such things. People expect you to splurge and throw away money when such tales have been broadcast. A Negro reckons you entirely by what you throw away—and if you fail to waste, he insults you by calling you 'cheap'."

"I'm so sorry, sweetheart. I'm so sorry because—because you don't just seem like yourself; like you were both of the other times I met you. What is the matter?" She kissed him, and stroked his hair.

"It's the business, honey. I'm loaded and it worries me."

"Please let me help you."

"Very sweet, baby; but there isn't a thing you can do. There isn't anything anybody but Santa Claus can do, and since I'm too old to believe in Santa Claus, there's nothing even I can do but 'take it.' " Sighing and taking her in his arms:

"Now we're going to forget all about my troubles, which are not bad yet; they are simply going to be and I know it, and that is what will worry me if I think about it. But I'm going to forget all about them during these two weeks that I'm here and just let you entertain me."

"Oh, darling, I'm glad. I do so want to make you happy."

"Of course you do. We've hardly had any courtship. You had to go out West there and file on the land—"

"But sweetheart, that was all right. That was just too delightful for anything. I enjoyed the trip and it gives me so much to talk about and to think about."

"Especially to talk about and let those you talk to put me in a spot by broadcasting that I'm rich."

"But Martin, darling, I tell you—"

"I believe you Linda."

"Others put it out and if they do nothing but talk about it when I'm in their presence, what can I do?"

"Nothing, baby, I suppose nothing, so let's skip it and have a good time while I'm here."

"My baby, my poor, hard worked and worried darling. I will be so unhappy if you continue to look so worried."

"I promise to douse the worry. I'm giving everything up for two weeks and having a grand, royal good time. How's that?"

"If you can forget old troubles and just do that, I'll try to do my share to help you have the good time."

"Then a good time it is! The first thing we want to check up on, then, are the dances. The white people invite me to their dances out there and when you and I are married and living there together, we'll go to some of them when we can dance together, but I've had too much sense to go waltzing around there holding their white girls in my arms."

"You'd better not."

"I don't mean it that way. Ninety nine of those who live out there would think nothing about it, but the one hundredth one could be a Southerner, with complete ideas about Negroes staying in their places (which is not at balls dancing with white girls, and I don't mean maybe). So since I still like to dance, and want to dance some more, I'll take advantage of the opportunity to do so while, and where, I can with impunity."

"And I want to dance with you, darling. Oh, my sweet, it is going to mean so much, these two weeks with you here with me, you and I together." Finding a dance program on the radio, they got into training by taking a turn around the room together.

Duke Ellington was advertised to play the first big dance, so they went in full evening attire, to the Metropolitan Ballroom, and had a glorious night.

For two weeks Martin Eden laid aside all cares. It was perhaps the first time in his grown life that he had, and he really enjoyed himself. To be engaged to a pretty girl, truly in love with him, and to go to theatres and balls and cabaret parties, made life worth living. But before he was fully engrossed in the business of having a good time, he had to give it all up and return to South Dakota and the laborious work that awaited him.

It was a cold and bitter winter. It had snowed early in December and the same snow stayed with them, with all the rest that fell between December and April, to make traffic difficult, nights cold and bitter.

With the coming of April, he was scheduled to return to Chicago to wed Linda. The winter was behind them, spring was approaching—and with it the first of Martin Eden's troubles.

For no reason whatsoever that he could see, Linda started an argument by mail with regard to his coming to marry her. Terry had bided her time. She liked few people and least of all, Martin Eden. Of Linda, her own sister, she was jealous. Her husband had gone almost into oblivion, as far as being talked about was concerned, while all she could hear on every tongue was Martin Eden.

Terry didn't like it, had never liked it, was a natural born trouble maker, and started out to make trouble—all she could, between Linda and her fiancée.

She chose to make trouble by a devious route. In this she had a good ally. That was her father, who also had a "bug" to pick with Eden, for something he knew nothing whatever about.

He had been warned that to get along with the Elder, meant to flatter and praise him; to make him think that he was a "king!"

He had started off by doing so, but had forgotten all about it in the interim. Meeting notes and commitments were the things that required all his thoughts and time and plans. He most assuredly had no time for tickling the vanity of a poorly paid preacher; he hadn't time to even think of him. And that was Terry's trump card!

It was on this she played by writing letters to him and adroitly criticizing Eden's failure to refer to him as "Father," for coming to Chicago and making a show without taking the Elder around and "showing" him off to the people, too. By first one little thing and then the other, she had succeeded by April, in working this child-man father into a state of bickering and unreasonableness. Linda, innocent and sweet, was being used as a tool for them to get back at him.

So Linda wrote, wondering if a mistake had not been made and if it was prudent after all to marry him. Maybe it was only a gesture, but it added to his worries, his overburden of troubles. The best way out was to catch a train several days earlier than he had planned and see what such letters were all about.

By this time, Eden had become very devoted to Linda. He'd began to feel that he was actually falling in love with her—and the way he dashed off to Chicago seemed a sure indication.

CHAPTER XVI

EDEN ARRIVED IN CHICAGO and after registering in, went directly to Linda's home and was relieved when she answered the bell. She received him coldly, but showed him into the parlor, careful to avoid his eyes. It was several minutes before he managed to get her on the couch beside him and down to common sense. He didn't know that Terry had been watching, and when she heard his ring, had called Linda and given her a sound lecture and a set of rules laid down on how she was to treat him.

Terry wielded considerable influence over Linda, the older, under certain conditions. Then, when she could inveigle father, as she had done in this instance, into supporting her, she could make Linda, with ways like her mother, do things, at least for a while, for which she was later ashamed.

As long as Linda could avoid meeting Martin's eyes, she could make some show of resistance. Also, as long as she could be kept from talking to him, she could hold out. Eden soon saw that what was needed was strategy, so began to apply it.

"So you're trying to make some of the things I predicted come true."

"What do you mean?" said she.

"Listen, Linda, and please look at me. I'm not afraid to look straight at you while I talk. If your conscience is clear and you're sure you are in the right, you can look at me and say so, can't you?"

"I'm not afraid to look at you." She looked at him then up to his shoulders, but no higher.

"I want to talk with you about the letter you wrote me. If

all the things you've been saying to me since last fall were true, then, they are true now. So why did you write me such a letter?"

"Because I wanted to. All I said was true."

"Then look me in the eye and say it." Still her eyes were downcast. "I dare you to look me in the eye and repeat what you wrote me." She didn't take the dare, but sat speechless, eyes still lowered.

Terry from her vantage point heard every word that was said, and could scarcely resist intruding and berating Martin. However, she feared Linda might side with him in the event of a controversy. She also hesitated to argue with him, shrinking from embarrassing questions he might ask. She could only continue to eavesdrop, hoping that Linda would "get that man told," as she had promised.

"Remember what I told you last fall up there in Dakota when you said so much about how simple it was and that it would have been such a mistake if I had not taken you up there and done what I did? Everything as far as I'm concerned is just like it was then. Nothing has changed—unless that something is you."

"I haven't changed."

"Oh, you haven't?"

"No."

"Then what's this all about?"

"It's you."

"Oh, me. How?"

"You know how. When you asked me to go with you, you—you—didn't say that you—loved me. That's what's the matter."

"Oh, that's what's the matter, eh? Then why didn't you bring this up last fall when I asked you to go; or at least last Xmas when we spent, I thought, two most lovely weeks together? You were sweet last fall, you were most lovable last Xmas, but now you throw all that out the window by writing me, for no reasons at all, as far as I can see, a most awful letter. And now you sit there like a cat has your tongue with your eyes down and last but not least, with your mouth stuck out like an evil old Negro."

Up came her head in a hurry and away went her resistance!

"It is not so! I can use my eyes to look any way that I want to look, and my mouth was not stuck out and I am not like an old, evil Negro," she cried with eyes flashing fire. Thereupon his heart leaped with joy.

"That's the spirit, Linda. I'm glad you did that."

"Did what?"

"Why, showed some fire. That's what you need, fire, honey, fire, more fire, lots of fire. Fire to stand up and fight for yourself, for if you'll fight for yourself, you'll fight for me and that is when I will love you, love you with all my heart. Oh, My sweet," and he put his arms about her. "My sweet, why deprive us both of all the honey you can be giving me, why, baby?"

"Oh, Martin. I said that I was through with you; that I was not going to love you any more because I don't think you love me; I think you only want to marry me for that land."

"If I'm not learning to love you, then I must be in love with somebody else. Do you think I love somebody else?"

"Maybe you still love Jessie Binga."

"Linda!" She sat up half frightened. "Linda, you don't believe that. You know that I have not been in love with Jessie since I met you. You are the only woman in my life and you ought to be ashamed of youself for acting like a spoiled child—like an ornery old Negro."

"But Martin."

"I have been growing more fond of you daily and I may be very much in love with you already and not know it. But it was agreed between us that you wait until I told you that I loved you of my own volition. You said you didn't want me to say it until I was ready; that you would hate me if I said it just to please you; that you wanted me to feel inspired when I said it. How can I feel inspired when you, above all people, treat me as you are doing? To please you, however, I will be a liar and a hypocrite this once, only I want you to know that I am before I say it. So what shall I do? Bend on my knee and say 'I love you, dear'. Is that what you want me to say?" She shook her head.

"Then you must trust me and believe in me, for only if you do, can I endure." She saw how much he needed her love. Her heart melted, and she placed her hands on his.

For answer he rose and moved, head down, to the window. Following, she threw her arms about him and begged him to look at her. When he did not respond, she stood in front of him and forced him to look at her. His eyes were tired and heavy.

"Oh, Martin, my sweet, forgive me: forgive me and look at me, please!"

Disengaging himself, he took his hat from the hall and started for the door. She held him by sheer force, almost screaming.

"Martin, oh, Martin, please don't, Martin please don't leave me, if you do I will die—Oh, Martin, please—please!"

He tried to let himself out, but the locks confused him. She managed to get between him and the door, where she pleaded anew.

"Please Martin. I can see it all now. You're in trouble, deep trouble. You are worried until you don't look like yourself; you are not yourself because of all this worry, and instead of helping you and comforting you, I've annoyed you and added to your worry. Oh please forgive me, darling, and come back in the parlor and let me help you, let me love you. If you do, sweetheart, I promise that I will never—no, never, make you unhappy and lose your patience again. Oh, say something Martin, do something, slap me if you like—even strike me, anything; but just forgive me darling and come back in the parlor and let me hold you in my arms." After a time, but without a single word, he let her lead him back into the parlor where she sat on his lap with an arm about his neck.

"Why are you so worried, Martin dear? Is it because—I wrote you that old mean letter?" He shook his head in the negative.

Terry, watching all this, with a suppressed oath sped upstairs in a passion and slammed the door of her room behind her.

"Then what is it, darling?" pleaded Linda. "Please tell me, Martin. You know how I love you, dear. That letter and all that I've been pretending was only a gesture. I didn't mean any of it, sweetheart. All that concerns me in the world is you—you, my Martin. I will do anything to help you, precious; anything that you ask me to—only speak darling and say what you want of me." She crushed his head upon her bosom so closely he could hear the beating of her heart against his ear.

After walking the floor impatiently for a few minutes trying to shut out Linda's voice from downstairs, Terry tore out of her room into her mother's.

"Can you hear how she's carrying on over that—nigger!"

"Terry!"

"After all I did to try put some sense into her head to keep that darky from making a fool of her! I wish you would take a look at her, and listen to the way she's carrying on. Just go to the door and take a look at what's happening. He isn't with her five minutes until she's forgotten all that I've been trying to put in her head for weeks—weeks, I tell you!"

"Will you go attend to your own business and leave your sister to attend to hers!"

"I won't do it, I won't do it! She's my sister and I'm not going to let that dirty niggah make a fool of her—I won't, I won't, I won't!"

Terry stormed about the room like an enraged tigress, swinging her arms and crying as she did so.

"Terry," cried her mother, recalling that was exactly the way her husband had carried on in all the years since he married her. "Will you please calm youself and go about your business and let Linda attend to hers."

"I won't, I won't, I won't!"

"Well, you will, you will, you will, or else—"

"What?"

"I'll go to the phone and call your husband and tell him how you are performing."

"I don't care." Nevertheless, she quit walking the floor and became much more calm than before.

"You know he doesn't want you meddling into Linda's and Martin's affairs. Linda is older than you and ought to know well enough what she wants to do."

"But she doesn't. That's where the trouble comes in. She's like a child, does not know what she wants to do and will let that—that shrewd darky make a fool of her, and I won't stand for it, I won't, I won't, I won't!" Stamping her foot she began walking the floor again, tearing her hair, and like her father, foaming at the mouth.

"Some day you'll end up in a padded cell doing the very same thing you are doing now."

"She promised that she was going to take his old ring off and put it away and send him right back to that wild country where he belongs; promised me faithfully, and now—"

"—she's down there doing just what I knew she would do when he showed up, when you were trying to put all that devil in her. The only thing wrong with Linda and Martin is you and your father. If—"

"But we're doing it for her own good—and you don't appreciate it."

"And you said she promised to take his ring off and put it away?" countered her mother.

"Yes, put it away. Not to let him see her wearing it. That's what I told her and she promised me that she would do it."

"Oh, *you* told her and she promised to do so? If she really wanted to break the engagement, the thing to do would be to take it off and give it back to him. You didn't tell her to do *that* though, did you?"

"I didn't say that I didn't."

"But you *did* say what you did. No, you didn't tell her to do that because then you knew she would have revolted; you knew that she would have refused to do it; and you knew that it was a beautiful ring and an expensive ring. So you would break her and Martin up because you're envious and cruel and mean just like your father and wouldn't hesitate to destroy your own sister's happiness to satisfy your own vanity. All because of your towering ego which Martin, because he's so hard worked and busy, has not appeased. That's all the matter with you and you know it!"

"Will you hush, mother—please hush this minute!" She screamed so loudly that Linda and Eden heard it downstairs and looked up.

"What was that noise, dearest," inquired Eden, looking toward upstairs. "I thought I heard somebody scream."

Linda knew who was "screaming," and what they were *screaming about;* but she didn't want him to know. So she racked her brain hurriedly for an excuse. She thought of one.

"Well, you see, they—they're putting on a play soon and Terry is in it. She's perhaps rehearsing."

"Oh, I didn't know Terry was an actress, though I imagine that she could be. She'd perhaps make a very good one. . . ."

"Oh *she* can act—yes," said Linda, nervously.

"What does she play best, *tragedy?*" and he looked at Linda with a faint smile around the curves of his mouth. The situation had been too tense in her own affair to waste much time on Terry, who was often performing.

"Oh, let's don't bother about Terry. As I said, she's perhaps rehearsing. We have our own troubles to think about, don't we, dear," stroking his hair and cheek. "I want to help my baby. How can I help you, sweetheart?" she ended, all her resistance gone. He shook his head in the negative.

"*You* cannot help me, Linda, except to drop this foolishness and get ready to marry me."

• "I want to marry you, Martin; but why—"

"You see," cutting her off, "to buy the relinquishments and finance the development of the lands, building houses on all three claims and all that is going with it; the expense of taking you and Mrs. Dewey up there, sending you back, buying you that ring, taking care of my sister and grandmother, has been considerable."

"Of course it has, Martin. I know that."

"I didn't have that money. Nobody piles up cash in banks to spend at will—they borrow it when they need it and have to pay interest on it and pay it back sooner or later. So that is what I'm having to do."

"Of course, dear."

"That is why I was sorry when it was broadcast that I was "rich" and all that tommy-rot. I knew that it would come back to annoy and embarrass me, that's why I didn't want it spread around. I can get along if nothing gets in my way. I knew I would have all this to contend with—every sensible man would know that; but in the midst of all my troubles of trying to get along and trying to make ends meet, you, who say you love me—"

"I do love you Martin, with all my heart."

"Then why don't you work with me instead of against me?"

"Oh, Martin, darling, I'm not against you. I—"

"Maybe not now; but how long has it been since you were so completely against me that after four months you meet me and don't offer to even kiss me; sat there like a spoiled child and did all you could to make me feel hurt and bad. I—"

"Oh, please, darling, don't tell me any more. I know I was wrong and I feel far worse than you do on account of it. I promise never as long as I live, to do it again."

"I believe you mean well, Linda. I don't believe you'd ever do a single thing again as long as you lived to hurt or make me unhappy. But there's two people in your family, and you know who I am talking about, that are given to developing ideas, who must be flattered and cajoled and made over and appeased, and this is their reaction through you. You would have never written me a letter like you did or met me the way you did. It wasn't you; it was those who 'love' you so much that if we aren't very careful, they'll ruin us and our true love before this is all over."

"Oh, Martin, darling please don't say that. Nothing in the world could—"

"Could? Did you say? It *has* already and you and I have got to stop now and appease them and be patient and put up with a lot that at least I don't consider necessary and that I know I don't need. I don't want that kind of love at all; the kind of love which tells you when the time comes that— 'I must now kill you—take your wife, or take your life or both, but I am doing it all for your own good! But I think you are mighty ungrateful not to thank me. So before I do all this, before I do it for your own good, please thank me and tell me that you are going to appreciate it'."

Linda sat silent. She knew that every word of it was true and that to appease those two in her family, she had been cruel and unkind to the man she loved. She decided not to try to argue back. She was sorry, by trying to do what Terry wanted her to, that she had forced the words he was saying, out of him.

"I don't mind this little quarrel, darling, and I believe you love me and want to do everything in your little heart to help me; that you are willing to endure any sacrifice and this might be necessary before the end. But what worries me is the times to come. Little blazes like this, can grow into a huge conflagration; a prairie fire like we still have up there in my wilderness, which can destroy everything before us, if given the chance."

"I'm asking you, who will be the medium through which this can and may happen to us, to remember well my words. It will be up to *you* and *you only*, Linda, in the years to come, to stand between me and those subtle possibilities that can wreck our whole lives—God help us!"

There was no answer that she could give to this. Martin Eden was right and she knew it. Her sister and her father had been mean and unkind to her mother; they made her life miserable. Yet in that peculiar fashion they felt that they had a right to do these things for her mother's and her "own good".

In her heart then and there, Linda decided to stand four square for this man of hers; she was determined that never would these two forces of evil be permitted to come, like wolves in sheep's clothing, with sweet words about "all their love" and disrupt their lives. Because she replied nothing to what he had charged, he was sorry for her. After all, there sat the girl he was going to marry. His heart was hungry and his soul was tired. He was young and he was *so* tired, because he had worked hard and worried so much. For years he had, off there in that wilderness, dreamed of love, a home, a wife and her care, and now that girl was sitting there before him, ready and willing to give him all this. So he decided to forget further warnings and to take her, be good to her and honor her, and do all that a husband is expected to do. Kneeling beside her, he whispered:

"I'm going to forget about the things that might come, and give my heart to you, Linda, if you will let me, if you want me to, precious. Do you want me to do this, Linda?"

She looked straight into his eyes and melted.

"Oh, Martin, my darling—my poor, precious darling!" And then she fell to weeping on his shoulders. She cried so hard he rose up, and taking her bodily in his strong arms, walked the floor for a full minute and then sat down, still holding her as he would a baby. After a time she had calmed enough to dry her tears and sit up beside him.

"Just a few more words and then we will go somewhere together and forget all the unhappy side, honey."

"Yes, Martin."

"We went through a terrible winter in Dakota this year; snow has covered the ground all winter up until last week. It's been with us and in our way since the middle of December and I lost some of my stock which I planned to sell and help meet some of the expense."

"Oh, Martin! You lost some of your stock? But you didn't tell me, dear. You didn't write me that you had."

"No, dear, I did not; because I didn't want to be misunderstood."

"Oh!" she was thinking of her father and Terry again. *They* would misunderstand anything, mix it up and make capital out of tragedy.

"Besides there was nothing that you could do about it. I felt that if I told you from that distance, you not only might have had it misinterpreted to you, but it might also have discouraged you. When we think in the wrong direction, mole hills soon become mountains and can grow higher into the air than Everest."

"Still I don't think it was fair, darling, for you not to tell me your troubles—all of them. If I'm going to be your wife, I should know all the sorrows as well as the joys."

"Yes, honey, you should and you will from now on; but after what happened, you see, it is well that I didn't write you anything more than I did.

"But now, honey, let's get down to the serious side of things. When are you going to marry me?"

"Do you really want me to marry you, Martin?"

"Of course I want you to, darling. Why ask such a question? I knew I wanted to marry you before I came to ask you last fall?"

"Honestly, dear?"

"Honestly, my sweet. Don't you believe me?"

"Of course I do!" throwing her arms about him. "But I just wanted to hear it, to make you say that you wanted to over and over again. Will you love me and always want to, my dear?"

"I shall always want to, my Linda."

"Then seal it with a kiss!" He obliged her—with pleasure.

"Well, you'll have to excuse me while I go and tell my mother." He rose too, and getting his hat, paused.

"And your sister," he added, whereupon she turned to look at him sharply, quickly. He smiled, and with a jerk of her head, haughtily, she hurried upstairs. He went outside.

Up there, she hesitated, and thinking what to do first, it occurred to her to go and tell Terry; to have that unpleasant matter over with, so knocking, called:

"Oh, Terry! May I come in?"

Terry lay stretched across the bed, weeping. She did not raise her head, but called through the door:

"Go away, please go away."

Linda entered, closed the door, crossed to the bed. Taking Terry by the shoulder she turned her over, roughly.

"Get up, you evil creature! Lying there, sorry for yourself. Cut out the self pity stuff and get busy."

"Oh, I hate you, I hate you, I hate you!" screamed Terry, sitting up. "How dare you promise me—"

"Skip it! What's a woman's promise to another—even to her sister, when the man she loves is involved?"

"He doesn't love you!"

"He does!"

"He loves only Jessie Binga!"

"You're a liar!"

"I hate you!"

"Go on and hate! He loves me. That's all that matters."

"What're you going to do about it?"

"Do about it? Are you crazy? What do you suppose I'm going to do? What he wants me to—marry him. So get up from there and begin to help me get ready."

"I'll never let you."

"Go chase yourself."

"What about father?"

"We're going to call him up."

"No need to. I'll wire him; I'll tell him that you've gone crazy. I'll tell him that the man does not love you; that he's only marrying you to get more land; to help him get rich; that he's going to work you to death out there in that wild country; that he's going to kill you; and that when you are dead and in your grave, he'll come back here and marry Jessie Binga, whom he loves and—"

She got no further, for Linda let drive her open hand, which took Terry on the cheek with a noise almost like the crack of a gun. Back she went on the bed, her face stinging as if burnt by fire.

"Damn you," cried Linda, all hell broken loose in her, "talking about my man like that! *I'll kill you, I'll kill you, I'll kill you.*" The next moment with both hands, she jumped on Terry and found her throat, encircling it with both hands, and squeezing, trying to strangle her.

They rolled across the bed. Linda, gone temporarily insane, was trying to finish her. Terry was trying to free herself and fighting back for her life. They fell on the floor on the right side of the bed, where Terry struggled to her feet, still unable to loosen Linda's hands.

Mrs. Lee, who had just gone downstairs, hurried up and burst open the door.

Locked in a death grip, Linda was still holding her sister's throat, while they surged from left to right, from front to back. They finally struck the floor again.

"Great heavens alive," cried little Mother Mary, horrified. "My God, my God, my God!" She gripped her hands together helplessly for a moment before she tried to part them. Then she rushed toward Terry, wheezing for breath, struggled again to her feet, dragging Linda with her, and staggered over against the wall. There Mother Mary caught hold of Linda and pried her hands loose from Terry's throat.

"My heavens, my heavens, my heavens! My own daughters fighting. Oh, what has come over this household? In all your lives, you have never, even at play, as much as struck each other."

Exhausted, Linda fell upon her mother's shoulders. Terry, after some effort, started breathing regularly.

"She did it!" pointing to Linda. "She struck me. I didn't strike her. She struck me!"

"But I overheard what you was saying to her. It was enough to make her strike you. I told you to keep out of her business and let her alone. Why were you upbraiding her like that?"

"Because she's my sister. I was doing it for her own good."

"Her own good, bah! Just like your father, always disturbing the peace—and all for somebody else's good. You were doing it because you are evil and envious and mean, that's why you were doing it. She ought to have struck you and choked all that devil out of you, you evil person! Now help me take your sister to her room and hereafter behave yourself and let her alone!"

Beaten, Terry fell across her bed and bellowed like a dying calf. Mrs. Lee, having seen her act like that before, decided to let her cry it out. Meantime she managed to persuade Linda to stand and walk. She took her to her room and put her to bed.

Terry's enviousness had not stopped in the house, persuading Linda to treat Martin Eden badly. It had been working overtime in the way of frequent letters. She knew her father. She should when she was so much like him. With his towering ego, he was no kind of business man at all. He understood the fundamentals of nothing that had any relation to business, commerce, agriculture or industry. He lived in a small world, and had a small mind, although a "big" preacher.

Eden, burdened with the weight of carrying his promotions

had forgotten and neglected to flatter the Elder and make him feel that he was a "king." So Dr. Lee had become peeved. Terry fostered this feeling with frequent letters criticizing Eden, adroitly. The Elder, somewhere in Southern Illinois, developed an ugly mood. He couldn't even determine what he thought Martin should have done. He only felt that he hadn't done what *he*, the Elder wished, whatever that was.

He was seeking excuses to justify his mood. Terry had played up Eden's old love for Jessie Binga. This provided an excuse. It was easy to conclude that Eden was only using Linda as a tool to secure the land. He let this play on his imagination until the mole hill was becoming a mountain. He actually pictured Eden killing his daughter by hard work and returning, when she was dead to marry Jessie Binga. Terry waited until Eden had returned that night to see Linda. She then called her father by long distance. She was very careful to "set him up" with "terrible" things about to happen and then called Martin to the phone.

"Hello, Dr. Lee," called Eden, cheerfully.

"What're you doing in my house!" shouted the Elder from the other end. Eden didn't understand. He wasn't expecting anything but a pleasant exchange of greetings.

"How are you?" he answered.

"I say, what're you doing in my house!" The others in the next room could hear him and looked at each other.

"I don't understand you. This is Martin Eden, I asked how you were and wish to say that I am in Chicago to marry your daughter."

"I don't approve it!"

"I can't understand what you're talking about, Dr. Lee. I said that I am Martin Eden, and I'm here to marry Linda. We wonder if you are coming in for the ceremony."

The Reverend thought Eden was kidding him. This made him more furious and he fired such a volley of words that Eden beckoned Linda to the phone, with his hand over the receiver.

"Maybe you'd better talk to him. I'm afraid I don't know what he's talking about." Linda knew, and looked at Terry meaningly.

"Hello, father." On hearing her voice he calmed somewhat. "This is Linda, father."

"Oh, Linda. This is your father."

"Yes I know. How are you, father?"

"I'm well but terribly angry."

"Oh, father, you shouldn't. Remember what the doctor said about letting yourself get excited. It's neither good for your heart nor your blood. A man died in Chicago, I just read in the morning's paper, by letting himself get so mad he ruptured a blood vessel. So be careful. We don't want that to happen to you."

"What do you mean by letting that man Eden into the house? I thought it was understood when I left there a week ago that it was all over; that you were not going to marry him."

"Well, father, I can't explain it over the phone. The best thing I think for you to do, since you feel as you do about it, is to come to Chicago and have it out with Martin."

"I don't approve of you marrying him. He's only marrying you for land so that he can get rich, then, when you're—"

"Father--please! Let's not go into all that over the telephone. Just you come to Chicago and it can all be discussed here in the home, pro and con."

"Well, all right, I'll come in; but be sure not to have him sitting up there when I get there. I don't want to do anything rash, but I'm a severe man when I'm angry and that man has got me mad."

"All right now, father. Remember what I said about not letting yourself get excited, and come on home. When'll you be here?"

"I'll be there tomorrow. I'm leaving on the night train."

"All right, papa. Sure stay calm now and don't get excited and I'll look for you home in the morning. By, by!" She hung up the receiver and turned to her mother.

"What a session!" Her mother looked pained. Linda went on: "Terry should stop writing him letters and upsetting him. She knows how he is, so I don't see why she does it." Terry went to her room upstairs, slammed the door. They heard her scream her husband's name:

"Glavis!"

"Yes, dear," replied Glavis, removing his pipe from between his teeth and getting up out of his comfortable chair, where he was trying to relax after a hard day's work.

"Go downstairs and throw that man out of this house," she yelled. "Throw him out! I've just talked to father and he doesn't want him here."

"Now, Terry, wait a minute."

"Get down there and throw him out I say!"

"But—but, Terry."

Downstairs, Linda, Mrs. Lee and Eden could all hear her. Linda and he had planned to go out so beckoning to her, he said:

"Let's beat it outside while there's still 'peace' in the family."

"Oh, I'm so embarrassed. I—"

"Skip it and let's get going." He helped her into her coat and put her hat on her head at a crazy angle.

As they walked down the street while she adjusted her hat, they talked.

"I'm ashamed of my family, honestly."

"Your mother is all right."

"Oh, I'm glad you think so. I'm glad at least one is tolerant and not so troublesome."

"Well, *she* is, isn't she? Only *she* doesn't run the place," and he laughed.

"Well, dear, I'm not marrying your father nor your sister. It'll all be over in a few days and with us in Dakota and those two back here in Illinois, we ought to get along fine together." She felt humiliated and hurt, so he took her arm affectionately.

"Cheer up, precious. In just a day or two now, we will have each other and we won't ever quarrel, will we sweetheart?"

"Never!"

"Being a preacher's daughter, how is it that you haven't married one? You would make a good preacher's wife."

"Who, me? Nevuh!"

"What do you mean?"

"Just what I said. Marry a preacher, nevuh! I've never even gone with one."

"I should be surprised."

"You should if you think I'd ever marry one. I've seen enough of being a preacher's wife, looking at my mother. Nevuh, for me—nevuh!"

"I really can't understand you."

"Well, when it comes to me marrying a preacher, I can understand myself—nevuh! Why, I'd rather be married to a gangster. I'm sure they're much nicer to their wives." Eden let the conversation drop, hurrying down to a movie on South Parkway.

The Elder arrived early, and being tired from loss of sleep, wasn't very agreeable with his family, especially, of course, his wife.

He had cooled off considerably by the time Martin Eden reached the house. Like some noisy dog, his bark was much louder at a distance, than his bite—when close-up. The reason was very obvious. He could substantiate none of the things he had visioned about Martin Eden and was really afraid to invite him to his study and ask nim some questions, because he was afraid Eden would ask him a few in return. He recalled him asking questions which had embarrassed others unmercifully. So he called a conference in the dining room with the family seated around the taable, including Eden.

"Now do you love this man, Linda?"

"Yes, father, I do."

"Then do you want to marry him and go and live with him up in Dakota?"

"Yes, father."

That settled it. The Elder was mostly bluff and make believe. With his massive pompadour, now almost white, his dark skin and Roman nose, an odd one for a Negro, and his six feet two, with his white collar worn hind part before, he commanded attention as a most extraordinary physical character. But when confronted by any mental problem he was, and never had been, very efficient. So after all the trouble he had caused the lovers, it took less than two minutes to settle everything; all of which should have been left to the contracting parties in the beginning.

"Well," said the Elder when it was all over. "That is that, and there is nothing more for the rest of us to say. When do you wish to do so?"

"We would like to tomorrow, father."

"Then it's tomorrow, so let's all get busy, getting ready. I'll select the minister." He rose to his feet.

"The first thing for the pair of you to do now, is to go to the city hall and get the license."

"Oh we have it already, father," advised Linda, promptly. Eden frowned at her. The Elder hadn't needed to know that.

"Already?" he repeated, looking at her.

"M-m," she nodded, happily, with her hands on the lapel of his coat, playing with the buttons. "We got it yesterday."

"Humph," he grunted, turning toward the front of the house, thinking how calling him and what had happened since, was only an empty gesture. He blamed Martin for this. For the present, however, he decided to let well enough alone, so put on his hat to look for somebody to tie the knot. Just before his departure Terry called him upstairs.

"You see," said she with suppressed fury; "You see what I tried to tell you? You see how he rushed in here like a cyclone and after wrapping Linda around his finger in five minutes, took her downtown and got the license without so much as to consult you, me, or anybody."

"Well, Terry," he started. What he was going to say, she cut off to get in a last thrust.

"Linda promised me faithfully that she—"

"Terry, be quiet and let *me* say something. I guess Linda is old enough to know what she wants to do. You heard me settle it downstairs, so call it off and let's have peace."

He patted her on the shoulder and started downstairs.

"Humph!" she sneered. "And he's even out talked you." He smiled at her indulgently, and went on his way.

FOR SEVERAL DAYS a warm wind had blown from the South. The winter was passing and spring was on the way, so rain was expected. It was uncomfortably warm.

Meanwhile, preparations for the marriage of Martin Eden to Linda Lee went on at fever heat in the Lee home on Vernon Avenue. Being a widely known minister's daughter, they felt they had to give her some kind of a wedding. They could have sent out invitations and had a pleasant little home, or perhaps even a church wedding, had Terry not decided to upset the apple cart. After what she had started was finally settled, it had to be hurried through, for Linda's time to get on her claim was almost up and they had to hurry to Dakota.

Martin Eden was sorry for Linda, for despite the fact that she had upset him unnecessarily, she was the kind of girl who was entitled to a respectable wedding ceremony, and he would have been glad to see her have it. He hated having it put through as it was now with a rush.

Terry had had a big wedding, gotten married in a gorgeous and beautiful costume, made to her order. So poor Linda, whom she imposed on so much, was compelled to get married in the same dress. It was not fair and it angered Eden, who couldn't, of course, express his anger. Since it was getting under way, he was sensible enough to let it go through.

Meantime, in keeping with his love of display, the Elder sought a bishop to tie the knot. Unfortunately, only one Bishop was in the City, and he was too ill at his home to leave it, so he had to be satisfied with the services of a fellow minister. The minister, however, was a brilliant man. Martin

Eden had heard him several times and liked the kind of sermons he preached and the intelligence displayed in the delivery of same. So he was glad to have Dr. Cook perform the ceremony.

Came his wedding day, still warm, the air sultry. The hour was set for 2 P. M. and he was surprised at the large number of guests assembled on such short notice. Many were well known and most were the best Colored people in Chicago. Having had no time to order a wedding suit, he was given Glavis' for the ceremony, and it being a bit too tight, he was not very comfortable as he waited for the great moment.

As the hour approached, the air was rent with a mighty clap of thunder. The lightning flashed and it became so dark that the lights had to be turned on. The lightning continued to flash and lit up the outside at intervals with a strange weird light.

Then, as the wedding march began, starting from upstairs, the heavens opened and the rain fell, coming down in torrents!

"My, God," cried one woman to another in an undertone. "Isn't this a terrible thing to happen at this particular moment?" The other looked out at the water which was coming down now in great sheets, and moaned.

"It ain't nothin' but an old superstition. It can't mean that that young couple's going to have a stormy life. Just look at them."

"M-m."

"Both in the flower of youth."

"And Linda, she's so beautiful in her wedding gown, ain't she?"

"She sure is—just as sweet as she can be."

Then again, a great clap of thunder, so loud the music of the wedding march was drowned out, and the lightning was so intense people present feared being struck.

All through the audience people were apprehensive. They were the high-up Negroes of the city, but superstition was there; expressions of anxiety were exchanged and people feared for this young couple, but wished them great happiness. Yet all were skeptical in their hearts, because of the great storm that made the house tremble.

It was depressing—to everybody but Linda and Martin, neither of whom seemed to pay any attention to the elements. They went through the performance, supremely happy, and could hardly wait for the kisses and the rice and the presents and all the ceremony which followed, to end. They were anxious to get away and be somewhere alone together.

After the ice cream, the wine, the cake and the congratulations, they slipped upstairs and donned comfortable traveling clothes.

Mrs. Dewey invited them to her quarters on the West Side to spend their wedding night, so as quickly as possible, they took a taxi and were whirled away across town. Twenty minutes later they were alone in their room at Mrs. Dewey's.

They had their wedding breakfast with Mrs. Dewey the next morning. The Elder and Terry came over to have it with them. That afternoon, Linda's girl friend's mother, a Mrs. Farley, invited them to dinner, where also the Elder and Terry joined in, this time bringing Mrs. Lee, who rarely left the confines of their home on Vernon Avenue. That night, Linda and Martin packed and started back to their future home in the West.

CHAPTER XVII

AFTER ONE OF THE WORST winters in years in the Rosebud Country, summer was one of the most pleasant and beautiful. Martin and Linda got along perfectly together, and were supremely happy.

Eden managed to get his promotions adjusted. He met his interests and commitments, was free of financial worries for a while. He was happy with his wife, who provided him with a bounty of affection, and he looked forward to a happy and peaceful future, with her at his side. Then one day they were notified of something that was to become the most bitter episode in their lives.

Eden had continued to farm his lands in Gregory County, and had not kept Linda on her homestead as much as he should have, but enough to hold it. So the thing that was to change the whole course of their lives in the near future, was started by one Eugene Crook, a white man and a banker. He filed a contest against Linda's claim on the grounds of insufficient residence.

The die was cast. Eden blamed himself. Linda was so untutored in the ways of the wilderness that he had hesitated to send her to her claim alone. She had been there only when Eden took her, but had established her residence, he knew, and knew also that he could beat the case—but it meant trouble, and trouble was not what he was looking for at any time.

During the late summer, the Elder came for a visit. He had laid aside his ostentation and other than being a man easily discouraged, and quick to be ready to give up and cry that "it can't be done," he was pleasant company for them. The trip was a new experience for him and he was delighted to find Linda happy and actually begun to admire his son-in-law.

Glavis called him "father," which Eden didn't get in the habit of. Years later he was sorry that he had not been a bit more patient with the Elder. But Eden had come up the hard way, had reached out and acquired all these lands to a large degree on nerve and was "up to his neck" in the responsibility of carrying on and holding same. This responsibility worried him, and because the Reverend knew and understood so little of what it was all about, there wasn't much interest in common between the two men. One, grown, with a child's mind, the other young with an old man's, they were so far apart in their points of view that it was difficult for them to be as sympathetic as could have been possible under different circumstances. And had the Elder been a man of any financial or business or industrial experience or appreciation, they could have gotten along fine.

In the West, the settlers don't mind moving houses ten, twenty, thirty, forty or fifty miles. Eden had bought a house, which a man had built with the express purpose of moving it onto a claim that he expected to get, but didn't, in the next county. So he bought it for Linda's claim, and while the Reverend was visiting them, he started moving it to Tripp County.

Moving houses, although done out West without comment, often runs into difficulties that worry and work the movers very hard; so hard in fact, that anybody other than a seasoned pioneer, would get discouraged and give it up.

It so happened, therefore, that Eden soon began running into almost endless difficulties. Having been out to her claim, at the further side of Tripp County, fully forty or more miles from where they had been living on one of Eden's places in Gregory County, it seemed to the Reverend an ungodly distance to move a house, anyhow. He started off cheerfully enough, and being, as described, large and strong and powerful, he was very helpful in the work. Soon, however, he became discouraged, and in a conversation one evening, after an unusually hard day, during the moving, with a sigh, he unburdened himself regarding the task.

"This is a mighty hard life for my daughter out here, Martin." If there was anything Martin Eden had no patience with, it was sighs in difficulties. He had learned that most efforts toward achievement became hard sometimes and that the most annoying thing to have around in the meantime was people who sighed. Still he was patient with the Elder. He had studied him and knew that he was a weak willed person. What perhaps annoyed him more than anything else was that he was expected to think the Elder was anything else but what he was. He was not surprised to hear him cry under fire; but it annoyed him to see him try to tie Linda up with it. Until he came for his visit, Linda had become accustomed to "taking" it without complaint. In two weeks the Reverend would be going back home, so he reckoned that he could put up with him that long.

"It is a hard life for everybody if we let ourselves think about it too much," countered Eden.

"There should, it seems, be some way to get around some of it—this house moving, for instance."

"There is, Reverend."

"That's what I mean."

"Exactly how do you mean it, for instance?"

"Well, isn't there people who make a business of moving houses?"

"There are."

"Then why can't we hire them?"

"Because they would charge me $150 to move it, and I can't, after paying for the house, afford it."

"Well, I have $20.00 that I could spare towards helping make up the amount. You can have that."

"Thank you, Elder," said Eden, "but I thought out all the cost of moving it ourselves before I started. We'll make it. We'll see it through."

The Elder sighed deeply and said no more; but Martin knew he was thinking that he, Martin, was hard headed; that nobody could tell him anything.

The next day was another hard day, but they went five miles. That night, the Elder was still sighing. They would have to get the house moving finished and get back to Gregory for the trial in the Eugene Crook contest case.

"Now what's all this about some contest on Linda's place?"

"It was my fault," said Eden.

"Oh, *your fault*," with relief, seeming to be glad that it was. So long as it could be charged to Eden, he quit sighing and got ready to say, "I told you so."

"We weren't fixed for staying on it as much as we should have stayed. I didn't want to send her there alone. My time was taken up so much by demands back there on my land to put through the crops. This was necessary so that we could make some money to help us along. So the man charges her with insufficient residence, hence his contest of her rights to the claim."

"Now you see, that's one of the troubles with you, Martin. You won't listen to advice."

"In what way did I need any advice? Reverend?"

"Why—"

"I knew as well, if not better than anybody else, what ought to have been done. I didn't need any advice and nobody offered to give it to me. It's our bad luck. I took a chance because I was trying to respect the fact that Linda was not accustomed to exposure as much as my sister and grandma, who have been living on their claims ever since they filed on them. During the cold, severe winter and all, they stayed on theirs. I didn't want to expose Linda to such rigors, so tried to make it as easy on her as I could. Result: Her claim was contested and we've got to get back to the Land Office in Gregory in time next week for the trial."

He knew that the preacher didn't know what he was talking

about, except that it was hard. Here were cold hard facts and conditions to face and difficulties to surmount. No faking or pretending could do him and Linda any good and that was all that the Elder had to offer. That had been his game, the game of make believe, of bluff, and because the people of the Negro churches over which he presided, knew as a whole, even less than he, he could deceive and cajole and threaten—and get away with it. Here realism discouraged him.

He didn't have a chance to be alone very long with his daugh ter during the moving of the house. They lived in it as they moved, so all were together, leaving the Elder little chance to get in a word of criticism to Linda about her husband.

Eden and his sister's husband (she had got married after filing on the land and her husband, a carpenter, was staying with her on the claim until she could prove up) went a few miles ahead one day to choose the best route for the next ten miles. This left the Elder alone with Linda, and a chance to get in some words.

"He's a good boy, a fine boy, daughter, but he's so hard-headed. Nobody can tell him anything."

"Martin isn't hard-headed, Father."

"Then—"

"You don't understand him. You don't or you could see what he has to do to keep all this going. That's a tremendous responsibility, and it's all on him."

"But he won't take advice."

"What advice, father? Nobody's advice could help him. Besides, I haven't heard anybody coming around to offer any. Giving advice about other people's business is confined largely to Negroes. There are no Negroes here, so there's nobody to give advice. The people who live out here just work—do things, solve their own problems. They are not looking for advice. Martin says that people who do things don't give advice; that the most they do is to express an opinion if an opinion is asked for."

"You're getting just like him—he's filling your head full of what he's filled with."

"Is there anything wrong about that, father? Shouldn't I think as my husband does? I'm satisfied with his ways. We love each other, we are happy in spite of all that seems so hard at times."

"I'm glad to hear you say that, but this is a hard life, daughter, a mighty hard life."

"Martin and you, father, are different types of men. You really haven't much interest in common."

"I don't see why. He's married to you, my favorite daughter. I want to help you both by a little fatherly advice. I—"

"I didn't mean it that way, father."

"Then in just what way do you mean it?"

"I mean that your lives have lain in different channels. You are a minister of the gospel, accustomed to an entirely different association than Martin. In a way he has to be like he is, otherwise he couldn't endure. By that I mean that he must face facts, and facts are cold and hard and, in a measure he must be firm and often seemingly severe, to be able to endure this realism. Your life is not like that; your association in the church is not like Martin's association out here in this new country. Can't you see, understand and appreciate these things, father?"

"Ugh," he started, trying to think up some excuse to disprove her logic. Then he thought of the house.

"Now to show you that he *is* hard-headed. I offered to give him $20.00 to help move this house."

"It would cost $150.00 to move it. So if he had taken it, it would still have cost $130 more."

"What of it? He's supposed to have money, isn't he? Why everybody in Chicago is talking about how 'rich' he is, so what would $130 mean to him?"

"A lot, father. Besides, Martin is not 'rich,' never has been and is terribly annoyed at being called rich. He had nothing to do with anybody broadcasting such a report."

"He's trying to do too much. That shows that he's hard-headed like I'm trying to tell you."

"I can't see where you get that at all."

"Well, here's one point to prove it. He's got four fine farms down there in Gregory County, hasn't he?"

"What of it?"

"What of it? Why, he should have been satisfied and let well enough alone. Why is he slaving, and got you slaving—"

"I'm not slaving, father. Why do you say that?"

"Well, he had enough land down there in Gregory County, enough for any one man. Why that home place of his is wonderful—magnificent. Why couldn't he be satisfied to have married you and stayed right there on that fine farm? It is enough."

"If he'd been, according to your idea, which is not his idea at all, (and it would seem that every man is entitled to think as he wants to) he would never have had the four back there; maybe only one and maybe none at all."

"Well, he's got this out here—and you've got to get up there on the witness stand next week and have some lawyer ask you a lot of questions."

"I don't mind answering them, father. Besides I have Martin to instruct me. He is widely informed on almost everything —especially on what concerns his and mine."

"Nevertheless it's a hard life, and no girl, out of a comfortable home like you have in Chicago, ought to have to put up with it. It's a hard life I tell you."

"Oh, well, father, I'm afraid you are like Martin said you were."

"What did he say about me? What did he say I was like?"

"He said you were not acquainted with the fundamentals of business, industry, trade or agriculture. He said that back there in Southern Illinois as a presiding Elder, you were only dealing with simple, church folks and their simple, spiritual problems, whatever those were. So he doesn't expect you to understand this life up here. He is very tolerant."

"Tolerant my foot! He's hard-headed and I'm surprised that you don't see it and agree with me. He should have hired somebody to move this house."

"But he prefers to move it himself and save the most of that money. He needs to use the money elsewhere. He estimates that he can move it for about $25.00, and that in expenses only, while doing so. There's $125 to be used somewhere else. Why don't you let him run his own business, father?"

"But can't you see that I'm trying to help him? I offered him $20.00 of my own money toward helping him to move the house. I'm offering all this for his own good and even you, my own daughter (I'm not expecting him to because he's hard-headed), can't seem to appreciate my sacrifice."

"Oh, papa, you seem utterly hopeless. It is nice for you to wish to help us, but Martin isn't asking for any help. He is standing on his own responsibility. He wouldn't accept your $20.00—even if he needed it! Are you ever going to learn that real men will not accept charity; and when they don't even need it, why try to make my husband a bad fellow, just because you don't understand what he really needs?"

"Well, what does he need?"

"To be let alone, father. He needs for you to quit sighing and telling him and me and yourself that our life is hard; to quit trying to tell him what he ought to do or ought not to do. In short, all Martin wants of you, is to be left alone. Quit trying to help us for 'our own good.' Our burden is *our* burden and we are willing to make any sacrifices that may be necessary. Just let him alone, father, and that is the greatest help that you can give him."

It was too much for the Elder, so beaten in an argument that he started and kept insisting on. There was only one recourse —tears, a flood of tears.

"Oh, he's ruining you—he's turning my own daughter against her poor old father. Oh, I can't stand it. I don't know what will become of me, of you, Oh, my daughter, the Lord only can help you, help us. Oh, my Father!"

Linda had to return to her childish ways to soothe her father. Thereafter, to keep him satisfied and to make him think he was helping and doing so much "for their own good" she continued to seem simple and helpless. Only by her so doing could he seem a strong, great man.

They finally reached the claim with the house, leveled it and made it permanent for the time being. Eden's sister and her husband returned to their claim, while he and her father returned to Gregory, to their work down there, and to the trial which came up the following week.

Other than sighing and getting a headache from trying to understand what the trial was all about, the Elder was more moderate from then on. But this was at Linda's expense and Martin soon observed it. To please her father, she had to dispense with what he had succeeded in putting in her since they were married and naturally he resented it. It was hard for her to play a dual role, so she played only the role that pleased her father. She flattered and cajoled him; told him how great he was, how fine looking, made him think that he was a "king" again and thus made his last days of the visit very pleasing for him.

The trial was heard and was over with and then they drove the Elder to Gregory to entrain for his return to Chicago. He was happy and pleased and he and Eden parted more like father and son than Eden had thought possible. He gave him seeds in bottles from the small grains they had grown on the farms, which included oats and wheat and linseed. He selected several ears of corn, just hardened and solid, which the Elder took with him back to Chicago and showed to everybody. He told them it came from his daughter's husband's lands.

CHAPTER XIX

EVERYTHING WENT ALONG serene and happy throughout the fall and into the winter, when new troubles beset them.

Came the winter, and a cold one, although not much snow, and it is never unpleasant in South Dakota for long, if deep snows don't come to belch up cold air, and keep the body uncomfortable.

Three months after they were married, Linda told Martin that she was going to have a baby.

"Oh, my sweet," said he, gathering her to him. "Won't that be wonderful!"

She wasn't so sure. She hadn't planned on it so soon, so was rather annoyed.

"But darling, people don't plan on when to have children. The children start when they get ready and you have to put up with the waiting and the inconveniences that may happen while you are waiting."

"But I didn't want a baby until we were better fixed, had a better house and were settled for good out on my claim."

"Forget all that, Linda, darling, and just let's rejoice with the fact that you are going to have one."

"My father'll have a fit."

"And why?"

"He will say that we should have waited until we were more conveniently fixed."

"Did my mother and father wait and have me when they were ready, and did yours wait until some selected time to have you?"

"I don't know, but I don't think so."

"They didn't. Nobody does, so let's forget all about your father having a 'fit' and get ready in six months for the blessed event."

Linda wrote Terry that she was going to have a baby and Terry answered by no means to do so. Linda asked what she should do, and Terry told her to "get rid of it."

Linda was horrified. She didn't think that she ought to. In the next letter, Terry sent her a recipe, to be brewed from smart weed. Linda wrote her that she was afraid to, and that Martin wanted the child.

Terry snapped back that she was a fool; that if she tried to have a baby up there where there was no maternity hospital to go to, it might kill her.

This correspondence took place while the Elder was visiting up there and after Linda gave in to him she tried Terry's recipe, which didn't work.

All this she kept from her husband, but they had discussed the question of telling him about it and decided negatively. They didn't wish to be burdened with all that he would be saying about it.

Linda's heart was too soft to keep secrets from her husband, however, so after the Elder returned to Chicago, she told him all about what her sister had written about getting rid of their unborn child.

From that day on Eden didn't want to hear the name of Terry. Neither did he feel any warmer toward the Elder, for he had observed Linda's having to change her ways to play down to him.

"I did not tell him about our baby, Martin," said she. "I remember that you asked me not to, so I didn't."

"I'm glad that you didn't. Your sister and father just can't seem to fit in to our scheme of things, our future, so the fewer secrets you have with them, perhaps the better. Had I tho't that Terry would try to have you commit the crime of abortion, I would not have let you tell her, either. The idea, to want to destroy our baby."

He was enraged and it was days before she could calm him. His fall commitments were due and past due again; he needed money badly. Carrying the load and trying to develop the lands in Tripp County with all their attendant responsibilities, was getting very hard on him.

Linda said that Terry had gotten rid of several; that Terry said she didn't want any children and wasn't going to have any.

"That is the greatest event we have to look forward to, Linda. If I couldn't have that to anticipate, it seems at times I would surely go crazy."

Eden moved to Linda's claim after Xmas. He sent grandma and Linda on ahead with a light load of furniture and such as was needed to sustain them, while he followed behind with heavier loads of farm implements, lumber, coal and other things. This delivered, he made them comfortable and prepared to return to Gregory County for the balance of their belongings and their stock.

This would be a heavy, tedious task, and he had put it off until the last, but it was something that had to be done. His sister had gone for a visit to Kansas and wrote him that she would come on through to Winner on her way back and take a bus to the town nearest Linda's claim when she returned. This would be before Eden could possibly get back with the final loads and stock.

The life of the settler is not an easy lot. It is filled with endless privations and sacrifices as to comfort and many of the conveniences that the present day average person is unwilling to forego. Yet *somebody* must make conquest of those undeveloped portions of the West; somebody tore up all the great prairies that once embraced the whole states of Ohio, Indiana, Michigan, Illinois, Iowa and so on down. This was what Martin Eden would think of when he was confronted with these raw conditions; somebody had done it before him, including his uncles in the settling of Kansas. What they and others had done, so could he.

Linda's time for delivery was approaching and he disliked to take any chance of not being by her side to attend her and comfort her when this happened. He wrote his sister and in reply she answered that she was cutting her visit in Kansas short so as to get back and stay with Linda. She advised him to complete his moving, for unless he did, more trouble would be the result.

When he was about ready to leave, Linda clung to him and begged him not to go; not to leave her because she was afraid.

"Olive will be here in two days, dearest," said he. "I don't want to go, but if I do not, we'll never get completely settled out here. So take it easy, don't worry, and wait for Olive. Everything will be all right after she arrives."

"I'll do my best, dear," she whispered.

"This will be the first time to leave you alone since we married, precious," said he, consolingly. "When I return from this trip, we will be able to relax into our lives here on your place with our baby and can take it easy from then on."

"I hope so, Martin."

"So just be brave and patient. You have everything you need in the way of food, clothing and fuel. What you may need after I leave, Olive can go into Carter and get it for you, so be sweet and wait for Olive and soon I'll be back."

He kissed her good by, repeating on the kissing several times. She clung to him and cried and made him feel that he might never return, but after a time he got off to the East.

Olive arrived and took charge and the two girls and grandma had it pleasant together. But for the elements, Martin would have been back before the blessed event arrived.

But a storm sweeping out of the northwest, covered the whole Rosebud Country deep with snow. The thermometer fell to degrees far below zero; Eden and Bill encountered almost everything in the way of weather and accidents on the way back with their loads and were delayed for days beyond the time he had reckoned on returning.

After days, however, he managed to reach Winner, the end of the railroad, and seventeen miles from Linda's claim. He arrived there late on Sunday night and left early Monday morning for the final trek to her place. When about half way, he met her neighbor who pulled up and said:

"I tried to get you by telephone in Winner, Dallas and Gregory Saturday, but couldn't seem to reach you."

"I was whipsawed between Dallas and Winner. We broke an axle and lost several hours before we could get a new one. Why?"

"Your wife had a baby Saturday."

"Oh, my goodness!" Eden's heart fell.

"She made it all right. Dr. Leach from Carter delivered it. A great big boy, weighed over ten pounds." Naturally Eden was relieved, but the next remark spelled the trouble which was never to end.

"When I couldn't reach you, the doctor was afraid and had her wire her father."

"Oh, my heavens," thought Eden—and he knew the worst was soon to come.

"She got a telegram this morning that they were leaving Chicago today and would get in Winner tomorrow night," said the neighbor. "Well, congratulations, old boy. I know you must feel mighty good now," and with a wave of the hand, was on his way.

Eden struggled on toward her claim, his heart heavy. He had been away when the blessed event arrived. At last, the Elder, forever wishing to humiliate and unnerve him, now had something on him, and as he struggled with his loads and his stock to her claim, he realized that he would never hear the end of it.

"They were leaving" he said to himself as he trudged on his weary way. "What could he mean by 'they'?" Could it be possible that the Elder was bringing Mrs. Lee with him? No, mother Mary never went anywhere. Then of a sudden he knew who the "They" included. *Terry!*

Cold sweat broke out all over him and he stayed in a daze until he reached her claim.

Arriving there, he ordered Bill to unhitch the teams and put the stock in the corral, the horses in the barn, and hurried up to the house. He met his sister, who came out before he reached the steps, her face clouded with what both knew was soon to cast its shadow across that home.

"Oh, brother, where have you been?"

"We slid off the road, one wagon got a broken axle; I was delayed. I couldn't help it."

"I knew something must have happened. You never would have stayed away, knowing that Linda's delivery was about due."

"I feel terrible about it. How is Linda?"

"She's doing very well, but I'm worried, so terribly worried. The doctor sent Old Lee a telegram about the baby. This morning we received an answer that he and that sister Terry whom I've heard you mention, were on their way, and Linda is worried, too. We had all of Lee last fall that we could stand, so I hated to hear he's on the way back here again."

"Yes, I'm in for plenty of trouble now and it's me that knows it," sighed Eden.

"The doctor had to deliver the child by Caeserian operation," said Olive, her face still serious and worried.

"Great heavens!" exclaimed Eden. "You don't say so!" She nodded her head up and down to affirm it.

"I met Marshall and he didn't tell me that."

"It was too large and she couldn't give birth to it. So there was nothing left but to deliver it that way."

More water under the bridge. More excuses for the Elder and Terry to loosen a blitzkrieg when they arrived. He would be fortunate now if their marriage survived this catastrophe.

Eden's throat became so dry he almost choked; her words had left him cold and speechless. He swayed for a second and she placed her hands on him to steady him. The next moment he staggered into the house and to the bedside of his wife.

She was asleep, both she and the baby which lay by her side. He uncovered the little one and looked at it. It was too young and funny looking for him to understand much about it; but he saw with pride that it favored him. His son. He felt so strange that for the moment he forgot all the trouble that was riding its way to his home. As he knelt there, admiring the little fellow, Linda's eyes opened, and turning slowly, fell on him. She smiled and called:

"Martin?"

"Yes, Linda. I'm here. I managed to get back."

"Oh, my husband. Why did you stay away? I waited and longed and prayed for you to return."

"Accidents beset us; the storm overtook us; we had all kinds of trouble. I did the best I could; I'm so sorry I didn't get back in time, darling. Forgive me?"

"Of course I forgive you, Martin, and I knew that something must have happened, but I'm so sorry, for had you been here, I wouldn't have let the doctor send that telegram."

"I know, my dear. And again I'm sorry. I'm sorry again because a telegram had to be sent."

"I didn't want to send it; but when the doctor realized that he'd have to operate to deliver the baby, he said he must at least tell somebody who was close to me."

"I understand, Linda. It couldn't be helped. Now don't worry and be very quiet. I'm sorry I didn't send you to Chicago to a hospital now; but I've had so much to worry me."

"I know you have, my Martin, and I'll be very quiet; I'm following the doctor's orders to the letter."

"Yes, please do, sweetheart. You will have to take it easy for weeks."

"What do you think of Junior?"

"He's wonderful, isn't he?"

"Just like you."

"I could see the favor—the first time I looked at him."

"He's a darling."

"I want to look at him some more. Can I—take him for awhile?"

"Not until he wakes up. He performs if he's awakened. He might even cry then; but he might decide to be quiet. He's the boss of this house now and must have his own way. You can look at its face. Are you glad that it's a boy?"

"I am, my sweet."

"The Dr. says most men worry their wives with talking and hoping that it'll be a boy; just like there didn't have to be a girl born now and then, also."

"I'd be happy if it had been a girl, but I'm happier still that it's a boy."

"You're a darling husband. You never said at any time what you wished it would be."

"I realize that there must be girls. All wives can not deliver boys just because most of the husbands want a boy."

"That's so sweet of you."

"Maybe the next one will be a girl."

"The next one, Martin?"

"Why, of course, dear. The next and the next until we have at least five."

"Five! Great heavens!"

"But we'll talk and think about this one now," said Martin.

"Yes, lets do."

"I've named him already."

"Why, Linda, that isn't fair. Why couldn't you wait so we could have given him his name together," he said this poutingly. She smiled, not disturbed.

"I didn't need you to help name him what I did."

"Well, what name did you give him?"

"The one you would have given him."

"Me?" said he, pointing at himself, then sighed. "I hope it isn't any old funny name and not two or three names. I would have given him a simple one."

"That's what I did."

"What is it?"

"Can't you guess," said she, tantalizingly. He shook his head, and looked skeptical.

"Martin, Jr."

He almost jumped and screamed for joy. The fact is that he hadn't thought of any name he'd wanted the child to have, if it had been a boy. The fact that he had been given his own name, made him too happy for words.

"Martin, Jr.! Just think of it. Me, a father, with a fine little boy and a lovely wife. We are now a happy little family, aren't we, dear."

"So happy, now that papa has come back." At this point they heard an auto which came to a stop very shortly.

"It's the Dr.," said she, seeking to adjust herself. "He's due at this time. He'll be glad you are here."

Two minutes later the Dr. was ushered into the room and shook hands with Eden.

"I've heard enough about you to know you. It's strange that we haven't met before."

"That's because I seldom go to Carter. My activities are from here, east."

"I understand. That perhaps explains it. But you're very well known in Carter at that."

"I wouldn't be surprised. Meanwhile, I want to first apologize for not being here when all this happened. We were trying to get the rest of our stuff and the stock out here from down in Gregory County. We ran into that blizzard, had some accidents and it seemed impossible for me to arrive until this morning."

"Naturally. Well, I was frightened when I realized that she couldn't deliver it in the usual way and when we are forced to operate, we must have the consent of the person who is the closest of kin, in the event the operation does not prove successful. When, therefore, I could not contact you, there was no alternative but to wire her father, which I did."

"Of course."

"Even then, I had to operate without anybody's consent, because the baby was delivered Saturday and I didn't get a wire from him until today, giving me consent. So you see what a spot I was placed in."

"I can appreciate the position."

"But since the girl, here," pointing to Linda, "came through like a brave soldier, I guess everything will be all right. She must, of course, be extremely careful and cannot be moved for weeks."

"I understand, Dr., and will obey instructions."

The Dr. then examined her and dressed the incision, checked her temperature, blood pressure, and pronouncing her fit, took his leave.

Matters went along evenly and there was no cause for any thing to the contrary. Eden talked with the Dr. outside before he left to go back to his office and was told that barring any unforseen developments, Linda would come through 100 percent. He said she would be herself again in less than sixty days, as she was healthy, blood pressure perfect and assured him there was nothing to worry about. All she had to do was to follow his orders, keep quiet, no exertions, and everything would be all right.

Little did he know, however, that at that very moment, there was nearing Winner, more trouble on the way to them than Linda and Martin would ever experience if she gave birth to a dozen babies, all to be born the same way.

After the Dr. left the next day, when he pronounced her condition as splendid, another car drove up and came to a stop. Out of it stepped Trouble, double Trouble, both crying, which forebode evil hours and days to come.

Eden met the car and helped them out and brought their luggage into the house, behind them. He didn't speak to them, as both were crying, and there was no chance, so he was at least relieved that long, of the storm which was to come.

Trouble entered the house and rushing into Linda's bedroom,

split at the foot of it, and fell to their knees on either side of the
bed, crying loudly as they did so, in unison:

"Linda! Thank God that you are still alive!" Poor Linda,
looking up, groaned audibly, and got ready for the worst.

The Elder bellowed in base while Terry was a contralto in
her delivery. The chorus didn't harmonize so well, but it offered
at least a contrast in tones, so the bedlam, without rhythm,
continued on for several minutes before the two took time out
to look her over and check on how next to proceed.

Olive, whom they had ignored, was holding the baby and
thinking they would wish to see it, had entered the room with
it in her arms. The child let out a little cry at this point, attracting its mother's attention, whereupon, hoping to get them off
the floor and to stop their crying, she pointed weakly toward
the child:

"Papa, Terry, my baby. Have you seen Martin and our
baby?"

She expected them to rush to it, take it from Olive's arms,
caress it and tell her that it was a wonderful baby; that it was
beautiful, and holding it, carry on over it, talk about it, praise
it. That was the way fathers and sisters and mothers did when
their sisters and brothers and sons and daughters had their
first babies, their second and third—but this was her *first* baby,
a fine healthy little fellow that weighed over ten lbs. at birth—a
baby for all related to it to be proud of.

Instead, these two deceitful hypocrites ignored the child and
only cried louder and louder. She closed her eyes and let escape
a deep sigh. She felt strangely weak and wondered why. She
felt so helpless, too. She opened her eyes for a moment and
saw Martin enter the door. To see him she had to look over
Terry's head, whose eyes were lowered as she cried. Martin
paused in the door way and she could see the sadness in his
face, and her wearied mind went back to some of the things
he had said, less than a year before. And now through the
unfortunate twist of fate, they were in the toils of a love so
great it would destroy two people "for their own good."

She saw by the expression on his face that he was helpless. Powerful, strong, courageous Martin Eden, to be crucified on the altar of hate—by tears! Her eyes seemed to plead with him to help save her from those jackals and for a moment something rose up in him. In that moment, he was tempted to stride forward, catch these two creatures by the nape of their necks and bump their heads together so hard as to make real tears by the pain of contact. The steely eyes that belonged to him; those eyes of grim determination, born to weather the storms that had come and were gone and the storms to come were tense for a moment, and then he thought of something; it was that he was away when the child came. Anything he did now to assert a husband's right would be charged up against him, and they had enough already charged against him to convict him for life. She saw him relax to that expression of helplessness, so she closed her eyes again and groaned with pain and mental anguish.

Terry and the Elder dried their tears long enough to wash their faces, unpack some luggage and eat their dinners which had been prepared by Olive. Eden went to Carter for something Linda needed, and the conspirators were alone with their victim. Just before the Elder entered, Terry came in, her eyes flashing, her tongue sharp. She sizzled in an undertone:

"You wouldn't do what I told you and wanted you to do, so you see what's happened! They had to cut you open and endanger your life to have that brat for him!"

"Please, Terry, mine is a sweet baby."

"Sweet your foot! No brat is worth risking your life for. You should have gotten rid of it as I do mine—then you wouldn't be lying here like this. I tried so hard, and you know it, to save you from all this mess, but you must believe that nigger instead of me, when I was doing it all for your own good, so you see what's happened—see!"

The Elder was coming now, so Terry had to hurry the last words before the "Holier than thou" arrived. Her attack was direct and to the point, while his went around the detour. Linda made a final effort to stay what she knew was coming. They sat on either side of her bed now. She reached out and putting her hand on her fathers arm, whispered:

"Listen, father and Terry. Don't blame Martin. He's doing the best he can. He's got so much trouble."

"I've tried to tell you all along, but you insist on standing by him, regardless. I told you that the man is hopelessly hard-headed, nobody can tell him anything, so his chickens are coming home to roost," chimed the Reverend.

"I tried to tell you that he only married you to get this old land and that he would kill you," added Terry, "but I didn't expect him to start out to do it so soon. He could at least have given you two or three years of freedom before he started in to finish you. But evidently he wanted to have it over with in a hurry so that he could have the land and be free that much sooner."

"Please father, please Terry, I'm sick. Please quit talking about my husband. I'm too sock to defend him."

"Of course you are, but its your own fault," cried Terry, sharply. "Father and I wore ourselves out trying to help you for your own good—but 'my Martin' was all that you could think of."

"What I want to know, Linda, is, why wasn't I told before—at least while I was out here, that you were going to have this child? Was it because I didn't count, your own father who loves you?" He felt sorry for himself, and finding his kerchief, started dabbing at his nose.

"But father, it was agreed between mama, Terry and Martin that you were not to be told."

"Now don't go trying to hang that on me!" screamed Terry. "I *did* agree not to tell father, but it was only because you wrote me such pitiful letters, begging me not to. But somebody must have had you write and beg me not to tell father and you don't have to be a good guesser to put your finger on who that person was," she berated, nodding her head up and down, knowingly.

"To think of keeping this from me and what could have happened," he moaned.

"She's lucky she didn't die there in that bed out here in this wild country, and if she had, he would perhaps have buried her on one of these hills and said nothing to us about it until after it was all over. I wouldn't be surprised at anything that niggah wouldn't do; this niggah that she 'loves' so much."

The baby began to cry out in the other room, and Linda called out weakly:

"Oh, Olive, my baby. Please bring it to me, dear." Swinging the baby gently and trying to get it to stop crying, Olive hesitated.

"Please bring it to me, Olive, dear. It'll stop crying when its mother holds it."

"But Linda, do you think you ought to? You've got to be so very careful not to exert yourself. You know what the Dr. said."

"I won't exert myself, Olive," whispered Linda, holding out her arms for the child. "Just give him to me, please. I know what's the matter with it."

Olive placed it in her arms, whereupon she bared one breast and let the baby nurse. At sight of this, Terry's eyes opened in horror. Her father, who was looking at the same thing, started to cry again, but quietly.

"The Dr. told me to nurse it at my breast. So it's all right."

"In this day and age—well, people!"

"But the Dr. told me to."

"No hospital would ever permit it."

"But can't you understand that there is no hospital around here to go to, Terry? After all, God provided a way and even if it does seem antiquated, mothers nursed babies at their breasts for thousands of years before the advent of hospitals and maternity wards."

Olive, seeing that their presence was injurious to her, interposed:

"Pardon me, Reverend Lee and Mrs. Glavis. I'm afraid you're going to injure Linda. You're getting her all excited and upset and the Dr. warned Martin especially against that. Don't you think it might be best if you'd leave her alone for awhile now?"

"Linda is our child, Olive, we are here to save her. We love her and she needs us, so she'll be all right. We have a few things we want to say to her and then we'll leave her alone, thank you," said the Reverend. With a light shrug of her shoulders, Olive retired from the room.

As Olive left the sick room, Martin came into the house. Laying a finger on her lips, she whispered in his ear:

"Her father and that Terry are about to drive her crazy in there. They'll kill her if you don't do something about it. They've been here for three hours or more and they haven't even looked at the baby. I overheard Terry lecturing her about not getting rid of it as she tried to get her to, before it was born and referred to the child as a brat. You'd better do something or we'll be burrying Linda."

Eden's manhood reasserted itself. He glared at them through the door and entering the sick room, paused momentarily.

"You know how hard I tried to keep you from marrying him less than a year ago and after nothing would do but that you just must, I then tried to have you get rid of this brat, but you—"

The Elder had heard Eden. Terry, whose back was toward the door was so engrossed in what she was saying, hadn't heard him. She looked over her shoulder and swallowed guiltily. Martin looked straight at her and she turned her eyes away. Linda groaned:

"Martin!"

"Well," said he. "Do you even *hate the child*, too? The helpless little baby. I know you hate me, have hated me from almost the moment you met me, but I'm not squawking about that. I'm a man and I can take mine standing up, but Linda and that little baby she's holding are helpless. You pretend to love her so much, yet you hate her baby because you hate me so. If you really loved her half as much as you pretend, you'd have at least looked at her baby. It's hers as well as mine, so if you really love her at all, how can you hate the baby so; such a young baby, too. Answer me!" his eyes flashed and he made a gesture at which both ducked in fright.

"Please, Martin, do hush. You musn't—" begged Linda, but Martin's ire was up.

Grandma and Olive, coming up from the rear, took Eden gently by each arm and drawing him away, entered the other room, closing the door behind them. No sooner than the door clossed, the conspirators were busy again.

"See what he's done to you, my child," began the Elder. "Just look at what he has brought you to."

"Brought me to, father! Martin has done nothing to me. I've just had a baby. I'm recovering like any other woman who has given birth to a child. Why all these accusations? What do you mean, anyhow?"

"You'll die a fool!" hissed Terry. "Don't you understand what father is talking about?"

"No, I don't understand what father is talking about; I don't understand what you are talking about. I'm all right. I've got my baby and my husband and the Dr. says I'm getting along fine."

"The older you grow, the bigger fool you get to be," cried Terry. "This man has deprived you of the little sense you once had."

"Don't you understand what she means, Linda?" The Elder's face was solemn. "Look at you, lying out here in this little old house in the wilderness and nursing your baby at your breast, when it should be in a nursery and you in a hospital."

"But I've explained that there are no hospitals, and of course there can be no nurseries out here, and I'm not the only woman who's had a baby in a house like this. Women are having babies all around me just like I've had this, many in not as good a house, and nobody is even thinking about it. I tell you that you both are all wrong about the whole thing. I—"

"Please hush up, Linda, and look around you. Whoever heard of a woman being operated on in a house? Why, you could have died like that!" and she snapped her fingers to emphasize her point.

"I understand all that, Terry. If I was going to die, I'd have died in a hospital having it the same as I would have here; but the fact to be appreciated is that I did not die but have my baby, and other than being a little weak, I will soon be well. The Dr. says so. He says that in two or three weeks I'll be able to sit up, and with Martin home and my sweet little baby, I'll be happier than ever."

"*Your baby*," screamed Terry in suppressed rage, "*your baby*, you keep crying about your baby, when you could have been dead—dead!"

"Oh, Terry, Oh father, I don't understand either of you. You talk of love, cry about it, and all you've done since you entered this room is to hate, hate, hate! You hate Martin, you hate our baby, you—"

"Calm yourself, Linda, and don't be so excited! We don't hate your baby. It's the excitement; the fear after receiving that telegram, that you might be dead—that you *were* dead. Think of the strain and suspense we labored under all the way from Chicago here. We—we simply haven't gotten around to the baby yet. Give us a little time, but—"

"Oh, you hate my husband, you hate Martin. He has done nothing to either of you, yet you hate him so much you hate his baby, too—and why?"

"Why!" exclaimed Terry, derisively.

"*Why!*" echoed the Elder, pointedly.

"Yes, *why?*" asked Linda, trying to be brave.

"Well!" from Terry, contemptuously.

"Well, well!" echoed the Elder, as if anybody oughtn't to know; oughtn't to understand.

"You don't understand him."

"Don't understand him," cried Terry, as if somebody was questioning her intelligence. "I *like* that!"

"What is there to understand?" inquired the Elder.

"That's what *I'd* like to know," said Terry.

"Then won't you tell me; tell me so *I* can understand, Terry," suggested Linda.

"That, you will *never* do! You haven't that much sense; it's *you* who don't understand, however, else you could see through it all."

"See through it all? See through *what* all? What ever can you mean?"

"Just what we've been trying to tell you and show you all along," hissed the Elder, dropping his "holier than thou" mask for a moment and becoming his real self. "*That the man does not love you,* never did, and never will!"

"Oh!" cried Linda, covering her eyes.

"*That he married you just so he could get this old land—more land to help him get rich, and—*"from Terry.

"*—will kill you to do so,—*" from the Elder.

"*—and when you are dead and in your grave, he'll go back and marry Jessie Binga, the woman he loves, and—*" sizzled Terry.

"*—always has, and while you rot and stink, he'll—*"

"*—go flying around all over the country with her and have a good time on the money you've given your life to help him get!*"

"*Now will you understand what it's all about and—*"

"*—let us help save you while there is yet time—for your own good, you fool!*" Terry finished with a yell. The door opened and Eden stood there looking at them. They started guiltily. He stopped at the foot of the bed and began:

"If I don't stop you two pretty quick, she'll die from all the 'love' you are trying to kill her with so you might have to take some of the blame if she dies. It sure is a wonderful love that the pair of you are showering on her, when a fool can see that the girl is weak and that what you are handing her is making her weaker, lying there helpless; that what you are doing is downright criminal.

"You consider you have the right to *even kill her*, if abuse of me can do it, because you," pointing to the old preacher, "are her father, and Terry, there, is her sister. But she's *still* my wife and I have a greater right to kill her—even if she must die, than you two. However, you don't mean to kill her. You simply hate me so until you've forgotten that she has just had a child. You seem to insist on forgetting this fact, and that no woman should be forced to listen to all the mean things you are saying about her husband, while lying there weak and sick and helpless.

"So, however, you choose to feel about it, *I* intend to save her from that thing you call 'love' and 'for her own good,' until she is well and strong enough to fight back if she wants to."

"Why, my son—" began the Elder, deceitfully.

"You don't mean that, Elder, and you know you do not. Lets understand each other, clearly. You, and your daughter, Terry, hate me more than you could a rattle-snake out there on those prairies. You hate me more than you could a rattle-snake that even *bit you*, so we understand each other, and knowing how you feel, don't expect me to believe any honeyed words you might utter.

"I want you to understand what everybody around here knows, that this is a new country. As you say, perhaps, a wild country. We haven't gotten settled well enough yet to build hospitals and nurseries and clinics, so we are having to get along without them until we can do better. During that time, our wives and mothers and sisters will have to keep on having babies, maybe. And they will have to bear them in their homes like they did thousands of years before all the conveniences you spoke of were even conceived. I was born in a house, so were you, Rev. Lee, also Linda, Terry and my sister, Olive.

"I was away when the baby came. God knows I intended to be here by her side; she knows it, the Dr. knows it. I apologized for this failure in the best way I could. I explained the misfortune that overtook me. Linda has forgiven me and until you two crossed this threshold, we were a united and happy family here with our baby. In a few weeks she will be well and our child that we both love and are proud of will be bigger and stronger, and we will all be as happy as it is possible for a little family to be.

"But because of my misfortune, I know that you, with an excuse now for being here, intend to 'get even' for all the wrongs which you have me charged with. And you are so anxious to get started, that you can't even wait until the girl is strong enough to listen, much less talk.

"Well, I'm telling you now that you can't get away with it, see? Do you understand what I mean?" He leaned toward them with such firmness that they cringed in fear. "She's taking no more of this abuse from either of you, under the guise of 'love,' do you hear me?"

The Elder had enough courage to say, without meeting the other's eyes:

"I'm sorry that you're feeling this way, Martin. What do you intend to do about it?"

"Do about it? Why sure. I'm taking you both to the hotel in Carter and putting you up there." He looked hard at them as he finished. Terry dared meet his eyes for a moment.

"Well, people!"

The Elder tried pacification.

"Why, Martin, you don't mean—"

"Just what I say, Elder, I'm taking the both of you to Carter to a hotel—and tonight, get me?

"Douse the tears, Elder, because I'm wise to them, and to yours, too, sister," he said to Terry.

"Now listen to what I'm saying. I'm driving you both into town and putting you up at the hotel. I saw in ten minutes after you came that she would never get well if I let you sit around her bed with all your tears and your 'love'—and your *tongues!* So I drove right into town and engaged a room for each of you and at my expense. So I'm taking you there tonight—*right now!*"

"Now listen, Martin," whimpered Terry.

"Please Martin," began the elder. "We—"

"I hear you but I'm taking action. You're not going to kill Linda, even if she is your own blood. So get up and get ready, else I'll carry you both out, and I'm strong enough to do so, too, if you get what I mean."

"But please, Martin," said Terry rising.

"I'll come to Carter and drive you out here and let you stay, if you douse your love and tears while here each day, as long as the Dr. says you may. I consulted him and gave him the low down on both of you, so I'm acting on his orders as well as mine, and his are, to get you away from this girl. I'm giving you five minutes to get your things together and be ready to go with me. You can see her every day you stay here, but no more of your 'love' and 'doing it all for her own good,' see? Now remember, you've got just five minutes to be ready!" and he was gone.

They were waiting when Eden returned, but in a last effort, the Elder began:

"Now, now, my son—"

"Cut the 'son' stuff, Elder," snapped Eden, picking up their bags. "You're my enemy. I accept you as such and enemies lose no love for each other."

"He misunderstands us so, father," said Terry, affecting sadness. Linda opened her eyes and called:

"Father, Terry, where are you going?"

Looking back and down at her, the Elder replied:

"To Carter, sweetheart. Your husband is putting us out."

"Putting you out!" cried Linda in weak surprise. Martin returning to see why they had not followed him, heard the last words. Linda called:

"Martin, dear, what—"

"I'm taking your father and sister to the hotel in Carter where they can be more comfortable. The Dr. says that being so near will upset and excite you and that is bad for your condition. I'll go for them tomorrow morning and bring them out every day."

"Martin thinks we hate him, Linda, dear," said Terry.

"We don't hate your husband, Linda. Do we Terry," tried the Reverend, turning to Terry.

"No, we *love* him," said Terry, sarcastically.

Eden kissed Linda.

"Now I'll talk to you when I get back, if you're awake, but don't try to stay awake if you feel like sleeping. Plenty of rest and quiet is your perscription, so remember what the Dr. says and do it. By, by, Honey. See you later."

In the outside room, Olive was walking the floor with the baby. Getting on either side of her, they peered into the little one's face.

"The precious little darling," chimed the Elder, smiling down at it.

"Just like its dear papa," echoed Terry, tickling it on the cheek. By the door, waiting for them, Eden smiled and shook his head at this.

Linda called Olive and Terry cried:

"Please let me hold it while you're inside. I'll take good care of it, the dear little thing." Olive hesitated.

"Oh," cried the Elder, reassuringly: "We'll take good care of it. Let me hold my little grandson." Olive handed it to him. It started to cry and Terry took it away from the Elder. Meanwhile, Olive returned:

"She wants the child," and held her arms out for it.

"Let me take it to my sister, please," begged Terry. Olive consented. Terry turned and said: "If Martin comes back in, tell him we are just playing with the baby for a few minutes." Terry stood at the foot of the bed, playing with the baby.

"I was telling father that your baby is so sweet; it looks just like its dear papa."

"Yes," agreed the Elder, affecting a fatherly smile. "He does—just like him. Is that why you named him Martin, Jr., dear?"

"And you hate it," cried Linda from the bed, weakly. "You hate it just like you do its father. Now give him back to me—let me have him, please!"

"Why, Linda! How can you say such a thing? Me, hate my sister's baby—you should be ashamed of yourself!"

"Give me back my baby, I say. I'm ashamed of you, both of you. You can't fool me, neither of you. You," pointing a finger at Terry, accusingly, "tried to make me murder it—murder it before it was born; you abused me for having given birth to it. Now you ask me to believe you love it when not an hour ago you were calling it 'my brat.' Give it back to me, I say—*give my baby back.*"

Seeing that she was working herself into a fury, Olive took the baby.

"Please let her have it. She's so excited she's liable to break the stiches in her stomach." She handed it to Linda whose whole body was trembling, pitifully. She gathered the child to her and turned back to Terry and the Elder.

"I'm ashamed of both of you. First you hate my husband and abuse him to his back unmercifully, and because you hate him so, you call my child a brat and hate it. Why don't you hate me; I don't want your love if you've got to hate my baby and my husband so. What can I do with such love?"

"Oh, Linda," cried the Elder, alarmed. "You must not say such words. We don't hate the baby. Please believe us that much."

"My—my husband was right," murmured Linda, aloud but more to herself than to the others.

"What do you mean, Linda?"

"That you must stay in town."

"But, Linda," protested Terry.

"You must stay in town. I can see why, now. If you tried to stay here and you continued the way you have started, I would soon die. So you must stay in town. It is best."

"We're going to stay in town, dear, but we don't want you to be feeling and thinking about us like that," beseeched the Elder. Linda, holding her baby close seemed not to hear.

"The thought of your hatred for my husband and baby is too much with both of you near, for me to stand. So you must go away from me so that I can try to forget, *so that I can try to forget.*"

"God help us," sighed the Elder.

"Yes, father," sighed Linda. "I will pray God to help both of you. Only *He* can. Please go now and leave me and don't come back until the Dr. has been to see me again. You've talked too much and made me talk too much and I begin to feel strangely weak and giddy—please go—" her voice trailed off into silence and her eyes closed. Olive took one look, then turning to them:

"I've been afraid all night that this might happen. Now don't either of you say another word. I'm going for my brother. You better come with me and let Martin take you into town. He's got to send the Dr., so hurry." They followed her out into the night, and the car dashed away and over the hills into Carter, returning a few minutes later followed by the Dr.

After reviving her the Dr., with serious face, turned to Eden and his sister:

"What's been going on out here? Why, I left that girl two hours ago in the best of condition for her illness. Now her pulse has increased; its beating 50% faster than it was; her temperature has shot away up—she's in a bad way. What's been going on around here?"

After some hesitation, Olive replied:

"We hate to expose family secrets, but her father and sister don't like my brother. When they arrived, knowing that he wasn't here when the baby came, they started abusing him to her while he was out."

"Oh, I understand. I *thought* something had been going on contrary to my orders. What is the matter with these people? They seem intelligent enough. I'm surprised." He turned to Eden.

"I had no idea when you explained to me tonight that you thought it best not to have them so close to her, that it had gone this far. This is serious. Another experience like the one she has just gone through, would make her develop pneumonia and she'd never survive an attack in her condition. I'm mighty afraid this one may throw her into it." Re-examining her, and shaking his head, he rose.

"There's no more that I can do now. It'll depend on her constitution to overcome the serious set back. I'll take a chance on her tonight, but I'll be back early tomorrow morning."

They thanked him and escorted him to his car. Just before starting the motor, he said:

"I'll talk to this preacher myself when I get back to Carter. I must check up on him. He evidently fooled me. I'd never have guessed that he could be so—so foolish. Well, good night."

"Good night, Dr."

The Elder and Terry couldn't think of retiring, much less sleeping, until the Dr. returned and they had a report on Linda, whom they were real anxious about now.

"Listen, you people," and he paused to look through his glasses from one to the other.

"Yes, Dr.," anxiously.

"Do you know that all the talking and, I understand, abuse you heaped into Mrs. Eden's ears since you arrived there this afternoon, has got her at the point of death?"

"No!" their jaws dropping in fear.

"I don't understand how two people, as intelligent as you both seem to be from your looks and your talk, could sit there by that girl's side and talk about her husband and the baby until she's more near dead right now than she was while under the ether."

"But, Dr.," began the Elder, raising his hand. The Dr. raised his for silence.

"Pardon me, Elder. I don't want to hear anything about family differences. I can't sit in judgement on who's right or wrong. Your son-in-law seems to feel very bad because he was not there Saturday when I had to deliver the baby by Caesarian operation; but he apologized like a man and explained how he was unavoidably delayed. That can happen out here. I believe him, and since he returned, the girl seemed to be happy and was coming along 100% until you two arrived.

"Now she's worse off than she has ever been and I'm greatly worried about her. She's liable to develop pneumonia and if she does, she hasn't one chance in a thousand to survive it, and it's all your fault, so that's all I know.

"I told Eden this afternoon when he came to ask me about you, that it would be all right for him to let you stay with her two or three hours each day, but to bring you back here every night. With the condition she's in now, I must countermand that order and forbid either of you seeing her again for at least a week. I'm sorry." With a curt good night he was gone.

Trouble looked at Trouble and both felt guilty. And then the thought of having to lounge around the hotel in this village with nobody to talk to, nothing to do, made both sick. So retiring to their rooms, they tried to make the best of a bargain that was bad, but which they had brought on by their own hate.

When the Dr. returned the next morning, Linda was still too weak for him to be optimistic; merely hoped for the best and told of the instructions he had left with the others, that they were not to see Linda for at least a week.

"That will be a good lesson for them," said Eden, after his departure.

"The best one—just what they needed," replied Olive. "I hate to see them have to hang around the hotel like that for days, however, without anything to do or anybody to talk to."

"But what can you do about it?"

"I'm not going to do anything myself, but I'm going to see what I can let you do for them. There's a Colored teacher at an Indian Day School in the next County, only about twelve miles from Carter."

"You mean the Barrys."

"Why yes, of course, the Barrys. I didn't know that you knew about them."

"I've met them."

"Go on!"

"Sure. They were up to my claim."

"You don't mean it!"

"Sure, they drove up one Sunday and spent the entire day and we had a most wonderful time."

"Well, well, I'm glad of that because by you knowing them, you can call to see them and it'll seem more natural."

"Well, what do you want done?"

"I want you to go down to Carter and visit with them every other day. Then arrange to drive them out to see Barry and his wife—" He broke off to do some calculating.

"Today is Wednesday. Arrange to drive them out to see the Barrys on Sunday, see?"

"Sure. That'll be nice. I promised to come out and see them myself, but haven't gotten around to it yet."

"Well, now, you make it a business to be in town tomorrow afternoon. Barry always goes there on Thursday and you'll pick him up on the street about four o'clock and then you can tell him of your plans to bring him some company on Sunday."

"That's fine. He'll be flattered to have them."

"And won't they be glad to be taken somewhere!"

In Carter, the Elder and Terry were left alone too long to find much happiness together. The fact is they never got along well together, except when one wanted the other to do something subtle or evil. Then they seemed to get along fine.

So left in the lonely little hotel in Carter, with no kind of a Negro in the town to "frat" with, the hours hung heavy on their hands. During this interim, they began to blame each other for being banned from seeing Linda.

"I knew," said the Elder, "when I heard that you stole in the room when I wasn't there and called Linda's baby a brat, that you were going too far."

"And you had no business doing all that crying. You ought to have known that would upset her."

"What about you? You certainly were doing your share."

"A woman is expected to cry, not men. She wouldn't have paid any attention to me, but when you loosened that blitzkreig of tears of yours, that started it."

"It wasn't *my tears* that upset her. It was that devil tongue of yours—and you know what a tongue you've got," he shot back, whereupon she jumped to her feet in a rage. She glared at him.

"Now don't you try to kick me around. Remember, I haven't ever taken any of your abuse. I've got a husband and if you go trying any bawling me out, I'll wire him to send me money and I'll go right back to Chicago, that's what I'll do."

"Now, Terry, why must we—you and I, quarrel? Maybe both of us are to blame."

"Well put it that way, because you know I'm not letting anybody put anything over on me,—and that includes you."

"I know, I know. We were both at fault, so just let it go at that."

"Then say it that way. You may lay mama and Linda out as you do when you get good and ready, especially mama; but if you come trying to put anything over on Terry Glavis, you'd better try doing it on the run, and don't let me catch up with you, else I'll get you told and *you* know that I know how."

"I understand, Terry, so calm yourself and quit talking."

"I'll quit when I'm good and ready. Besides, how'd you get that way, anyhow; telling me to quit talking. My mouth's my own and I'll talk all I want to and I'd like to see you stop me."

"Please, Terry," he admonished, because she was raising her voice loud enough to be heard.

"Well, why'd you start me? It was you who started this argument, accusing me like you did."

"Terry! We're the only Negroes in this white man's hotel. Are you going to stand there and keep running off at the mouth so loudly that he comes up and asks for his rooms? Where would we go—and think how Eden would take it—he'd be tickled to death."

"Well, I doubt it," her voice much lower.

"What do you mean?"

"What I said."

"You mean that he might not laugh if the man asked us for our rooms?"

"That's what I mean."

"Well, I never!"

"He isn't that kind of a man." When the Elder opened his eyes in surprise at this, she went on to explain.

"I'm not changing with regards to him. I hate him, always have and always will; but give the devil his dues. He isn't little like you, for instance."

"Like me! Little like me? Well, people!" The Elder could find no words to describe his indignation.

"I mean that he *isn't* like you, little and mean, and wouldn't do little, ornery things like you. He'd be sorry if you and I got put out of this hotel for acting like the niggahs we are. I don't hate Eden that way; I mean for being little, for he

isn't little. I hate him because he's smart—too smart and too
shrewd and too scheming. He's a scheming niggah and a
shrewd niggah and that's why I hate him. He can think out
more angles in five minutes than you could in five years, though
you won't admit it, for you've never admitted the truth when
it is inconvenient for your needs. You hate him, too; and
and that's why you hate him."

"It's a lie!"

"What!" "Do you mean to call me a liar, you—you!"

He took her by the arm, with his free hand raised as if to
cup her lips. "Terry, for God's sake, will you hush, for heaven's
sake, *hush!*" He glared at her and she calmed down.

"Them white people's going to put us two niggahs out of
this hotel, so help me God."

"I've hushed. Now why don't you?"

There was a knock on the door, and their hearts leaped,
and through their minds flashed the words:

"There he is! I told you to shut up." Both gulped and their
throats became dry. It was a terrible moment. Terry beckoned
to the Elder to go to the door, but he beckoned her. The
knock was repeated, but louder. They could stall it no longer.
Terry called anxiously:

"Yes?"

"Please open the door!" The tone had a familiar ring, yet
they weren't sure, so Terry called:

"Who is it, please?"

"It's Olive, from out on the farm. From Linda."

"Linda!" they almost yelled in fright. She was dead! was
what flashed through their minds—and *they had killed her!*

"Linda!" Both rushed for the door now. Terry got there
first. The Elder followed, catching Olive by the arm and pulling
her quickly inside. Olive looked at them in surprise, while they,
in chorus cried:

"Linda, did you say Linda!" Don't tell us that she's—
she's dead!"

Olive started in surprise and looked from one to the other.

"Linda, dead, what do you mean?" Thereupon both fell to their knees, and with upraised faces, grasping one of Olive's hands, the Elder offered the prayer, Terry acquiesced.

"Yes, Linda, dead—and *we* killed her, yes, *we killed her!*" They lowered their eyes then and he continued, this time penitent:

"Oh, Lord, God, our Father, have mercy on our souls. It was us who killed Linda. Nobody but us, dear God. We hated her husband and we hated her baby, so we abused them through her while she was weak and sick and helpless and her body couldn't stand it, so she died. *We* killed her, dear Lord, *we did it,* so try to have mercy on our poor souls."

By this time, Olive had recovered from the surprise. With a yank, she pulled both to their feet and when they were able to stand, she had something to say.

"You two miserable sinners. You abused poor Linda enough to have killed her; but she isn't dead."

"Not dead!" they shouted.

"Quiet," cautioned Olive, looking around. "This hotel is run by white people, you know, and they're not used to noisy Negroes as guests."

They calmed down.

"Linda is not dead and whatever made you think so, I don't know. Must have been your guilty consciences," said she, a bit of censure in her tone.

"Linda is still very sick and the Dr. is not sure she will escape that attack of pneumonia. It all depends on her; but that is not what I came here to see you about."

"No?" looking up, in relief.

"No. I came to advise that I wish to drive you into the next County, Sunday, about twelve miles out, to visit with a Colored, Indian Day School Teacher and his wife and have dinner.

"Oh, my, how nice," exclaimed the Elder, his face lit up with genuine joy and relief. He turned to Terry, whose face was wreathed in a smile of delight:

"Why, Olive! How very nice of you—an are we glad!" She was so enthused that she actually threw her arms about Olive and embraced her sincerely.

"I'm glad that the suggestion pleases you."

"Pleases us—that isn't the word," cried Terry.

"A colored teacher, did you say?" asked the Reverend.

"Yes, delightful people. They have a government job and teach. In fact, Mr. Barry, which is his name, has charge of this Day School and he and his wife both teach. They live at the school, which is about twelve miles northwest of here. I met them last fall and later they paid me a visit at my claim. I promised to return the visit but hadn't done so. I met Mr. Barry on the street awhile ago, told him that you were visiting your daughter here, and before I could tell him that I would like to bring you out, he invited us, so we will drive out Sunday morning, and attend services."

"Services?" asked the Elder, wonderingly.

"Yes, regular church service," replied Olive.

"Church services out here?" asked Terry, in amazement. "Why, I—"

"Oh, there are churches all over the reservation. Mostly catholic missions, but since it has been turned over to settlers, they are building quite a few new ones."

"Indeed!" exclaimed the Elder in great surprise. "I had no idea that such was the case. And they have a church out at this school?"

"Yes," said Olive. An Indian Church."

"An Indian Church," cried Terry.

"Yes, it is an Indian church and they have an Indian preacher."

"An Indian preacher!"

"Well, we are learning something, daughter," said the Reverend, turning and looking at Terry.

"We sure are. An Indian church with an Indian preacher! We'll sure be able to say we saw something that almost nobody in Chicago ever saw," chimed Terry.

"Never even heard of," said the Elder. "I'd never heard of anything like it: I know it'll be interesting. To hear an Indian preacher, too."

"Now here is another surprise—he preaches in Indian, the original Sioux tongue."

"Oh!" cried Terry, swinging her body in delight. "Oh, Olive, this is getting more interesting the more you tell us about it."

"Just what is it like, Olive?" inquired the Elder, enthusiastically. "In the original Sioux tongue—isn't that wonderful! Can you understand it? How does it sound, anyhow?" Olive smiled.

"You won't understand it altogether. It doesn't sound anything like any other language you ever heard. There aren't many words like the current languages. They seem very limited and all the words, the most, as far as I can see, anyhow, end with a double E.

"But they have hymn books and all the Indians can read their language in printed form. Many of the older ones cannot even speak English and of course they couldn't read it; but they seem to be able to read the hymn books and sing from them in their language."

"Well, I do declare," ejaculated the Elder.

"They accept their services almost like the ordinary people of our group. The women react to the sermons very emotionally and while I don't recall seeing any of them shout, they listen to the sermon with the most rapt attention, and sway and look at each other. When they sing, they're almost like our people in country churches back in Southern Illinois and all over the South."

"Well, we sure consider this a privilege and a pleasure," said the Elder. All had been so absorbed in what they were talking about that they had forgotten to ask Olive to be seated. Finally they invited her to sit down.

"How is Linda?" asked the Elder, his face serious.

"We really thought she was dead when you called her name awhile ago. You liked to scared us to death," said Terry. Olive smiled.

"I hope I never have to go through a scare like that if I live to be a hundred," breathed the Elder.

"I think I'd die the next time myself," said Terry.

"As I said, her condition is too serious for me to hazard an opinion. The Dr. said that he hoped by Sunday to be able to say more about it. He is still out of patience with—well, I dislike to say it, but—"

"We understand," said the Elder.

"But when I come for you Sunday, I hope to bring you better news," said Olive, rising, preparatory to taking her leave. "How are you getting along down here, anyhow? Is the hotel comfortable?"

"Not bad at all," said Terry.

"And the meals?" inquired Olive.

"Very good," acknowledged the Elder.

"Listen, Olive," ventured Terry, confidentially. "Father and I got to arguing just before you came and during the excitement, each of us raised our voices louder than we are accustomed to, you understand?"

"I see."

"Neither of us seemed to be aware of how loudly we talked, so we were cautioning each other to lower our voices and we got afraid that they'd come up here and put us out." She paused to laugh. Olive joined with them. Terry imitated her father in the next sentence. "Papa said: 'they goin' come up here and put us niggahs outa this hotel'." The Elder beat her to the climax of the joke by relating it himself.

"But the funniest part of the joke on us was, that when you knocked on the door, we thought it was the white folks coming to ask for our rooms, and—" they were all laughing so he couldn't finish, but Terry picked up:

"You liked to scared us to death," and all leaned over against the wall in the laugh on themselves. Olive was the first to find her voice.

"I wondered at the silence. I thought I heard your voices as I came up and then all of a sudden everything was so quiet, like nobody here at all. So I wondered."

"Oh, by the way, Olive," said the Elder, his face becoming serious, "About the—difficulty out there. We're awful sorry about it."

"We sure are," said Terry, sincerely. "I hope you can forgive us."

"Well, it isn't for me to—"

"We understand," cut in the Reverend.

"But I do hope there will be a better understanding from now on. Anything like this can be so—so very unpleasant, and I'm sorry."

"You can bet that we are more than sorry," said the Elder. Olive was moving away now. She didn't want to be drawn into a long discussion regarding it.

CHAPTER XX

THE DR. CAME early the following Sunday and after checking Linda's condition, said, with a sigh of relief:

"Well, she's past the danger of pneumonia. But under no circumstances must you expose her to another experience like she went through Tuesday night."

"I understand," said Eden, following him out of the house and across to his car.

"How soon will it be convenient to let her father and sister come out to see her?" The Dr.'s brow was wrinkled; it could be seen that he would have preferred that they not see her until she was able to sit up—even walk again; but he realized that they had come a long way and maybe did want to see her and might behave themselves.

"I might take a chance on letting them see her Monday; but only if they promise to keep their mouths shut and under no circumstances say anything to upset her." He was thoughtful a moment, then turning to Eden: "I'll drop by the hotel and explain to them myself when I get back to town. That'll be better." Stepping on the gas then, he rolled away.

In town he found them waiting and very anxious about Linda. They rose and stood anxiously, while he, taking off his glasses, polished them with his kerchief, replaced them and said:

"Your daughter, Elder, and," turning to Terry, "your sister is convalescing very favorably and 'll probably escape pneumonia, unless she has another session like you brought out when you came in from Chicago. Your son-in-law seems to want to let you see the girl and because of this, I've decided to permit you to do so Monday—but for only a little while."

244

"Oh, thank you, Dr."

"But I'm not going to take any chances. I'm not going to allow you or anybody else to gamble with that girl's life."

"Why, Dr., of course not," they echoed.

"But you *did* gamble with it last Tuesday; gambled with it so ruthlessly that we're all lucky that she isn't a corpse today. I'm surprised at both of you. Two intelligent looking people, sitting by the side of that very sick girl and laying her husband out to her—ah, now," raising his finger as they start to protest; to advance an alibi. "You are the guilty ones. Eden didn't tell me this—Eden doesn't even know that I was told, nor was it his sister nor his grandmother. It was *Mrs. Eden herself!* Just this morning when I told her that I might permit you to see her, she became almost hysterical and begged me not to let you!"

Both started, and looked at each other, breath coming short.

"I can see that you're surprised, but I'm telling you only what she said; how she reacted to my mention of your names. She said: 'please don't let them come, Dr. My relapse was all their fault. I was doing all right and was so very happy after my husband got back and I had him and my baby both with me. I was so happy I didn't mind being sick at all and wasn't worrying over how soon I would be well again. And then they came. I saw evil in their eyes as they entered the door. They talked of love and doing so much for my own good—yet they hated my husband so much that they even hated the baby, our little baby. Then they started in and they lambasted my husband for everything they could think of; they called my baby a brat, and my own sister abused me because I didn't murder it before it was born. Oh, it was the worst thing I ever experienced. I suffered such mental anguish; I tried, like a wife, to stand up for my husband, but what chance did I have? Me weak, and sick and helpless against two of them, well and strong—and mean!'" He paused now while Terry and the Elder stood with bowed heads.

"So you see just how it stands."

"That was what *your own daughter* told me, not a half hour ago, and, according to her wishes, I shouldn't let you see her at all. But on talking with Eden, outside, he said that he didn't want to see you have to hang around here day and night without being permitted to see her. He said that if you'd promise me to keep your mouths shut while you were with her—not to even imply anything like you talked about, I might let you come Monday, so if you promise not to annoy her and set her back, I may then let you come to see her every day." They dared raise their eyes here and breathed a sigh of relief.

"I have a patient north of here who has a new baby, too, and then I have another about ten miles north of that one who also has a baby. So here's what I'm going to do:

"I'll take you with me and leave you with Mrs. Eden and let you stay with her until I return, in about two hours on the way back from seeing my other patients. Then I'll bring you back to town with me."

"Oh, thank you, Dr." said the Elder, profusely. "And I promise you—"

"I'm not exacting any promises. I'm exacting behavior. It isn't your fault that your daughter is alive today. You did more towards trying to kill her than having the baby by caesarian operation would do if she had a dozen children that way. So I'm not taking any chance with you or this daughter here until the girl is strong enough to walk."

"I swear, Dr., that we won't—"

"Just behave yourself every day until she's walking. That's all I'm asking and what I'm going to have as long as I'm her physician. Good day."

The Elder and Terry fell into each other's arms and gave up to their tears. They dried their tears presently, then bathed their faces quickly, when they heard a motor drive up and espied Olive getting out of the car to come for them.

They had a wonderful day at the school, where Barry took

them around and showed them the Indians, the way they lived and much that they could never have known except for such a visit. They stayed late into the night. Barry was from Kansas and knew many ministers that the Elder knew, and all the Bishops. They told Olive, at the hotel, that the Dr. would bring them out when he came to see Linda the next day and take them back when he completed his calls. So with a pleasant good night, Olive returned to the claim.

After the Dr. went north to make his calls, leaving Terry and her father with Linda, the Elder ventured out to the barn and corral, and finding Eden, sought pacification.

"Terry and I are very sorry for what happened the other day, son. We *were* excited when we arrived and was afraid that she might be dead."

"I appreciate how you were feeling," said Eden, continuing his work.

"Oh, thank you, my son, thank you; now I'll go inside and play with the baby. Will that be all right?"

"Oh, sure."

"And we'll be very careful regarding Linda."

"I'm sure you will. You understand, however, that you are responsible to the Dr."

"We understand. Well, I'll go now."

They violated none of the Dr.'s orders, and on coming in and checking her on his way back, the Dr. was relieved to see that their visit had no ill effects on his patient.

CHAPTER XXI

TWO WEEKS WENT BY. After the first week the Dr. relaxed and permitted the Elder and Linda to stay as long as they wished. Since the house was small, it was more convenient for them to continue to stay at the hotel in Carter. Olive would drive them in at night and the Dr. would bring them out when he came to make his call every morning.

At the end of three weeks Linda had recovered sufficiently to sit up and eat what she wanted. The baby was thriving, could laugh, lustily; knew most of those who came to see him, and everything was apparently serene and dandy.

The third Sunday, they had the Barry's down from the school for dinner and it was a most pleasant gathering of race people away out beyond where the masses of them lived.

On Monday, Eden consulted with the Dr. and informed him that he needed to go to Gregory County to prepare for the spring seeding and other important matters, and asked if it would be safe to leave Linda for two weeks.

"She'll be able to come out in the yard and meet you by the end of that time, at the rate she is recovering, so go ahead. If anything develops, which I can't see at this time, you'll be in touch with your home, so I'll wire you."

"Thanks, Dr." and Eden was relieved. He went into the house. They were gathered in the bedroom, the Elder playing with the baby, Terry talking of events back in Chicago with Linda. . . . All was well, everybody apparently happy.

"Well, folks," began Eden, "A man must eat, so must his wife and baby," and he looked from first one to the other with a happy smile. "So I've got to get my work under way."

"Of course, my boy, of course," said the Elder cheerfully.

"So I explained the matter to the Dr. just now and he told me that Linda should be well enough to walk in two weeks, and since I plan to be gone two weeks—"

"Two weeks!" exclaimed Linda from the bed. "But, Martin, dear! I don't want you to go. I want you to stay here until I'm well enough to go with you."

"Oh, precious, you must stay here. We've had such an awful time, moving and tearing up and all that. We're fixed well enough here for you to be comfortable now. So you must be a good girl, stay right here and continue getting well. Then in two weeks when I come back, the Dr. says you will be well enough to meet me outside, throw your arms around me and kiss me, standing up. Just think of that and what it'll mean to us all!"

"Yes, dear," she agreed, "but somehow, I don't seem to want you to leave me."

"Why, Linda, you know Martin has his work and yours and the baby's living to make," offered the Elder. "You must let him go, for he cannot neglect his work. That is important."

"Yes, papa, I understand that. Still, I wish he didn't have to go. I wish he'd stay here until I was well enough to walk, even if he couldn't take me and the baby with him."

"To hear you talk, Linda, one would think you were afraid of being—kidnapped," said Terry. "Father and I are staying two weeks longer, so that'll make it just right."

"Of course," chimed the Elder. "When you go outside to bid us goodby, you turn right around and welcome your husband."

"Sounds all right, but I just don't like to see him go away. I don't know why. He is often gone, and last summer I didn't seem to mind it at all, but now—"

"Well, you didn't have the baby last summer, Linda; this little lump of sweetness," said the Elder, pausing to kiss him fondly. "So that's what's making the difference. But Terry and I will be here with you. We'll look after you."

Martin walked over to the Elder and taking the baby, fondled it. It started to cry and Linda remarked:

"You see, even *he* doesn't want you to go away," which brought a laugh as Eden handed the baby to the mother and after kissing both again, and bidding all a fond goodby, left them. The Elder and Terry followed him to the door and waved at him as his wagons moved to the east, then, turning, met each other's eyes, and something passed between them. Linda, holding her baby and looking through the window, and waving at her husband, turned just in time to see it. She started; her smile died on her lips and she became cold with fear. She *had seen something!*

They started toward her room. In the few moments it took for them to get to her, she passed through a series of emotions. She had *seen something* in the exchange of that expression between her father and Terry; something that didn't bode her husband, not yet out of sight, any good, and through her mind flashed the question: *What kind of a man and a woman were her father and sister!* She sought to hide the fact that she had seen that subtle *something,* as they came up beside her, wearing smiles that seemed more like horrible sneers. She knew that something would start happening soon. What *would it be* and *how soon* would it start? She didn't have to wait long. She steeled her nerves for the worst. And then, on the spur of the moment, she decided to make one last try to save her home, to save the union of husband and wife. She turned as they came up, both on the same side of the bed this time. They paused and smiled down upon her, more a leer than a smile. She reached out and placing a hand on them, cried:

"Listen, father, and you, Terry. You mustn't be hard on Martin. He borrowed money to purchase and develop these lands. He's burdened with debt, it is hard and worries him. Honestly, he has the biggest heart and is as good to me as any husband can be, but he's loaded with debt and the strain on him is terrific. You must bear with him."

Knowing in her heart that whatever answer they might make, they didn't mean her husband any good. When she saw the leer become almost livid with rage and hatred, she almost swallowed her heart. With Martin gone, and her left at the mercy of these two, nothing but a miracle could save her. Her eyes, while she still tried to look up at them and into theirs for sympathy, half closed, hopelessly, and she waited for the worst.

"My daughter; my poor, Linda, darling," said her father, like the arch hypocrite he was. "Of course we will bear with your husband, with Martin, won't we, my dear?" turning to Terry who stood looking down with eyes that seemed to flash fires of hatred.

"Why of course we will, Linda. Of course we will bear with your husband."

They took seats now, deliberately, and made themselves comfortable.

"Being burdened with debt and worries, is, of course, his own fault," said the Reverend, adjusting himself for what Linda knew would follow—a lot of words. Her husband was gone now, but she could still hear the wagons in the distance.

"That is true, father, and he admits it." It was natural for her to try to defend him.

"Then why," chimed in Terry, "should he place the burden on you?"

"On me?" cried Linda, turning to her. "What burden on me? What are you talking about?"

"You've been forced to make many sacrifices, terrible sacrifices. And those sacrifices were all for him, were they not?"

"If I'm making any sacrifices, they are for us. That, then, is my duty and if it is, I don't mind it."

"Oh, we understand about that, all right," said the Elder, "Don't we, Terry, dear?"

"Why, of course, father. We understand everything, perfectly." Linda shifted hopelessly and looked at her little boy. Oh, if he were only older; big enough to go and call the next town through which Martin would be passing; call and leave word for him to come back home—to hurry—anything to save her; but she was still too weak to go anywhere; to leave the house.

Olive had taken Grandma and was gone up to her claim, and did not plan to return until the end of two weeks. That was to be in time to meet her brother when he was due back. Linda waited to see what they had planned.

"It is so unfair, and very thoughtless on his part, to make you put up with the crude life out here when you have such a comfortable home in Chicago. There you could recuperate in so much more ease, with so many more conveniences." The Elder looked around the room, a sneer on his face—it was akin to contempt and angered Linda, she shot back:

"I'm content to recuperate in all this—inconvenience which you imply, father. If it's a burden, it's *our* burden. We put ourselves in it and we're willing to put up with it." Her words were short, with an effort at firmness.

"My brave girl, my wonderful daughter," cried the Elder, "that's the right spirit; the kind of spirit to fight your battle with; the kind of spirit to have to win. We're proud of you!"

Linda looked straight at him, and he knew she was looking right through him.

"What're you trying to get at father? What's behind what you're talking about? You're not fooling me. I saw something in both your faces as you stood in that door, watching Martin start away. You don't mean him any good, now what's on your mind—speak up, tell me just what it is."

"Why, my baby, how can you say such things; how can you even imagine that I am thinking evil. Really, Linda, you're hard on your poor old father. I—"

"I'm not hard at all and please don't start crying." As Terry started to say something, raising a silencing hand, she cried:

"And please, Terry, and father, too, please don't tell me that you're planning to do something for me for my 'own good'. Anything, but not that, please."

"I was trying to compliment you for standing up for your husband. That's the wifely spirit. I'm happy to see my daughter so brave and resolute."

"There's more behind this; but until you show your hand, I'll say 'thank you, father. I'm very glad to hear you say that'. Now go ahead, please, and tell me what's on your mind."

"Well, Linda," interposed Terry at this point.

"All right, Terry, let's have it. I'm listening."

"Well, father and I had discussed the possibility of you taking a trip home, as quickly as you were strong enough, to stay until you have fully recovered."

"Oh, that's what *you and father* have been discussing. Did you talk it over with Martin?"

"Well, not exactly," cut in the Elder. "We were going to—in fact we wanted to; but in view of the unfortunate misunderstanding following our arrival, we were really—to be truthful, afraid to say anything to him about it."

"But he's hardly out of sight before you take it up with me, so what?"

"We thought," said Terry, "that we'd best talk it over with you first and then if you decided, we could let you take it up with Martin."

"I'll take it up with Martin when he comes back—in two weeks," said Linda, hoping that would be the end of it. Terry started to speak, but the Elder interposed:

"Now, Terry, Linda has spoken and said what she would do. Her husband is the boss, so let's go no further into it. Now let's leave Linda and her baby alone awhile and you and I take a walk across the prairies." The sun was shining brightly and the prairies, as all three looked out, seemed to shimmer, as they stretched almost endlessly in every direction.

Terry caught the hint and a few minutes later they were walking together, he and Terry, across the wild prairies.

"It really is a beautiful day, isn't it," began the Elder.

"It is," agreed Terry. "Truly a beautiful day, father." They approached a tall hill, that, in the center of Linda's claim, rose high above them like a slender mountain peak.

"That's a strange hill," said the Elder, pointing at it.

"Right in the middle of Linda's place, too."

"Almost in dead center, it spoils the looks of it, I think."

"I don't know what any of it is all about, I'm not a farmer and don't take any interest in farming, so I don't know whether it spoils the looks of her place or not. The whole country seems wild and worthless and desolate as far as I'm concerned."

"If you'd seen his places down in Gregory County, you'd understand what I mean. His lands there have no ugly hills, reaching high into the air like that," pointing again to the hill. "That is what I mean. This is all wild, while his places in the next county are either level or gently rolling, and with it all under cultivation, is so much more beautiful than this."

"Well, skip the hills and tell me what's on your mind. You didn't bring me out here to talk about that hill."

"No, of course not. I brought you out here to talk over some plan to get Linda away from here."

"You know how I feel about it. I'm with you in any effort to break him. It's unfortunate for anybody to hate a man as much as I do him, and because he's married to my sister, who is so much in love with him that she's blind, makes it more unfortunate."

"You shouldn't permit yourself to hate, Terry."

"That's why I'm so much like you."

"Our reaction to him is mutual, and I'll never be happy until I've made him suffer for the way he has treated me," said the Elder, his anger coming up. "What I have in mind is to get Linda away from here and to Chicago and give him a good scare."

"That'll scare him all right. He'll be afraid that he might lose some of this land and I can see him crawling to you on his hands and knees, begging you to let him have her back. When he does that, for her sake, I'll try not to hate him so much—but until then, I'm willing to go any limit to get even with him, regardless of the cost."

"Well, to put your deal over, we've got to be very clever. I believe she'll be well enough, regardless how the Dr. feels about it, to travel soon."

"But if he objects, and you try to over-ride him, he may wire Martin. It is Eden who is paying his bills you know, and if we start anything, we've got to see it through quickly, else we'll be messed up."

"I've thought of all that and here is my plan:" Altho' they were on the wide prairies, with nobody visible for miles, the Elder looked around, very carefully, before he started to explain.

When they returned to the house, they talked about what they had seen in walking over her claim; of the strange high hill, the weather, and then the subject of her going home was brought up again.

"Wouldn't you like to see old South Parkway and all the jitneys and cars and busses and Negroes milling up and down it? Go see some good pictures and a stage show down town now and then—and even go to one of the night clubs on Garfield Boulevard or State around 55th street, dear?"

"Why, of course, I would father. If we have a good crop this year, am sure Martin will take me and the baby to Chicago just before Thanksgiving and stay until after New Years'. That's the way he says he tries to do every year."

"But you need a trip sooner than that, sweetheart. Now if you could go to Chicago real soon—say in about ten days, for instance. You'll be well enough to travel in ten days, and that would seem to be the right time to go."

"In ten days! Oh, father, you can't do that. Surely you wouldn't think of such a thing. Take me away before Martin comes back—father, you *wouldn't* do that, surely you wouldn't."

"There, there, Linda, calm yourself and don't become so excited."

"But father," she cried, in a startled voice, fear gripping her vitals. "You—"

"Why don't you listen to what I'm trying to say first, Linda, before you go to getting all excited and trying to upset yourself."

"Why not let father tell you what he has on his mind, Linda," argued Terry. "He's your father. Do you suppose he's thinking about anything except something for your own good?"

"For my own good, for my own good! I told you never to say those words to me again—ever! My own good. You came near killing me when you first came, which was to be for 'my own good'—oh, God, have mercy on me!"

"Linda," cried the Elder, laying a hand on her and trying to get her to hush. "Will you please listen to what I have to say? Surely you can trust your own father; surely you can listen to what I have in mind?"

"I ought to, father, but—"

"Please be quiet then, Linda, for a few moments and hear what papa has to say."

"Now just be quiet a few minutes, dear, and I'll explain all about it." He paused, and as he did so, he changed.

"Now on second thought, suppose we forget all about making the trip, maybe, until Martin comes back."

"Oh, that'll be fine, father. I'm so glad you decided to wait, and, if you do, I'll—I'll ask Martin to—let me go," cried Linda, clasping her hands happily, as she finished.

Bowing and rising, the Elder continued:

"So you see, you were getting all excited for nothing. Why don't you put yourself in the hands of your old father, precious? You know how he loves you. You've always been my favorite daughter. You are all that I have to live for. Do you begrudge me some happiness while I'm with you?"

"Why, of course not, father." She held out her arms to him and he let her embrace and kiss him, then straightening to his six feet two:

"Well, it's time we all had something to eat. So, Terry, get off of it and let's go cook dinner." Unseen by Linda, he winked at Terry. She nodded back that she understood. After removing his coat in the kitchen, while Terry tied an apron around him, he said in an undertone:

"We started too soon after Martin left."

"We did." Terry was taking plenty of time to tie the apron.

"I saw that she was going to get all upset and would perhaps tell the Dr. about it when he came, and he'd get in touch with Martin right quick, see?"

"I'm listening. . . ."

"So I decided right quick, if you noticed, to wait awhile; until about the middle of next week, maybe."

"Go on, . . ."

"That Dr.'s costing Martin $6.00 a trip."

"Yes?"

"He was thoughtful enough to have Linda checked carefully before leaving, and the Dr. agreed to cut his visits to one every other day, starting next Monday."

"I've got you, Steve."

"According to that, he'd make his second trip about Wednesday. . . ."

"Yes?"

"I'll have things ready and on Thursday we're taking her and making our get away, get me?"

"Got you twice, father."

"Okeh. So mum's the word from now on. Say nothing more about it. Meantime, we'll soften her up, making over the baby a plenty, you understand?"

"My eyes as well as my ears are open. Am sorry now that I called it a brat when I came."

"That's hard for her to forget."

"Of course."

"Call it *our darling* from now on."

"Hey, why're you so quiet out there?" called Linda from the bed. "Talk loud enough for me to hear."

"We were playing," called Terry through the door.

"Playing?" came back Linda's voice. "Playing what?"

"Bean pie hot and bean pie cold, bean pie—" Linda cut her off with a laugh. Terry and the Elder exchanged glances.

"We haven't played that for years. I'd almost forgotten it."

"We had, too." called the Elder. "That's what we were doing. Saying it low to see if we could remember. Now we'll come back in there and see if we can remember it well enough to play it for you."

"Please do." To do so, they had to touch the palms of each other's hands. They had to stand close together and face each other. So at the foot of the bed, her father and Terry took up their stance and started:

"Bean pie hot—"

"—and bean pie cold—"

"Bean pie nice and—"

"—bean pie old—"

"—bean pie brown—"

"—and bean pie round—"

"That's wrong, Terry," cried Linda, holding up her hand. "You made a mistake. That line, the last line, doesn't go like that. Now come over here and let me play it with you." Linda prepared to have a little fun. Meantime, the Elder thought of something; something that he decided right quick to get off his chest. Telling his daughters to play the game between themselves, he put on his coat and went for a walk.

It turned out to be a longer walk than he anticipated. Having started, and feeling good, however, he wouldn't turn back. So he continued over the hills, which rose on the south and west of Linda's claim. The trail he took led through a valley, and then to a small house that stood behind some trees. A rare thing to see, were trees on the open prairies. On this claimstead lived a settler by the name of Hood whom he had met while exiling in Carter.

Hood had a car and made a side-line business of hauling

people to and from the railroad. He was home and when the dogs began barking, he came out of the house and greeted the Elder as he approached.

"I came to see if you could possibly make a trip to the railroad around, say, next Thursday. Have you anything booked for that date?"

"No, am sure I haven't, Reverend Lee."

"Well, if you can manage, don't book that afternoon. I've something coming up and may be able to use you that day. So if you don't have to lose any money by keeping that date open, save it."

"Okeh, Reverend Lee. Will I hear from you before then?"

"Drive by Eden's place about five o'clock Wednesday."

"Thanks, I'll be there. Good bye."

"Good bye, Mr. Hood." The Elder started away. Hood thought of something.

"Hey, Elder?" coming up to him on the run.

"I can drive you back to your daughter's claim if you wish me to. There'll be no charge for that."

"Thank you, Mr. Hood, but I feel like walking—in fact, I'm enjoying it."

"Well, I just happened to notice that you were, so I can give you a lift if you like."

"I'll walk, thank you." After a step, he paused. "Oh, pardon me, Mr. Hood," turning back and meeting him half way—"I just happened to think of something else."

"Yes, Reverend Lee," from Hood, looking up at what he thought the most extraordinary specimen of Negro manhood he had ever seen, one who impressed him very much.

"For reasons of my own, I'd appreciate it if you didn't say anything about my plans to use you next Thursday to anyone."

"I shall say nothing about it, Elder."

"Thank you. That is all." Then again, "Well, so long, Mr. Hood."

"So long, Dr. Lee."

When the Elder got back to the house, he found Terry in the kitchen. He laid a finger across his lips for silence.

"Father?" from Linda. "Is that you?"

"Yes, dear, it's me."

"Where've you been?"

"For a walk, sweetheart."

"For a walk? Where?"

"Over the hill, honey."

"Over the hill? What hill?"

He entered the bedroom, kissed her on the forehead, tickled the baby's chin, and Jr. laughed.

"You haven't said what hill, father?"

"Maybe the hill to the poorhouse." He laughed. "You're so inquisitive, honey. You've learned that from your husband."

"Have I?"

"You weren't that way before you married him."

"No, I guess not. Maybe I did. I'm learning lots of things from Martin."

"I'll say you are."

"He asks lots of questions," said Linda.

"He embarrasses people."

"Some people."

"Many people, I fear."

"I wouldn't say that. He doesn't seem to embarrass the people up here, the white people, I mean."

"No?"

"No. They seem to like it and ask him questions. Only Negroes seem to be embarrassed when he asks questions."

"It isn't right. People don't want you asking them all about their business."

"I'm afraid it's because they have no business is why they become embarrassed when Martin asks them questions about themselves. Many would have him think they're 'big shots' but when he questions them and they try to answer, it turns out that they are 'small time'. That makes them mad."

"Well, Martin has some funny ways. I could never ask people questions about themselves like he does."

"You and my husband are very different in almost every way."

"You think so?"

"I know so."

"In what ways, for instance?"

"Every way—there is no parallel."

"Well, do you mean to imply that he's smarter?"

"Not smarter, exactly. He's more exacting; more thorough. He likes to go to the bottom of everything in which he's interested. You don't. In fact, you like to take most things for granted."

"I don't like to meddle into other people's business, if that's what you mean," snapped the Elder.

"He doesn't meddle into their business. He only asks them questions that anybody can answer, and as I said, the white people seem to like to answer. They turn in then and ask him questions about himself, where he's from, what he is doing, et cetera."

"And does he answer them?"

"Oh, promptly. If he's fond of asking questions, he's even more ready and glad to answer them. Martin is a smart man, father. Everybody says so; by everybody, I mean the white people around here. It's only Negroes, Negroes who would like to have you think they are high and mighty, who don't altogether like him; who object when they are asked questions about themselves by him. If they were honest and truthful they wouldn't object. It's because they are not is where the rub comes in."

"Well, guess I'll get into the kitchen and help Terry with the dinner."

"A fine time to help me when I have it almost ready," came Terry's voice.

"I'm closing this door, Linda. I'm afraid the odor may make you cough and is not so good for the baby."

"All right, father. Meanwhile, step on that food. I'm feeling the pangs of hunger."

"Where were you?" from Terry in an undertone.

"Up to see Guy Hood about taking us to the railroad next Thursday."

"Yes?"

"Yeh. Everything's jake. He'll be by at five o'clock Wednesday afternoon, to find out if it's set."

"Good."

"Mum's the word. I asked him not to say anything about my plans, as I wasn't sure. He'll be afraid to, for fear he might lose the job."

"I get you."

"That's enough now. Remember."

"I remember."

Sunday night of that week, Linda had a strange dream. She dreamed that Martin came home that night and when she awakened the next morning, she reached out to touch him and he was not there. Only then did she realize that it was only a dream. She did some calculating. In seven days he would be home—one more week and her husband would come back to her and their baby.

She sighed and longed for him; but a week wouldn't be so long. She'd be patient and wait.

The Dr. came on Monday, again on Wednesday, and at five o'clock, Guy Hood came by. He blew his horn and Linda heard it.

"Who's that?" looking toward the window.

"I'll go and see," said her father, and went outside.

"Well?" asked Hood, as he came up.

"Right here tomorrow night at eight o'clock. Come prepared to drive to the railroad."

"Okeh, Elder." Then the Elder thought of something.

"Oh, by the way, Mr. Hood?"

"Yes, Elder," lifting his foot, which was about to step on the starter.

"I wonder if you'd do me a favor."

"I'll be glad to, Rev. Lee."

"Please drive to Carter and get me a quart of good whiskey."

"Sure."

"Here's $3.00, I guess that'll be enough. If they have Canadian Club, please get that."

"Canadian Club? Fine. I'll be back in less than an hour."

"I'll be waiting, Mr. Hood."

As the Elder walked back to the house, he was smiling. Linda would ask who it was and what he wanted. He hated that. It reminded him too much of Martin. Now she had his habit. No sooner had she heard his footsteps, than:

"Father?"

"Yes, dear?"

"Who was it?"

"Guy Hood."

"Guy Hood? What'd he want?"

"I had him go to Carter to get me some—whiskey?"

"Some whiskey, father? What'd you want with whiskey?"

"I feel that I'm going to have a cold."

"Oh, a cold. Well, whiskey might prevent it. I'm not used to you drinking whiskey."

"I'm not used to being out west. That's why."

"Well, I guess that's right. Lots of people drink whiskey out here who never would have thought of it back east."

"We'll have your dinner ready shortly, dear, so be quiet now while we dish it up. I'll bring it to you."

"All right, papa."

Terry had been standing waiting impatiently. She jerked her head toward Linda:

"Just like *him*—asking a thousand questions." He shook his head in disgust.

"I had Hood go to town and bring the whiskey," said he in an undertone, "so that I could have an excuse for him coming here. It occurred to me while I was out there that she'd ask me a dozen questions when I came in, so that was the quickest way I could think myself out. We may need the liquor, however, before we get out of this God forsaken country."

"I'm going to take a big drink of it myself as quickly as he gets back with it," said Terry.

"You?" looking at her in surprise.

"Yes, me. This place is enough to drive a woman to drink, even."

"You're telling me!"

"What time is he coming for us tomorrow?"

"Eight tomorrow night."

Terry sighed relief.

"The train leaves Winner at 11:30," said the Elder. "I didn't want to be hanging around there for hours."

"I understand."

"What're you all talking about out there?" called Linda.

"Dear, dear," cried the Elder, as he entered her room with her meal on the tray. "Can't we do a little talking between ourselves without worrying you with it?"

"Pardon me, papa. I didn't mean to meddle."

"You were not meddling; but sit up now and eat your supper, and quit asking so many questions."

"All right, papa," said she, and patted his cheek. "Please don't be mad at me."

"I will be if you don't get out of the habit of asking so many questions. I didn't raise you to ask questions, so I don't see why you got to get so far away from what I taught you."

"I'll quit asking so many while you're here, papa."

"And after I leave, I still want you to stop asking so many."

At this hour, Martin Eden and Bill had completed their work in Gregory County and with wagons, loaded, pulled away from his home place, heading for Dallas, nine miles away, to spend the night.

"If we get out of Dallas tomorrow morning early, we can

make Winner for tomorrow night, which will be Friday. Then instead of getting home Sunday afternoon, I'll pull in there Saturday around noon, and surprise my wife and the kid." So with the heavy wagons, loaded to the guards, they rumbled on toward Dallas, where they arrived in two hours and put up for the night.

They were delayed until noon the next day, leaving Dallas, but at seven o'clock at night, they were pulling into Colombe, nine miles from Winner, where he planned to eat, feed his horses and get out to Winner where they would arrive around ten thirty or eleven.

And at this very hour, seventeen miles northwest of Winner, pandemonium had broken loose.

"We're taking you away from here, Linda," said the Elder, firmly.

"Taking me away from where? Why? What do you mean? My husband will be back Sunday, what—"

"We're not arguing with you about your husband or anything. We're wrapping you up along with the baby and taking you out of this hell hole, so don't try to argue with us. We decided to do this immediately after that rascally husband of yours left. So we're pulling away from here within the hour, so just keep quiet while we get your things together. We're going and taking you with us!"

She observed that they had been quietly getting their things together during the afternoon, but remembered his lecture about asking so many questions, so had refrained from inquiring what it was all about. And now like a bolt of lightning out of a clear sky, she realized what they were up to. She was to be taken away—kidnapped, as it were, by her own father and sister.

"I won't go!" she screamed.

"You don't have to," said Terry, firmly, coldly. "We're taking you. You're sick you know, and we expect to carry you to the car, and aboard the train."

"I'll scream, I'll fight, I'll—"

"Then we'll tell them you are crazy and they will help us. This, as father says, has all been thought out in advance—even *before* that niggah of yours left. So don't try to stop us. We're doing it for your own good, so that is that."

It was all too sudden, too horrible—too everything, to even try to understand. Linda realized too late that she was helpless. There wasn't a thing that she could do. They were going to take her away before her husband could get back; she wouldn't be allowed to even leave him a note. She sighed, clasped her baby to her breast and prayed for a miracle to happen.

But no miracle came to Linda's rescue that night. As they had said, within the hour they were carrying her to the car, where she was bundled, wrapped in blankets, with her baby, in the back seat along with Terry, while her father sat by Hood. A few minutes later they were spinning down the trail that led to Winner and the railroad.

Arriving there, they went to a room in a hotel to wait until the train pulled out.

CHAPTER XXII

It was ten thirty when Eden and Bill pulled into Winner and stopped in front of the only livery barn left there. Long since garages had taken the place of livery barns, for the Auto had almost replaced the horse. But when a settler had horses and wagons, there was but one way to move them, and that was by driving them hitched to a load. One Livery barn was enough to take care of this trade in Winner.

With the horses up for the night, he was leaving the barn when he encountered a man he knew.

"Hello, Eden. How're you comin'?"

"Well, Joe, just so so."

"About to get settled up near Carter for good?"

"Yes, about to. Am trying to get home, to the wife and kid, by noon tomorrow."

"That's fine. Come to think of it, I read where you'd become a father."

"Yes. A man at last."

"At last, old boy. A guy can't call himself a real man until he becomes the father of a child, is what I say."

"I agree with you."

"Oh, by the way, Eden. This seems like a coincidence, but I just saw some Colored people drive into town about an hour ago." Eden started and his blood ran cold. Suspicion jumped into his mind.

"Yes?"

"Yeh. Guy Hood, who lives out North of Carter, drove them in."

"Is that so?"

"Yeh. There was a man and two women. One of the women seemed to be ill. I saw the man carry her into the hotel. I think there was a baby, too, and the other woman was carrying it."

Eden was chilled clear down to his toes. So the Elder and Terry were playing their hand—he cursed himself for ever having trusted them. His soul was on fire as he started away, then it occurred to him that he didn't know where they were. There were several hotels in the town. He turned back to Joe.

"By the way, what hotel did you see them going into?" he asked.

"The Ulmer."

"Oh, the Ulmer."

"Yeh. That's where I saw them go into, as I said, about an hour ago."

"Thanks, Joe. Think I'll drop by and see them. So long."

"So long, Eden."

By now he was burning with rage. At last he would assert himself. He would go to the Ulmer, pick his wife up, and with their baby, hire a car and drive straight back to her claim that night. Great beads of perspiration were standing out all over him. Tonight he would fight—if necessary, he would die! So he hurried toward the hotel.

When Reverend Lee deposited Linda and her baby, with Terry to watch after her, in the bedroom of the hotel, he chanced to walk down into the lobby. Here he lingered for a moment, then stepped out into the street and looked around. He hadn't decided which way to walk, when he heard two wagons. He looked quickly; then he sought the shadows. It was his son-in-law, Martin Eden, and his hired man, Bill, pulling into town. He was frightened. He trembled all over. If Martin heard that he was in town and learned the truth, he not only would take Linda away from him, but he would forbid her to ever have anything to do with him or the family again. But worse—he might *kill him!*

The wagons rumbled by. They drove about a block and

stopped in front of the livery barn. Then the Elder did some fast thinking. Hood was gone, so there was no way to escape by his car. He would be afraid to stay in Winner with Eden in town. *What was he to do?*

While standing there, trying to decide on a plan of escape, a taxi drove up and stopped by the curbing. It was a new car, and the duco paint glistened in the night. He found himself looking at the car.

"Taxi? Taxi, Mister?" said the driver—then a thought came quickly to the Elder's rescue!

He could use that taxi! thought he; he could use it *right away!* He stepped forward.

"I have some urgent business in—in" he couldn't think where, and was forced to pause and raise his hand to his chin to try think where.

"Colome, Dallas, Gregory?" suggested the driver.

"Gregory," he cried. "What'll it cost to go there?"

"Ten bucks to Gregory."

"How long will it take to drive there?"

"Aw, an hour, maybe. Of course, if that price is too high—"

"I'm not thinking about the price. Come with me and help me with my luggage. I have a sick woman. I want to get her to a—Dr. in Gregory."

"Yes, sir!" and in a flash he was out of the car and at the Elder's heels as he burst into the room where the women and baby were, half out of breath. He called Terry to one side, after asking the driver to excuse him.

"Eden's in town. Just happened to see him drive in when I went outside," he whispered, pausing for breath.

"No!" exclaimed Terry, frightened, too. *"What'll we do?"*

"Just hired this man to take us to Gregory. That's about 35 miles east. He'll get us there in time to catch the same train that'll leave here in an hour, see?"

"Yes, but—but if he comes here and finds we're—" The Elder started, then Terry laid a hand on his arm:

"Leave word with the clerk, if anybody calls, to tell them that we went back to the claim, see?"

"Fine, Terry! Now we must move fast. He may be down stairs by the time we get there, even!"

Giving the driver the luggage, the Elder picked Linda up in his arms, Terry took the baby and they hurried downstairs. Terry stopped at the desk.

"If anybody comes and asks for us, tell them that the—the sick woman took a relapse and we are driving her back to the claim, please."

"Very well, madam. Sorry."

"Thank you." In the car, the driver pulled out for Gregory, and they were gone.

A half hour later, Martin Eden called at the hotel and was given the message that Terry left with the clerk. He went back to the livery barn, sat alone in the office and thought some more. At this moment he heard the train that left at eleven thirty, pull out.

"Why would they go to the trouble to come away down here, then turn right around and go back?" he asked himself. He was not satisfied; it seemed so indefinite. Yet there was nothing he could do about it, so a half hour later he went to bed and arose early the next morning and pulled out for the claim.

Martin Eden was not superstitious and he didn't believe in dreams. Yet he had had the strangest dream the night before, which he kept thinking of as he rumbled on west to where he thought his wife and baby were waiting for him.

He had dreamed of Joe meeting him in some town, which was not clear, but Joe said to him in the dream the same things that he told him the night before. In his dream he went to the hotel, but they had not left. He found them there in a room. He did not pick up his wife and start back home with her, but he did talk to her. As he recalled the dream, he remembered the Elder coming to the door in answer to his knock. His jaw dropped and his eyes opened wide with fright when he saw that it was Martin Eden. He remembered standing for a moment looking the Elder straight in the eyes. Then he crossed to Linda where she was lying on the bed.

She was not well, he could see, and she was too exhausted to talk, to say much. The Elder and Terry slunk by the wall at the other side of the room, keeping their distance and saying nothing. Linda lay, her eyes half closed, with the baby by her, side, which he looked at and touched on the cheek. She opened her eyes, and looked at him dully.

"Oh, Martin, you."

"Yes, me, darling. I just happened here. I was on my way home. I was trying to surprise you by getting back a day earlier than I promised." Her answer was only a sigh, which was nearer to a groan, and she closed her eyes again.

"How is Junior?" said he, and touched its face with his finger again. She opened her eyes, weakly, tried to smile and looked down at it. The little one woke up then, and after a few mumbles, looked up at its father. His little eyes opened wide as if he recognized him. Martin reached down and picking him up, held him suspended.

"When he opened his eyes and smiled, and looked at me, he seemed like he wanted to say 'da, da'," said Martin, and both smiled happily up at it. After a spell he laid it down between them.

"So you decided to go home for awhile," said he, stroking her forehead.

"Yes, dear," she sighed weakly. "For awhile."

"I hope the trip doesn't set you back too much," said he, simply.

"I—I didn't want to go until—" she replied, but he cut her off to save her the effort of trying to talk.

"I got back, I understand, dear. I'm not criticising you, and you have my consent to go," said he.

"Thank you, darling." Her voice seemed hoarse and she coughed a little. He looked down at her and was worried. He was conscious that his home was being broken up, but he was powerless, it seemed, to do anything about stopping it. He was vaguely aware that Linda had nothing to do with it; that she had been taken from her home by virtual force. All this seemed clear as he dreamed it, yet he couldn't understand why he made no effort to step in—to do anything. After a time, he recalled that he sighed, and turning back to her:

"Have you any money, dear?"

"Yes, Martin. I got a check cashed."

"Oh?" His one word was a question. Then he went on: "How much?"

"Fifty Dollars," said she, and he started. "Was it—for—too much?" He relaxed.

"No-o. You'll need it."

"Are you—pressed, dear?" she asked, anxiously. He shrugged his shoulders.

"I've been pressed for so long now that I seem to stay that way to keep from having to get that way," he laughed, a weak hollow effort at a laugh, and turned back to the baby.

"You'll take good care of Junior?"

"Yes, dear, the best I can."

"And you'll write me as quickly as you are well enough to do so?"

"I will try to when I get there; I wish I could write you every day. As soon as I am well enough, I will. You must write to me, however, every day, Martin, every day."

"Not every day, my sweet. That will not be convenient. But I will write as often as I can."

"I—I want to come back as quickly as I am well enough. I hate to leave you, dear Martin. It seems—oh, that I—I have no feeling, somehow. Everything seems to be in a hub-bub; vague, strange, indefinite. I feel I'm in the toils of a terrible night mare. I see you, yet, yet—" and then she was quiet. She lay with eyes half open, gazing at nothing, like a person who has died. He placed his hand on her forehead. This seemed to revive her and she looked up at him, oddly.

"Please be quiet and try to remember that the main thing is to get well."

"I—I am not ill, physically, but I'm awfully sick, mentally. I think it must be because they are taking me away, away from you, Martin, dear, and I don't want to go—I don't want to go!" She started crying. He found her kerchief, damp from the tears she had already shed.

"I can't leave you out here alone, Martin. I'm your wife and you need me. I don't want to go, I want to stay here by your side. You need me, you need your wife. I—"

"Quiet, dear and take it easy. Just quit trying to think and forget everything until you are well and strong again."

"But I can't get you out of my mind, Martin, you and what is happening to me. You don't seem to understand. I am not going on a visit. They're taking me away from you, don't you understand, Martin? They're taking me away from you and I can't stand it. I don't want to go. I'd rather die here in your arms than to let this happen to us—oh, Martin!" He had to take her in his arms and hold her close until she had become calm again.

"Quiet, dear, and take it easy. Don't get yourself all worked up like this."

"Oh, Martin, I feel just like I want to die."

"But you must not let yourself feel that way. You have so much to live for, precious—everything. Think of Junior, here, our son—our own darling little baby. Think not so much about me, for I am well and strong and can manage and will get along. Think only of Junior, and take good care of him."

"All right, Martin, I shall try to do as you ask me. You are both mine, and for you two I shall go on trying to live, but it is so hard, dear, and is not right that I should be taken away from you when I don't want to go."

"There, there, precious, everything will be all right. I must go outside for awhile now, but I'll come back and help you on the train, so try to go to sleep now and forget about everything."

His dream continued. He remembered going outside and walking around. He thought of Deborah, and of her warning of the evil things to come in his life, and they *had* come. Yet, Linda was his wife and she had born him a son. This was his life; his destiny was ahead of him; he had to endure his troubles.

Somewhere he remembered stopping, and a soft prairie wind was blowing, which was soothing to his burning brow. Then he tho't on. This time it was of a tall, powerfully built, dark man, whose head was almost as white as snow. By his side walked a woman, her eyes burning with hatred, a tall slender, brown woman. Then he recognized them as the Rt. Reverend Dr. Lee and his daughter, Terry Glavis, both arch enemies of his. The man with the massive pompadour, a fine head of hair which had almost completely turned white, posed as a disciple of the Christ who was the son of God. And Martin Eden was he whom the Gods would destroy. His head ached so badly that he laid his hand on his forehead, and cried out:

"Oh, God, what have I done that all this suffering should be heaped upon me?"

He remembered staggering through the darkness of the night until he got back to the hotel to assist his wife to the train,—then of a sudden he woke up.

Half way to his claim, he met the Dr., driving furiously. He stopped the car quickly and cried:

"Your wife, she's gone! I was there and the house is empty, deserted. They have all gone, your father-in-law and your wife's sister, they have all gone."

"Yes, Dr. They *have* gone and have taken my wife and baby with them," said he, sadly, for after he lived again through the dream, he concluded that he had been the victim of a hoax, and wasn't expecting to find her there when he got to her claim. He only *hoped* that he would. The Dr.'s words had destroyed that hope, so he became quickly resigned to what had happened. It was the tragedy in his life that Deborah had said would come!

"But—the girl, she—"

"Take it easy, Dr., and try to forget. They—her sister and father, they hated me. They have always hated me so much—and I don't know why, that they would almost murder her to injure me. So they're doing this to me because they despise me and want to injure me all they can."

"I never heard of such a thing in all my life—and such people." The Dr. placed a hand on Martin's shoulder. "I'm sorry for you, Eden. God knows I am. I'm sorry for your wife, too. She loves you .dearly, passionately. When she is well enough, she'll leave them, come back to you and bring her baby with her."

"Thank you, Dr., I'll try to endure, and I hope she will come back."

"She will—she must," and with another kind word and a pat on Eden's shoulder, the Dr. continued on his way, while Eden rumbled onward to her claimstead, with his heavy wagons, loaded with other goods necessary for the development of the land, and to make the house more comfortable—the house which was a home no longer.

CHAPTER XXIII

AT HOME, IN CHICAGO, the Elder and Terry went to work at once on Linda, to "change her over." "Poor Linda," as had been the case during the Elder's visit in the west the fall before, had the alternative of giving in to them, or being driven crazy, trying to stand by her husband and uphold him. So she chose, suffering agonies the while, to follow the line of least resistance.

Terry set herself up as a censor and when Linda poured out her heart in the first letter to her husband, Terry read and promptly destroyed it right before her eyes.

"Now write another, this time the kind you should. We're looking after you from now on. You will write him the right kind of letter; the kind that will bring him to his senses. So while I dictate, you write it."

Linda wrote the words Terry dictated. She knew that Martin, when he received it, would know it was not from her heart. She knew he would see that Terry had dictated it; but she had the choice of doing what Terry said (in which her father concurred) or of being driven to insanity, trying to be faithful to Martin.

Matters settled down to a routine. The Elder went back to his charges in Southern Illinois, leaving Terry on guard, with instructions to "look out for Eden."

He came. In two weeks. He knocked on their door. Terry answered and on seeing him, cried:

"You can't come in here!" and promptly slammed the door in his face.

Linda, who was sitting in an easy chair upstairs, holding Junior, heard it and called:

"Who was it?"

"Your niggah," said Terry, shortly.

"My—my—what?" shrieked Linda, her mouth wide open, her eyes bulging until they would seem to leave their sockets.

"I said, your niggah," repeated Terry. "That *thing* you married and dare call 'husband'."

"Oh, my God, my God, my God!" moaned Linda, and seemed on the verge of fainting. Terry held her up. Her mother rushed in and cried:

"Quick, Terry, get some water! I'm afraid she has fainted. She might even die." Mrs. Lee, tears flowing, tried to comfort Linda, but was so nervous she was not much help. Terry returned with the water and they gave her a drink.

"Please—please, mother, take Junior and care for him and put me—put me to bed. I—I can't stand it—I can't stand it!"

In bed a few minutes later, she whispered, sadly:

"Oh, mother, isn't it awful—awful!"

"Yes, Linda, it is. Oh, I'm so sorry. If Martin had only been at home when the baby—"

"We have been over that time and time again, mother. Martin committed no crime; storms and accidents overtook him and he couldn't help it, I've explained all that over and over again."

"I know you have, sweetheart; but it was his failure to be there that gave them the excuse to bring you here—at least the excuse to go out there."

Linda sighed. "It didn't give them any excuses after that. All that has happened since is their doings. To think, my poor husband, knowing the letters Terry made me write, were not my letters, left his work and came all the way here—to have Terry slam the door in his face! Oh, God will punish my father and Terry for all this. Just as surely as they have done it unto my husband and me, surely will the lord do it unto them."

"Shut up all this noise about something being done unto us," said Terry, walking up. "You know how I tried to prevent all this from the beginning. If you'd listened to me then, none of what you're going through now could have happened."

"If I had listened to you, I wouldn't be married to my husband, if that is what you mean?"

"That's exactly what I mean."

"The fact that I love him, am satisfied with him in every way, have a baby and love it, means nothing to you at all?"

"Nothing."

"Nothing at all. Then, when Martin calls on the phone or dares try the door again, won't you tell *him* that? You don't dare, because then he would go to the courts, seek a—a—you know what that writ is called, that makes people deliver others—that's what *I* mean."

"Since you *would* marry the niggah, and you have that—"

"Please don't say it again. Please don't say that, Terry, and hurt me more, unless you want to injure me unto death—make me suffer even more than death itself, for death is final. It ends all things. We grieve a little while and then we resign ourselves to the inevitable. From death we know there is no escape, no return; but as long as there is life, there is feeling and I still have some feelings, Terry. So please don't call my baby a brat again."

"I'll spare you that, but you got some of that from Martin."

"Maybe I did."

"But *we* knew you before *you met him* and *we* know you best. *We know you well enough to realize that you are going to let us handle this 'affair' of yours from now on!* Now what I started to say when I was so ruthlessly cut off and 'lectured'—was, that *we are going to let the niggah—yes, I want to call him the lowest and worst name I can think of* and referring to him as 'niggah' pleases me. We are going to make him sweat plenty before he gets you back. So let me have my say.

"We are not planning to keep you away from him for good. But we intend to keep you here until he comes to *us* and makes his peace. He is going to come to *us on his knees* and beg *our* forgiveness and then we—"

"—which is what *he'll never do!* Never until the longest day he lives, I live, you live—never!"

"That's what *you* think."

"Not what *I* think. What I *know!*"

"Oh, what does what *you* think, and even cry that you *know* matter? I say, that niggah'll come to papa and me on his hands and knees, and crying like a baby, beg us to let him have you back. He won't do it because of you, oh, no. We say that he loves Jessie Binga, nobody else; but he loves land and riches better. To get that old land you have, back, is why he'll come to *us*, because only through you can he have it back."

"You are the meanest woman that God ever created; that he ever put breath into."

"I am *your sister*, who loves you, who is doing all this for you—"

"Go on."

"Just as sure as you're lying there in that bed, this darky'll come around and do what we demand that he do, before we'll consider letting him have you back," said Terry, full of confidence.

"That would give you great pleasure."

"And father, too,—especially, father."

"And because neither of you know the mark of a man."

"Don't call that darky a man; call him by his right name," snapped Terry.

"His right name is Martin, and just as true as you are sitting there, I'm telling you that you may even destroy Martin Eden as you have broken his heart, broken up his home, you'll never humiliate him; you will never hear a word from his lips that even borders on appeasement. Do with me as you wish, but you'll never bring him to his knees before you."

Terry rose to her feet. The persistence with which Linda held out about what Martin would never do, began to annoy her.

Glavis was a hen-pecked husband; but he was not a malicious

man. Through Terry, the Elder could persuade Glavis to do certain things that Glavis would rather not do; but they feared to try enlist his direct aid in their fight on Martin Eden.

Nevertheless, Glavis could be used as a "means to an end—their end!" Going downstairs, Terry phoned him at where he worked.

She told him that Eden was in town, and that her father had left strict orders that he was not to be permitted in the house without the Elder's consent.

"Don't you think, Terry, that you and your father are going a bit too far—a lots too far?" he started to protest.

"Now, Glavis, neither my father nor I have any intention of keeping Linda away from her husband, permanently. But you know what happened to make us have to go out there and bring her home."

Glavis, listening, his face annoyed, didn't know all the truth about this; only as they had related it. He *did* know, of course, that they had received a telegram, and had rushed to South Dakota. So he listened to Terry's plan, since he had her word that they did not intend to deliberately separate a man and his wife.

"The Negro, as you know, is crazy to get rich. He'd do anything for money. Now since Linda *would* marry him, has this baby and is crazy about him, we plan to make him worry some and get afraid before we give her back. You understand?"

"Yes, I understand, Terry, but you're playing with fire."

"Will you shut up and listen to what I have called you to say?"

"O, all right, Terry. Now exactly what do you want *me* to do? I certainly don't want to be asked to do something that Eden can blame me for, later. I hope you'll respect that. I consider Eden and Linda's business their own, and I'd rather not go having anything to do with it, one way or the other. But go ahead, what is it you were starting to say?"

"I just wanted to tell you that I'm expecting him to call Linda on the phone, and as Linda is still sick, I'll have mother answer and tell him to call you, see?"

"Go on, I'm listening."

"When he calls you, you are to tell him to call you again when you get home, understand?"

"No, I don't. Why can't I tell him if he does call me, to call Linda. I don't want to be meddling in this man's affairs and you know it. You—"

"Will you please hush and promise to do what I am asking you?" she shrieked. He had been called to the phone at an officer's desk, who had much use for his telephone and couldn't have it tied up indefinitely. So with a "Pardon me, please," to the man sitting there, forced to listen, he had to reluctantly agree to her demands—and went back to his work.

As Terry suspected, Eden, after going to a restaurant and having a bite to eat, called his wife at the Lee home. Terry had her mother answer, standing over her as she did so. The mother, ever subservient to the will of her husband and Terry, did as instructed and told him to call Glavis.

Eden called Glavis, who told him to call him at his home about seven that night. He was relieved that Eden did not go into any long colloquy over the phone.

At home that night, he listened with a frown on his face, while Terry explained her plan to have him invite Eden to the house the next evening for dinner. As Terry outlined it, it seemed fair enough to him. When Eden called at the appointed hour, he was a bit surprised to be invited to the Lee home the next evening for dinner.

"Now, my dear. Although Linda seems to be recovering very satisfactorily," said Terry, fixing at her husband's collar and tie, lover like, "she isn't really well at all and should have the attention of a specialist."

"What for?" cried Glavis, threatening a revolt. Although he was "going along" for the sake of peace in the family, he saw that it was a plan to humiliate Martin, and as he reckoned, correctly, Eden would never accept humiliation. Though he was married to what he often, in moments of anger, thought of as a "creature," he could be cajoled, so Terry proceeded:

"Will you please listen to and do what I ask you to, my husband?"

"Oh, well," with an impatient shrug of his shoulders, "now what?"

"I simply want you to say that we think Linda should have the attention of a specialist. Then give him the impression that it will not be best to keep Linda sitting up long. In other words, papa and I want to manage this so that he will be more careful with her, when we let her go back to him. But we want it managed so that he won't know when that will be. . . . We feel that if we can have our way for a little while—"

"—you'll break them up completely. Whether you feel that way or not, I'm telling you that you're playing with fire, trying to adjust Linda's and Eden's marriage to your way of thinking. You don't know men well enough, because you've always made them do as you wanted them to, else they had to quit coming, and father is almost as bad."

"Well, then, what?"

"I mean that Martin Eden is a man of his own convictions; I don't think he's as crazy to be 'rich' as you and father think he is. My opinion is that you could make him lose everything he's worked for and he would take it on the chin without a flinch; but he's not going to let you and father humiliate him, regardless how you handle this."

"Well, Mr. Smarty, will you or will you not, do what I ask?"

"I will do it on condition that I don't have to be responsible for what happens. I'll tell him what you want me to about the specialist; I'll imply that it will not be best for Linda to sit up too long after the meal, which, as I can see is an invitation for him to leave—early."

"Yes?"

"Yes," said Glavis. "And then it will be up to father and you to carry on your dirty work. If you promise to leave me out of it from then on, I promise to go that far—but no further."

"I promise, my husband," said she, sarcastically, and followed him with her eyes, wearing the same expression, when with a grunt of disgust he turned and went across the room for his pipe. Terry went to Linda's room and sat beside her sister on the bed.

"Now," as she took the seat beside Linda. "I have arranged to let your husband come to the house tomorrow evening for dinner." Linda listened without enthusiasm. Since Terry had said that she didn't intend to keep her away from Martin forever, she decided to do just as Terry wanted her to—until she got back with her husband! And, then, until the longest day she lived, she would never again, subject herself or her husband to the will of her father or Terry.

She listened patiently while Terry went on:

"Since I am doing all this for your own good, although you persist in being ungrateful, and don't believe me, I must ask you, if you want to go back to him very soon, to let me handle it as I see fit for the present."

"What do you want me to do now?"

"Just restrain your emotions and not start any argument when he comes tomorrow. You may, of course, return his kiss and let him hold the baby."

"Then what?"

"Sit beside him and eat your dinner and still restrain your emotions."

"I'm listening."

"You should be checked by a good physician, to see what

condition you're in at this time. Glavis will suggest that at dinner, and imply that you should not sit up long after you've eaten.

"Which is his invitation to leave."

"Well," said Terry and Linda knew what she meant.

Accordingly, Eden came to dinner; he kissed his wife, who restrained her emotions. He was allowed to hold his baby and play with it until dinner was served. He was seated by his wife at the table, by Glavis, who did what Terry asked him to when the meal was over, viz.: suggested that Linda should be checked by a specialist, whom they knew that Eden would send to the house next day.

After the meal, Glavis told Linda that she shouldn't exert herself by sitting up too long. Eden caught the hint and in a few minutes, kissed her good night, promising to send a good doctor on the morrow, which, of course, he did.

Terry persuaded Linda not to seem too well when the specialist (a Colored one who could use Eden's money) came. He went through the process of examination and found, of course, that he should come again. When he came again he announced that he should give her a series of checks (and pile up as big a bill for Martin to pay as would be possible).

Terry waited impatiently. She was expecting Eden to call and beg to see her. She expected him after this, to say a lot about how wrong he had been; to fall upon his knees and beg her forgiveness, in answer to which she would tell him that he would have to make his peace with her father. But if he asked her that, would she agree to forgive him? She would say yes to that. Terry waited. But nothing like this happened, as Linda predicted. All that happened was that Eden called after two days and asked if he could tell his wife and baby goodbye, as he was returning to Dakota that night—and that was all!

Terry was surprised—taken aback. "The fool!" thought

she, almost aloud. He had put her on the spot. She had been sure that Eden would come to her and beg her to give him his wife back. Now, before she could formulate any new plan, Eden had called. He kissed his wife good-bye without any any sort of appeal to Linda's emotion, and returned to South Dakota, leaving Linda and her baby on their hands to be taken care of.

CHAPTER XXIV

BACK ON THE ROSEBUD, Martin hired a mighty steam tractor, drawing twelve plows to turn the soil on his sister's and grandmother's places upside down. To do this he had to supply the fuel, to be hauled from Winner. His sister and Grandma provided the men their meals and in two weeks, that which had been a wild prairie since the beginning of time, lay black, with the grass surface upside down. Flax, seeded in the black, dull earth, sprouted and commenced to grow. This work not only absorbed his time, his energy, but it also took every dollar that he could beg, borrow and steal, had there been any place to steal any.

Anyway, it so depleted him financially that he had no money to send Linda. Terry, who had looked for these letters with their usual money order began to fret.

"Why doesn't he send money to take care of his wife and kid?" said she, fretfully.

"Why didn't you leave them up there where he'd *had* to take care of them? Then you wouldn't be so disappointed when you fail to find money in his letters," countered Mrs. Lee.

"The dirty rascal isn't even writing her very often any more—the nerve of him!"

"Why should he? You and your father 'took over,' as the gangsters say, so they're *yours* and *his* burden now, not Eden's," argued Mrs. Lee, which made Terry boiling mad.

"She's his wife—he married her; he gave her that child. He should send money here to feed them, to buy them clothes and medicine. He knows what it takes to take care of a woman and a kid. Glavis doesn't make enough to do it, neither does father, so what's the matter with him?"

286

"You," said Mrs. Lee, calmly.

"Me? What do you mean by 'you'?"

"Just what I say, *You.*"

"Will you please explain, mother, exactly what you are talking about?"

"I mean that you meddled into your sister's married life, stole her and brought her here away from her husband. You refused to give them half a chance to even talk privately together when he was here. You have stood in their way at every turn, so now it looks like he has decided to let you two take care of her. That's what I mean when you ask what the matter is with him. The answer is, as I said, you."

"Ah!" she screeched, throwing her hands into the air and walking the floor faster. After a time she paused and thought a moment, then turning, looked straight at her mother and cried:

"I know what I'm going to do!"

"What?"

"I used $6.00 of my husband's $22.00 salary last week on her and that kid. She needs more this week than she did last and I thought that nigger she's married to would send it."

"But he didn't."

"I can't afford to use any more of Glavis' money on her. Father's got to put it up."

"He hasn't gotten over the expense of the trip. It'll take him six months to get caught up on that alone. Please don't ask him for anything. If he sends it, I won't be able to eat."

"Well somebody's got to provide Linda's keep—so who's going to do it, unless it *is* father?"

"Ask somebody else. I'm sure I don't know."

"Well, I'm going to write to father—tell him just what a burden she is on Glavis and me. He'll have to do something."

In Southern Illinois, Reverend Lee found a letter waiting

for him when he reached Carbondale on Saturday, for his quarterly conference there on the morrow. He saw that it was from Terry, and sighed before opening it. He dreaded to get letters from his home any more.

Like Terry, he'd begun to realize that things had not worked out as they expected. Martin Eden had come and gone back to Dakota, leaving his wife and baby for them to take care of. And he was not able to take care of the burdens of home very well, without having a married daughter and a baby thrown upon him. His life of bluff was being called. He had, in running away with his daughter, "dished it out" a plenty in taking her away from her husband and home. Now he was being forced to "take it" and it wasn't pleasant.

He was called home, commanded by Terry, to please be there by Tuesday. It was about Linda and her baby. When he went home, he recalled, unhappily, he was supposed to bring money—and his "pickings" had been poor. He had tried to argue, to the contrary, while in Dakota, with Eden, who insisted that Negroes were "small fry" and would keep anybody depending on them, on the "ragged edge"—and now that was right where he was!

That Sunday Mrs. Dewey came to the house to see Linda and the baby. She'd heard all about the "kidnapping," and was not surprised. She had often delighted in telling the Elder to his face that he was an "awful sinner" and "would burn in hell some day."

"Well, Linda. You married Martin. What're you doing here—staying here so long?" she asked, when they were seated close together on a couch. The baby was at their feet in the rumble that Terry had been forced to pay $6.00 for the week before.

"Ask Terry; ask my father."

"M-m. But Martin married *you*. He didn't marry Terry nor Glavis and he didn't marry your father."

"I was sick when they brought me home and my husband was away. . . ."

"Meaning that you couldn't help yourself and your husband being away, he didn't know?"

"That was how."

"Is your husband providing for you?"

"He was before he came here."

"Oh, he was *here!*"

"Yes, didn't you know?"

"I didn't, Linda."

"They only let me see him twice; just for a little while, and then never alone."

"Isn't that a shame—a shame before God."

"I'm awfully unhappy."

"You must be. Well, since he went back, what's happened?"

"He—he doesn't write much any more." Linda was nearing tears. Mrs. Dewey shook her head sadly. She didn't like Linda much because she had ways so much like her mother. But now she forgave her those ways and felt sorry for her. She reached in her purse and finding a $5.00 bill, handed it to her.

"Oh, Mrs. Dewey, as badly as I need it, I can't accept it."

"I understand all about the mess you're in, so keep it. Terry and your father have been allowed to have their way, which is not working out, I can see, as they thought it would, and you and this darling little one are caught in the middle." She reached down and picked up the little fellow.

"Just like his father."

"Everybody says the same thing."

"And them old mean people done took you away from your da, da!" she said playfully.

"What's his name?"

"Guess?"

"Martin Junior."

"Why, Mrs. Dewey. You guessed it. How did you?"

"It was the only one you could have given him to fit."

"I named him before his father saw him."

"He's a darling. I bet Martin's crazy about it."

"Worships him."

"And can't have him nor his wife. Now listen, Linda, say nothing about that money I've just given you. If I find you have, I'll not give you any more. I think I understand why Martin isn't sending you any, and I don't blame him. He's doing just right and I know all about the angle here at home." After a pause to think.

"When's your father coming home?"

"He's due in tomorrow night."

"Tell him I want to see him when he comes in. Tell him to come and see me Tuesday afternoon."

"I'll tell him, Mrs. Dewey." At the door, Mrs. Dewey kissed her, continuing:

"Tell him that I said to just come on over, get there about two o'clock; not to bother about calling, don't waste a nickel, to just come on over."

"Allright, Mrs. Dewey. Good bye."

"Good bye, my child."

The Elder returned to Chicago, arriving Monday night as he wrote he would. He heard the bad news from Terry, and together they indulged in laying Eden out, but not for long, nor was the laying out they gave him very convincing. The shoe was on the wrong foot; was too tight, and was hurting.

When they came downstairs, and he was alone, Linda approached timidly and told him what Mrs. Dewey said.

"What does she want?" he asked, impatiently. Nothing was a pleasant subject with the Elder these days. His judgment of everything was bad and he was missing, it seemed, everything that he tried to shoot at.

CHAPTER XXV

"So you've been at it again, eh?" said Mrs. Dewey after she had greeted the Elder, made him comfortable, cleared the decks for action and sat down to face him. He knew she had "something on her chest," so he looked across at her with a slight frown.

"At what again, Ida?"

"Don't try to look so innocent, Newt Lee. You can't fool me because I know you."

"Well," and he tried to appear indignant.

"I know that you and Martin Eden are not setting well; knew you wouldn't from the beginning. He, with his practical slant on life and you with your make believe, bluff and pompousness, that has carried you along, were destined to disagree from the beginning, but—"

"Why, that sonofabitch," cried the Elder, springing to his feet, as mad as a hornet! "That dirty sonofabitch. I'm sorry I didn't kill him, shoot him dead when I had a chance, the dirty sonofabitch!"

"So you've been getting 'religion' since I saw you last."

"Dirty sonofabitch," the Elder kept on saying. He had risen and was now walking the floor impatiently.

"You went out there and got to meddling in Linda's business; doing something for 'her own good' and got in trouble. Now he isn't kicking in with the dough, so you've got the precious daughter that you 'love' so much on your hands to take care of while you 'get even', and the shoe's pinching your foot, eh?"

"Damn him, God-damn his soul!" sang the Elder, continuing to walk the floor, his rage all out of bounds. He presently stopped in front of her.

"I've got my pistol loaded, Ida, and if I see him again, I don't care where it is, I'm going to aim it straight at him and 'doi, 'doi, 'doi!" imitating the sound of a revolver exploding, "straight into his head, his heart, his belly, the dirty sonofabitch!"

"He was too busy to 'praise' you, eh, to flatter you; to make you think that you were a 'king,' and that was how it all started; started before he married the girl." She continued tauntingly. "A king without a throne. It's time, therefore, Mr. King, for you to abdicate."

"It's a lie! I'm not vain. I've never sought praise and flattery. It's not so."

"Of course you haven't, dear. You've simply demanded it, but, of course, you'd never admit it. You've never admitted a mistake yet—according to your philosophy, you couldn't make one. Yet you've made a big one this time, a colossal one, and it's eating you and you 'can't take it'." She was the one person who could speak her mind to the Elder or Terry, and not have to be crucified for doing so.

"He neglected Linda. He would have let her die out in that wild country, but for me rushing there and saving her."

"Went out there and abused her husband, when his back was turned, so violently the Dr. made you go to town and stay in the hotel." He stopped short, and looked at her.

"How'd you know that—that is, how'd you know we stayed at the hotel? Who's been talking?"

"You made a crime of Martin's misfortune in not being home when the child came. The Dr. wired you, because he didn't understand, and this gave you the excuse you'd been waiting for, praying for. So you went out there and 'started to work.' But you were overly anxious. Then to actually save the girl's life, they had to rush you two niggers off to town, put you up in a hotel and keep you there so that the poor child *could get well!*"

"It's a lie—Martin Eden's lie! Who told you all this, anyhow?" puffing with embarrassment.

"Wouldn't you like to know," she went on, more tantalizingly now than ever.

"He must have told you when he was here—sounds like something he said."

"Sounds like the truth, that's what you mean. You and Terry had it all figured out. All you needed in the beginning was an excuse. The telegram provided that. After arrival there, you set to work at once and almost drove the girl crazy in two hours. Then they threw you out of the house and only let you come to see her after two weeks, and then for only two hours a day. They only did this when you promised to be good and behave like a good little boy—until Martin turned his back and had to go away to work."

"It's a lie, I tell you—a lie! And that sonofabitch told you; but I won't listen to it, do you hear, I won't listen!"

"Oh, yes you will. You're going to listen to all I've got to say, and that's a plenty. You've committed the greatest travesty on your own daughter—and all out of spite and meanness—that has ever been committed on a woman in all the history of devils like you."

"He's a scoundrel! All he's thinking about is money; the man's gone crazy trying to get rich. He—"

"And you've gone crazy, trying to 'get even.' Better that a man lose his mind trying to achieve material possession, than to lose it trying to hurt other people like you've done. And now you try to put the blame on the one you've tried so hard to injure."

"I say that it's a lie, a bare faced lie! All I did was to try to save my daughter's life."

"Well, *you have her here on your hands now.* You brought her back after stealing her like a kidnapper while her husband was out trying to make her a living."

"That's another lie," he screamed. "Another lie!"

"Was Martin home when you left with Linda and the baby? Answer that question and quit trying to make all that you did out a lie. I asked you if *Martin Eden was home* when you brought Linda away?"

"I won't answer," he dodged. "It's none of your business. I—"

"You mean you *can't* answer; that you don't dare answer because *you know he wasn't*. Of course, you were doing all this for the 'girl's own good.' Well, you've had your way, so what are you squawking so loud about?"

"He's left her on our hands, he—"

"*Left* her? Did he *bring* her there?" she stuck her face into his as he came striding by like a big, bad wolf.

"Will *you* quit asking me such confounded questions!" he cried, stopping to stamp his number thirteen foot.

"Will you quit trying to stall through all the devilment you've done and quit trying to put it on the victim of your perfidy? Will you quit trying to pass the buck and sit down there and talk sense and admit the truth, so I can see if I can help you out of the mess?"

He paused, his breath coming short.

"Well, what do you want me to do? What do you want me to say?"

"Nothing. Just sit down there and listen to me."

"Oh, all right," and still breathing deeply, sank back upon the chair. She resumed her seat in front of him.

"First I've got to tell you why you're so mad," whereat he sat quickly erect. She pushed him back.

"Take it easy, please, and listen to me. I can't do you any good until you acknowledge the truth, if you have to by just being quiet and saying nothing. Now.

"You and Terry stole her out of her home and came tearing in here, thinking that Martin would soon follow her; you were right, for he did. You wanted him to be like you are, a hypocrite, and come kowtowing to you, begging your forgiveness

for something he hadn't done. If you had ever tried to understand men, you'd have known that neither he nor any man,
would ever do that. But you've been able to threaten and scare
poor helpless preachers all your life, and if they didn't do as
you wanted them to, you'd 'fix' them. You've 'fixed' a many
a one. So you were out to 'fix' Martin Eden. You were unable
to understand or appreciate that there was as much difference
between Martin Eden and the preachers you've been kicking
arou. 1 for thirty years, as there is between day and night,
so you blundered. That's why you've been cussin' like a sailor.

"Now what you are so mad about is that Martin Eden came
here. You had Terry run him out of the house, refuse to let
him see or be alone with his wife. As I said, you were bent on
being appeased; you wanted him to humiliate himself and lie
to you by telling you and Terry how great you were—in
short, to pretend to be anything except what he really is,
then you would let him have her back."

"You seem to know all about it."

"He didn't do that and he isn't going to. You thought you
would frighten him into doing so because, as you put it, he's
'crazy' to get rich and fearing that he might lose the land, he
would do just what you two wanted him to. But he didn't.
So lo and behold! Instead of doing so, he went back to South
Dakota—and isn't even sending Linda the money you expected
him to."

"Go on, you're proving very interesting—most interesting."

"So you've got the girl on your hands, with a baby, to feed
and take care of. You have no money and neither you nor
Glavis make enough to take very good care of yourselves and
wives, much less Linda and Eden's baby. Your bluff didn't
work and you've been called to Chicago to see what can be
done about it."

"So now what?" Secretly, he was hoping that she could
offer him a way out.

"The way out is to get from between Linda and her husband. When he comes again, let him come in the house and take Linda back there where she belongs, if she wants to go. Simply mind your own business and let Martin's and Linda's alone. That's all there is to do, so be patient, put up with it, now that you got yourself into it. Take care of her until Martin comes for her and then let him have her. Now go make your peace with God, and I repeat, mind your own business and let Linda's alone."

She rose and he followed as she turned for one more word of warning.

"You remember what I've been telling you for years, Newt Lee. That you'd better quit sinning. You better start taking heed of what you preach yourself, otherwise you're going to be called on to answer to your maker for the sins you've been committing. You're just completed the biggest one—parting a man and his wife, and the wife—your own daughter."

"You've said enough for one day, Ida, so will you please hush."

"Not until I finish what I started out to tell you, that if you keep up this awful sinning, the devil's going to get you sure, and you'll burn in hell some day. Now good bye and behave yourself."

She let him out, and as he rode back to the South Side, he felt better. He would let Martin Eden have his wife when he came for her—when he even wrote for her, and he would never stand in their way again.

CHAPTER XXVI

Out west in the meantime, Martin Eden was slaving almost night and day. The problem of agriculture in the west, where irrigation is not practiced, is that of sufficient rainfall at the right time to produce a substantial crop. It was dry that summer, and although Eden had seeded grains on more than 500 acres of his lands, drouth was wreaking havoc with same. Between the worry over approaching crop failure and the loss of his wife and baby, he lived in an almost perpetual nightmare. It failed to rain for two months, and during this time the air became filled with the odor of dying crops, being killed by drouth and hot winds from the South which blew for days.

Then along toward the end of July heavy rains fell all over the Rosebud Country, breaking the drouth. However, all the early seeded crops had died; for them, the rains had come too late. The roots of the flax seed crops that he had seeded on Olive's and his grandma's land, still survived, and when the rains continued to fall, the flax took on new life and started growing all over again. This gave him a new hope, and with new hopes, he began to form new plans.

The Elder had decided to get out of his way and let him have his wife back and no longer interfere. But Martin Eden didn't know it. During the siege of drouth, he had no plans at all to get her back. But when his crops started all over again and it became apparent that he would have some kind of a harvest after all, he began to formulate a plan to get her back.

As they had kidnapped her, so he planned to reverse the action. He would steal into Chicago, and enlisting Mrs. Dewey's assistance, re-kidnap his wife and baby.

During the balance of the summer, all through the fall and into the winter, he did nothing mentally but work out the plan to kidnap his wife. He thought it out from every conceivable angle. And with all this planning, it never occurred to him that they were waiting to *give* her back for the asking. He dared not reveal his intentions even to Linda, for he decided that she had gone over to their side to have peace. He thought that if they had any suspicion of what he was planning, they would act to forestall such effort.

For more than nine months he had given most of his thoughts to formulating his plan to steal her back. During this time he weighed the possibility of resistance to these plans. In his heart there had grown up a hatred for the man who had done all this unto him. This grew, it thrived, it continued growing until by the time spring came again and he had completed all the details for the execution of this plan, he was so bitter against his father-in-law, that he decided to kill him if he interferred.

Years before he had tried to conceive how one must feel to commit a murder. When he read of executions for murder, he had often tried to picture how the one executed could have worked up a feeling that could drive to committing such an act. And now here was he, at this terrible gateway himself. He had suffered so much on account of this man's vanity, that to kill him—shoot him down like a mad dog, became a maddening desire.

Yet he would not do so if he could avoid it. If he could, through some ruse, persuade Linda, or have Mrs. Dewey do so, to meet him at Mrs. Dewey's home, and could be alone with her for one night, it would not be necessary to kill her father.

When they married and went to Mrs. Dewey's house for their wedding night, he discovered that Linda was a virgin. He was forever thinking of that. She had waited all her life for him, and how he wanted her. She was his by divine right and if her father tried to stand between them further, he was determined to kill him.

Beyond seeing the Elder dead at his feet, he could think no further. He couldn't seem to see prison walls for life— possibly the electric chair! He could get no further than the death of this arch hypocrite who had taken his wife. He would kill him and after that—all was blank.

He secured a revolver and secreted it on his person. He prayed that he would not have to use it. All that he wanted was Linda and his baby.

By the time he sold his short crop and the few cattle he had fed on grass (for the grass was plentiful that year, due to the continuous rains, after the drought was broken) he had only $200.00 left. But that was enough to bring Linda back. With her and his baby near him, he would find a way to get along.

So at last he set out for Chicago, where he arrived twenty four hours later, and went directly to Mrs. Dewey's apartment.

"Martin Eden, of all people," she cried, kissing and embracing him fondly, before she closed the door. She ushered him inside and closing the door, embraced him again and then sat him down where the Elder had sat during their colloquy of almost a year before.

"Why didn't you write me that you were coming, Martin, and I would have had everything ready and waiting for you," she said, glad indeed that he had come for his wife at last.

What she meant, but he did not understand, was that she would have had Linda and the baby there with her; that she would have kept them there after he arrived. She knew that he would dislike to meet the Elder or Terry, so she would have saved him any humiliating embarrassment.

Martin Eden had done all his planning with a view of kidnapping his wife. He had been convinced over a year ago, that Terry and her father meant him no good. If he could have one night alone with Linda after all that they had been through, it would be a repetition of their wedding night and no power on earth could stand between them after that.

He had reckoned thus, so what she meant about "having everything ready" he never had the least idea of. And, not knowing that he had formulated a plan of stealing Linda, she never stopped to explain that they had decided long ago to give her back and keep their hands off ever afterward. She took it for granted that he knew, hence her failure to say more about it.

He didn't waste time or words in coming directly to the point.

"I've come for my wife, Mrs. Dewey. They were, the Rev. and Terry, out there. When they entered the house I saw evil in their eyes and Linda saw the same thing. They started, as quickly as I stepped outside, venting their hatred on me so violently that she collapsed. The Dr. made them stay away for two weeks, so that she could have a peaceful mind and continue her recovery.

"When at last she was able to sit up and I had to go about my work, they promised to look after her until I got back, which was to be in two weeks. A few days before I was due back they stole her away, and when I returned home, they were gone and had taken her and my baby with them."

"Yes, I understand, Martin, but—"

"I followed her in about two weeks, but Terry slammed the door in my face when I called at their house. I was allowed to see her but one hour while here, and then under guard. I was allowed to bid her and the baby goodby, also under guard, Terry's guard. Since then I've been driven almost insane. Only God in heaven knows how much I've suffered.

"So for a year I've been planning, planning how to see her—alone. Just a little while alone with her. Just one night, and then I need worry no longer.

"Now Mrs. Dewey, I don't want her to know I'm here. I noticed when the Elder came to visit her during the single year we were together following our marriage, that he pestered her. It was all about 'his love' and her 'old father', until she had to become as she used to be, simple and helpless; given to praising and flattering him, to get along with him. She must have become that way again by now and I don't want to go to her house and take a chance of being put through all I went through last year.

"I have, therefore, planned a way to avoid all this."

"Yes, Martin, but—"

"I have planned a way that you can help me, Mrs. Dewey, and if you still have a heart and a soul as you did have, I beg of you to help me, Mrs. Dewey, please."

"Of course, Martin, but—"

"Please don't say 'but' Mrs. Dewey. Just say that you will help me. That is all that I ask and I—I feel that I will just die, if you don't."

She was trying to explain that all he had to do was to call Linda, or she would call her, and that Linda would come flying; but being convinced that the forces of evil were still at work to humiliate and destroy him, he was so far away from what she was trying to tell that she had to give up and listen to his plan.

"I love Linda and am sure she still loves me. But I don't want to be put through anything I have been through before to see her. I didn't wire you or write you because it is *my* trouble. I didn't want to burden you any longer than necessary, and that isn't going to be long. I have everything thought out as to how she and I can be together again—just one night, that is all, and then it'll be all over. Our troubles will be at an end and we can go back to So. Dakota and start all over again.

"So that's the story, Mrs. Dewey, my sad story. If you have the same kind heart you've had since I knew you, then again I ask, will you help me?"

"You know that I'll be glad to help you, Martin; help you in any way I can. What is your plan?"

"I know Linda well enough to realize that if I can be alone with her for one night, the fight is won. One night with her away from their influence and she'd go back there and spit in their faces the next morning if I asked her to. But for a year and a half she's been there, under that roof and their influence, and to avoid any long, drawn out colloquy with them, my plans are to have you act as a sort of go between and get her over here." He paused now as he could see that she was thinking.

"You don't have to do this, Martin. All you've got to do is to go right to the house and see her. The elder happens to be home, and if you go there, he'll admit you and let you see Linda and your son, who has teeth and is able to walk a little now. You and she can then adjust your differences and nobody will interfere with you."

This was as plain as words could explain, but all the Elder and Terry had done to Eden had played upon his mind until he didn't understand what she was talking about even now. He had worked out his plan to steal her so completely that it had become an obsession. He reckoned that it was the only way to get her back. His nerves were on edge. Any thought of going to the Lee house and meeting the Elder and having to even look at Terry, was as far out of his mind as heaven from earth. But he didn't wish Mrs. Dewey to know how bitterly he despised the two. It might prejudice her against him, so he countered:

"I would have to kowtow to him and Terry and play the dirty hypocrite. So please don't ask me to do that, Mrs. Dewey. In fact, I know you wouldn't if you could realize just how much I have suffered. Only God knows that, and only God knows how I feel toward those two people. It is better that I never have to meet either again. At least, not in their house. I don't want to—in fact, I'm afraid to. I'm afraid of what might happen; what I might be tempted to do if confronted with either of their evil faces in my way again.

"No," he went on, his face haggard and worn and tired, "the way I've planned it will be the best, I'm sure. So it's all up to you, Mrs. Dewey to help me as I see it."

"All right, Martin. I'll help you and in your own way. I can see that it would not be—to your best interest to have to go there. I can see that your suffering has affected you. Linda is your wife. She has your child and you want a chance to settle the differences, if there are any, between you, and all there are, if any, have been developed there in the Lee home. Now exactly what do you want me to do?"

"I want you to call her on any excuse you care to make up and have her come over here to see you. I will be here, and then—" He broke off and she understood the rest.

"I think I know a better way. You see, if I call Linda and ask her here, I could not ask her to come alone. It would arouse their curiosity and they would be trying to find out what I want to see her alone about."

"I see, and that is true."

"And if I asked her just to come over, the Elder would sure come tagging along with her."

"Yes, he would. That's true, also. He'd be glad for an excuse to come over."

"Exactly."

"So?"

"I can call her and ask her over, just as you wish me to, and if he comes with her, I can assure you that he will not try to interfere."

Again she was trying, indirectly this time, to make him understand that there were no barriers in the way. But still he did not understand, because for more than a year he had thought of nothing else but of the Elder standing between them and trying to force him to kowtow to him in order to meet her. He could feel the revolver, tucked away in his clothing; of his decision to shoot him dead the moment he threatened to stand further between him and his family. As he viewed it, the only way to avoid killing the father of the girl to whom he was married, was not to have to look into his face again until he and Linda were reunited.

"No, no," he cried, hastily. "I don't want to take my chance of having to meet him—I *must* not meet him." She had no idea how important those words were. How little could she guess that for these two men to meet at this time, meant almost sure death for the Elder, and the end, perhaps, of Martin Eden.

"Please tell me the other way," said he, and waited.

"All right, here it is. Do you remember Mrs. Farley—you must, because she had you to dinner the day after you and Linda married."

"You mean Blanche's mother?" a bit of a smile on his face.

"Of course, Blanche's mother."

"Oh, yes. A very fine woman. I rather liked her. Her husband is head waiter at some hotel downtown."

"That's her. Well, she likes you, too; is a friend of both yours and Linda's and will be glad to do as much for you as I would."

"I'm glad to hear that. Dear Mrs. Farley, a stout, Irish looking woman."

"She *is* Irish—that is, part Irish and the rest, niggah."

"Now my plan is for you to go over to Mrs. Farley's, who'll be glad to see you, see?"

"Yes, I understand," seeming to warm to it and anxious to hear more.

"Instead of me calling her to come over here and having the Elder come trailing with her, to be in your way, as you insist that he would be, she can call and he wouldn't likely follow her to Mrs. Farley's house, understand?"

"Of course I do. It's a splendid idea! You can call her now and tell her that I'm on the way over."

"Oh, no, no. I don't want to do that. Don't give her anything to think about in advance—just go right on there and surprise her. She'll be too glad to see you and hear what you want her to do, to do any thinking after you get there," cautioned Mrs. Dewey.

"Yes. It is better that she have no time to think."

"Of course not. If I called her and told her that you were on the way to her house, she might get to thinking and before you got there, would be calling up Linda, and—"

"Of course, of course."

"So just go right over and after you have greeted her, explain what you want done and she'll call Linda before anybody can do any thinking at all."

"Fine, dandy, Mrs. Dewey. They said you were a smart woman and the way you've doped this out, proves it."

She followed him to the door, laying a hand on him.

"Now, Martin, my boy. When Linda comes, don't rush her. As you said, she has gone back to her old ways, which is the only way she could get along with her father and Terry. Yet she has only gone back to what is natural with her, for those are the ways of her mother. Linda looks like her father, you know, but she has ways like her mother—subservient and helpless. If she had the proper fire she'd never have let them bring her away from you—even if she was sick. In fact, had they not known she could be made to do as they wished, they'd never have attempted to bring her away—but that's history and you are interested in the present.

"So, for your own good just take it easy after she comes. In fact, when you get to Mrs. Farley's tell her that you want to take her and Linda downtown to a show. She's crazy about pictures—spends half her time sitting up in some theatre, looking at them. So when you tell her you want to take her downtown to see something first run and a revue and band in the bargain, she'll fall for that like a ton of bricks."

"Great! I'll buy a paper on the way over and pick out the show I will offer to take them to."

"That's the thing to do. Then, after the show—in fact, lump them all together. Make it a show and then a dinner, by which time you should have Linda where you want her and can then talk about her spending the night with you."

"If this goes through, Mrs. Dewey, I'll have you to thank for it," said he, gratefully, tears of emotion welling in his eyes.

"It'll go through, Martin. All you're to do is what I've asked you to—exactly as I've said, and soon everything will be all right."

"Let's hope so. God knows what'll happen to me if it doesn't." As hopeful as it seemed, his decision to shoot the Elder dead had not altered an iota. But he was not thinking of murder now. He was thinking of Mrs. Farley, who lived far out south on Wabash Avenue. Kissing Mrs. Dewey goodby, after promising to bring Linda and the baby to have dinner with her before they returned to So. Dakota, he hurried away and caught the elevated for the South Side.

CHAPTER XXVII

On the way to Mrs. Farley's, he purchased a paper and checked the theatrical page for the most popular show in the loop. He thought about his previous acquaintance with Mrs. Farley and her daughter, Blanche, who had married about the same time Linda and he married, and went with her husband, to live in Mississippi. Mrs. Farley seemed fond of Linda and they were very close friends. He remembered, as the Elevated train rumbled noisely on its way, that Linda used to talk about her and how she, Mrs. Farley, liked her 'tea'.

A few minutes later she met him at the door, kissed him motherlike and then sat with him in the parlor while he told her his trouble.

"Why, of course, I'll help you, Martin. I think anybody who knows the truth about you and poor Linda, would do the same thing. She stood up now and was close enough for him to catch the odor of her breath. In spite of his unhappiness, he had to smile inwardly. He could see that she had had a "nip," but he was relieved to see that she was not intoxicated.

"You know, Martin," she went on. "That dirty old Negro that she calls father, ought to be took out and shot."

Eden looked at her, his face immobile.

"As many women as he has, has always had; and the way he has treated his wife for thirty years—then to up and meddle with Linda's marriage is a shame. He's sinned enough to be shot down like a dog and if I was a man and he treated me as he has treated you, I'd take a gun and shoot him right through that old white head of his. The dirty old rascal! He is, without doubt, the ornerest nigger in all Chicago—and has been since before you was big enough to know a girl from a boy." Having exhausted her vituperation for the moment, started looking for a nickel to put in the phone. Observing her doing so, Martin handed her one.

"Oh, thank you, dear. I'm so sorry for you and Linda. Your home all broken up by that old black, proud, pompadoured rascal—and all because you were too busy to make over him!

"What he did was the dirtiest thing that has ever happened in Chicago, even, since I can remember! A preacher, calling himself a minister of the gospel; a man of God—breaking up his own daughter's home for spite!" She turned and started to the telephone, but thinking of something else, turned and coming back, laid hand on him and continued:

"And that homely Terry. She's just as bad. Between them they're two of about the most despicable people I ever knew. Poor Linda, just like her mother; my poor cousin, they've made slaves out of both she and Linda all their lives." He interposed:

"Being so glad to see you, Mrs. Farley, and so happy at your agreeing to help Linda and me, I forgot to tell you that I want to take you both to a show and after that, to Morrison's for dinner."

"Oh, Martin, no!"

"Yes, to a show downtown." He had forgotten to mention it. He was glad now that he remembered it before she called Linda. He then named the picture that he wanted to see, and on the same bill was a Colored Orchestra.

"Oh, Martin, you darling! That's just the picture I've been wanting to see, and with that band on the same program— that's too delightful for words!" She turned and coming back to him, cried:

"Let me kiss you again for that," and she did, with a loud smack. Turning to the phone at last, within a minute she had Linda on the other end. After the usual greetings and a bit of gossip.

"Listen, Linda. I'm going downtown to the Chicago Theatre to see the show that's there. I'm too excited to remember the name of the picture, but they have a colored band on the bill, too. So I want you to put on your clothes and come right over here and go with me."

"Oh, Mrs. Farley," Eden could hear. "That's too wonderful for words! How can I ever thank you? I haven't seen a picture in weeks and now to think you want me to come over and go with you to see such a good one! They always have a good show at the Chicago. Oh, you darling! I'll be right over. You can almost hold your breath, because that's how quickly I'll be there."

"All right, baby. Make it snappy. I'll get dressed and be waiting for you."

She came back to Martin, feeling so happy over it that she kissed him again. She had thought of something else.

"Listen, Martin, dear. You go into the parlor and stay there. If Linda gets here before I'm dressed, just you stay there and let me answer the bell and let her in, see?"

"Of course, Mrs. Farley. That's the sensible thing to do. I'll step into the parlor and wait."

"That's a good boy."

He hadn't been in the parlor twenty minutes before he heard somebody mount the steps, looking out, and, caught a flash of Linda. A moment later he heard the bell ring, and adjusted himself to await the great moment.

He saw Mrs. Farley, about two thirds dressed, hurry across the back parlor from her bedroom and down to the front door. Pausing on the way there, she stuck her head in the parlor, and cried:

"There she is! Now you just sit tight until I'm ready for her to see you." A moment later, he heard his wife's voice for the first time in more than a year.

They exchanged a kiss after the greeting, and then more words.

"No use to ask you to rest your things, Linda. Just come on back with me to the bedroom until I finish dressing, then we'll be ready to go." Placing Linda in front of her, she made a back hand wave two or three times, which Linda could not see, for him to hide. Mrs. Farley dared not turn 'her head; but Eden had become wise when he heard her invite Linda to her bedroom, and had hid himself, although he could see them as they passed by.

In a few minutes Mrs. Farley came out of her room on some pretext and saw that he was out of sight, as she wanted him to be until she brought Linda into the parlor. They exchanged a few nods to indicate that everything was understood. A few moments later she came out again with Linda following her.

"I want you to meet the gentleman," said she to Linda, "who's been kind enough to ask us to the show."

"A gentleman!" exclaimed Linda, her lips parting, her mouth remaining open in surprise. "Now this—"

By this time they were in the parlor and Linda looked around for the "gentleman." Martin stepped forward. Her eyes fell on him and she let escape a little scream:

"Martin!"

"Yes, Linda," said Mrs. Farley, calmly. "Martin, your husband. Now take a seat, you two, over there together.

"While you two do some talking, I'll go check on the work I'm running away from, and when I come back, we'll go right downtown to the show."

They were silent for several moments, as if a bit afraid of each other after such a long absence. After a time, she looked at him a bit strangely. He could see that she had been 'made over' since he'd seen her. He had not written her for two months, and before that for three months. She was looking at a new man and not understanding that he had been dying slowly, because he wanted her so badly; she misunderstood it all. She had long since begun to fear that, after all, he did not care for her; and worse, he didn't care for his baby. With this misunderstanding between them, she didn't know how to greet him. Finally, he found his tongue, and hesitantly, began:

"Aren't you—glad to see me, Linda?" She lowered her eyes uncertainly. She didn't know what to say, but answered by asking a question:

"When—when did you—you come?"

"This morning. About two hours ago." He waited for her to say more, but all she managed was:

"Oh," and waited for him to speak. He was so afraid that he might say the wrong thing. She was afraid that all her father and sister had preached was at last true and she did not speak, because she too was afraid.

"You must—must give me a chance to talk to you, Linda. I'm afraid—afraid there's a great misunderstanding somewhere."

"There is no misunderstanding, Martin. You simply never loved me, that was all."

"Oh, Linda! How unfair!" his face was drawn and pained.

"But you don't," she dared argue. "You simply do not and you never did.

"I'm sorry to hear you say that, Linda."

"But it's true, Martin. All too true," she persisted. And then again fear entered his heart. He decided that they'd better go. He feared she might so misunderstand him that she'd go back home, completing the crucifixion that had been started over a year before.

"Please don't let us quarrel. I haven't seen you for a year and then not alone. I had Mrs. Farley send for you to come here and I want to give you time to—to quit thinking that way. So let us postpone the talk and go downtown, to see a show, then have a good dinner, and maybe then we can talk and you will believe me."

Taking her by the hand, he helped her to rise. The touch thrilled both and neither knew how badly each wanted to throw aside all restraint and fly into the arms of the other.

Eden asked to be excused a moment and called to Mrs. Farley that they were ready. A few minutes later, they left the house and were aboard a roaring elevated train, on their way to see the show.

"How's Junior?" he asked, softly. She looked up with the first smile she dared to indulge.

"Oh, he's a bad boy—and such a big boy. He's walking now."

"Oh, great goodness! My boy, walking," as if to himself. There was pain in her eyes.

"You don't care for him, either." She didn't believe her last remark. He decided to change the subject. Looking at her sitting there beside him, he remarked:

"You're stouter."

"Yes," she answered, glancing down at herself and running her hand over her side.

"It becomes you," with an expression of admiration which seemed to please her.

"So Junior's walking?"

"M-m. And has teeth." She smiled again.

"Isn't that wonderful! I'm so anxious to see him." Again she looked at him with pain in her eyes.

It was a good picture. Linda sat between them. Before it was over, he dared let his hand rest against hers. She did not draw away and by the time it was over, had relaxed considerably.

They liked the show so well that when they came out, Eden bought tickets for that night's performance of a stage play at another theatre. They took a bus out South Parkway to 47th Street, where they had a delightful dinner.

They decided to take a taxi back to Mrs. Farley's. While they were at the table, waiting for dinner to be served, Mrs. Farley went to the bar, had a stiff drink and came back to the table "happy," and talkative.

Arriving there, Mrs. Farley left them alone in the parlor.

"Won't you rest your things, dear," said he, and he took them to the hall tree and returned to sit beside her.

"How do you feel by now, dear? All right, maybe?"

"Yes, I feel all right," and waited for him to say more.

"Did you enjoy the show?"

"Oh, very much."

"And the dinner?"

"It was very nice, too, thank you."

"You don't have to thank me, Linda. You are still my wife."
She couldn't think what to say, so waited for him to say more.

"Have you forgotten that I'm still your husband, Linda?"

"How could I ever forget that?"

"You seem to have."

"You mean it the other way, that you've forgotten you had a wife—and a son."

"I've done nothing but think of you, every day, every hour in the day, since last I saw you."

"I don't believe you."

"You seem to have quit believing me. Yet I've never told you a lie in my life. I tried to be a good husband. I'm still willing to keep on trying."

"You have a funny way of showing it."

"Do you mean, because I—I haven't written you so—often?"

"Of course."

"The letters I received from you were not your letters. They were not the kind you wrote me before we were married. In fact, they didn't read as if you wrote them at all. Still they were in your handwriting, so you *did* write them. They were void of feeling, kindness or sympathy. There was no heart throb in them. So I was afraid to write you as I wanted to. I didn't know who might be reading the letters I sent. . . ."

"Now you lay off of my people, please," she protested, with vigor, frowning at him.

"Did I say anything about your people?"

"No-o; but you were throwing out a strong hint."

"I only hinted that somebody might be reading my letters

to you other than you, so I decided that I shouldn't write many, and to wait until I could see you."

She wanted to say something. He was looking straight at her, and she had to turn her eyes away. He always looked at people like that, she remembered—straight into their eyes. She couldn't meet his eyes as she always could when they were together in Dakota. During those memorable days, when she looked at him, she always had to smile.

"What we need is to have a long talk together, Linda. A long talk with nobody to—well, just you and I to sit down together and talk. I haven't changed a bit since I went away and came back to the claim to find you gone," he sighed, sadly.

"I asked you to leave my people out of this, if you please," she cried, impatiently again, and moved away from him a bit.

"Dear, Linda, why be so impatient and unkind to me? I haven't mentioned anybody's name since you came here this afternoon. Why do you keep asking me to leave somebody's name out. What body, dear?"

"Well,—ah—you—you keep hinting at somebody and I don't like it."

"You used to be the sweetest, and the most agreeable girl I ever knew. Now you are just as impatient with me as you can possibly be—without any reason that I can see at all. What is the matter, dear? Are you—afraid of me?" She had never been able to meet his eyes unless her conscience was clear. And her conscience was *not* clear as she sat there beside him.

"It—it isn't me at all. It's you. You don't love me. If you had loved me, you—we—well, you just don't love me, and that's what made everything like it is." She was on the spot, and was engaging in subterfuges to try to get out of a crack.

"All right, since you insist, it is agreed that I don't love you. Then what?"

"Well, what?"

"Since you married me, are still my wife, wouldn't it seem

fair and reasonable that I be given a chance to prove that I do love you?"

"Well, yes. You should have that chance."

"Then I propose that after we return from the show, instead of going back home, you—you stay here with me tonight. Mrs. Farley will give us a room.'"

She seemed to be thinking. He waited anxiously. It seemed that his whole future life—their future lives, hung on her decision. When she turned to him, she had made it, but before giving him her answer, she wanted to call her father and tell him that Martin was in town; that she was at Mrs. Farley's with him and would not return home before morning.

Oh, cruel fate, what a terrible thing! Enter again, fatal misunderstanding. She did not know that he thought her father was still standing between them, and that the only way he could have her back was to kidnap her. She meant to be fair to him, to give him a chance to prove that he loved her, and she had a picture of herself, locked in his arms all through that night, listening to him as she used to—oh, how much she wanted him!

But she had reverted to her premarital subservience to her father.

Now if Linda had said all she meant, the story would soon be ended. She meant: "I'm going to tell father that you are here and that I won't be home before morning." That is what *she* *meant* but she did not say it, so the misunderstanding continued and as we shall see, grew infinitely worse.

"Excuse me a few minutes while I go and call my father!" and she felt his muscles contract. She started and looked at him.

"What's the matter?"

"Please don't, Linda," he almost begged her and his face was pathetic. She couldn't understand him at all.

"But, I'm only going to call father and tell him that you are here."

"Please don't Linda, I beg you not to." His eyes were as she had never seen them before. She almost recoiled in fear. Yet she *wanted to give him the chance he asked for*, and she didn't know that *he* didn't understand.

"But, Martin," she said, kindly. The expression on his face was growing more terrified than ever. She began to fear now that he had lost his mind. He was beginning to foam slightly at the corners of his mouth. Then, between clinched teeth:

"If you call him, it means the end of everything, Linda,—everything," he hissed and begged all in one. Her face was contracted; *what was the matter with her husband!*

"I don't know what you are talking about," she said, moving away from him, nervously.

"Everything will be all right between us by morning, Linda, I know it will." She noticed that he was trembling. *What had come over the man?* Had he *gone mad?* "If you just don't call him now; just wait 'till in the morning, Linda, and you can call him—you can even go back home and you can take me with you if you want to; but please, Linda, don't call him now. Please give me a chance, Linda, please." The more he talked the more he trembled, and the white was coming out of his mouth. Still she hesitated to conclude that her husband *had* gone mad!

"Give you a chance? That's what I'm doing. That's why I'm going to call my father and tell him that you are here."

She started toward the telephone again but he caught her by the wrist and whirled her face about. She was face to face with little short of a raving maniac.

"No, no, no!" he shrieked, so loud her ear drums trembled. "It shall not be, it *must* not be! I have waited for you, cried for you, prayed for you and you are mine! Oh, God, I want you *so* much, Linda."

He stepped between her and the telephone. For almost the first time,—and the wrong time, she became angry and decided to fight back.

"I forbid you to use it—I forbid you to call him—I beg you

not to call him, for if you do, Linda, it will be the end—*do you understand what I'm trying to tell you?* It will be the *end*—of everything!"

She was angry now. She considered him ungrateful, but most of all, she'd concluded that he had gone crazy, so stiffening, she said, coldly:

"Will you please stand aside and let me use that telephone?" In mortal anguish he moved away, and stood with his back to her, trembling like a leaf.

She crossed to the phone, put her nickel in the slot, and got her home.

"Father," she called.

"Yes, Linda," he answered.

"Martin is here," said she, still trying to give him his 'chance'.

"Well, bring him to the house."

What he remembered then was that the Elder wanted him to come there so that he could be lectured by him; have to listen to Terry scream and charge him with all the sins since creation; accept humiliation which he never even thought of enduring. It was more than he could stand, more than he *would* stand. All the suffering those two had put on him, had left him a broken man. He felt himself going around and around. Was this the way men felt before they committed murder?

Afterward he came to feel more sorry for unfortunate men who committed murder under certain stress. If they felt as he did then, little wonder that they could kill. It would be easy. Living through such a tragedy was a terrible thing. He rushed to the telephone, snatched the receiver out of her hand, and screamed into the speaker, hoarsely, but with murder in his voice:

"*I don't want to come to your house, Reverend Lee!* Do you understand? *I don't want to come to your house!* You've taken Linda from me; you've wrecked my home, my life; I can't have my baby. You've driven me insane, do you hear? *And I don't want to come to your house!*"

Standing by, Linda again misunderstood everything, the same as Eden was misunderstanding her. Again, in addition to having lost his mind, he was an ingrate—as she saw it. After she decided to spend the night with him, their first one together for fifteen months! And now it was all being thrown to the winds by this man she called husband; the man she had loved more than anything else in the world!

So *she* became angry and snatching the receiver out of his hand, angrily, called:

"Oh, father. Please come and get me. I'm at Mrs. Farley's. Please come and get me, father—quickly." He tried to wrest the receiver from her hand and it fell with a thud against the wall, while they struggled for it.

At Reverend Lee's home, in the meantime, the family, including Glavis, had gathered around the Elder, and all could hear Linda struggling. Naturally, this time the concern about her was real. He could hear an occasional word, as they struggled into the parlor, knocking open the door, which banged loudly against the wall, and resounded through the telephone.

"Go get my sister!" screamed Terry, loudly. "*Go get my sister!*" She turned to her husband, beating him with her fists and forearms. "*Why do you stand there like a fool!*" Go get my sister do you hear? Go and get her quickly!"

There was no alternative. Two thoroughly frightened men rushed frantically into the street. Vernon avenue was a quiet thoroughfare, and at night no Taxi drivers wasted gas to drive through it, so they had to run two blocks west to South Parkway, where the street is constantly filled with jitneys.

They got into the first one that drew near the curbing and ordered the driver to rush to Mrs. Farley's address on Wabash Avenue. There was extra money if he could get there quickly.

At Mrs. Farley's home, foaming at the mouth and apparently gone temporarily insane, Eden got ready to meet Reverend Lee. He reached for his revolver, withdrawing it and turning toward the front door.

Knowing that her father would rush there as quickly as a taxi could bring him, Linda screamed long and loudly:

"You shall not—*you must not kill my father!*" She reached to try take the revolver from his hand and struggled with him for the possession of it. Bitter and unhappy to remember, was this desperate struggle between two people who once really loved each other. One, driven insane by the evils that had been forced upon him, now broken and out of control, after a life of perfect mental and physical well being. The other, his wife, who not five minutes before, was picturing herself in his arms, drinking of the love that had once meant so much to her. Hers was a struggle to prevent a murder, and therefore justified.

Hearing the excitement downstairs, Mrs. Farley rushed down, and seeing Linda and Eden locked in a death struggle for possession of the revolver, screamed loudly and fell to the floor in a dead faint!

Meanwhile, the Elder and Glavis reached the house, and pressed the bell vigorously. They had to stand there impatiently and wait as they heard the struggle inside.

"God help us," breathed the Elder, trembling all over, cold sweat covering him like the morning dew a lawn. Glavis pushed the bell harder and could hear it ringing.

As they struggled, Linda managed to get her finger on the trigger of the gun, and womanlike, with no realization of what it might do, she pulled it. It exploded, the report of which they heard outside. She pulled it, as they struggled for possession, three times!

Outside the men groaned and knew not what to do.

Inside, the third bullet plowed the flesh of Eden's forearm, near the funny bone, and glanced off into the wall. The impact with the bone chilled him and rendered him almost unconscious; enough to make him relax his hold and sink to the floor with a groan.

There on the floor before her, Linda looked at her husband dazedly. She became conscious after a time of the bell ringing loudly. Picking up the gun, she staggered toward the door, which she managed to open and the others rushed in. She fainted into the arms of her father.

"Thank heaven, you are alive, my daughter—alive!" His voice was hoarse, but he held her as the gun fell to the floor.

Glavis picked it up nervously and helped the Elder inside with Linda, closed the door and advanced far enough to see both Mrs. Farley and Eden lying stretched on the floor. He concluded that both were dead,—killed by Linda.

"Great God Almighty, father," breathed Glavis. "Both dead, and Linda—"

"Hush, Glavis," said the Elder. At the sight of what he thought were dead bodies, "Quick! Carry that revolver and lay it beside. one of them and let's get Linda home—out of this!"

Glavis laid it beside Eden. He was half way to the Elder, who was holding Linda in his arms preparatory to departing. Glavis changed his mind, and picking up the gun, wiped it with his kerchief, and laid it beside Mrs. Farley. He hurried to catch up with the Elder, who had reached the front door and was waiting there for him to come and open it.

"Now, father," said he. "Stand here and keep the door partly open while I go out and find a taxi, then come back and get you and Linda."

"Please hurry, my son. Oh, heavenly father, please save us; hurry my son; please hurry."

In less than two minutes Glavis rode back with a taxi. With the cold air on her face, Linda had recovered sufficiently to open her eyes. They assisted her to the cab and whirled away towards home.

Inside, Eden recovered, and though his arm was numbed, he was able to regain his feet, look around and try to remember what happened. He felt his arm, which was plastered with blood, but seemed to have stopped bleeding. He went to the bathroom, removed his coat and rolling up his sleeve, with relief, saw that it was only a flesh wound and had stopped bleeding. He bathed it and tied a thin towel around it, by which time the numbness had passed and he didn't feel much worse for his injury.

Returning to the parlor, he found Mrs. Farley turning over. He helped her to her feet, and she looked up at him, half dazed.

"Martin," she said, reaching out and touching him as if he were a ghost. "What—what—happened?"

"A misunderstanding," Mrs. Farley."

"A—a misunderstanding?"

"Yes, Linda and I had a misunderstanding about—well, the same thing. You know."

"You—you mean, her father?" He nodded in the affirmative.

"Yes," said he. "Her father. I guess that's the end of it. All of our troubles have been on his account. So I guess this is—the—end," he sighed as he finished.

"The end, Martin, between you—and Linda?"

"Yes," nodding and sighing.

"I guess we—we just can't make it."

"Oh, isn't that just too bad," said she, sympathetically. Then she looked at him more closely, and pointing to his arm:

"You—you had an—accident?" He nodded again.

"How?"

"Well, it was my fault I guess. But the truth of it is, it is well that I, only, was injured. Which is only slight."

"But you must call a Dr."

"Oh, no, Mrs. Farley. I'll go to one in a few minutes."

"But—what—"

"Oh, I'd been through so much I decided to—kill him if he interfered further."

"Oh, Martin!"

"Show's the stage to which a man can be forced if he lets something play on his mind long enough, strong enough."

"And you—you had decided to—kill him?"

Again he nodded in the affirmative.

"So?"

"I reached for the gun after we struggled for possession of the telephone. When she saw me do so, she realized that in the condition I was in, I would shoot her father, so she rushed in and tried to take it away from me."

"Oh, my God. Think of it. And I thought you were getting together splendidly."

"We were, until she said she was going to call him and tell him that I was here."

"And then?"

"That started us—I went, oh, I think I lost my mind, as I recall it now; but anyway, in the struggle for possession of the gun, she got hold of the trigger, pulled it and kept pulling it. The last time she did so, the bullet hit me on the crazy bone and sorta knocked me out. I was half conscious and remember their coming, her father and Glavis; them carrying her out of the house and to home, I guess."

"And so now, you—you're not going to—"

"I'm not going to try any longer. I'm afraid that she is so completely under their domination it is useless to try to live with her again. I could never quit hating them, as they have so persistently hated me—so I say now, 'what's the use?' "

"I'm so sorry."

"I am, too; and especially for you. Now don't go charging yourself, as we so often do when we try to help somebody, and feeling that we hadn't any business trying to do so. You tried to help two lonely people find the happiness their love held for each other. That was a fine and noble act. If it failed, then please don't blame yourself. Linda and I could have made it all along. We could still make it. But it is a known fact that no man could ever go with her before I came, because of that peculiar, interfering love that her father claims to have for her. That alone is to blame for this, so let's forget it, and let me thank you for the help you tried to give."

"So sad—a tragedy. What are you going to do now?"

"Right now, I don't know; but I'll return home in a few days and try to start all over again."

"You're young. You can and you will succeed yet. You'll find some nice girl, who won't be burdened with so much 'fatherly' love. She will love you, be good to you and make you happy."

"I hope so, Mrs. Farley. But now I must take this injury to a Dr. for dressing and then I'll decide just what I will do before I return to Dakota." He kissed her good bye, went to a Dr.'s office and had his wound dressed.

He then found a room for the night, went to bed, and on awakening the next morning and trying to still the pain of disappointment that had ended a year of waiting and planning, he suddenly decided to go to Southern Illinois.

CHAPTER XXVIII

WHEN HE LEFT Chicago he was undecided as to where he was going. He had bought a ticket to Carbondale, but he had no thought of Delia when he did so. He did think of Jessie as the train sailed over the former prairie lands, and he decided to go to her.

She and the man she married had not stayed together long and she was home. He had even exchanged a few letters with her the fall before. Like a woman who feels that she has missed something, and because it had been she who married first, she wanted to see him.

He considered any future with Linda as a closed chapter in his life and being lonely and discouraged, he wanted to give up for a few days and to forget all the harrowing emotions that he had been through. He wondered as the train rumbled into Murphysboro, if the old love with Jessie might be renewed; if the old fire had a chance to kindle—burn again. Any way, she was the one woman that he could talk to and who would be glad to listen to his story and give him some comfort in these unhappy hours.

At least, it was some consolation to have somebody to go to; somebody who had once loved him and somebody who knew why his present marriage had failed.

As stated, he found Jessie at home. He was glad to see her, she to see him. She was idle; she could give him all her time. He decided to stay three days, and she was nice to him and tried to make his stay a pleasant one.

When he related what had happened, she expressed sympathetic concern.

"I understand everything, Martin. Everybody knows that Linda was never able to keep a beau on account of her father. You were the first real one she ever had. We did think that after you married her and she had a baby, that he'd let her alone, but—"

"The way of the transgressor is hard," he sighed, cutting her off, and tried to smile through it.

"What are you going to do—about your son?" she asked.

"I haven't any plans yet."

"If they raise it, they'll teach it to hate you."

"No doubt; but until I get back home and try to check up on the wreck that my life seems to have come to, I'm not going to do any planning. I'm just going to relax until then and get myself together."

"Yes, dear, try pull yourself together. You're too much of a fighter to stop now."

"I'll never stop. That I know—even now. Only when they lay me beneath the cold, cold, earth, will I stop. However bad my misfortune, I know that I will go on and on—I *must* keep going on."

"In spite of all the mitigating circumstances, I still can't understand how any woman could let her father break up her home. I don't think you could find another woman in ten thousand that would let anybody do that to her."

"I think it is because of too much love. I've known men whose mothers have pampered them to the point where they have ruined them; made them impossible for any woman to ever live with—and it was all because of too much parental love."

"Yes, and while I suppose the Elder loved Linda in his way, it was your failure to flatter him in the beginning that started it and in the end, it broke up your home. I still believe that if you'd gone on to the house there in Chicago, and not tried to get together the way you did, that they'd have given her back to you."

"I never thought of it that way."

"There might still be time enough," said she, and looked up at him.

"No, that phase of my life is a closed chapter. I'm going to start all over again. I don't know now where I'll end up— maybe in bankruptcy, if we don't get a better crop this year."

"By the way, what about her claim?"

"I haven't decided about that, either."

"Well, won't she have to go back there and live on it—to, what'd you say that was, that you're supposed to do?"

"Prove up on it?"

"Yes, that's it; prove up on it."

"I suppose so; but as I said, I haven't done any planning since last night."

"I understand, dear, and we'll quit talking about it."

"Yes, please, let's do."

Martin stayed there three days. Jessie and he tasted of that something both had missed, and he returned to his home at the end of that time.

During his stay, they formulated a plan whereby she would come to So. Dakota that fall, if the crops were good. If she liked it (though it was not agreed upon), in the minds of both, there was a feeling that she might take Linda's place.

His winter seeded crops, the winter wheat and rye, matured before drought came, and he had some revenue, but the spring crops failed again. He experienced what he had gone through the year before. The air became filled with the odor of prematurely dying crops, but this time no great rains fell to break the terrific drought and Martin saw himself sinking lower and lower, until he reached a place, financially, where nothing but a miracle could save him.

Days came and days went and he had nothing to do but sit and look out over that wide expanse at dying crops, and sniff of the odor of same as they struggled to resist the inevitable results.

He gave up early, the plan to send for Jessie. He gave up almost everything and just sat there, listening to the persistent south winds that blew and blew and blew, always hot, day in and day out. Then came grasshoppers—millions of them. Pestilence!

During this time he found solace in reading. He read everything he could find, to help forget what was going on around him. He read, among other things, a novel by Jack London, which dealt with writing. Said London, the way to write was just to get a pencil and paper and start writing, and to keep on writing until one had written something; something that somebody might read.

Then out of the maze of conflicting events a thought came to him, an inspiration. Why didn't *he* write something? Write what? he asked himself. A story? What story? Then suddenly, a startling idea! Came the answer! "Your own story, Martin Eden! *Your own story, your life of hell—the work of an evil power!*"

If Jack London had learned to write just by writing, so could he. London said he wrote 10,000 words a day. If London could do 10,000 a day, so could he, said Martin Eden. He always felt that he could do what any other man could do—under the same circumstances.

But he knew that if he was going to write anything, he would have to learn more than he knew right then. To write, one can describe people and things only as well as that particular phase of life is known. He was satisfied with the plot he had in mind, which was to tell a story of himself, anonymously. That was the kind of story, the "Autobiography of an Ex-Colored Man" was.

In that story some light skinned colored man went over on the "other side" by passing himself off, married a wealthy and beautiful white woman, and as a Caucausian in the end told his own story and published it, anonymously.

Martin, as well as Deborah and her father, had found the story far more interesting than the current novel. For reasons which each respected, they never discussed the story. Was it because Deborah was in love with Martin? A love that could not be admitted or debated?

He decided to tell his own story—even in the first person, but give himself a different name. He decided to begin the story back in Southern Illinois where he was born. He decided, as the author of the "Autobiography of an Ex-Colored Man" had done, to tell the intimate side of his life. He would end the story as his life with Linda had ended. It would not, therefore, have a happy ending.

But to learn something about how to tell his story!

So he started to develop his literary education, preparatory to beginning his story, which had to be got underway quickly. In fact, he couldn't even wait until he finished the home training that he decided on, which consisted of just plain reading— reading and weighing and checking and double checking what he read. To keep on reading and writing, too, and comparing what he was trying to write, by way of construction, with the way what he read was written and constructed, was the hardest angle of this work.

So Martin Eden bought himself a thick tablet. It was the cheapest kind of ruled paper, and he sat him down and started to write. Jack London, he recalled again and again, had written that was the way to write, by just writing.

He kept in mind that Jack London wrote 10,000 words a day. So Martin Eden wrote 10,000 words the first day, too. It was jumbled and clumsy, and after trying to read it he wondered what it was all about. The fact was, and he admitted this to himself, it didn't read anything like the smooth, well written and well edited stories that he was reading in novels, magazines and what not. He was not, therefore, satisfied with what he had written as his first day's work. There was but one thing to do. Write it all over again.

So he turned the tablet over the next day and wrote it all over again. He read it. It was better than the first day's work and he was more satisfied with it—yet by comparison with the stories running currently in divers magazines, he knew it was not nearly good enough.

So after many weeks of reading and making several starts, he finally whipped something into a semblance of a plot. He consulted a white woman he knew, who had been graduated from college, and who kindly agreed to help him. He consulted a lawyer, who was also a college graduate, and he agreed to do half of it. Others had started to assist him, but after trying to labor through his tangled thoughts and involved sentences, had gradually dropped out, leaving the woman and the lawyer the only ones to see him through.

Meanwhile he wrote and wrote and re-wrote. Finally, having put a mass of words together, which were hard to straighten out, yet in which there was a definite and interesting plot, he turned half over to the lady, the other half to the lawyer. They spent weeks rewriting it and finally gave it back to him in two hundred double spaced typewritten, legal size pages.

He called his story "THE CONQUEST," being the Story of A Negro Pioneer, by the Pioneer.

The first publisher he sent it to, kept it so long he began to hope that they would accept it. He had also read a great deal about "rejections" and the familiar "We have read your manuscript, and sorry to advise that we found it unavailable for our needs, so are therefore returning it," etc., etc.

The rejection he received from a Chicago publisher was in the form of a letter saying all that, and ending with a paragraph which wasn't incorporated in the current rejection slips. They had added: "Regretting that we cannot write you more favorably, we beg to remain, Yours Very truly, John Doe & Co."

Meanwhile, it soon got around that he was writing a novel of the Rosebud Country. The report became widespread and everybody was interested. All the local papers, and then the Sioux City, Iowa, and Omaha papers carried a story about the book he had written. Everybody began asking for it, waiting

for it to appear—seeming to forget that it would be up to some
publisher first, if it was ever to appear. And all Martin Eden
had, after his months of writing, rewriting, editing and re-
editing, was a rejection slip—which he didn't have the courage
to show.

He told only one person that his work had been sent back.
"What'd they send it back for?" asked that one, greatly
surprised. He didn't seem to know that most scripts are sent
back. It's surprising how many people are ignorant of this
fact—especially when they've developed ideas about writing
something. Many just take it for granted that the publishers
are waiting for it,—what they are "thinking" about writing.

Martin's heart was broken when his came back, but like
many before him, he got over it. He wrote then to one big magazine publisher, who answered that he would like to see it. He
read it, and Eden had cause to believe, might have considered
publishing it, but that it was too long for a short story, and
he didn't care to publish it in serial form.

Among derelicts and ne'er-do-wells, who hung around the
Rosebud Country, was one by the name of Roy Harrop, who
years later, ran for President on some kind of ticket. He was
interesting and reminded Eden of a Socialist.

"Why don't you publish it yourself?" said he.

"Publish it myself?" repeated Eden, surprised. "Never
heard of such a thing."

"It's been done," insisted Harrop.

"But how?" inquired Eden, interested.

"Well, I don't know," said Harrop; "but you can find out
by writing Hamilcar's Editor." Hamilcar; let it be understood,
is the name of a famous man, whose name is only Hamilcar,
for the purpose of this story.

"Hamilcar's Editor?" repeated Eden, "did what?"

"Published his own book." He called the name of the book
and Eden had heard of it.

"So if you write to him, he'll perhaps tell you who printed
his."

Eden wrote him that same day, and in a few days, received a reply to the effect that a printer there in the City of Nebraska where he lived printed his, and that he had turned his letter over to them.

He sent his script to the printer referred to and got a reply back that they would be glad to manufacture a book from the same; that it would total about 300 pages and could be made for about 50¢ a book.

At least that was a start. Eden was happy to know that such a thing could be done, so proceeded to follow up the idea. He had some wealthy white friends who figured conspicuously in the development of his story. They had read the script and liked it and were very anxious to see it published.

He went to Dallas, where they lived at the time, to see them. He had shown and read the letter from the Nebraska printer, so they inquired if he had any money.

"No cash."

"I suppose not. You're what we call land poor—more land than you can pay taxes on. Well, how much do you need to go down there and see this company?" Eden told them.

"Come on over to the bank."

Over there he was advanced money to make the trip.

He left the same night, finding himself at the printer's office the next morning.

He presented, as he always had since coming west, a strange novelty. He interested the printer right off. Coming out of the Northwest where all knew few Colored people lived, with a manuscript for a 300 page book, was something out of the ordinary. His personality and something about him impressed them. They printed the first chapter, made up a half dozen first class dummy copies to show the size and general appearance, and he returned to the Rosebud and displayed it.

He had plenty of land which he was having a hard time to continue to hold, but cash had long since become almost a stranger to him. Now he was going to have a book. What would he do with it? An answer was waiting—sell it himself—use his power of persuasion, to get people to order copies.

So he became forthwith a high powered book agent—selling his own book—and took orders for 3,000 copies at $2.00 per copy in less than three weeks.

The printers demanded a certain amount in cash with the order, and a guarantee of account for the balance. Back to his friends he went, with orders for 3,000 to be printed at 50¢ a book and to net $6,000 on delivery.

Anybody with any interest, and they were most assuredly interested in seeing the book come out, would sign a guarantee of account when shown orders for the entire edition, sold in advance. So they put up the cash for him and executed the guarantee of account.

Martin went back to the printer. He bought new suits, and in a few weeks the book came out, and he returned to the Rosebud, made delivery and found himself on his feet again quickly.

He advertised the book. People from Iowa, Nebraska, Eastern So. Dakota and Minnesota had been to the Rosebud in large numbers. They had relations and friends there, so sent for copies on seeing ads. Martin Eden, therefore, was soon receiving enough orders and checks through mails to resume his farming out of income from his book.

Because of so many persistent failures due to drouth, he had conceived an idea of how to resist it; to raise a crop if it rained during any time of year at all. And it always rained enough during any year to mature a good crop, if the moisture could be conserved in the earth until it was needed. His solution to that was extremely deep plowing.

This would take powerful tractors and tractors cost money.

Two important angles in the story have been somewhat neglected—first, the Stewart family; second, Eugene Crook, the banker, who had filed a contest against Linda's claim, and whose bank had since gone broke.

The Land Office at Gregory had found in favor of Linda.
Crook appealed to the General Land Commissioner in Washington. Eden was in so much trouble in the meantime that
he neglected to retain a Lawyer in Washington to appear before
the Commissioner. Due to his default in not retaining counsel,
the Commissioner decided in favor of Crook.

Eden appealed from the Commissioner's decision to the final
court, the Secretary of the Department of the Interior, and
there it was awaiting final decision when Martin's book
appeared and he began to recover his financial equlibrium. In
the meanwhile, the Stewarts were continuing to farm part of
Eden's land in Gregory County, finding it hard to make a
living, in view of the droughts that seemed to persist, year
after year.

With plans for deep plowing to store the moisture up when
it did rain, on which the plant roots could draw during dry
weather, he drove down to the Stewarts, who welcomed him
gladly. Old Jack, who was getting along in years and not so
active as of old, greeted him cheerfully, with:

"Martin Eden, my word!" grasping Eden's hand and shaking
it, heartily. "My, but you're looking well." On hearing his
name, Deborah came out of the kitchen, smiling all over, with
her hand stuck out.

"Why, Martin," she exclaimed, looking him up and down.
"I'm so glad to see you."

"And does he look well, Deborah," chimed Stewart, walking
around and looking up and down at him, admiringly.

"I'll say. A regular Jim-dandy," cried Deborah, joining her
father in admiration of him.

"It's the clothes," said Eden. "Tailored clothes and other
things that go with them can change a man's looks and that
is what's making the difference."

"Whatever it is, sure becomes you," said Stewart.

"It makes looking at you, as you used to say, 'easy on the
eyes,' Martin," added Deborah.

"We read your book," said Stewart.

"And it sure was interesting. Remember, I said that you ought to write one," said she.

"He said he hadn't enough experience then to write one," recalled Jack.

"Yes, that was *then*. Well, according to the book, he's acquired plenty since," and she laughed.

"Your book is selling well. Is that how you've managed to come out, like this," he said, pointing at the clothes

"I guess so, Stewart."

"It *was* that. You haven't taken it out of the land. You're a regular soldier of fortune, Martin, you are that."

"Oh, no, just a child of circumstance; but I'm down to see if I can interest you in helping me put an idea over."

"I'm always in for anything you suggest, Eden. I've always been. We've got no money, but there's four willing minds and hands available if they can do any good."

"That's all I need from you. Now here's what it is," and he outlined his plan to buy the powerful tractor, supply gasoline and the machinery and try his new way of farming, with Stewarts to do the work.

"Deliver the tractor, stick around and we'll put your ideas into effect starting this spring—right now."

A few days later, the tractor was turning furrows 12 inches deep. As so often the case, plenty of rain fell during the spring and early summer. It was usually the middle of the summer when it got dry and often failed to rain for weeks, and drought then destroyed the crops.

There was plenty of rain that spring which enabled the Stewarts to plow deeply with the least amount of power. Over 400 acres were plowed and seeded to crop, and got off to a good start before dry weather, the arch enemy of the west, set in.

By harvest time, when half the crops had withered and died, the Stewarts harvested one of the finest the Country had ever seen. Eden came to help them with the harvest and they lived in unwaning enthusiasm during the entire period.

"Every acre in the country," said Eden, sitting between Jack and Deborah one night, "can be made to produce like that. Very soon this persistent drought is going to ruin every farmer who has come here, unless he resorts to what we're doing."

"I believe you."

"Lord, if through any twist of fate, I should become rich, I'd buy every farm that's soon going to be foreclosed and sold for the mortgage. I'd then go back east and lobby the Congress into damming the White river so that water could be brought into this country through huge aqueducts. Then after plowing all cultivated lands 12 inches deep, I would flood the whole area with waters when needed and make the Rosebud one of the richest and most productive countries in all the west.

"A section through which I used to run out in Idaho, when I was on the road, which at that time was a vast wilderness, producing nothing but sage brush and jack rabbits, is now through irrigation and deep plowing, one of the richest producing sections in America. Some of these lands which twenty years ago were just worthless alluvial rock formation, are now producing fruit and alfalfa so profusely that the land sold as high as 1,000 dollars an acre.

"Out there the individual farms are not large. No farmer tries to cultivate as many acres as we do here. As I said, if by any twist of fate I become rich, I'd try to buy half the lands in these two counties. I'd divide large numbers of these farms into ten acre tracts, go back east and take a thousand Negroes off relief, bring them out here and settle them on these ten acre farms. This would be somewhat like the way they are helping them by housing projects in the cities the country over, except that mine would be a Housing and Farming Project.

"I would interest capital in investing in food product factories to develop mills on another scale, but much like those in North and South Carolina to process the cotton that is raised locally. This would bring the city to these poor people and I would help them by helping myself. That's the kind of charity I've always believed in—help people to help themselves; but to help the helper at the same time.

"Some day, whether my dream comes true or not, something like this is going to happen in these drought ridden sections of the west. We have fine soil, and enough rainfall every year to produce a bountiful crop. But the moisture necessary to change all this ends in the Gulf of Mexico, whither it flows through the rivers, and evaporates into the air from the thinly plowed lands, the way we've been trying to farm out here."

CHAPTER XXIX

ON LINDA'S HOMESTEAD, the strange hill that rose high into the air, from the center of the claim had been named, and it was now known the country around as Mount Eden.

Geologists had been sent to the Rosebud Country to check and see if there might be coal, oil or any kind of minerals in that section. Oil was being found in states like Illinois, where for generations nobody had the least suspicion that there was anything but coal, which had been discovered years back.

As has been described, the land was smooth and level right up to the foot of this peaklike hill, where it shot almost straight into the air for a thousand feet and could be seen towering twenty miles around from every direction. At the foot of it, a white rocky substance which gave indication that the peak was almost solid rock, cropped out at its base and reminded one of lime rock.

Other than that, it was just a high hill and nobody thought anything about it. Since Eden had gotten back on his feet again, and Stewarts had been helping him in the manner described above, he had persuaded Deborah to drive out to the claim now and then. It was his hope that since Linda was history, but the claim still in her name, when the contest was finally decided, he might send Deborah to try buy it from Linda, through her father.

Deborah had gone there several times during the summer, spending sometimes two or three days there, and would be in position to claim residence if it came to that.

Then came one day a telegram from his lawyer in Washington that the Secretary of the Interior had reversed the

Commissioner and Linda had won the last round. The claim was hers now, free and clear of any litigation. As we know, Linda was Rosebud history and Eden never troubled to remind her that she still had a claim. Meantime, among the many people who had read Eden's book, was Eugene Crook.

At about this time, a lawyer whom Crook knew, and who had acted as his attorney for the bank before Crook's bank went broke, met him in Winner.

He had been appointed to a good position in the department of the Interior and was in charge of the Engineers and Geologists who had been sent to the Rosebud in connection with the survey. They had just completed a check up for oil and mineral deposits in Northwest Tripp County and had made a most important discovery.

He had been told of the contest Crook had filed against Linda's claim, by Crook's lawyer in Washington, and was interested in this strange hill that reposed in the middle of that claim.

In meeting him in Winner one night, Crook told him about losing out finally for possession of the claim.

"This Martin Eden," said Crook, showing the other the book, idly, "the author of this, tells one of the strangest stories I have ever read. Reads like a true story."

The lawyer examined the book. "I'd like to read it. May I?"

"Sure, take it along. It'll hold your interest."

"Thanks."

The next morning, on meeting Crook, he said:

"That's a true story, Eugene. Now that claim you've just lost out on, belongs to this preacher's daughter, and according to this story she should be there at home with the preacher in Chicago."

"Well, what is that to me?"

"Everything, man. Now listen to me." Thereupon Eugene Crook and the lawyer, two hours later, had a well laid plan for important action.

Through Martin Eden's idea of deep plowing to form a reservoir to store up moisture and combat the effects of drought (which had reduced three straight crops to a pitiful minimum) Stewart shared in the biggest crop he had raised since coming to the Rosebud Country.

"We owe you a debt of gratitude, Martin," said Deborah, "that we will never be able to pay."

"What do you mean?" he said, looking at her with a question in his eyes.

"Why, we've done so well this year that papa says I should take a trip back to our old home in Indiana for a visit."

"A splendid idea," said Eden, smiling enthusiastically. "I second the motion."

"Thanks, Martin."

"And are you going to?"

"Well, I'd like to," a bit timidly. She had never had a vacation, nor a trip in her life; they had never been fortunate enough to have that much money.

"Fine. When have you planned to go?"

"Next week, if you think you can get along without me."

"We *will* get along without you."

"If I go then, I'll have to give up the trip to your place near Carter, and I hate to neglect that."

"What is there up there that could be of any interest to you, Miss Stewart," he inquired, "except to oblige me as you have been doing."

"We go fishing in Willow Creek."

"In Willow Creek?"

"Yes. Haven't you ever been?"

"No. You mean the creek about five miles east of the place up there?"

"Yes. It has all kinds of fish in it. Not only do you catch lots of fish and have fun, but it's a delightful place to row on."

"Row on? Why, it's just an insignificant stream as far as I've been able to see."

"That's where the surprise comes in. It has many very deep holes, deep enough to row on. The Farnhiems have a boat, so we row out into the middle of the hole and fish. Some of the pond-like holes are almost large and wide enough to have a boat race on. So you see if I go to Indiana, I can't meet them up there and go fishing next week as I promised to."

"Well, it will be too bad to have to give up your fishing trip. But since you can go fishing another time, you take the trip now and have a good time, and when you come back, maybe we'll all go a fishing."

"Farnhiems say," she went on, "that it is a most treacherous stream, however; and that any time the rains are heavy along the White River north of there, the Creek gets all out of its banks. Three bridges across it at that spot have been washed away on the road from Winner to Carter."

"I know that they can't keep any bridge across the thing, and there isn't any across it now. They have a good place to cross, however."

"Yes, there is never any water where they cross, except, I suppose, when it rains. I've often wondered at the deep fishing holes north and south of the crossing, with water many places more than ten feet deep; and where they cross it is always dry and hard, except, as I said, when it rains heavily. I've noticed it when going up to your place north of Carter."

"Well, Deborah, I suppose the people who knew you back in Indiana will be glad to see you again," said he, changing the subject.

"On my way back, I thought of stopping in Chicago."

"In Chicago? Bully. There's lots to see in the Windy City."

"Yes, I know; but I have some relations there."

"Some relations, Deborah? Where do they live? On the north or west side, or would you know what side? And who are these relatives?"

"A grandfather."

"Indeed!"

"He lives on Vernon avenue."

"That's on the South Side."

"Oh, then you know where it is."

"Oh, very well—in fact how well *do I know* where it is. That's in the Colored section. Are you sure that's the name of the street?"

"Yes, that's where I've been sending my letters, and he always answers them. That's the name of the street all right."

"That's unusual. It's right in the heart of the colored district. But there may be a few white people who own their homes and still live on the street."

"Yes, I suppose so. He owns his home and has lived there for a long time, that I know."

"Then that's perhaps his case. Was living there when the colored people moved in and didn't move out like most of the white people do, so that perhaps accounts for his still being there."

"No doubt."

"When's the last time you visited him?"

"Oh, I've never visited him. In fact, I've never seen grandpa. I really wouldn't know him if I met him on the street, but if I call on him at his home, that'll be different. I will then, of course, get to see him."

"Naturally. Well, I've got to get out to Tripp County with Bill, so if you happen to leave before I get back, here's hoping that you have a good time and find your grandpa. Good bye."

"Thank you, Martin, and good bye."

As he went out she smiled after him happily, and looked very sweet. After getting into the car, he thought of something and came back to her.

"What is it, Martin?" she asked, looking at him in an anxious fashion. "Has something gone—wrong?"

"Not exactly," pausing as if he didn't know just how to start.

"This may sound kinda funny, coming from me, and yet it was that about which I really wanted to see you and tell you."

"Tell me something, Martin? Then come in and sit down."
He turned, still wearing that expression. She was more anxious
than ever to know why his face was so serious.

"I dreamed of you last night."

"Oh, only a dream," smiling and relaxing. "I thought
something had really happened."

"It *did* happen—in this dream."

"But you don't believe in dreams, Martin, and neither
do I."

"But you said you had a dream about me once. Before I—"

"That wasn't a dream, Martin. I didn't tell you that it was.
I don't believe in dreams any more than you do."

"Not a dream?" said he. "Then—"

"Mine was a premonition. It just came to me; came to me
while I was as wide awake as we are now."

"Oh, I thought it was a dream and remembering how it all
came true, I thought to tell you about the dream I had. I
sure don't want *it* to come true."

"Well, it's interesting to be told that you dreamed about me.
You may tell me what you dreamed. I'll be glad to hear it."

"Well, since it was only a dream, I don't mind. Especially
when I remember that my dreams always go by contraries.
Nevertheless this was such a terrible dream it frightened me.
I was still frightened when I woke up."

"Oh, and it was a terrible dream, eh? Well, go on, tell me
about it. You've got me all curious now."

"I dreamed that you were—killed."

"Oh," she laughed now. "So I've been killed."

"You won't be; but I have a feeling that something unusual
is going to happen; and that you will in some way be mixed
up in it before you get back," he said, smiling and turning
toward the door.

"Well, anyway, that's interesting. I'd like to get mixed up
in *something*. But your feeling that something is going to happen
to me before I get back is not so cheering. You didn't dream
that, too."

"No," said he, pausing on the threshold, "that was a premonition,—my premonition," and he laughed as he went
across the yard to his car.

She waved him good-bye from the doorway again, and he
drove away over the hill and out of sight.

Eugene Crook and the lawyer boarded the morning train
at Winner, following their night session, for Chicago on an
important mission; a mission of intrigue.

When the train reached Gregory, they did not notice a
girl who got on board and took a seat directly behind them.
She didn't know the men and they didn't know her. It was
just a coincidence.

She became sleepy after about an hour and was annoyed.
She didn't ride trains often enough to care to get sleepy when
she happened to take a trip, and tried to throw it off. Then she
gave in to it and tried to sleep. In this she was not successful
and became more out of patience with herself. Ahead of her
she heard the two men talking.

"I'm taking you on this trip entirely on a hunch," the
lawyer was saying. "From the story, as Martin Eden tells
it in his book, the man we should see is his father-in-law, this
Reverend Dr. Gee, whom we have learned is by right name,
Lee."

Deborah started, and sat up, ears wide. "Martin Eden,"
she said to herself. "What did these men have to do with and
why were they talking about Martin Eden?"

"It's a long chance, and a thin chance; but what he says
about this Dr. Gee in his book, doesn't read like fiction at all,
but like plain facts," said the lawyer.

"Martin Eden," echoed Deborah, "Dr. Gee and 'his book' "
—was all true—every word of it. This she knew. But of what
interest could such a thing be to these men? They were talking
again now and she decided to play dumb, so lay back and
closed her eyes, ears wide open.

"And if the preacher is as Eden described him, we should
have a chance," said Crook.

"A big chance. Now read this paragraph," whereupon he produced the book.

"I was told," read Crook, "that if I wanted to get along with the Elder, the thing to do was to praise him, flatter him—make him think that he's a 'king'." They laughed heartily.

"So now we, as he says elsewhere in the book, are 'hipped' and it's up to us to do some thinking, on our way to Chicago and some planning too," said the lawyer.

"Let us figure how to approach and flatter him, to praise him, and—"

"—make him think that he's a 'king'."

Deborah was listening, eagerly. Her drowsiness was gone; she could keep awake now, all the way to Chicago. Whatever these men were up to, she didn't know. So she hoped that they would talk more. They did.

"Between now and tomorrow morning we'll decide on a mode of proceedure to tickle the old boy's vanity. Meanwhile, getting back to the place, are you sure that there is a great manganese deposit in that hill? Manganese is very valuable and rather rare."

"My experts advise me that it is one of the most valuable manganese deposits in the world. Of the highest quality for alloy, and is worth millions—almost untold millions!"

"Great goodness!" exclaimed Crook. . . . "It sounds fantastic; I'm afraid to even believe it."

"I'm not, for I know that it is so," said the lawyer. "So you see how much it means for us, for you to get possession of that claim. And this old Negro preacher, according to this story, seems to offer, through his daughter, the best way out."

"And you don't think anybody knows about it or has any idea that it is there?"

"Nobody but my Geologists. Since it's on private property, and doesn't have to be reported, they've agreed to say nothing about it if we cut them in on the deal."

"I'll sure do that," said Crook, "if I can get the old man to do business."

"Well, that's the least of my worries, cutting the boys' in. The contract between you and me takes care of us all, if and when we get the land. It's up to us now to get the old man to make the girl sign a relinquishment."

Deborah, listening, started, but didn't rise. It was all clear now, however. They were on their way to Chicago to double cross Eden, because of what they deduced from reading his book. In it, as she knew, he had told his own story, changing the names of people, places and things. She immediately recognized the Elder, Linda—and even herself.

He had hinted at her love for him, his for her, but because she was white and he was black, it was against the Customs of Society, and he couldn't return a great love that he might have had.

So, by an ordinary twist of fate, she was overhearing a plot, a plot to undermine Martin Eden and secure lands that he had bought. They were out to secure same through a hypocrite, who would make his daughter, Martin Eden's wife, betray him.

Most of what she had seen through the medium of second sight, had already happened to Martin Eden. Now the major thing was in process of taking place. These men were on their way to Chicago to have the Elder complete the tragedy of Martin Eden's life by betraying him through his wife. They were talking again:

"Just how will we go about this, anyhow," said Crook. "I don't know anything about Colored people. Martin Eden's the only one I ever knew very well and he would be too smart to fall for any kind of hoax."

"Washington's full of them. Many seem to have a great deal of education and the government departments have quite a number on the payroll. The best way to dope this thing out, however, is to study this book. It gives you a better insight into Negro life than we could ever get otherwise."

"And especially, as regards this particular Negro, this preacher, I mean," said Crook.

"It doesn't seem conceivable that a wife could—would betray her husband, even if they are parted, as she will have to do in order for us to get the land," said the lawyer.

"No, but it won't be her. It will be this old preacher. Eden says in his book that while the old man's great on show, he never actually had $500. in real money at one time in his life."

"Say," cried the lawyer. "There's an idea."

"Yes," answered Crook, "Where?"

"About the old man never having actually had any real money."

"I don't get you!" from Crook. The lawyer sat up with a new idea.

"Listen," how much did Eden pay for that relinquishment when he bought it for her, anyhow?"

"$1,500."

"Fifteen hundred dollars, eh? And he paid the government fee, built and moved that house from Gregory and put it on it and built a barn and made other improvements."

"Yes," said Crook. "Has got between $3000 to $3500 in the place I'd say."

"Call it $3500. Quite an investment in the name of a wife that's not living with him. Yet she holds title to the claim and only she can execute a relinquishment."

"What's on your mind, anyhow?"

"I was thinking what we ought to offer them."

"Oh, that is timely and important."

"Yes, now I learned something about Colored people there in Washington, and according to my information, they aren't accustomed to much money."

"No, I've heard that myself."

"Of course," said the lawyer, "one like this Eden—"

"Oh, he's an exception to the rule, of course."

"Of course, so we can't take him as a criterion; but about what I was starting to tell you. They say that if you give them much more than they are used to handling, you spoil them. So I was thinking that if we went to offering this preacher anything like what Eden has invested in the place, we're less likely to get it than if we offered less."

"I agree with you."

"A whole lot less."

"Yes, *a whole lot* less."

"I think we should start off at about $500.00."

"And raise it a hundred at a time, if he bites, and we have to "

"Then we have the matter of an offer for it settled, yes?"

"Okeh."

"Well, that's enough for the present. Let's go up ahead and have a smoke? The news butch carries a pretty good brand of cigars."

"Okeh," said Crook and they went forward to the smoking car.

Immediately they were out of sight, Deborah sat up. She started to thinking. She had been staying out there on this claim and it was understood that after the crops were sold, Eden might send her to try to buy a relinquishment from Linda. The plan had his consent and he was to supply the money with which to pay her.

But unless she did some deep thinking, and executed some quick action, Linda might sell the relinquishment without his knowledge or consent and before she could get to her. And the place was rich!

"Oh, what can I do," she cried, to herself, but almost aloud. She stood up and walked to the other end of the car. She was trying to think herself out of a most difficult situation. The man she loved,—for she still loved Martin Eden,—was about to lose the chance he had worked for all his life,—his big chance, the chance to make enough money to do all the things he said he would do, if by any trick of fate, he became rich. He could, under the circumstances, perform a great human service.

And now the chance was right in his lap—but about to be snatched by two strangers, one a man who had tried to beat her out of her claim and failed.

She walked back and forth at the rear end of the car, which was empty, and tried to think of some plan of action. She simply *couldn't* let it happen—yet *what could she do* to prevent it?

She recalled, as she walked back and forth back there, other passages from his story. The more she thought of it, the more she became convinced that the preacher would make Linda do it. The Elder must have understood that by this time, all was over between Linda and Martin, so he had the best possible excuse to make her sign a relinquishment which would mean money for him.

If she went to them, and told them about its value, they wouldn't, perhaps, believe her, or believing, would proceed out of spite and hate, to injure Martin in some other way.

And most important of all, these men were on their way to see her, and whatever was to be done, might be completed before she could even tell them.

After a time she gave up. She was determined to do something, or try to; but she couldn't decide then, so went back to her chair and sat down.

"Oh, Martin, if you hadn't been so honest about being faithful to your race, and married me," she sighed to herself. "This was the place you would have put me on. It would have been all free and clear now. You would have been happy and we would have children by this time, perhaps more than you and she had, which they took away from you, too."

She was distinctly miserable all the way to Omaha, where she changed cars and lost sight of the two men, whom she saw enter a Pullman from Omaha for Chicago. She could only afford to ride in the coach.

All through the night she tried to formulate some plan of action. Finally, being unable to arrive at a better one, she decided to call on the Lees, too, and offer them more money; money that she didn't have. But she would wire Martin, if they agreed to sell, and he would get it and send it to her.

She fell off to sleep and when she awakened, the train had just crossed the Mississippi River. Three hours later it was pulling into Chicago.

She hid away in the station to watch, and saw Crook and the lawyer go by. She concluded that they would most likely go to a hotel before calling on the preacher. This would give her time to get to Linda at her home, first. She remembered then that Eden said Vernon Avenue, where her grandfather lived, was in the middle of the Colored section. She decided to go there first and ask him about them. Lee being a well known preacher, she was sure that her grandfather could help her find his house.

So she took a taxi, with orders to drive to her grandfather's number on Vernon Avenue. The driver thought she said "Vernor" Avenue, which is on the far West Side of Chicago. It took him a half hour to drive there and more than $2.00 cab fare.

He drove its full length, could find no such number, and stopping the cab and opening the door, he said:

"I'm sorry, Miss, but there is no such number on Vernor Avenue. I've tried—"

"Vernor Avenue?" she cried, amazed. "I didn't say 'Vernor' Avenue. I said 'Vernon' Avenue."

"Oh, great goodness, that's away out on the South side, miles and miles from here; out in the nigger section."

She started, and was angry—not because of driving her away from the street she wanted to go, but because of the ugly word he used. She had never forgotten the lie Richards told on her in which he quoted her as using it.

"Well, this is something," she cried, getting out of the cab in burning indignation.

"I'm awfully sorry, Miss. If this cab belonged to me, I'd drive you back there without charge. But—"

"Needn't bother. Your mistake may cost me dearly; but you perhaps made an honest one. I want to get there. There's an elevated over there. Since you seem to know where it is, maybe you'll be good enough to tell me how I can get there."

"I sure will," apologetically. "I'll be glad to. Just step in the cab, please, I'll drive you to the elevated station and tell you on the way, exactly how to get there."

"Thank you," said she getting back into the cab.

It was about six blocks to her grandfather's home on Vernon Avenue from the elevated station where she got off, so she took a cab. It was a beautiful day and from the time she left the elevated station, all the way to Vernon Avenue, she saw nothing but Colored people. She looked at them curiously. They were all colors, many as black as night, others as bright as she was.

Even after turning in on Vernon Avenue, she still saw nothing else. By the time the cab stopped, she decided that her grandfather must be the only white person on the street.

After leaving the cab and checking the number to be sure she had come to the right house, she looked around her. It was a beautiful, warm fall day, pleasant outside and re-freshing. Many people were going to and fro on the street, some sat on their porches, while others looked out of windows—and they were all colored. She smiled and went up the steps with plans to ask her grandpa how it happened that he still lived there when all other white people had moved away.

CHAPTER XXX

THE HOUSE HAD A large, wide door, the place was clean and well kept, a fact that she noticed. She had observed that many of the houses where the Colored people lived were not as well kept. She was glad to see the neat porch with flowers, deftly arranged, a small lawn with the grass cropped, no weeds—in short, the whole place was as industrious white people would keep it.

She pushed the bell and waited. Presently she heard foot-steps and a moment later the door opened—and she recoiled. Her mouth opened so quickly and so wide that the woman who had opened the door looked at her oddly and inquired:

"Why, what is the matter?" looking her up and down. She recovered her equilibrium quickly enough. But what had made her start so quickly was that the woman standing there before her looked so much like her mother, that she frightened her. The only difference was that this woman was colored!

After recovering, she advanced a step, and in a timid, apologetic voice said:

"Pardon me, but does a Mr. Nelson Boudreaux live here?"

"Yes," replied the woman, "he does."

"Thank you," said Deborah; "And can I see him, please?" The woman hesitated, before speaking.

"Well, he's asleep right now and I hate to awaken him. He's rather old, if you don't happen to know, and he usually takes a nap about this time. If it's very important, however, I could call him; but if you could come back in say, about an hour, I'd like that better. He'll be up and around then."

"I'm awfully sorry," said Deborah; "but it is *very* important

351

that I see him. In fact, *most important*." She was thinking about
Eugene Crook and his lawyer and of Reverend Lee and Linda.
The woman was speaking again.

"Well," she sighed, "I hate to wake him up. He's so much
better off when he can sleep until he awakens. I could take a
message, or I might even attend to what ever you want to
see him about. I'm his daughter, you see."

Again Deborah recoiled, and staggered back two steps, her
mouth open wide.

"His daughter?" She raised her hand to her mouth.

"Why, yes—but what's the matter? Are you—ill?" her
tone was kindly.

"Why, no—no, I'm not ill and—"

"Then why do you keep starting like that? That's twice
you did that way in the few moments you've been standing
there. I really can't understand you. I'm afraid you *are*
ill."

"Oh, no, really, I'm not and there's nothing else the matter.
I—I guess that I—"

"Come in the house," said the elder woman opening the door
wide. Deborah stepped across the threshold.

"Step into the parlor and have a seat. I'll get you a glass of
water. Maybe that will help you." The parlor was very large.
It was one of the first mansions, built in the eighties, that
Negroes ran the white people out of when they began to invade
the neighborhood.

Being one of the "better class of Negroes" of Chicago,
Boudreaux, who had lived there for many years, had pride
and was careful to keep the place neat and comfortable.

The elder woman hurried away to the refrigerator, and pouring her a glass of ice cold water returned to find her still
standing. She was looking at the pictures on the piano, and
had just had another shock. For there on the piano was *a
picture of her mother!*

"*What mystery here?*" she asked herself.

"Why don't you take a seat?" said the other, handing her the glass of water, which she drank to the bottom. "*What does it all mean?*" she was asking herself.

First, a woman opening the door looks so much like her mother that she is frightened at the sight of her. And now, before her, propped against a small easel on the piano, was *her own mother's picture!* There could be no mistake about that. It was *her mother's picture all right,* for *they had one back in So. Dakota that was made from the same negative!*

Before she could make an excuse for not sitting down, she heard footsteps coming slowly toward the parlor, and heard the woman saying:

"Oh, father, you up?"

"Yes, daughter, I wasn't so tired, slept too much last night. So I didn't sleep long. Such a pretty day, thought I'd get up and take a stroll outside."

The old man had not seen Deborah. The woman hadn't either, because her back was turned, when Deborah experienced the biggest shock of all, for the man standing there was her grandfather, without doubt—and he was *a colored man!*

She steadied herself with an effort and was glad that they were exchanging words and hadn't seen her have the other shock.

"Well, I'm glad you're up and I didn't have to awaken you," and then turning toward Deborah:

"This young lady has been inquiring for you. This, Miss, is Mr. Nelson Boudreaux. Are you sure now that he is the person you want to see?"

The old man had stood, looking hard at Deborah. Adjusting his glasses on his nose, he advanced a step.

"Listen, young lady, and look at me. Isn't your name Deborah? Deborah Stewart?" She was calm now and strangely happy.

"Yes, grandpa Boudreaux, this is Deborah," and she permitted him to take her in his arms and kiss her.

Presently he held her at arm's length and looked at her with admiration. His daughter did likewise.

"Well, I declare! Bernadine, this is your neice, Deborah Stewart. Can you imagine it being her, all grown up like this?"

"Laura's daughter! My dear child!" and reaching out her arms, she embraced Deborah fondly.

"We talk about you and think about you, but we've never seen you before."

"No, grandpa, we've never seen each other, but here we are together at last," said Deborah, happily.

"But—how came you to be here now?"

"Oh, I'd almost forgot; but I'm here on such important business that I hardly have time to tell you about it."

"Is that so? I'm sorry; but since you don't seem to be mad after seeing what we are, can I ask you if you dislike us now because you see that we are—are colored?"

"Why grandpa, how can you ask such a question? Dislike you—I love you both and I'm so happy now that I've met you at last."

"But, Deborah," cautioned Bernadine, "do you understand what father means? We're Colored people—Negroes, do you understand? While you, you're supposed to be *white*, aren't you?"

"Yes, auntie, I *was supposed* to be white. I never knew that grandpa was a colored man until just now."

"And you—you don't hate him after you've—you've learned the—truth?"

"Hate my grandpa, why, no! I'm glad that you are all Colored—oh, *you don't know how glad I am* that you are; but I can't take enough time now to tell you all about why."

"Thanks be to the Lord," sighed Bernadine, tears in her eyes. "We didn't tell you before because we—we thought you might hate us when you learned the truth. And now that you don't hate us, please kiss me again, Deborah, you're such a sweet child."

Deborah flew into her arms, kissed and caressed her, and then putting her arms around her grandfather, kissed him again and again and caressed him.

"Now as big a hurry as I am in, I must take time enough to tell you a story.

"I'm in love with a—Colored man—have been since the first I met him, and he loves me, I know. But because he thinks I am white while he is colored, he refuses to return my love. I even proposed to him but he turned me down and told me why he could not marry me. He is the finest man that ever lived and father and I both love him.

"As I said, I even proposed to him, but he told me that a marriage between a white girl and a colored man could not be, and then he came here to Chicago and married a colored girl. The colored girl loved him and they were getting along fine and had a baby. The girl's father came to visit them and while she was still recovering from having the baby and her husband was away, this man stole his daughter and brought her here to Chicago. The girl and the baby are still here.

"He held this man's (his name is Martin Eden) wife as a pawn to wreak vengence on him."

"Martin Eden! Why, we know him. He married old Reverend Lee's daughter down the street. We not only know all of them, but we knew that something has been wrong, because the girl's at home, in the next block now, and has been there quite a little while. We have all wondered exactly what the matter was."

"Oh—oh! Such a coincidence! But I must finish my story, so that you will know why I'm here.

"If Martin Eden had known, or had I known, that I had Negro blood in my veins, he would never have left South Dakota to find a wife in his own race. For there all the time was I, and he would have asked me to marry him long ago."

"If I could have only known," said Boudreaux, "I would have written you then, and—"

"Of course you would have. But how could either of us have known such a thing, under the circumstances? So you see why I'm so happy because now I know that I'm a colored girl at last, and when all this trouble is over and settled, I can tell Martin the truth and he will marry me. He will love me as I want him to and I can give him the great love that has always been in my heart for him."

"Such a strange story," sang Bernadine.

"But I must get to what is about to happen—happen to this man that I love so much.

"He bought his wife a claim. Now she's away and the claim is valuable—valuable beyond the realm of wildest dreams. They don't know it, neither does Martin Eden; but two white men do, and they are in Chicago right now to *get it from her;* for a song. To do so, they're going to see her father; all she has to do is sign a paper. But she will betray her husband, Martin Eden, when she signs this paper. Nevertheless, I have the feeling that her father will make her sign it." ·

"What!" cried Boudreaux.

"Oh, Grandpa, I can't stay here longer to tell you more. I'm here to see this wife of his. I will offer her more than they plan to pay her and hope she will sell it to me so I can prove up on it and give it back to her husband, Martin Eden."

"But, Deborah," began Boudreaux.

"I can't tell you more now nor listen to anything you want to say. I must get to this girl before they do and it's too late." She said the last words on the way to the door.

"Please come out on the porch and point the house out to me and I'll get right over there before they do—if they haven't been there already."

They showed her the Lee house across the street in the next block, and tapping each fondly, she hurried away.

"I'll be back as quickly as I've done something." She crossed the street and walked rapidly toward the Lee home. When within a few paces, she saw the door open and Crook and his lawyer stepped out the door, followed by the Elder. Shaking his hand, seeming well satisfied, they came down the steps and went up the street in the same direction that she was walking.

Her heart sank. She slowed down and looked at the preacher and noted what a fine specimen of humanity he was. He glanced down at her a moment, then stepping inside, closed the door.

She continued down the street in a maze of bewilderment and heartache. Things had been happening to her so rapidly in the past hour that she was finding it difficult to keep her wits together. She had the feeling that the men ahead of her carried a relinquishment to Linda's claim, and by all odds that settled it. Yet she couldn't seem to give up; to admit defeat. She was conscious that she *ought to do something*—yet what?

At the next corner, there was an ice cream parlor. She went in there and ordered a drink. Taking a seat, she tried to think what she ought to do—what could she do? She was desperate; the situation was desperate. Now, since having discovered that she was colored and not white, the way was clear for Martin to marry her and she knew he would; but he had been betrayed. He didn't know it, and if he did, he could not help himself. It was up to *her* and *her alone* to help him; to help him *now*— and, oh, how much she wanted to!

She couldn't think of any way to change what she was positive had happened, so all upset, she left the parlor and started to retrace her steps. As she came out she met Mrs. Lee and Terry, whom she didn't know, of course, but they were holding between them, what she thought was the cutest little boy.

She smiled at it, in spite of all the worry, waved her hand, and the little boy waved his back. She looked back over her shoulder at the women and the little boy, who crossed the street and walked eastward. They were taking the boy to the park for an outing. She, in the meantime, walked back up Vernon Avenue in the direction of the Lee home.

When about a half block from it going south, she met

Reverend Lee going north. His brow contracted. He was trying to remember where he had seen her, which had been during his first trip to South Γ∖koˌta—but he couldn't recall where.

After passing him, an idea jumped suddenly into her mind. *Why not call and see and maybe have a talk with Linda?* She quickened her pace and hurried toward the house.

After passing the girl whose face seemed familiar, the Reverend looked back over his shoulder and watched her. His curiosity aroused, he followed her, at a consistent distance, in the hope that he might find a chance to speak to her.

In front of his house, she looked up to make sure it was the right place. After seeing Crook and his companion come out, then going on by, she wasn't sure now which one of three houses, all just alike, the Lee home was. The Reverend trailing her, caught up, passed, then turning back and tipping his hat, said:

"Pardon me, but could I help you, madam?"

"Why, yes," thinking quickly, guardedly. She didn't want to say much to him because the inspiration to call and see Linda had come when she saw him leaving. So she didn't wish him to be there when she talked with Linda.

In the fast thinking she was doing, she remembered Martin Eden saying that he met Linda in Murphysboro. She turned to him now with a forced smile.

"I'm looking for Linda Lee, whom I used to know slightly in Murphysboro. She—"

"In that house," said the Elder, pointing at it. "That's my home. I'm her father. Come on up and I'll let you see her."

"Thank you, sir." She was thinking fast as to how she could get rid of him after she got inside. He unlocked the door.

"My daughter is not feeling so well. I'm in a hurry, as I have to be down on Michigan Avenue very shortly. I'll bring her a little medicine when I return."

"Thank you, sir. And you say she's not feeling so well?"

"No, a bit upset this morning," swinging the door open. She stepped inside.

"That's too bad, really. I hope it isn't serious."

"Oh, no, and you can see her, but I'm afraid you'll have to do so in her room."

"Oh, I won't mind that."

"Then follow me and I'll take you right up to her."

"That is very kind of you and many thanks." He stopped and knocked on the door of Linda's room as Deborah came upstairs behind him.

"Who is it?" called Linda, through the door.

"It's me, Linda. There's a young lady here to see you. I've explained that you don't feel so well and she understands and says that it'll be all right. I'll let her in." He opened the door and made a gesture with his other hand for her to enter.

Before he closed the door, she thanked him with a smile. Looking over her head he called:

"I'm going downtown, Linda. Will be back in an hour or so."

"Very well, father."

Deborah was relieved when she heard him open the outside door and close it behind him. She could hear his footsteps on the side walk and in a moment he was gone.

Deborah had toyed with something about her purse in a play for time, then with a "pardon me, please," crossed to where Linda lay on the bed and paused beside her. Linda looked up at her.

"Who're you?"

"Why—"

"Seems like I know you. Haven't I met or seen you before somewhere?"

"Yes, you've met me."

"I thought so. Where?"

"In South Dakota."

"In South Dakota?" repeated Linda, in surprise, and sat up. "Oh, yes, I remember. Your brother use to work for—"

"Your husband," said Deborah, evenly, and looked hard at her. Linda started, as if she were pained, or was it a guilty conscience? She sank back on the bed.

"Well, what do you want?"

"I—I've come to see you—about your—claim," ventured Deborah.

"My claim?" repeated Linda, and seemed vague.

"Yes, your place in Tripp County, north of Carter, in So. Dakota, you understand."

Linda repeated listlessly:

"My claim. I have no claim any more."

"No claim any more!" cried Deborah, laying a hand on her, turning her over and looking hard at her. "What do you mean?"

"I mean what I just said."

"Please, say it again please. I'm afraid I don't quite understand you."

"I mean that I haven't a claim any more. I mean that I just sold it."

"You!" cried Deborah, grasping her wrist, "*sold your—* claim?"

"Yes," sighed Linda, as if very tired. "I sold it about—an hour ago."

"Sit up, you, and listen to me. You don't know what you are saying—you *couldn't* have done such a thing."

"Please," cried Linda, trying to wrench her arm free. "You're hurting me." Deborah relaxed her hold on the wrist, but continued looking hard at her.

"I meant what I said, which was, that I sold my claim. That is, I relinquished it back to the government." Again Deborah grasped her wrist and glaring at her cried:

"You mean that you relinquished it to Eugene Crook; to the man who tried to *beat you out of it!*" She squeezed the wrist so tight that Linda's face was distorted with pain.

"Will you please," she cried, "let go of my wrist!" Deborah relaxed it, but looked at her so hard that Linda, rubbing the wrist, was half frightened.

"Well, what if I did?" trying to be defiant. "It's none of your business, is it?"

"I'm *making* it my business, see!" and finishing, she smacked Linda hard on the cheek, a sharp, stinging slap.

"Well, people!" cried Linda, holding her cheek where Deborah had slapped it. She started up, but pushing her back roughly, Deborah cried:

"Sit down, you, and listen to me!" Her tone was commanding, sharp and severe.

"Well!"

"Yes, I'm *making* it my business because I know all about it, and I know all about you, too, do you understand what I mean?"

"No, I don't. I don't even know who you are, but I'd like to ask what concern it is of yours; and by what authority you come smacking my face and twisting my wrist."

"Then, I'll tell you why."

"Please, by all means do. You, a white girl."

"I know all about it because before Martin Eden left So. Dakota to come to Chicago and bring you back there to file on this claim, I proposed to him. I loved him and he loved me, only—"

"Well, I never!"

"Now don't get me wrong, but most of all, don't go getting Martin Eden wrong, either. I said that I loved Martin Eden and before he came here to bring you out there the first time, I proposed to him—I asked him not to come here for you; I would homestead the claim for him, and that I'd be his wife and I'd have been a good wife.

"Now I know I'm justified in what I've just done," cried Linda indignantly, "I know now that my sister and my father were both right about him from the beginning. He was false all along, a liar, a cheat and a fakir. I—"

"Another word like that from you and I'll—"

Deborah drew back and Linda ducked. "Now you keep quiet

for a few minutes and listen to me and you'll know a whole lot more than you do now."

Deborah drew a chair close to the bed and continued:

"As I said, I proposed to Martin. I didn't say that he proposed to me, for he didn't. I didn't say that he said he loved me, for he didn't say anything of the kind. My woman's intuition told me that."

It was all so bewildering to Linda, she sighed and shook her head to indicate how she felt.

"It's a long, long story, but you're going to listen to it because it involves mostly you and the man you married, Martin Eden. I'm involving myself.

"Now, I know what you are thinking. You're thinking that I am a—a white girl, running around after a colored man, and that my character is bad and all that. You started to justify your act of an hour ago, by accusing him of a lot of things because of what I said. That's what *I* said, not he. When you've heard what I'm going to say, you're going to feel mighty bad. You're going to regret from now until you're dead the act you've just committed—betraying your husband. But in defense of myself, I want to say that I am not a *bad* girl. I couldn't be a bad girl and a virgin, too. So that is that."

Linda, indignant, started out of bed with: "I'll not be insulted by you another minute, I—" Getting her by the shoulders, Deborah shoved her back on the bed roughly.

"No, you don't! I said it was a long, long story, and you're going to listen to it, or you'll be treated worse. So just be patient and hear me through.

"I was about to say that you're going to be so sorry for everything you've done, and allowed to be done by your sister and father, to him, that you'll wish that you were dead, for you've done an awful wrong."

"I don't know what in the world you're trying to tell me; I don't know what it is all about."

"Here's the first of it. I want to explain that I *was* a white girl."

"You *were* a white girl?"

."I mean that I *thought* I was a white girl until a little over an hour ago.

"No," cried Deborah, "I'm not insane. Just give me a little time and I'll explain everything. I meant just what I said.

"I *did* think I was a white girl, and I'm supposed to have been one all my life. My father and brothers back there in So. Dakota and Martin Eden, too, *still* think that I'm a white girl.

"That was why Martin couldn't admit that he loved me. Yet I know he did because we had so much interest in common.. I was good to him and he was just as good to me. No two people in all the world were ever so naturally adapted to each other in every way as he and I.

"But as I said, he didn't then, and he hasn't since, said one word of love to me. Even though your folks stole you away from him and have kept you away all this time, he still ignores my love for him. However, he doesn't know that I'm not a white girl any longer. Nobody knows that but you and me, for I only found it out a little over an hour ago.

"You still think I'm crazy, don't you? Well, to get that part of the story over with, here's what happened.

"I was on my way back to Indiana, where we lived before we moved to So. Dakota. It happened that I was on the same train with that man, Eugene Crook, who tried to beat you out of your claim, and failing, has now secured it by having you betray the man you married."

"I don't like that word 'betraying' which you keep on saying. I didn't betray my husband. He betrayed me."

"We'll get to that in time and when we do, I'll leave it to you to say who's been right. Meanwhile, lets get back to Crook, the man who wanted your place.

"I was in the seat just behind them on the train from So. Dakota. I imagine they got on at Winner, while I boarded it at Gregory. They got to talking, and after hearing them mention Martin's name, I naturally listened closely to all they said, until they got through and went into the coach ahead to smoke.

"They talked about Martin's book—incidentally, he wrote one, in case you haven't heard."

"I've heard about it. They told me all the things he said about my father and my sister and me. In fact, in it he talked about everybody."

"Which gives you another excuse to justify what you've just done. Yet you haven't heard all my story.

"As I was saying, I overheard their conversation and that they were coming here to see your father to get you to do what you admit having done. Now I'm getting around to my side of the story and how I happened to find out that I'm no longer a white girl, as I have been thinking I was.

"I was on my way to Indiana, but have a grandfather here whom I've written to but had never seen. I planned to stop off and see him on my way back from Indiana. But after I overheard this plot to get your land, I decided to stop off and see my grandpa today, and then you, in the hope that I could in some way stop or delay you in committing this travesty." She dabbed at her nose, for tears were threatening. After a time, Deborah managed to go on:

"When I called to see my grandpa, who lives across the street in the next block, and whose name is Nelson Boudreaux, I found that he was a colored man!"

On mention of Boudreaux, Linda started up, then looked closely at the other. She knew old Nelson Boudreaux as almost everybody in Chicago did—especially everybody on Vernon Avenue. She had been seeing him all her life and remembered that he looked so much like a white man, people wondered why he didn't go over on the other side.

"So that was what I meant when I said that I had thought that I was white. When I saw him for the first time in my life, I knew differently.

"I haven't had time to talk to him and find out how we got all mixed up like this. All I know is that I was supposed to be white when I was born, and have been raised to think that way, so that is that, except that I'm glad now that I am colored. I'm so glad I am, that if I didn't have to try to do something about what you've done, I'd be shouting for joy. Of course you wouldn't understand that either."

"By that I mean this," said she, using her forefinger now to illustrate. "Had Martin Eden known that I was a colored girl, he'd never have come to Chicago to take you out there. He felt that he *had* to marry a colored girl. You didn't know that and I'd bet that he never said anything to you about it in all the while you were with him."

Linda's silence acknowledged it, her eyes glued to this strange girl, who was telling her things she had never even suspected.

"He found you, he was nice to you, he married you—a girl who never understood him, and let her father and sister abuse him shamefully. They kept up their abuse until they had succeeded in breaking up your union. Now, on top of all the misunderstanding and the abuse you forced on him, you climax it by letting them make you betray him. I don't believe that any woman in all the history of womanhood and marriage, has betrayed a man as shamefully as you have—and that man your own husband!

"And yet that's what you've done to him." Tears ran down her cheeks; her body shook with sobs.

"I say that he loved me and it was cruel that fate let him make such a sacrifice. Before he married you, he boarded with us and that's how I came to know so well the kind of man he is. He was ambitious. He spoke repeatedly of his people and sympathized with them. They meant well, but 300 years of slavery had made them, even though free a long time, irresponsible, carefree and dependent on others to give them jobs and look out for them. He talked for days when it rained and they couldn't go to the fields, of how, as a little boy, he didn't want to be like that. So he started to struggle while he was a mere child to change it, insofar as he could.

"Instead of wasting his adolescent years, he struggled and

saved, went up there to that Country when it was new and undeveloped, and made conquest.

"I saw that his greatest aim in life was, first, to succeed so that he could have security; then to marry a nice girl and bring her there and love her. He pictured children, little boys and girls that he would raise off there where they could be free of this terrible environment which you see all around you here. I could have given him all that and stood ready to do so, but I was white while he was black, and he said it couldn't be.

"So he left me and went in search of that wife of his own blood. He found you and married you, tried to live with you, and in his book he says that you tried to be faithful and good, too. But your father and sister had made you subservient to their will, so he awakened to find that he was expected to please them, and to do so he would have had to conform to their idea of life.

"That wasn't fair and you knew it then, you know it now; but however you might feel at this time, it is too late now. You have this day betrayed him and sooner or later you're going to be called upon to pay—to pay this debt with interest!

"He said when I told him that I loved him and asked him to marry me, that it was against the custom of society and that he couldn't transcend those customs. I asked him to disregard those customs and their social laws; I loved him, I understood his needs and I would dedicate my life, my health and my strength to caring for him and helping him.

"Now isn't that what he needed? Isn't that what he was looking for? Isn't that what he hoped and prayed for in marrying you? And did you give it to him? You did not! Instead, you've betrayed him for a mess of pottage—and Linda Eden, you'll pay! Pay with your blood and soul until the longest day you live. . . . There is no escape from the hell you've put yourself in. Try to justify any act you've committed against this man, and see if you can escape your own conscience.

"Just before he was about to leave and come to you the first time, that was when I told him that I loved him and proposed to him. I didn't do so because I was brazen and immodest. I did it because just before he came, I had a strange premonition. My father says that I am psychical; that I have the gift of second sight; that I was born that way. Any way, I experienced a strange premonition and Martin Eden was the center of it. I saw that a storm was about to envelop him; and I knew in that strange way, by this gift of second sight with which father says I'm endowed, that the only way he could be saved from that terrible something that would soon overtake him, was not to come to Chicago. I, therefore, sacrificed my modesty by telling him that I loved him; that I would homestead the claim for him, and that if he wouldn't come to Chicago, this terrible something that I had seen couldn't happen to him.

"I knew that he couldn't accept me; I knew that he wouldn't take me. But it was the only way I had to try to save him from all this, which you know now already *has* happened to him.

"He left me and went his way. He had to walk to his little claim house. A high hill rose between our house and his and he had to cross over this to get to his house. When he reached the top of that hill, as if from nowhere, a mighty wind swept up into his face. Oh, what a mighty wind that was.

"I knew when he left, that this wind would meet him, this wind from nowhere, for it was the forerunner of the storms that were to meet him; to struggle with him, overthrow him—and in the end destroy him." She took a few steps, then turning, pointed a finger at Linda.

"That storm, Linda, *was you!*

"I stood there at the window and I saw Martin Eden struggle against it. It drove him away back and it seemed that it must surely fell him. Even to this day, I can't understand how he endured and kept his feet—but he did. Not only kept his feet, but finally forced himself through it and disappeared over the hill.

"That was the courage that is Martin Eden. Because of it,

I've had another premonition; the feeling that he *will* survive even this tragedy that you have put upon him, for brave men cannot fail, they cannot be whipped—they will not die!

"You know the rest of the story. I passed out of his life then and you entered. Because he loved me, he couldn't at once, turn that love to you. Half of love is understanding. I understood him. Me, a white girl; but you a colored girl, did not.

"You know that he tried to love you; you know that he soon became fond of you. He was kind to you. He was faithful to you—did everything he knew to make you comfortable and happy. And for all that, you have betrayed him. Oh, what a terrible thing you've done! And even yet, he does not know it.

"He'll find out from Eugene Crook, who was a banker, but whose bank has since gone broke, because he stole the people's money and gambled it away in speculation. He is under indictment now as well as under bond. As he beat the people out of their money, so he tried to beat you out of your claim, the claim that Martin Eden bought for you. The claim that he put you on and trusted you with.

"Eugene Crook failed in his effort to beat you out of your claim, not because of you or anything you did, oh, no. But because of the man you've betrayed. He fought your fight; fought it after you were taken away and held here. He fought it all the way from where it was when you left, clear up to the Secretary of the Interior, at Washington, D. C.—and in the end, won. Won for you.

"You didn't know that the Secretary of the Interior decided in your favor, closing the contest case Crook filed against it while you were still in So. Dakota, did you? No, you didn't know it—but Eugene Crook did. And when he knew that he had lost for good in an open court, he read Martin's book in which he told his own story, his life of hell.

"Gene Crook then knew whom to see and what to do. You know the rest of that story, too."

Linda's head was bowed now. Deborah's story had been a revelation; a revelation—that came too late!

"Another thing you didn't know, and not even yet does Martin—but Eugene Crook does. He knows that the strange, high hill, in the middle of the claim you held, which he has bought for a song, has the richest deposit of manganese ore in all the world—and is worth millions!"

Linda recoiled, her mouth wide, speechless!

"You wouldn't know, of course, what manganese means, so I'll explain. It develops an alloy, the finest ingredient for the tempering and softening of steel.

"That is something that nobody knew until a few weeks ago, not even Crook. I heard the man who was with him explain that nobody knew but the geologists who made the discovery, and this lawyer and Crook.

"So Crook, who failed to steal your claim because of Martin Eden, will soon be a very rich man. In discussing you and your father, I heard them agree that Martin had put about $3,500 into your claim, but that since your father wouldn't understand about so much money, they were going to offer him $500.00, which is the amount I imagine they paid him.

"You know, feeling as I do, if I were guilty of what you, through permitting yourself to be weak and not standing up for your husband, had done, I wouldn't want to go on living.

"Why, only a few weeks ago, Martin said that if by some strange miracle of fate he should become rich, what he would do. He would buy all the land he could in that Rosebud Country. He would go to Washington and lobby for a bill to have the government dam White River, 60 miles northwest of the Rosebud, and when it was dry and the crops needed it, bring the waters down and flood the country through the medium of mighty aqueducts.

"For three years the Rosebud has suffered severely from drought. The country has sufficient rainfall, if it falls at the right time—but it hasn't fallen at the right time for three years. Three short crops in succession haven't done anybody up there any good—and most of all, Martin, who always seeds such large crops. Things have been so bad with him, due to these failures, that he was on the verge of going broke. And with all the trouble you've put on him, his life has been miserable.

"It was during the height of this misery last fall that he conceived the idea of writing the book—and turned in and wrote it. The story impressed everybody who read it as being so true to life that it became popular and is selling well. With the profits from this, he has been able to redeem himself considerably. With a relief, for awhile at least, from the burden of worry, and the profits from his book, he put one of his ideas, which pertained to deep plowing to store up moisture, into effect—with splendid results.

"We've just harvested and threshed the largest crop ever grown on his lands in Dakota, which is how my father, who is working part of his lands on shares, was able to give me money to make this trip.

"Now if you had been a good wife to him and stayed out there on your claim where you belonged, just look what would have happened! This immense fortune from the manganese deposit on the claim you gave to Crook so that your father's hatred for Eden could be satisfied, would soon be available to help Martin, help so many poor people of our race to help themselves. Think of that plan of his to buy all these lands, divide them up into ten acre tracts and come back here and take a thousand poor colored families off relief, settle them there where they could make an honest living. Where they could have a cow and pigs and chickens, with a garden to raise more vegetables than they could eat. Food product factories to employ them a few months each year to make some extra spending money.

"He said he would keep all policy bankers and vice racketeers away from them and help send everyone who stole in there and tried to start it, to the penitentiary for life. He pictured a substantial church, one for about every 500 people. Between playing policy and losing much of their little earnings on one hand, and being bled white by a thousand miscellaneous preachers operating no end of little churches in empty stores here in Chicago, poor innocent and helpless children go hungry, stay out in the street until all hours of night, and land in jail before they're old enough to know what life is all about. He says the race is going right to the dogs.

"His program is simple and easily understood. It's the philosophy of common sense. All he needs is some money to put it into actual practice. He talks always of practical charity with regards to his race—our race. He believes in helping people to help themselves. And to think that right here on the claim that he bought for you, was the means to realize all these ends.

"All these wonderful things can never be done now just because of you. Because you insist on being weak and simple and not standing up like a woman and fighting for your man, these poor helpless people of your race—our race, must go on, staggering helplessly to God knows where. From the earth must come all things on which life depends to subsist. What Martin Eden would do for a thousand Negro families on relief today, would mean almost a new race of the same people, twenty years hence. Oh, what a sin you have committed, what a terrible wrong you have done. You—" She was cut off by a scream from Linda who fell over on the bed, her body shaking with sobs.

"You, his wife, the woman he trusted even before he married you, has made all this impossible. For five hundred Judas' dollars, you have destroyed this great possibility. Think of the millions, they said, maybe, untold millions, lying hidden in that worthless looking hill, that would have been used for posterity—but all goes now to a white man. It'll mean just a few more rich white men, added to a procession of already rich ones, while struggling in the dust of nowhere are those poor helpless members of our race, right under your eyes, stumbling on and on to the kingdom that will never come." Wet with tears of remorse, facing Deborah, Linda grabbed her by each arm.

"Oh, please hush—hush! I can see all the wrongs I've caused and how I've made my husband suffer. I know I betrayed him, but if you stand there and keep telling me over and over again about it, you'll drive me insane—do you hear!" She relaxed her hold on Deborah and walked the floor crying.

"You were right. You've been right in everything you've said. I take all the blame and don't deserve any consideration. I admit that I've been a weakling and because of my weakness I've sinned. I was unfit to be Martin Eden's wife in the beginning; I was unfit to be any strong, courageous man's wife and I stand bared at last before my maker; I'm ashamed of myself, ashamed of what I've done. I'm ashamed to go on living—and I want to die, I want to die!

"Oh, lord, God, my heavenly father! Please try to forgive me—not only for what I have done; but for what I am about to do. Please, God, dear Lord, try to forgive me that."

Anger gone and fear entering, Deborah watched her.

"What do you mean—about that dying and what you're going to do? I—I don't want to be the cause of you—you doing something to yourself, because of what I've said. Another wrong can't right the ones already done. You—"

Linda by an obvious effort, becomes strangely calm, now. She looked straight at Deborah, with an expression of peculiar determination; like a person who has thought and deciding to do something, but doesn't want to say any more. She raised a hand and laying it gently on Deborah, said:

"Please go now, dear. Try to forgive and forget me. Don't blame yourself for bringing me to see my sins of commission. Sooner or later, it had to be, and I forgive you as I've asked you to forgive me. Remember me only as an unfortunate woman without the strength of her convictions, and if I chose to 'pay the price' it is not your fault."

"But—I can't let you—"

"Please go, I say. Go—now!" Thereupon Deborah recoiled in fright. Linda ushered her firmly toward the door, and pushed her gently into the hall.

Outside, Deborah found herself in a quandary. She called Linda loudly to open the locked door, and not to commit an act.

"Go away, please. There is nothing more you can do. Please go your way and let me alone."

Deborah ran along the hall and opened all the doors upstairs. If there was any other person in the house, she would tell about Linda. All upstairs rooms were empty. She hurried downstairs, calling out loudly enough to be heard, but there was no response.

She hurried into the next block and told her aunt and grandfather what she feared Linda would do.

"She ought to kill her old daddy," said Boudreaux. "He's the one who's made all this mischief. He deserves to be killed."

"But, grandpa," cried Deborah, "If she kills herself, it will be my fault. It was I who worked her into such a state by the things I told her. Please help me to prevent maybe a terrible thing from happening."

"Of course I will; but what can I do? She's locked in the house, there's nobody in there but her. What—"

"Call the police station, father," said Bernadine. "Tell them—"

"I know what I'll do. I'll go down there. That's the thing to do. I'll take a taxi down and see the Lieutenant. I know him. I—"

"Then hurry, grandpa," cried Deborah, "Please hurry before it's too late!"

Bernadine, helping him find his hat, got him into the street. Not seeing any taxis in sight, he hurried as fast as his old legs could carry him to South Parkway.

CHAPTER XXXI

When Deborah left the house, she didn't look North. If she had, she would have seen the Elder, who was on his way back home from downtown, and feeling very good. He called to the girl and waved his hand, as he would have liked a bit of conversation with her. He had tho't about her, that she was "easy on the eyes," and he hurried back home in hopes of finding her still there. He was disappointed when she failed to hear him.

"Well," he sighed. "Maybe she'll come back," and with this hope he entered the house. Inside, he listened a moment. Nobody home, except Linda upstairs. A few seconds later he was knocking at her door.

"Yes?" came Linda's voice. There was an odd note which the Elder didn't notice. He was happy. He was about to satisfy a twenty years' ambition and he had hurried home to tell the family about it—especially Linda. Something Linda did that day, had made this happiness possible.

She opened the door and the Elder, almost bursting with anxiety to tell what was on his mind, stepped inside. The sun had shifted during the past hour. It was hardly dark enough to turn on a light; but coming out of the day light, it seemed a bit dark to the Elder.

During Linda's brief life in the West, her father had occupied the room. There was an old roll-top desk, upon the top of which there was a litter of useless articles. Yet nobody ever cleaned it up.

Among these articles was an old knife which her father had found and brought home, many years before. They often used it to cut card board, wall paper and divers things. It was a

374

knife with a handle, but nobody ever thought to close it. It had an unusually long blade.

When Deborah left, Linda went to the old desk and sat down reviewing the things Deborah had said. She thought of her husband, Martin Eden; recalled her short life with him out there in the Rosebud Country. She lived through briefly, their happy days together, his incessant struggle to get somewhere. And then she lived through the night they had stolen her away; his trip two weeks after to Chicago, and Terry's refusal to let him see her, except for an hour, under guard,— Terry's guard.

Then she remembered his last trip; his effort to steal her away and how she misunderstood. It became clear to her afterward, but she knew then that she had remembered too late.

By the time she heard her father's key in the front door, she had lived through the worst part of it all, what had happened that day. She hadn't wanted to sign the relinquishment, but like everything else, she had been persuaded and after a time, had signed her name to the paper which betrayed her husband so shamefully.

She felt odd now, just as Martin Eden felt the night he was shot. Words are inadequate to describe her feeling at this stage of her life. She was conscious only that a great wrong had been committed; a wrong that needed to be righted, and it was her duty to right it. She sat there, her hand played with the knife, first unconsciously. Then in a vague way she became conscious of it and turning it over, looked at it. She took hold of the handle and raised it up and down. When she heard her father, she laid it down, near the side of the desk, out of the way.

"Aw, my daughter, how are you by this time?" throwing hat on the bed. Linda closed the door and stood before him. She looked at the hat and recalled that a hat on a bed was bad luck.

"At last it's done and we'll soon have it?" he said with a happy sigh.

"What's done?" said she, looking down at him, "and what are we going to have so soon?" Her back was at three quarters' angle, with the window in the background. A ray of light shone through the window and lit his face, but hers was dark. He couldn't see any change in her expression.

"Why, the car, my dear. We are going to have a car at last. A pretty, brand new automobile, and now baby, won't your daddy show these Negroes something—oh, my!

"What a thrill, oh, what a thrill it gave me when we agreed on the down payment and I knew at last that we were to have that car. Isn't it wonderful, dear—simply glorious, and I'm so happy I don't know what to do." As his eyes met hers, she forced a smile, the kind of smile she had seen once before on *his* face. At her bedside when Martin Eden left to go to his work, and he and Terry were alone with her, just before the kidnapping.

Turning his eyes away again, he continued:

"A fine new car, all our own, with you my precious, to drive it. They've agreed to teach you to drive. And soon, honey, you'll be driving your old daddy to Southern Illinois; around to his churches, and back here more often. Aw, baby, we're going to show these darkies something now, sure enough. After forty years, hustling around on foot, I'm now going to ride, and ride and ride. Aw, I tell you, daughter, it's wonderful!"

"Yes," he heard her say in that strange tone. "Yes, father, as you say it *will* be wonderful—*wonderful!* How did you buy the car, father?"

He sat down and looked up at her in surprise.

"How did I buy it? That seems like a silly question to ask me. How do you suppose that I bought it—that is, made the down payment?"

"I asked a question, father. Will you please answer?"

He looked up at her again, this time a trifle annoyed. "Why, Linda, if I wasn't so happy, I'd say that you are acting strangely. Such peculiar questions. Why?"

"I'm waiting for you to answer me, father!"

"Well—what? Oh, you're being funny. Why, out of the money Mr. Crook paid me for your place, of course."

"I see. Out of the money you had me sell my birthright for; out of the money you made me betray my husband for. That's how you made the down payment, isn't it?"

He looked up at her, his mouth open, amazed.

"Say, what's going on around here? You know, you seem to be acting strangely, talking the same way." Rising now, annoyed.

"And talking about that man—not your husband; only the man you married." He circled around her to get a better view of her face; to study her more close. She looked up into his, strangely calm. Was it the lull before the storm? As he circled, so did she.

"The man I married, yes; but my husband, nevertheless. Yes—*my husband*, I say!" She almost shrieked the last words.

"Now listen here, Linda," began the Elder, becoming alarmed at the way she was acting. "What's come over you? You weren't like this when I left you, only about an hour and a half ago. What's—"

"No," she almost hissed through clenched teeth. "I am *not* like I was when you left me. I have changed, because when you left me I hadn't learned the truth. But the truth has been told to me since. I know all about how you've used me at the expense of my husband and now I hate you, father—God, how I despise you!" She advanced toward him, her eyes half closed, an evil purpose lurking in them. Her breast was heaving. Thoroughly alarmed now, he thought she had suddenly lost her mind.

"Hate and despise me," he shrieked, terrified as he backed away from her. He glanced over his shoulder toward the door and she circled to get between.

"Yes, I hate and despise you and I'm going to make you pay, not merely for the sins you've made me commit, but for the wrongs you've done to my husband, Martin Eden."

"Martin Eden! You mean that scoundrel. I—"

"Hush!" her back against the door. She turned the key and threw it across the room, where it slid under the bed and out of sight. "Don't ever speak his name thus again!"

"What—what ever has come over you, my child? Who's been here to—to change you like this," he whimpered, terror stricken, backing away with her following grimly.

"Was—was it that—that white girl that I let in the house? Surely—"

"Yes, it was that *white* girl who told me the truth, the whole truth; told me everything, so now at last I know, I *know!*" she hissed.

"Bu—but—what could a *white girl* know to tell you; what could *she* know about Martin Eden?"

"Everything. Everything because she loves Martin Eden. She loved him before he came to see me; she's loved him since. But because she was white and he was black, he refused to return her love. He walked away from her after she proposed to him; offered to marry him and dedicate her heart, her soul and her body to him, to watch over him—to love him until she died. That is what that pretty white girl offered him and he *refused* it and came here and paid court to me and married me."

"Oh, so he's got a white girl running after him, eh—" sneered the Elder.

"Shut up, you wretch, and hear me through!"

"She is *not* running after him, nor he after her. Unlike me, she has the courage of her convictions; the strength of will to stand up and fight for the man she loves. Yet he left her to come and marry me because he respected the fact that a colored man could not marry a white girl and be true to his race."

"Oh, *is that so?*" said the Elder, derisively. "He was afraid to marry her because she is no doubt, a strumpet—" The rest of his speech was cut off by a burning smack on his cheek that stung until it brought tears to his eyes.

"She is *not* a strumpet! She's a nice girl who fell in love with Martin Eden out there because she couldn't help it. But it turned out that *she is not*, after all, a white girl, but old man Nelson Boudreaux's (the Creole up the street) granddaughter!"

"Boudreaux's granddaughter? Then where does the white part of her come in. What—"

"Her father *is* a white man. She's been raised as a white girl and never knew she had any Negro blood in her veins until a few hours ago. Had she known this, and Martin Eden known it, also, you'd have never had a chance to make his life as miserable as you have.

"When *you* are dead, and I am, too, she'll marry my husband and take my baby and raise it as their own."

"Linda, *what are you talking about?*" he begged, circling again to reach the door.

"The things to come, father. The things to come, for you and I are not much longer for this earth. You've sinned too much by making me sin, and you've lived long enough, and today you're going to die!"

"Linda, my darling daughter—"

"Your *unfortunate*, your *miserable* daughter, you mean. I say, father, you've lived too long, so today you are going to die—die!"

"Oh, merciful father," whimpered the Elder, "What has come over my child, my favorite daughter. What—"

"Only the truth, father. The truth which has come too late. I cannot right, not only the wrongs I've done so long, but the wrong you made me commit today, which was a colossal wrong."

"Listen, Linda, believe me, I was only trying to—"

"—buy the car you have wanted so long. So you had me accept five hundred Judas' dollars; $500 for the land Martin had invested seven times that much for—"

"—but he—"

"I want to tell you all about this sin we committed today, and then we, you and I—will go to face our maker!"

"Oh, Linda, please—"

"Hear me through, father. Know the whole truth before the end." She cried, raising her hand and staying further speech by him.

"On the train, on the way to visit her old home in Indiana, that girl overheard this man Crook, who you know tried through all courts to beat me out of my claim. She overheard him and that man who was with him talking about this land. That high, strange looking hill on it contains the greatest manganese deposit in the world and is worth millions—"

"Why, Linda! Wha—"

"Shut up and listen!" she commanded again, with a dramatic lifting of her hand.

"She heard them say that Martin had invested $3,500 in the claim, but because you are a Negro and never had much money, they would offer you $500, which they did, and as you know, you took."

"But, Linda, if the land is worth so much, they'll surely give us some more. I'll—"

"You'll not live long enough to get anything or do anything. I've signed the land, my birthright, away and betrayed my husband and I don't want to live any longer to regret it. But before I go, you're going to precede me."

"Oh, Linda, don't talk that way. Death is a terrible thing. Let's wait awhile. Come, let's sit down and talk it over. I'm sure Mr. Crook, who seemed like such a nice white man, will—"

"I'm not interested in how nice Mr. Crook is. He is not nice. He robbed his bank up there; he's been indicted and is under bond. You know he tried to beat me out of my claim and only failed because of Martin Eden. *He* was the one who fought the contest which you know all about, through all the courts, and then after losing, this Crook came to you. He had read in the book Martin wrote that to please you was to 'flatter' you; to make you feel that you were a 'king'.

"Well, he flattered you. I listened to him doing so. He played

on your ego and vanity, and because you never made any real
money in all your miserable life, $500 seemed like a fortune.
So you know the rest. You made me sign it away, as you have
made me do all the other mean things to my husband. And
now the hour glass is running low—the time draws near,
father."

"Linda, will you let me talk, let me tell some things I have
done for you. I—"

"Did you take the contest the man Crook filed against me
when he tried to get my place, all the way up to the Secretary
of the Interior, where it was finally decided in my favor? No,
you know you didn't. Martin Eden did that.

"Did you pay a white woman $1,500 in cash for the relin-
quishment to the place in the beginning? No, Martin Eden
did that.

"Did you move the house 40 miles across the prairies and
put it on the place; the house where my baby was born; the
house that you kidnapped me from when my husband's back
was turned? No, you know you didn't.

"Did you spend $2,000 in cash to improve it so it could be-
come a home and a place to live? No, Martin Eden did that.

"Did you steal me away from my husband when his back
was turned? Yes, *you* did that.

"Did you make me sign a relinquishment today, which gave
the land to the white man who tried to beat me out of it, and
failing, because of the fortitude of Martin Eden, came to you
and gave you five hundred Judas dollars to make me sign
away millions that Martin Eden, if he had, would spend for
posterity? Yes, you did that.

"All you've done in your long, miserable, hypocritical life
is to make other people suffer because you insisted on being
vain and egotistical. You're a coward, a dumb bell and a fool
and I—"

The Elder has managed to maneuver himself into position
where he could dash for the door, only to find it locked, with

the key gone. When he saw that the key was gone, he faced her, great beads of perspiration, as cold almost as ice, all over his body. She became hysterical and laughed loudly. And as she did so, the conviction came to him that he didn't need to die. How could Linda kill him?

After all, she was only a girl, a weak woman that he had wrapped around his finger for years, so why let her excite him? He would make a dash for her, overpower her—and go free!

He hunched his shoulders for action, but she had read his mind while this plan was forming, and when he hunched his shoulders and started toward her, she turned quickly, dashed across the room and seized the knife. She gripped the handle, half closed her eyes, and prepared to meet him with a thrust.

He rushed for the door, shrieking in panic, tried to open it. She advanced with the knife drawn, for a quick thrust.

When about six feet away, she pointed the finger of her free hand at him:

"Once I heard Mrs. Dewey say to you, when neither of you knew that I was near, 'Newt Lee, you're the world's most awful sinner and you're going to burn in hell some day'. Well, father, that day has come, and—"

She darted forward and before he could recoil, his back against the door, she was on him with knife raised. It descended like a flash into his heart, as she shrieked:

"You're going to pay!" Lifting the knife again, brought it down on his breast with all the strength in her arm.

"You're going to pay," raising the knife, dripping with blood, "Pay, and pay and pay!"

Time and again she raised it and then sank it to the hilt in his breast, each time crying, "You're going to pay!" until the blood spurted out of his mouth and spattered over her. Then at last his heart stopped beating and he slid down against the door, to the floor. He struggled upward just long enough to meet her eyes, gasped once, and then rolled over on the floor, dead.

Linda seemed only then to realize that she had killed her own father. With a wild scream she staggered against the foot of the bed, dazed.

She thought in a vague, far off way of Deborah. She wanted to see her and tell her that she had righted the great wrong her father had done to Martin Eden. In a monent this desire became an obsession; she *had* to go tell Deborah. She also decided to tell Deborah to take her child back to So. Dakota. She wanted to tell her to marry Martin after she was dead and to be good to him as she had wanted to be. She wanted to tell her to raise Junior to be like his father, brave and strong; resolute and courageous!

She was positive that she had to see Deborah and tell her these things and then she would kill herself. She started around her father's body and remembered that she had locked the door and thrown the key away.

But she knew where it was. It was under the bed. She got on her knees and found it and unlocked it with her free hand.

She still carried the knife. She *had* to keep that; after she told Deborah to marry her husband and take care of their little boy, she would kill herself. She had decided to do that before her father came back. At that time she hadn't planned to kill him, too; it was after he returned and said so much about the car, to be bought with Judas dollars, that she made up her mind to kill him first, then herself. She wanted to die here in her own room. But she remembered that she had things to do.

She *had* to go to Boudreaux's and tell Deborah about her baby. She had to do this before she died because if she didn't Terry would raise it to hate its father.

With these things going through her bewildered mind, she went down to the front door. She seemed unaware that she was spattered with blood; that she grasped a bloody knife in her right hand. All she had in her mind was the plan to see Deborah and tell her what to do. Then she would come back home and kill herself, and everything would be righted.

She opened the front door, and as the sunlight and the breeze struck her face, she decided to hurry. Deborah might go out and not be there to receive her instructions. She rushed down the steps and paused at the curbing before going into the street, without thinking about cars. It would be nearer to Deborah's, if she went in a diagonal direction.

At this moment, Deborah and her aunt Bernadine, left to go to the Lee home where Boudreaux would be arriving with the officers. It took a half hour to round up a squad, and at this same moment they entered Vernon Avenue, three blocks below the Lee home, with sirens screaming, which brought everybody into the street.

A half block away, Terry and Mother Mary with Junior between them, were returning home. They were just in time to see, but not recognize, Linda, in her orange colored negligee, spattered with blood, her brindle-like hair disarranged.

Going north on the avenue, a wealthy white woman from the Gold Coast on the North Shore, was driving home. She had been to see an old servant, who was ill three blocks up from where the Lees lived. She became drowsy after the car reached a speed of about thirty miles an hour, yawned and closed her eyes. On the other side of the street, a long transportation truck was going in the opposite direction, and just missed Linda, who without looking to right or left, stepped into the street.

Missing the truck, Linda stepped directly in front of the powerful limousine, too quickly to avoid being run down. Less than six feet away the driver saw her coming directly toward him and making no effort to avoid a collision. He applied the brakes so hard that they screamed like death, while he swerved the car toward the sidewalk. The woman opened her eyes just in time to see the front right wheel strike Linda, as she rushed pell mell into it.

Loud was the woman's scream, like someone dying—and there was! It was Linda. The front right wheel raised the car a foot or more high into the air, then dropped down after going over her body.

Everybody who had been attracted by the police sirens saw it. Most had seen Linda, like a tragic apparition, dash into the street, heedless of the traffic that was moving up and down.

The police officers were the first to reach her and drag her body from under the heavy car. As they did so, the bloody knife she had been carrying was exposed.

The officers tried to keep the curious away. A little boy insisted on telling a story.

"What're you trying to tell us, son?" inquired the sergeant in charge.

"She come outa Reverend Lee's house across the street with that knife in her hand and it was bloody then, and she had blood all over that—that night gown, her face and her hair."

The Sergeant detailed two of his squad to guard the body, and with two more, followed by the crowd, hurried to the Lee home. Arriving in front of it, they met the two women and Linda's little boy standing on the porch, looking across at the accident that had just happened.

"Who was hurt?" asked Terry, as they stopped. The little boy said:

"That is the house, right there, Mr." pointing to the Lee home. They started up the steps and were stopped by Terry who said:

"This is my house. I asked you who was hurt? What do you want here?"

"Please step aside madam, and let us enter this house. A woman was just killed across the street, and the boy there," pointing to the lad who had given him the information, "said she came out of this house."

"This house!" screamed Terry, mouth agape.

"Have you the key, Madam? She had a bloody knife in her hand when the car that killed her struck her. We fear that she may have killed somebody in here before she left."

"Oh, my God, it couldn't be my sister, *it couldn't be!*" cried Terry, fumbling for the keys.

"I saw your father go in the house about a half hour before she came out," said a man who lived across the street and knew them.

Deborah, weeping in the arms of her aunt was back at the Boudreaux home.

"Oh, it's all my fault, my fault," she sobbed, her resistance gone.

"No, it isn't, baby," consoled her aunt. "You—"

"If I hadn't gone over there and told her about all the wrongs she had done to Martin Eden and upbraided her so strongly about it, she wouldn't have—oh, auntie, I'll never get over it."

"It was something that *had* to happen," said Boudreaux, standing near them. "It wasn't your fault. It was Reverend Lee's. That old man's been the biggest sinner in Chicago for years and at last his chickens came home to roost."

"Oh, father. You oughtn't say that," cautioned Bernadine, frowning up at him. "The man is dead."

"I know it's bad to talk about a man after he's gone, but according to the bible: 'As you sow, so shall ye reap'. The old man sowed the wind and today he reaped the whirlwind."

"But I'm so sorry I went there. This will be an awful thing on my conscience. Think of it, two people dead because I went meddling—"

"But, honey, you weren't meddling," insisted Boudreaux. "You simply went over there and told the girl the truth. The old man happened to come back at the wrong time and she killed him for all the sins he'd been committing for the last forty years."

"Wonder what happened to Linda," said Bernadine. "She must have gone crazy and ran into the street."

"She was perhaps temporarily insane," said Deborah, "but she was coming over here to see me. That's what she was crossing the street for."

"See you?" the others echoed in chorus.

"Yes." said Deborah solemnly. "She was on the way here

to see me and tell me to—to marry Martin, now that I'm a colored girl, and to take their little boy and raise it."

"But—" they started to speak.

"My father says that I was born with the gift of second sight. I don't know, but all my life I have seen things that are going to happen before they happen. Last night I had a premonition. I had a premonition before Martin Eden came to bring Linda out there. I had another before he left to go marry her and bring her to Dakota. I saw that something was going to happen to him if he did. I told him it *would* happen. The only way that he could prevent it happening to him, was not to go to Chicago, but to stay there and—marry me."

She bowed her head for a moment while they listened and waited for more.

"Always when something is going to happen, a wind blows. Now if it is going to happen to others, near and dear to me, I see the wind. It comes from nowhere. It doesn't blow all over; it seems to be confined to the object it foredooms. When something big is going to happen, or if it's something that may last through years, it blows harder and covers a wider area. If it is something quick and tragic like what we've just seen, it may be just a strong whirlwind.

"Last night while on the train, it was warm and I raised a window. Just after the train crossed the Mississippi River, I was awakened. The moon was shining and I looked out into the night, when of a sudden, I saw it. That wind from nowhere. It was a whirlwind that looked like the tail end of a cyclone. It was coming from the east and it was roaring and loud. But nobody stirred on the train, for they didn't see it, didn't hear it. It was coming. It was only I who heard its roar, and in a few moments, felt it pass through the car, just as if there were no car at all. I felt it go over me and was chilled.

"It didn't linger, but I knew then that soon something was going to happen. The Wind from nowhere had come and gone, but it struck me squarely and chilled me. What has just happened in the street and across the street was what that wind meant.

"It is now over, this wind from nowhere. It will never blow again; I know it will not and I shall feel its breath no more. It has gone its way forever, and will never blow again in my life time."

"You can see, Deborah," said old Nelson Boudreaux, "It wasn't what you did. It was the hand of fate, working in a mysterious way, God's will to be done." As he finished, the spell under which she had been laboring was gone and sorrow returned. He placed an arm about her, and she leaned on him and hid her face as she dried her tears.

"Now with regard to the land, Deborah," said Boudreaux. "Will he—lose it?" Boudreaux's reference to the land caused Deborah new excitement. The tragedies had made her forget. She started quickly, her nerves tense.

"Oh, the land!" she cried. "The terrible things which have just happened made me forget. I must act—I must do something—and quick!" She walked across the floor, thinking hard. She stopped presently, biting her lips in vexation, and shaking her head sadly, murmuring loudly enough for them to hear:

"I don't see how it can be saved. She told me that she had signed the relinquishment and the men have it. All he has to do now is to return to Gregory, present the relinquishment with his application pinned to it at the land office; they accept her relinquishment and file him on the land. This is the way it's done. Millions of acres of lands in the west have changed hands that way. There's no way that I ever heard of preventing it; of getting between the holder of a relinquishment and an applicant who holds the relinquishment. There is no record of a relinquishment until it is filed.

"He will more than likely take the night train back to Gregory."

"What time would that put him there?" inquired Boudreaux, wishing there was something he could do to help her. He was proud of her. She impressed him as being intelligent and smart.

"Late tomorrow afternoon; around six o'clock."

"Would the land office be open when he got there?"

"Oh, no, it closes at four thirty P.M." Suddenly something occurred to her.

"What day of the week is this?"

"Today is Thursday," replied Bernadine.

"Thursday," cried Deborah, becoming more excited as she dared entertain a new hope.

"That would put them there on Friday," said Boudreaux. "Friday after the land office has closed, according to what you say. He would then file his claim on Saturday."

"But the land office doesn't open its doors on Saturday at all. He can't file his claim until Monday. Oh, maybe there is some way to prevent this—this travesty yet. Maybe there is, but *how*, I don't know; I can't think."

"Maybe you can figure some way out. You have over three days. In short, you have three full days and four nights," suggested Boudreaux.

"Whatever I do, I must start acting quickly; start acting—now!" She walked back and forth again. Presently, she paused, her face sad but still not beaten.

"Will you both please excuse me for a half hour. I—" She heard a clock, but couldn't see it. Boudreaux sensed what she wanted to know.

"The clock is over there," said he, pointing at it across the room. "It's almost five o'clock. It'll soon be dark."

"Five o'clock," mumbled Deborah. "The train to Omaha, which connects with the only one to the Rosebud, leaves at 9:30."

"You have over four and a half hours."

"Four and a half hours? I started to say that I was raised in the open and can think more clearly in the open. I'm going to walk outside and try to think what can be done."

Her aunt let her out and she turned back with the first effort at a smile since the tragedy.

"I'll be back in an hour or less."

They wished her Godspeed and looked after her as she walked away.

"Remarkable child," said Boudreaux.

"Wonderful."

"I was so happy when, after seeing that we were colored, she didn't become angry and walk out."

"My heart was in my throat. I liked her from the first, and I would have been heart broken, after finding out it was Laura's child, had she walked out as we would have expected her to do."

"Wasn't it a strange coincidence that she should have fallen in love with a colored fellow? About the only one in the whole country up there," said Boudreaux as they took seats.

"I wonder in that mysterious second sight with which she's possessed, if she didn't feel infinitely nearer him; that maybe, she was the same as he. She said it was only he that objected to returning the love. She said she had never been conscious of being white; that she was just drawn to him and has suffered agonies ever since as a result of the division he set up."

"As I've said, 'God works in mysterious ways, His wonders to perform'."

"From the way she described him, I imagine they must be perfectly mated, even in the way of ages."

"Let's see," said Boudreaux. "Just about how old should she be, anyhow?"

"She said he was twenty eight, and was almost three years older than she."

"She, then, must be about twenty five," trying to connect it with her mother.

"She'll sure make him a good wife."

"She most assuredly will. That girl's intelligent, she's smart. He'll go places now, sure enough."

"I sure hope she'll think out some way to save that land for him. To think that poor Linda—"

"Just shout for joy that her old father's at last out of the way. He was the old rascal that brought about all the trouble. I always said that a niggah preacher—"

"Father!" cried Bernadine. "Please don't say such things. The man lies a corpse in the morgue now. He has paid the price with his life. Even *you* can demand no more."

"No," said Boudreaux. "No more; but it was too bad Linda didn't stick that knife in him before she signed that paper, giving that dirty white man who tried to beat her out of it and lost, that valuable piece of land. I'll never be able to feel sorry for the old rascal when I think of what he did, only today— this morning."

"Well, papa, it's nearly your supper time. I'll go in the kitchen and prepare it."

"Fix something good so we can give the girl her dinner when she gets back."

"Which reminds me," said she, pausing. "Put your hat and overcoat on and go to the grocery. Buy a chicken and a small pound cake. I'll fry the chicken and put her up a nice lunch to eat on her way back to Dakota."

"All right, daughter. Glad you thought of it."

At this moment Deborah found herself walking alone along the street in the dusk. She didn't know where she was going, not even which way.

She didn't know how far she had gone. She only knew that she hadn't thought of any way to prevent Eugene Crook from filing on Linda's land, and she was tired and sad and discouraged. Then she looked around, heard sacred music, and found that she was in front of a large church. Someone inside was playing the pipe organ, a soft hymn that thrilled her strangely. After listening for a few moments she walked up to the entrance.

She saw that the huge doors were not locked. She pushed one, walked through a narrow foyer, and opened another door, which led into a huge auditorium. At the front the pipe organ rose high up behind the altar and someone was playing it. Lifted up, she felt a divine inspiration and walked quietly to the altar and stopped. There was a statue of the Christ behind it, and before she was fully aware of what she was doing, she was on her knees before the altar. She offered up a little prayer and asked the lord to guide her and help her find a way to save Martin Eden; to forgive Linda and her for the tragedy she had inadvertently caused.

While kneeling there, she recalled something she had which might help her. A long time ago when they were hopeful of securing a claim in the Rosebud Country, she had got a booklet from the land office, which contained transcripts of procedures relative to homesteading, and the acquisition of a homestead, its laws and usages. She had placed that booklet in her bag when she was leaving, perhaps to show people back in Indiana, if it came to that, something about homesteading. There was something in it, she recalled, about relinquishments. She closed her eyes and thanked the Lord for giving her an inspiration, then went quietly out of the church.

She hurried to her grandpa's home. They had given her a key as she was leaving, which she used now to enter. The large house was quiet. She could hear her auntie in the kitchen preparing the meal. Boudreaux had not returned, so she stole noiselessly up to the room to which they had assigned her.

It was a large, comfortable room and she looked around it admiringly and wished that she could spend some time in it; that she could sleep one night in the large, four-poster bed—but enough of that, thought she. Digging into her bag, she found the booklet she was so anxious to consult.

It didn't take her long to find the chapter relating to relinquishments. Eagerly and nervously she read down through it, and finally came upon the paragraph in which she was so much interested:

"If a person, entering onto a claim, in the flesh, meaning in the person and establishing a bona fide residence thereon, and can prove by responsible witnesses that they did establish this residence on a certain date and a certain hour; and, whereas, another person, desirous of obtaining this self same tract of land, and who offers a relinquishment, signed by another who had previously entered on same. If, therefore, the person who has established a bona fide residence in person, can prove, through the proper affidavits, that they established a residence in person as above described, between the time this relinquishment was executed by the previous holder of said lands, and before the other, offering the relinquishment with his usual application attached thereto, then the land in question shall become legally the property of the person who established the residence. See: the case of Richard Rowe, versus Gustave Sabolsky, etc., etc."

Deborah raised her eyes from the transcript and tried to understand if she had read correctly. It excited her. Out of a maze of conflicting incidents, here seemed the possibility of a way out. She read the paragraph over and over again until she had committed it and could say it without reading.

She rose and began an effort at deductions.

Eugene Crook, with a relinquishment in his brief case, signed by the late Linda Lee, the name under which she had filed on the land before marrying Martin Eden, was perhaps still in Chicago. He would most likely take the train back to the Rosebud that night. If he had figured out that he could not file his claim before Monday morning, at 10 A.M., and decided to stay in Chicago and go back later, so much the better.

But she was making her deductions on the theory, which was the safest way, of his going back on the same train she would take.

If she went on through to Winner, and to the claim, where she might even find Martin, she could establish a residence ahead of Crook, and have two full days and three nights to prove it. She would notify the Farnheims and the Trouts and the Johnsons and the Giltzow's that she had jumped the claim and invite all of them there to see her on the same, living in the house. She had already lived there, so this would help substantiate her claim as that of a bona-fide resident.

The possible success of this plan would depend on Crook not becoming wise to her plans, and going through to Winner, where he had operated the bank that was closed. But he also might go try establish a residence before she could. With this and a relinquishment too, the claim would, in view of its now known value, be thrown into litigation to last for years and years.

After considering the matter from every conceivable angle, she reached the conclusion that she would have to beat Crook to the claim, enter the house and prove that she was there first. In this respect, she had the inside track, for if Martin was there (and he had left Gregory County to go there, before she came to Chicago) he would drive Crook off, whereas she could go right into the house and establish residence forthwith—and in comfort.

Restraining her excitement as much as she could, she went downstairs, finding her grandpa and auntie with the meal about ready, sat down to the table and told them in detail what she had learned, and what she would try to do. Naturally they were pleased.

"Now let's forget all about it and enjoy this delightful meal, then I'll go to the station an hour earlier and secret myself to watch every person who boards that train. I must see if Crook and his companion do, for if so, I'll know that I've got to work fast. I'll send Martin a telegram to meet me in Winner—most important—and if he does (in his car) we should beat Crook at his own game. But Crook might know of this same clause and protect himself by making a dash for the place, and try to get ahead of me."

"The train reaches Winner at seven thirty tomorrow night. In thirty minutes after it arrives there, I plan to be on the claim. Until then, there's nothing more that can be done, so let's eat."

When the meal was over and she insisted on helping her auntie with the dishes, she talked of the future.

"Whether we win the claim or not, I'm sure that Martin, when he is told that I'm a colored girl, will ask me to marry him. Maybe I won't have to do the proposing this time," she laughed, joined by her aunt.

"I'm sure you will love each other dearly," said Bernadine, and smiled at her, in a motherly fashion.

"If he proposes to me, I'm going to ask him to come to Chicago to be married."

"Oh, that'll be dandy, dearest. Then grandpa can—"

"Oh, no, grandpa cannot give me away. That will have to be my own papa. He still lives and I'm his heart."

"Of course," said Bernadine, sorry that her father couldn't do so. "But we will have to cut in and be a part of the family somehow."

"Do you know why I want to be married here in Chicago? There, dear auntie. I won't make you try to guess. I want to be married in Chicago so that it can take place in this house."

"Oh, Deborah, that will be wonderful. I do wish so much you would."

"I will demand that Martin bring me here for the wedding. I will even make it a condition of acceptance."

"Please do, dear Deborah, oh, please do. It will make us so happy."

"And I like the fine large room upstairs so much. I'm so sorry I can't sleep there tonight. I will never be satisfied until I do. So I want to picture Martin and me, after we marry, spending our wedding night in it."

"Oh," cried her aunt, enthusiastically, "that will be delight-ful—and you shall do so. I'll even put new furniture in it. I—"

"You'll do nothing of the kind. I want to sleep in it just as it is. That's why I want so much to be married here in this house, right there in that large front room."

"Oh, Deborah, you've made me so happy." She took Deborah in her arms then and smothered her face with hot kisses. "I'm going to love you more than my sister had a chance to. Poor Laura. She died when you were just a little thing."

"Yes, dear auntie, she did. I can just barely remember her. But getting back to my wedding. I should strike myself. I'm taking so much for granted. Supposing Martin shouldn't want me after all; supposing—"

"Oh, dear, dear, please don't joke. Of course he will want you. Oh, how happy will he be when he learns that you are, after all he's been through—one of—us."

"Oh, auntie, you darling!" Deborah threw herself into her arms again and both cried for joy.

Boudreaux came in while this was going on and they had to do it all over again for his sake. He was happier than they, went to the cabinet and poured himself a big drink and tried to get them to partake.

"I'm going to get good and drunk after you leave," said he, his arms around Deborah.

"Now, father, you'll do nothing of the kind," admonished Bernadine.

"I'm not letting you do anything foolish and take a chance of dying. You're going to stay sober, at least until Deborah comes back with Martin Eden and I've given her the most beautiful wedding a colored girl ever had."

"Oh, please, Aunt Bernadine, don't," cried Deborah, going into her arms again.

They wanted to go with her to the train, but she wouldn't let them. She wanted to steal into the station and go into hiding to see if Crook and his lawyer took the same train.

After purchasing her ticket, she found a good spot where she could see everybody who went through the gates to get aboard that particular train.

From her vantage point, she saw Crook and the lawyer purchase tickets and engage berths in a Pullman, then watched them go through the gates and get aboard. She knew that she would worry until she reached Winner, until she was on the homestead north of Carter, ahead of Crook.

XXXII

Out of omaha the next morning, on the train that ran to Winner she saw Crook and his partner again. They continued in a Pullman to Norfolk, where she saw them change to the coach. No Pullmans went through to Winner, and she found herself in the same coach with them again. There were only two coaches, that one and a smoker. All day they were going back and forth to the smoker, so there was no way for her to keep from being seen.

By the time the train left Bonesteel, at the eastern edge of the original Rosebud Reservation, the coaches were almost empty. People continued leaving the train at each station. After leaving Burke, Crook and his lawyer came back to the coach to get their belongings, preparing to get off at Gregory. As they were picking them up, the lawyer looked straight at her and touching Crook, said:

"Say, sit down a moment, don't look back. I want to talk to you."

Deborah was watching them closely and straining her ears. She knew they were talking about her, with their heads close and a glance back at her.

"Do you see that girl back there?" said the lawyer. "Don't look now. I don't want her to know that we are talking about her. Now take your time, get up and go to the rear for a drink of water, and you can see her going and returning. When you get back, we'll talk, and now hurry. We'll be in Gregory in a few minutes and will have to decide before we get there, what we are to do."

"I get you," said Crook, rising and pretending nonchalance.

As he started down the aisle, a mighty clap of thunder barked from the skies, which startled everybody.

"By God! Did you hear that?"

"Sounded like a bomb exploding," said the lawyer.

"Can it be that it's going to rain on the Rosebud this late in the fall," asked Crook, going to the window in the seat behind theirs and looking out into the night.

"It's been mighty sultry all day. It's possible."

"Well, guess I'll get me a drink of water," said Crook, turning into the aisle, carelessly.

As he came down the aisle, Deborah pretended to be reading a magazine she had. She could feel his eyes studying her as he passed by. When he reached the water cooler, he coughed loudly. She started to turn, but before she could, she saw the lawyer look back at him. She knew it was to see and study her face so she never let on. As Crook came back she still acted oblivious.

"You saw her," said the lawyer.

"Sure did; she's easy to look at. I noticed that, too."

"That isn't what I'm talking about, fellow."

"No," said Crook, turning to him. "Well—"

"Don't you remember seeing her before?" asked the lawyer, still in an undertone. Crook started to turn and the lawyer hurriedly placed a hand on his arm.

"Don't look now, for heaven's sake."

"Oh, excuse me. Well, what?"

"If I'm not mistaken, that same girl was on the train when we went into Chicago; in a seat just behind ours."

"No!" exclaimed Crook.

"Yes," insisted the lawyer. "It's the same girl; and the same girl we met when we came out of the preacher's house in Chicago. I happened to look back and saw her pause at the same house."

"You don't say so," said Crook, alarmed. "Did she go into the preacher's house?"

"I don't think she did, because when we turned to go over to that wide street (I believe it's called South Parkway) I looked back toward the preacher's house and saw her coming on down the street this side of it."

"Well, that should leave us in the clear."

"I'm not so sure about that. She could have gone back later, but that's the same girl and she might be trailing us."

"Maybe, but that doesn't mean anything. We have the relinquishment, signed, sealed and delivered, so what?"

"Sealed and delivered might not, in this case, be so good for us."

"What'd ya mean?"

"I mean that my being a notary public and placing my seal on the relinquishment, together with the date when she signed, might possibly prove a boomerang," said he, his face worried. The train whistled for Gregory and there was another ear splitting clap of thunder.

"Well, here we are," said Crook. "This is Gregory. Let's get off." The lawyer pushed him back and cried, loud enough to be heard above the screeching of the brakes.

"No, let's not get off here. Let's continue on to Winner. I want to consult some records I have there on procedures. I seem to remember something that might make a quick move on our part necessary."

Crook sank back in his seat. Deborah had strained her fine sense of hearing to the limit. She managed to hear all he said—and knew that if they didn't already know it, they would find out shortly after reaching Winner what she already knew. She felt chilled. When they found out, they would make a break to jump the claim. She *had to beat them to this!*

She sat quietly, and as the train pulled out, there was another mighty clap of thunder, so loud it seemed to reverberate around the world. It was followed by a flash of lightning that lit the dark outside like weird daylight. There was another mighty clap of thunder, and suddenly like a cloud burst, the rain came down.

Never since she came to the Rosebud had she seen it rain so hard. It came down in torrents, and as the lightning flashed she could see water on the ground, seemingly an inch deep, although it hadn't been raining five minutes. It was falling so fast the earth could not absorb it fast enough. Meantime, Gene Crook and his lawyer friend were talking.

"What should I do," asked Crook, turning to him anxiously.

"I don't know right now. As soon as I consult this booklet on homesteading rules and usages, I'll know."

"Do you think Eden's wise to our game and is trying to do something to keep us from getting it?"

"I wouldn't know, but it's dollars to doughnuts that girl back there is up to something."

"It doesn't seem possible. How could she know anything about what we are doing?"

"How did she happen to be on the same train with us going to Chicago; how did she happen to be coming along that street where the preacher lived and looking up at his house just after we came out? How does she happen to be on the same train on the way to Winner, when we had tickets for Gregory. That girl's up to something or I'll eat my hat," persisted the lawyer Meanwhile, the rain continued to fall in torrents.

"After all, we're not the only ones who have read the revelations of Martin Eden in that book of his. My hunch was right about going in there and getting the relinquishment through the old man, wasn't it?"

"It sure was—right to the letter, and we didn't have to pay him any more than we planned to offer in the beginning."

"We might have saved a couple hundred and got it for three C notes," said the lawyer.

"Wouldn't be surprised," agreed Crook. "He seemed to be so glad to get it."

"When you pulled out that roll and counted him off fifty ten spots, he was looking at it, his eyes wide and excited, and licking his tongue like a stew, waiting for his first drink of liquor after a prolonged drunk."

"That gal may be working through Eden. He may have sent her in to buy this relinquishment, too," suggested Crook.

"That's it,—that's exactly what he's done."

"But we beat him to her. We got there first," smiled Crook.

"We got there first and got a relinquishment, all right, but how do we know if she didn't go there later and persuade them to have her sign another? Eden's a pretty smart egg you know, and that girl back there don't impress me as being anybody's fool." Being behind them, she saw them turning, and lowered her eyes before they could focus their's on her. After a glance, they went on:

"That may be possible. If so, it won't work, because I had sense enough to put down the hour, as well as the date, on the one *we* have," said the lawyer.

"Well, that makes us safe as far as the relinquishment is concerned. I have a feeling that she hasn't got one, else she'd got off back there at Gregory."

"And that's what's worrying me—her going through to Winner. I don't like that at all, as I can't make out what she's up to. But if I'm not mistaken, she's planning to jump the claim."

"She could have done that already. How—"

"But, don't you see, that wouldn't have done any good as long as Eden, as the old preacher's daughter's husband, stayed there. She couldn't have got anywhere jumping the place— but now that the girl has executed a relinquishment, that can make a difference. That's why I'm burning up to get to Winner and see what that passage is, that covers this very sort of case." Crook looked out the window as the train began to move slower.

"What a rain, what a rain!" he cried, turning back to the lawyer.

Meanwhile, Deborah Stewart was doing some deep thinking. She checked on the telegram she had sent Eden from Norfolk to meet her at Winner. She realized that unless Eden happened to be in Carter he would hardly get it—than he might be up at Olive's and his grandma s places. But even if he happened to be at Linda's place, and not in Carter that afternoon, he couldn't get the telegram until the next morning. They had no telephone at Linda's place, so the wire would have to be mailed. The rural carrier would have left early that morning, long before she sent the message. So Eden wouldn't be at Winner to meet her, and how then, *would* she get out to the place?

As she looked out the window, she shuddered. No automobile could he depended on to get over those slippery roads during such a rain. Now *how would* she get to the claim? Then she started! If she could hire a saddle horse she could make it. A saddle horse? And then her heart leaped for joy!

She had hired one during the summer. It was cheaper for her. She had hired the mare, whose name she recalled was Dolly, which had a whinnying habit and was forever rearing upon her hind feet when ready to start—especially if it was to run.

She had kept her for three days while on the claimstead, because she could visit the Farnheims and the Giltzows and the Johnsons and return to Winner when through. The man had charged her $10.00 for the three days she kept Dolly. With her plans laid, she waited patiently for the train to reach Winner.

It was still raining when the train arrived there, but as the passengers were being discharged it let up. She saw Crook and his companion rush to a taxi and drive away. She looked for Eden, but as she suspected, he wasn't there, so she caught a taxi and hurried to the lone Livery Barn that remained in the town. She was relieved to learn that Dolly was in her stall, and ordered her saddled at once. They even had a riding costume, a bit too large for her, but she had worn it before, so she called for that, went in the private office and changed into it, rolling her clothes into a neat package so that she could take them with her. She had some clothes at the claim which she had made there during the summer and fall.

"Got any slickers?" she asked the attendant.

"Sure have, Miss. Want one?"

"I think I'll need it," said she, with a laugh, looking out where the rain had slackened but was still falling. The man got the slicker.

"You're not going out until this rain stops, are you?"

"Oh, yes," she cried. "I won't mind a little rain. We always need it so badly up here that I feel like getting out in it every time it falls, and getting good and wet." The man laughed.

"Mighty bad night, though."

"I know it; but I've got to be where I'm going right quick, so I'm starting right now, rain or no."

"Well," said he, as he assisted her into the saddle. "This mare'll take you if anything can get you there."

"I know it," replied Deborah, adjusting herself to the saddle as the man opened the door. Dolly whinnied, and knowing that she always followed a whinny with a rear up, he cried:

"Look out!" and was frightened. But Deborah was used to the animal, so rode into the air. After another whinny, she came down, set for the ride to the claim, and dashed out of the barn into the dark wet prairie night.

She rode up to the corner where stood the Ulmer Hotel, from which the Elder had made his last dash from Tripp County with Linda. As she reached it, where she would take the street that led into the road for Carter, she met a motor, coming in the opposite direction, which attempted to turn the same way she was going. The car skidded on the paving, and hurtled toward her. Only by bringing the mare to a quick stop was she able to avoid an accident that might have injured her steed. Dolly whinnied loudly, and reared up on her hind legs, just as a clap of thunder and a flash of lightening lit the skies. In the flash, she saw that the car contained Crook and his lawyer—and they saw that the rider of the horse was she.

They managed to right the car, got underway and quickly passed her as she rode out of town. It was paved to the corporation line, so they soon left her behind.

"Can you beat that," said the lawyer, after they had the car under control.

"Beat what?" asked Crook.

"Beat what?" repeated the lawyer, who was at the wheel. "Why, that girl."

"The girl. You mean?"

"I mean the person on that horse we nearly collided with when we skidded back there was she."

"No!" exclaimed Crook.

"Yes," cried the lawyer.

"Well, I'll be dammed."

"Nobody else but her. I saw her face when the lightening flashed just as plain as day. It was she on the horse, and after what we read in that booklet, it's a race for possession between her and us."

"Between her and us."

"We should be able to beat her to it."

"Maybe."

"We've *got* to beat her there."

"I'll try to."

"If it wasn't for all this rain, it'd be a cinch."

"But the rain has fallen and we're going to run into water a foot deep as quickly as we leave the paving."

"That's hellish luck."

"Sure is; but it's our only chance."

"I've been afraid Eden might get into this before it was over," said Crook.

"If tomorrow was any other day but Saturday or Sunday, our relinquishment might hold."

"But the little gal back there's got until Monday to beat us to it, if she gets there first."

"And if Eden's there, they'll use the house, while we have to depend on the tent we have."

"A tent is accepted as residence in a case like this," said the lawyer, hopefully.

"But a house is better."

"Well, if Eden doesn't happen to be up there and we get there first, we'll break in and take possession. We won't let her in when she gets there."

"Well," said Crook, with a sigh. "It looks like it's up to the first one who gets there, so let's take it as easy as possible." As he finished, the lawyer applied the brakes, and cried:

"Well, here's the end of the good roads. Trouble starts from here."

"Well, it's stopped raining at least."

"That's something to be thankful for."

As they bumped off the paving onto the dirt road, they ran into a long stretch of water.

"Take it easy fellow, before you kill the motor," cautioned Crook, looking around. In the distance he could hear the mare's hoofs on the paving.

"This sure is hell," sighed the lawyer, as the car slid from right to left, the wheels throwing water all over everything.

On the side of the road rose a ridge, and along this ridge they saw Deborah, astride Dolly, pass them by. For a few yards they could see the mare's tail, raised in their faces, while they sloshed and labored, frightened stiff for fear the coil would get wet and stop them dead.

Then for twelve miles, it was nip and tuck. Wherever the land rose and was rolling for a stretch, they would pass her, only to have her catch up and pass them wherever it was level, or if they had to cross a draw. All the while, the men in the car, hoping for fate to favor them, were in a state of agony and fear.

They dared not at any time, even where the ground rolled over smooth hills, give the car much speed, because they were in danger of skidding off the dirt road, turning over and being wrecked or killed.

Meantime, Deborah had thought of one important thing.— Crossing Willow Creek. In view of the heavy rain that had just fallen, if it had rained North along the White River as it had rained all the way from Gregory, Willow Creek should be out of its banks. If so, Crook and his lawyer could never cross it, and Dolly would swim it. She would be safe. So she took it easy as they passed her and within the same mile, maybe, she'd pass them.

The rain was definitely over, for the sky began to clear and the moon shone through the fleeting clouds and one could see far ahead, for night.

Just before they reached the creek, which Crook and his companion hadn't thought about, the land rose for fully a mile. The rain which had fallen had ran immediately off, leaving the way clear and solid for a car. Striking this, they soon overtook Deborah, who had passed them a mile back while the car was struggling uncertainly through a puddle of water that swamped the road. Now with the moon shining and lighting the landscape, as they passed her, they waved at her tauntingly.

Deborah smiled grimly, and did some hoping, too. At least she knew what should be waiting to welcome all on the other side of that long rise and fall of beautiful land.

On reaching the summit, they took new hope. The road was good and solid. The rain had fallen so hard it had made these sections of road more solid than before the rain.

They sailed down the long slope, at 30 miles an hour. Crook looked at his watch and said:

"Well, looks like we ought to beat her now, all right."

"If the road continues like this, we should be there in ten or fifteen minutes," said the lawyer, as he gave the car a little more gas.

Behind them, her heart in her mouth, Deborah was praying. Everything depended on Willow Creek. It should be swollen and out of its banks. She prayed that it would be.

The long slope the car was sailing down ran right to the creek's edge; but the road, to seek a shallow place to cross the creek, took a sharp turn to the left just before reaching the Creek, and they were almost there when Crook happened to think of it.

"Look out!" he cried, when it came to him. "There's a sharp turn right ahead of us. If you don't slow down, we'll keep right on going when we get there, except that it won't be on wheels. The car will turn over and roll the rest of the way." The lawyer reduced the speed and then Crook thought of something else.

"Good God," he shrieked, "we're coming to Willow Creek. Oh, Lord, I'm afraid we're sunk," and perspiration broke out all over him.

"What're you talking about! What do you mean?" cried the lawyer, glancing at him sideways.

"You'll soon see," moaned Crook. "We haven't one chance in a thousand to make it now."

"What *are you* talking about, fellow?" snapped the lawyer, frightened and impatient, as they went around the curve that lead down to the crossing.

"Oh, God, have mercy on us," sighed Crook, deeply. "We're sunk. I hear the rotten Creek now. Right ahead of us is Willow Creek, the most treacherous stream in the whole Rosebud Country when it rains. It's out of its banks after all this rain and we can never get across it."

"But the bridge," cried the lawyer.

"There ain't any. They've built three and the first big rain like this that came along washed each one away down the valley. The state plans a suspension bridge, to begin at the foot of the hill and rise 50 feet above it, those are only plans, they won't do us any good now."

"There it is," said the lawyer, as they came down toward where the crossing ran. "Just as you said. It's wider than White River—"

"—and deep as hell," Crook finished for him.

They drove as close to it as they dared, stopped the car, and getting out, looked out over the creek, which was now fully a quarter mile wide. As they did so, they heard the hoof beats of Deborah's horse riding toward them. Crook got a quick and daring notion.

"God damn our luck," cried the lawyer, stamping his foot, and swinging his right arm in disgust.

"That damned little girl, she's tripped us. She knew this Creek would be out of its bank like this," said Crook, fairly hissing the words.

"Damned right she knew it," snapped the lawyer, "and she's been laughing at us all the way from Winner as a pair of fools. Watch what she does now. She'll make that horse swim across, leaving us standing here like a pair of dumbbells while she runs away with millions!"

"The horse may swim the river all right; but I don't intend her to be on the horse."

"What're you going to do?"

"Just watch me. This is where Eugene Crook and chivalry part company. I'm going to take that horse away from her." No sooner were these words out of his mouth, than up rode Deborah. Crook, his head down, started toward her. She seemed to have sensed what he would do, so drew on Dolly's reins. With a loud snort and whinny, up went Dolly into the air and coming down, just missed Crook's head by inches as he fell back.

Quickly Deborah turned the mare around and rode back fifty yards, then halting, turned. Dolly got set, whinnied loudly, and rising high on her hind feet, stood suspended while Deborah, patting her neck cried:

"Take it easy, Dolly, we're going through."

The next moment down came Dolly, like a base runner, off to a good start. Desperate enough to commit murder, Crook got in the horse's path, to be snatched out of the way just in time by the lawyer.

"Fool! Do you want to be killed?" That gal knows what she's doing, look out!" He fell back, pulling Crook, just as Deborah leaning low in the saddle like a jockey, dashed by, throwing mud in chunks into their faces as she went through without hesitation, and plunged into the swirling waters of Willow Creek.

The rushing waters carried the brave mare and rider so far down stream it looked as if they would be lost. But when they got over one of the deep holes, the current wasn't so swift. Dolly finally found her equilibrium, and once set, swam against the waters. After a few minutes of struggle, her feet found land again about a hundred yards down stream. A minute later the mare, crawled upon land again and stopping to shake the water off, trotted up to where the roadway came out of the water opposite where the men stood. Deborah raised her hand to give them the razz, as she cried, loud enough for them to hear:

"Well, so long fellows, I'll see you in jail. Better luck the next time!" With that she tightened the reins, and Dolly leaped into the air, snorted and dashed away into the night toward Linda's claim five short miles away. She was soon lost in the gloom of the night.

CHAPTER XXXIII

In their hotel room in Winner, after Crook and his lawyer returned from Willow Creek, they talked to each other, two disappointed men.

"Well," said Crook, "We still have the girl's relinquishment. I'll present it with my application, immediately the land office opens in Gregory on Monday morning."

"There's nothing else left to do, in spite of the fact that it will be the same as offering a check at a bank without a signature."

"Nevertheless, I'm going to present it. It *might* be accepted."

"It is possible," sighed the lawyer, without enthusiasm, and then both went to bed.

Monday morning found them at the land office, the very first to enter. They did not see the girl as they expected, and were a bit surprised. Crook offered Linda's relinquishment with his application pinned to same in the regular order, which the clerk took, and retired to the office of the local commissioner. Like two men, being tried for murder, awaiting the return of the jury they sat anxiously. After a time the Commissioner came forward. In his hand he had a mass of papers, which he unfolded as he came to the counter. On top of the mass was Crook's application and Linda's relinquishment.

"I'm sorry, Mr. Crook, but a rare incident has developed regarding this particular claim."

"Pardon me," said the lawyer, stepping forward, "but we don't quite understand you. I'm Mr. Crook's lawyer."

"Thank you, sir," said the Commissioner.

411

"I want to explain that in the twenty five years that I've been connected with the Land Office Department, this is the first time that advantage of a particular clause relative to relinquishments versus prior residence has been exercised. Now let me first read you this clause."

In spite of the fact that they had read and knew all about what the clause explained, they listened patiently to the commissioner while he read it to them and gave each a copy.

"Now you have a relinquishment signed by Linda Lee, dated last Thursday and signed by her 10:45 A.M.

"In this morning's mail, I received a registered letter from one, Deborah Stewart, enclosing an affidavit to the effect that Linda Lee was killed that same day at 2:55 P.M. The affidavit is supported by this": He handed them a page of a Chicago newspaper, which carried an account of the tragic death of both Linda and her father.

"Another affidavit, witnessed by several persons living in the vicinity of the claim attests to the fact that claimant, Deborah Stewart, established a residence on this land during June of this year. In view of the fact that Linda Lee had not been on the land for more than two years and died before you offered this relinquishment, signed by Miss Lee, Deborah Stewart's application, supported by her residence as a bone fide settler on the claim, must be accepted instead of yours moreover, according to these witnesses, she has made a considerable amount of improvements on the claim during the summer.

"So I must return your application and the relinquishment which, due to the death of the signatore, is void and unacceptable. Sorry, gentlemen."

Outside, the two men faced each other.

"Can you imagine it?"

"That little gal sure took us for a buggy ride."

"Well," said Crook, with a disappointed sigh, "that is—"

"—that," said the lawyer, and the pair disappeared up the street.

Deborah, however, had not "pulled a fast one." It was simply an unusual coincidence in which she and Martin Eden fared the best, after all the bad breaks that he had been getting. In short, it "just" happened.

Deborah, riding away from Willow Creek the Friday night before, arrived at the homestead a few minutes after leaving the river. To her glad surprise she saw a light in the windows. With a suppressed cry of delight she bounded off the mare and knocked loudly. She heard somebody start inside, and a chair fall over. Until the door was opened, she feared it might be somebody that Crook and his lawyer had sent to jump the claim. Her heart was in her mouth, but the next moment she swallowed an "Oh!" It was Martin Eden.

"Deborah!" he exclaimed, his mouth open, his eyes wide. "*You!*"

"Oh, Martin!" she cried. In that moment all that had propelled her gave way. She swayed, but stepping forward quickly, he caught her in his arms, carried her inside and laid her on the bed.

He took off her beret, her shoes, her slicker and unbuttoned her blouse at the throat. Then he started a fire in the stove. When he returned to the bed she was looking up at nothing, her eyes open, blankly. She looked at him for a moment, still blankly, then reached out her hand and touched him as if to see if he were real.

"Martin," she called in a low voice. "Is this—you?"

"Why, yes, Deborah, of course. It should be I, asking if it is—*you?*" looking at her costume, which was still wet. Coming back to herself, she exclaimed, a little louder:

"Oh, of course! You must be wondering at me—like this.

"I have a long story to tell you, Martin. Such a long, *long* story, and a sad story, then a glad story." She remembered in that moment, that she was Colored, and smiled because she knew he would be so happy when she told him; then more than happy too, when she told him about the land and the hill which was a tower of manganese—the richest deposit in all the world—and valuable beyond the wildest dreams!

"I was in a part of the rain that fell tonight, Martin. My clothes are wet, my skin is also, so do you mind going out and putting that horse I rode here in the barn? And remove the saddle and feed her while I change to dry clothes and make myself more comfortable?"

"Why, of course not, Deborah—I'll be glad to."

"By the time you get back, I'll try to be ready." She thought of who she was again and smiled so sweetly at him that he was almost tempted. Before stepping outside, he dared turn and look back at her. Holding her arm taut, she shook her little hand at him smiling beautifully.

Outside he took his time after giving the mare plenty of oats and rubbed her down while she was eating, then bedded the stall floor down with hay.

Inside Deborah removed all her clothes, took a hot bath as best she could in a foot tub, donned the gown she left there, found a worn kimono, got back into bed and waited for him to return. He took so long she was beginning to get impatient when he finally returned and knocked lightly on the door.

"Come in," she called, softly, "I thought you weren't ever coming back."

"I wanted to give you sufficient time," said he, drawing a chair up close to the bed.

"And now what happened? I thought you were in Indiana having a gay time by now with old friends."

"I haven't been to Indiana, that is, I mean I never got there," said she calmly. "I stopped in Chicago, where something happened—*everything* happened. So much happened, in fact, it is going to take most of the night for me to tell you. But if you promise to be patient, I'll try. When you have heard it all and *understand it all*, I—but you must hear it first.

"On the way to Omaha, I happened to be in a seat behind two men who were talking. One was Eugene Crook."

"Crook," he echoed, and his brow contracted.

"They were talking about you and your wife and her father. They had read your book and the lawyer insisted that the story was true. They were on their way to Chicago to see the preacher. They planned to persuade him to have your wife sign a relinquishment. I heard them say that they were going to offer him $500 for it.

"When I overheard their plot to get this land, I decided to get off in Chicago and go see grandpa and then your wife, Linda, to try persuade her not to do this terrible thing. But a taxi driver took me to Vernor Avenue instead of Vernon and when I finally got to my grandpa's on the South side, I had lost two hours. I told grandpa and my aunt about it and they said your folks lived right down the street in the next block. I rushed down there, arriving just in time to meet Crook and his lawyer coming out of the house and could see from the way this Reverend Lee bid them goodby, and the expression on their faces, that they had got what they went there for.

"It was true. I managed to get in the house about a half hour later and found your wife alone. I had a long talk with her and upbraided her severely for the way she had treated you. I told her she would never have a peaceful moment thereafter for betraying you as she had. She became remorseful, then hysterical and said things which led me to believe that she would do something desperate. I tried to persuade her not to, but she drove me out of the house. I went back to my grandpa and told him what I feared she was going to do—most likely to kill herself. He went to the police station, and as he returned with a load of policemen, we met them just before they drove up in front of the Elder's home. As we left grandpa's house we saw Linda run out dressed only in a long pink negligee, spattered with blood.

"Her face, her hair—in fact, her whole body was spattered with blood. She carried a knife with a long blade in her hand and it was bloody, too. But I must go back to my trip on the way to Chicago.

"I was awakened after crossing the Mississippi River by one of those premonitions such as I had about you when you were leaving to go for her. I looked out of the car window and saw that wind from nowhere whirling toward the car. It met the train and passed through the car as if there were no walls at all and swept over me, chilling me. I knew then that something bad was going to happen.

"Linda was coming to see me when she left her father's house. She was going to bring me a message that concerned you and your son. She was hysterical and had no equilibrium. She ran right out in the street, without regard to traffic, was run down by a car—and killed!"

He started violently, and lowered his eyes reverently, his face sad and sympathetic.

"Back with my grandpa and my aunt, I was terribly overcome. I blamed myself for what had happened, for there was more than one death."

He looked up with a question in his eyes.

"Yes, before she left the house she killed—her father."

Again Eden started, but he couldn't lower his eyes, feel sad or reverent. He swallowed and nodded and remained silent.

"I was terribly depressed; but I wanted to try save the land. So I went into the street and walked, I don't know how far. Presently, I found myself before a large church. I went in and before the altar, I tried to pray. While there, something came to me. I went back to my room and consulted a booklet relating to land affairs and found something that showed me I could beat Crook at his own game if I acted hastily.

"I caught the night train out of Chicago. Crook and this Lawyer were on the same one. They were going to get off at Gregory but the lawyer suddenly looked at me. I saw them whispering together and peeping at me and instead of getting off at Gregory, they came through to Winner. They went somewhere and apparently found out what I had already learned from reading the booklet in Chicago. It related to a squatter's right over an application in conjunction with a relinquishment.

"They took a car out of Winner, while I hired that horse, and we had it nip and tuck all the way to Willow Creek. They had to run through so much water standing over the road in all the low places, that it delayed them. When this happened I would pass them, but when we reached high ground, they'd pass me. This continued all the way to Willow Creek, where they arrived first.

"The old Creek, however, was all out of its banks—they couldn't cross and were stuck. As I rode up, Crook made a dash for me. He was going to take the horse from me by force and ride it across the creek himself. But I saw what he was bent on and reared Dolly into the air, almost striking him when she came down. I rode back about fifty yards, and turning, Dolly reared high up on her hind legs, snorted and whinnied and almost ran over him as he tried to stop us. Then she plunged into the creek. The water carried us away down stream before I could get control, but I finally managed it, and we made the other bank, rode back to the road, waved at them across the creek and came on here."

"My, my, my! What an adventure and what an experience you've had, Deborah," said he, finding words inadequate to express his feelings completely. "But now, about the claim. You say that my—that Linda signed a relinquishment?"

"Yes, Martin, but it is void. Wait," and finding the booklet, she read the paragraph to him.

"Do you understand now, dear—or, Martin?" she asked looking up at him.

"You mean, that—that by your being here, on it," gesturing a bit with his finger, "that—"

"It takes precedence over his relinquishment. That's what this paragraph explains. So instead of Crook getting the place, I already have it."

"Oh, Deborah, that's wonderful. I'm so glad its yours, and—"

"But after I prove up on it, Martin, it will be yours. I'm going to sign it over to you."

"No, Deborah. It is yours—free and clear. Yours to keep and do what you wish with it. You know I would so much rather you have it than that dirty Crook who tried so hard to beat Linda out of it."

"But I don't want it that way, Martin," she said, softly, daring to lay a hand on his. "Meanwhile, you haven't heard *all* of the story. I've saved the rest to tell you last. I hope you won't be angry after I've told you. I've hoped that you might—be—glad, Martin." This was said more softly than ever, and he couldn't understand the expression he saw in her face.

"Poor Martin," she whispered, tears in her eyes, which were softer than he had ever seen them before. "They treated you so badly; they seemed to misunderstand you on purpose—and in the end they tried to destroy you altogether."

"Well, Deborah, I've managed to live through it somehow and now that the place was saved by you, I—"

"It shall be yours, Martin. I could not think of keeping it, after all I've learned about how they tried to steal it from you. You bought it, you paid the money, you improved it, that cost money. So—"

"Just don't say any more about what I've done, Deborah, but let me thank you for what you've done. I—"

"But I haven't told you all the story even yet, Martin." He looked confused and she realized that he was thinking maybe the place hadn't been saved after all.

"Oh, no, it's not about this place. That's settled just as I explained. It's—about me, Martin," she said softly and smiled again, until with great difficulty he refrained from catching her in his arms. "Now I'll tell it and I won't keep you in suspense any longer, dear."

"When I reached Vernon Avenue on the way to Grandpa's

house, I saw nothing but colored people—colored people everywhere and no white people at all. I found his house, which was a
nice place, well kept and beautiful; more attractive than most
of the other houses in that section.

"When I knocked on the door it was presently opened by a
woman who looked just like my mother. I was a bit bewildered,
for the woman that looked so much like my mother was a—a—
colored woman.

"After while, Grandpa came and asked if I wasn't Deborah
and I said, yes. He was in a shadow and I couldn't see his face
so well. But when he walked into the room and I could see his
face closely, I started again, more this time than when I saw
the woman—for *my grandpa was colored too!*"

It was Eden who started this time. His mouth hung agape,
and he experienced a series of emotions before he calmed again,
as if he were afraid to believe what he had just heard. All the
while, she lay there half afraid to smile too much, yet hopefully
waiting.

"Deborah," he started, and his voice was hoarse from pent
up emotion. "I—I want to be sure."

"Yes, Martin," she said in a low voice, which was very soft,
very inviting.

"You went to see your grandpa, and when you saw him, he
turned out to be a—a—colored man? And then he—he introduced you to—your aunt. The one you said looked so much
like your mother, and—"

"She was my mother's sister. That's why they looked so
much alike. . . ."

"And *she* turned out to be—*a colored woman?* Then—then—
Deborah, you—you are *not* a—*white girl* after all?"

She shook her head this time.

"And that—that makes you—you, *just like me,* Deborah?"
said he pointing a finger at himself.

She nooded her head, almost bursting with anxious restraint.

"Just *like you,* Martin. . . ."

"*Oh, Deborah.*" He looked at her with something in his face she had never seen before. Still he didn't take her in his arms as she expected.

"Martin? What—what is the matter, dear?" Tears were in his eyes as he looked at her.

"I—I'm all confused. I don't believe I'm awake. This must all be a dream. But if *it is a dream*, Deborah, and you hear me and can answer, may I say something, dear; something that I have wanted to say for years and years but didn't think I would ever have the chance to say it."

"Please do say it now, Martin. *Anything you want to say.* If it is a dream, it is a happy dream; the dream that I, too, have waited for so long. The dream will come true, it will come true *now!!* If you speak, Martin.

"I want to say, Deborah, that I—I love you, dear. Oh, how much I *do* love you; how much I *have* loved you. I have waited for you, cried for you. I love you, Deborah, I love you, oh, *so much*, my dear."

"Oh, Martin, *how long* have I waited to hear you say those words, oh, *how* long! You haven't yet asked if I love you, Martin. But you must know that I do. But I want to hear myself say it now, too, since that terrible barrier which has stood between us has been at last removed. I want to hear myself say it and I want you to hear me say that I love you, too, Martin Eden. I love you so much it will take all the rest of my life, if I live to be a hundred years old, before I can get through telling you how much."

As he looked at her he was so overcome he seemed to have lost his speech.

"Take me, Martin," she said, rising to a sitting posture in the bed. "And hold me in your arms and kiss me, Martin, kiss me—*forever!*"

So he took her and he held her and he kissed her. In after years they joked about how long this went on. They were so happy she forgot to tell him about the riches that high hill on *their* place held.

When the sun rose the next morning, it fell on Martin Eden's face and awakened him earlier than it did Deborah, who, in the other room, with the bed in the shadows, slept peacefully on while he rose and dressed.

He went out and after feeding Dolly, strolled out and paused to look across the wide prairies, shimmering in the sunlight. As he surveyed the vast expanse, stretching seemingly, endlessly, from where he stood, it thrilled him strangely; seemed to arouse a feeling of drama within him. And then his eyes fell on Mount Eden, the strange high hill, rising like a sepulchre, high into the air above him, eighty yards away.

Curious, he strolled over to it and for the first time, climbed its sides to the summit and gazed for miles and miles in every direction. To the south, he could see far into Nebraska; across the Keya Paha, winding its narrow way through the sand hill county that began beyond its wings on either side. He could see the Twin Buttes that rose also high into the air, to the southeast, across the Keya Paha.

He shifted his eyes to the north and 20 miles in that direction, he could see the White River, wending its way southeastward where it emptied into the mighty muddy Missouri. He raised his hand to shade his eyes as they shot across rolling prairies seventeen miles southeast to Winner, which seemed so very small at that distance, flanked, as it were, on all sides, by the vast prairies.

Then, as he turned to look for Carter, directly to the south his attention was arrested by a voice, very faint at the distance. It was that of Deborah's and as he looked, she stood in the doorway, of the claimhouse, beckoning to him.

When he arrived at the house, he found breakfast, which she had cooked, waiting. In good health, both ate heartily, and after she had cleaned the dishes, she took his arm and asked him to stroll with her to "Yon hill," as she described it. After they reached it, walked around it and inspected the strange, white substance that cropped out of it, she told him the story of its wealth.

"So, Martin, you see why I went through so much; I wanted to save it for you so badly, I almost died with fear and anxiety. I told Linda what you wanted to do; of the souls you wanted to save, and I'm sorry she did not live long enough to see you realize this ambition and to commence this great work.

He bowed his head and was sorry for Linda.

"She was a good girl, Martin, and it's too bad fate dealt so unkindly with her. Before—the end, she wanted to tell me to take you and her baby and to be good to both of you. She was coming to tell me when—it—happened. She was going to ask me to raise your son to be like you—brave and strong, resolute and courageous! And with God's help, I will try to do what she wished done, Martin. And I will try to be a good wife to you and make you happy, dear, happy all the rest of our lives. Kiss me, Martin, please kiss me, dear!"

So they kissed and went then unto the little house on the claim. After one week they went to Chicago. Old Nelson Boudreaux and his daughter met them at the train.

A week later, after they had taken Martin Junior to raise, Martin Sr. and Deborah, who was once white, walked down the long stairway in the Boudreaux home to the large parlor below and were married. Then after their wedding night in the room she liked so well, they went on their honeymoon to a far country. When they returned they began their life's work, out there in the Rosebud Country.

As their wealth began to accumulate out of sales from the great manganese deposit, they bought more than a hundred thousand acres of Rosebud lands. They manned mighty tractors, equal to compound locomotive power and had the lands plowed deeply. When the rains came, it was stored in the deep plowed soil to feed the roots of plant life when it was dry. Crop failures were no more. All plant life flourished and crops were ever abundant. Huge yields were harvested from the fields, year after year.

When this had been well established, the farms were divided into ten acre tracts. A modern village was erected in the center of every four square miles, with a school and a church, a small theatre and other needed buildings, including neat little project houses with enough room for all the families who were buying ten acre tracts.

Then Deborah and Martin went East, where unfortunate families of their race had been forced on relief. They selected from them the worthy and industrious ones, brought them hither and permitted each to buy and pay for out of earnings, ten acres of rich, deep plowed land. And with each purchase they supplied a cow, a horse, chickens and pigs. Each family then grew its own food. The women were able to make their pin money from eggs and chickens and milk; the men were given work in huge food product factories and manganese alloy plants that were built, where they were given a few days work each month.

Twenty five years hence, a great Negro colony will call the Rosebud Country home and be contented, prosperous and happy.

Martin and Deborah raised Linda's child and many of their own. They taught all to think and to conserve and to help others who were willing and anxious to help themselves—the philosophy of common sense. And so together they worked and continued to plan and prospered and lived happily ever afterward.